Saxton, Judith.

First love, last
love.

DATE DUE		
NOV 03 2006	OCT 18 2007	
NOV 17 2008	OCT 09 2008	
	APR 17 2010	
DEC 21 2009		

BAKER & TAYLOR BOOKS

First Love,
Last Love

Also by Judith Saxton

This Royal Breed
A Family Affair
All My Fortunes
Family Feeling

Judith Saxton

First Love,
Last Love

St. Martin's Press
New York

Library of Congress Cataloging-in-Publication Data

Saxton, Judith.
    First love, last love / Judith Saxton.
        p.   cm.
    ISBN 0-312-08779-9
    1. World War, 1939-1945—Wales—Fiction.   I. Title.
PR6069.A97F   1993
823'.914—dc20   92-34391
                                                           CIP

First published in Great Britain by HarperCollins*Publishers*.

First U.S. Edition: March 1993
10 9 8 7 6 5 4 3 2

For Brian, my favourite proof-reader

Acknowledgments

I should like to thank David and Pat Fuller of Norwich who got me information which I badly needed and put me in touch with Amanda Bringloe, who loaned me material on Pakefield Church which I could not have got from any other source; Adelaide Hunter of Brundall, who told me about Lowestoft in wartime; and Edwin Newson, of Pakefield itself, whose knowledge of his area and particularly of the school was invaluable.

I followed a long trail through Manchester, searching for information about the Jewish Hospital – now defunct – in Elizabeth Street. It started with Mike McQueen who passed me on to Ruth, who put me in touch with Mrs Wyn Lancaster, who knew just who could help me, so the trail ended with Sister Meta Servos of Prestwich, who had been deputy matron at the hospital and shared her vivid memories with me – many thanks, Meta.

Once more, Beryl and Alan Hague told me about the Americans flying in Britain and made the war years come alive again when they took me round the Aviation Museum at Flixton. I had a short but intensive lesson in how to fly a B-24 and have considerable respect for the men who actually took on the Liberators – they were some airplane!

The staff at the American Memorial Room, Norwich Central Library, were helpful and knowledgeable as always, guiding me through their stock and searching the shelves for the books which would be most use. They recommended *Courage, Honour, Victory* by Ian Hawkins, a beautifully written and researched piece of work, which I would recommend to anyone as reading for pleasure; as research it was a real bonus.

First Love,
Last Love

I

1930

It was a cold day with a bitter breeze that would have driven even the hardiest holidaymaker off the shore, had the summer visitors not gone long since. In fact the child crouching on the tideline, apparently impervious to the weather, had the beach to herself. Her bare feet gradually sinking into the soft gritty shingle, she was absorbed in sorting through the detritus cast up by the waves, searching for anything which might appeal to her. Tiny bits of driftwood carved by the sea into odd shapes were always a good find, or shells, or black and spiky egg-cases, light and dry as tinder.

The wind was biting, though, and Sybil's skimpy gingham dress was no protection against its chill. Already her thin little arms and legs were blue-tinged beneath their fading summer tan and although she occasionally interrupted her search to rub vigorously at her icy flesh it made very little difference. She was cold and likely to remain so until she abandoned the beach, and her search, and went indoors.

'Just one more lot,' Sybil said to herself, rubbing the back of one hand across her nose and then wiping the resultant snail-trail from her knuckles on to her faded pink skirt. 'Just one more, for Lizzie.'

Lizzie was her big sister, at twelve, two years older than Sybil. Lizzie was beautiful with her thick, fair curls, large blue eyes and clear, creamy skin. But despite her looks she was a sickly child, prey to every cough and cold, every measle and mump, that stalked the East Anglian coast. In winter Mother might wrap Lizzie in flannel and rub goosegrease on her chest, she might prepare evil-smelling concoctions for Lizzie to inhale, worse ones for her to swallow, but as far as Sybil could see it made not a jot of difference. Georgie, who was thirteen and almost a man, and Sybil herself, seemed impervious to the ailments which descended on Lizzie like a swarm of gnats as soon as the bright summer days began to fade into autumn. And now Lizzie was suffering from a nasty cold, unable to leave the house until the fever relaxed its grip, so Sybil searched on, knowing that something pretty would make up, a little, to Lizzie for her enforced incarceration.

The tide, creeping further up the beach, suddenly enveloped Sybil's toes, creaming spitefully close to her skirt. Her mother would not be pleased if Sybil went indoors wet, but the child was still reluctant to give up and go home with – she glanced rather reproachfully at her small pile of treasures – nothing particularly exciting to show Lizzie.

'I ought to go . . . but just one more shuffle,' Sybil promised the gods of wind and water. 'If I'm a good girl . . . just *one* nice thing for Lizzie!'

And as though the fates had been listening, had saved this treat for when Sybil was almost at the point of giving up, in the very next tangled heap she found the doll. It was a tiny doll, the sort that a child can hold easily in one hand, no more than five or six inches from the top of its round baby head to the tiny toes on its feet. Its body was made of cloth and stuffed with something lumpy and wet but its head, legs and arms were pink and healthy-looking, the eyes bright glass, the face perfect in every detail.

Sybil sat back on her heels, clutching the doll, everything else forgotten. The shells, the egg-cases, the piece of driftwood which, with the exercise of considerable imagination, could have resembled a legless dog or crouching cat, all counted for nought beside her remarkable find. A doll! Henry and Dora Cream worked hard, but they had no money to spare for luxuries such as dolls, and Lizzie was the sort of child who would enjoy the possession of such a toy. It would be as good as Christmas to see her face!

Carefully, Sybil got to her feet. She began to trudge up the beach, never taking her eyes off the doll gripped tight in her wet and sandy paw. It was bald and small featured, just like the baby next door had been a few months ago. Now he was starting to crawl and looked far less angelic to his neighbours as he grabbed the nearest piece of furniture and found his feet, only to topple, screaming, as soon as he tried to take a step.

At the top of the beach there was a stretch of grass, with the thatched church to Sybil's right and the cottages in which she lived to her left. A sandy lane divided the two, and if you went straight on between the church and the cottages you came to the smart houses where the summer visitors stayed, and to the village proper – the pub, the shop, the hall where they held dances in summer, the memorial column carved with the names of men who had died in the Great War, where the local youths foregathered to stare and whistle at the local lasses.

But Sybil had little interest in the village and less in the lads who hung around the war memorial. Lizzie, tossing her bright mane of hair, might look consideringly at the boys, but Sybil knew that she herself was plain and would probably never get married, though such things were supremely unimportant when you were ten. She preferred going to the shop with a penny clutched in one hand for cushies, the brightly coloured boiled sweets which lasted and lasted if you sucked and didn't crunch. Georgie crunched but Sybil and Lizzie sucked – they could make one boiled sweet last an hour that way. She would have liked the cinema shows at the Grand in Lowestoft too, but they would have to wait until she was older. Her weekly penny would not run to sweets and the cinema. Anyway, she was an avid reader, and if she could do without sweets her penny would buy quite a big bundle of second-hand comics from Alfie Holland, who acquired these treasures from the big houses where his father worked as a jobbing gardener, and sold them to anyone who could afford his price.

Sybil trudged up the slope of the grass and glanced, as she always did, at the church. It was an odd church, with two naves, which meant, Dad said, that it had once been two churches. Many tales of the two parsons and their two congregations enlivened Sunday evenings when Dad got to telling Mum about those far-off days when one church had been called St Margaret's and the other All Saints; stories of tricks played and tempers frayed, of wonderful victories for one side or the other, whilst Mum listened as she knitted or sewed, and smiled, and told Dad that he was dreadful to talk so, she did not believe a word of it, and Dad would have to answer for his lies one of these days. But she said it with her voice softened, and she would shoot a comical glance at the children, sitting spellbound by their father's eloquence, to show them that it was a joke, that she did not mean it, that it was just Dad's way.

And even now, though the church was simply All Saints, people still came to draw and paint it. One particular artist had taken Sybil's fancy because he liked to chat as he worked, and he told her that the strangeness of a thatched church so near the sea attracted artists and their customers alike.

'I never know, from one year to the next, whether the church will still be here to paint, you see,' he explained gravely, colourwashing a blue sky. 'And when I explain, people want to buy the pictures just in case.'

'In case it goes into the sea?' Sybil said. 'Oh, but not a church; God wouldn't let a *church* go under the water.'

The artist, perhaps mindful of the position of Sybil's own home, said she was probably right and Sybil, remembering the stories Dad sometimes told of the village under the sea, of being out in his fishing boat and hearing the church bell chime beneath the surface – and Mum's eyes saying, *It's just one of Dad's tall tales, so not to worry* – nevertheless felt a frisson of fearful excitement chase up her spine. And it made her look long and hard at the church, perched on its grassy cliff above the beach, surrounded by its old, leaning gravestones.

Did it ever wonder, that little thatched church, whether it would see next summer from atop or beneath the waves? Did it cower lower, tugging its thatch closer to its windows, hunching its grey flint shoulders against the howl of wind and lash of rain? Did it surmise that no one bothered to patch its seedy, sparrow-filled thatch because by this time next year it might be fishes who tapped against the stained glass, currents which stirred the reeds, limpets and barnacles which clustered on its eaves in place of the cheeky, darting sparrows?

But today, despite the cold and the wind, the church looked solid enough and the grass, which had been mown only days before by old Bill, the sexton, still showed the remains of its summer green. So Sybil gave it only a cursory glance before turning towards her own home – the end dwelling in the row of fishermen's cottages which faced the church.

They were built of flints and roofed with wavy, lichen-patched tiles whose original red had faded to a pinky gold. The windows were smallish, the door leaning, the wood cracked and swollen from the constant attack of the salt wind. But we never use the front door, Dad would say when Mum suggested a bit of work on the house, and besides, I can't spare the time, the mackerel are running.

That made Mum laugh, of course, and she would tell Dad he was just lazy and promise to do it herself one day. Only Mum was busy too and the better Dad did at the fishing the harder Mum had to work, since she sold the catch inland, at villages too small to have a fish shop of their own. As she got nearer the cottage Sybil could see, round the side, the door of the rough shed Dad had built out of odds and ends of driftwood to house the cart. Sybil simply accepted the cart as she accepted her home, her parents, her life, but Georgie could remember it coming, and how Mum had cried into her handkerchief and Dad had run his hands along the shafts and gone off to an inland farm where he had got the old horse for a song, he always said. Sybil wondered which of his songs he had sung for Beattie, but when she asked Dad named a different one each time, so she could never tell for sure. But I reckon it was Danny Boy, Sybil told herself. When Dad sings Danny Boy I'm sure any farmer would want him to have his old horse.

There was no sign of life at the cottage as she approached, skirting the building to go in by the back door, but that did not mean that Mum was not busy making their tea. And if Mum was frying potatoes and fish on the blackened range, then Lizzie would be sitting on the big wooden chair with the soft, faded cushions, a handkerchief in one hand, curling a strand of her rich gold-coloured hair across her upper lip and humming to herself whilst she watched from her comfortable seat every move that her mother made.

Georgie and Dad must be out still, Sybil thought, seeing the empty shed where, later, the cart would stand. She stopped for a moment to throw a handful of grass to the hens which clucked and pecked around the tiny yard. They rushed for it as though it was corn, pushing and jostling, then turning away, disappointed, when they realized they had been tricked. Stupid things, Sybil thought, and stamped at them, and then of course the hens managed to convince themselves that she was hiding their glorious potato-peel mash in the scoop of her skirt and ran towards her, two of them actually rising several feet in the air, their horrible scaly feet spread, their inadequate wings flapping, as they tried to spy just what it was she was carrying so carefully. Sybil, being small, was not too keen on hens at head level, but she tried to ignore them, thinking about her find instead. She would have loved that little doll – but it was poor Lizzie who had the feverish cold whilst she, Sybil, had been enjoying the beach for hours.

If Georgie and Dad are out, Sybil thought, approaching the back door through the milling feathered bodies, they won't see what a fine present I've brought back for Lizzie. On the other hand, if I walk in now how can I possibly hide the doll? Even if I don't show her she'll see it, she's bound to. Sybil's dress had no pockets and the doll's extremities extended fore and aft from her small paw. But there was always her knicker-leg. All the girls used their knicker-legs instead of pockets; Sybil was convinced that the only reason for the elastic was so that your possessions did not drop out of their hiding place. Yes, there was plenty of room for the doll up her knickers. So since neither Georgie nor Dad was home to admire her cleverness in finding it, her generosity in giving it to Lizzie, she would keep the doll out of the way until they arrived home.

Being the youngest did have its disadvantages and one was that, sometimes, she felt she was a bit of a nuisance to Lizzie. This fine present would make up for all the times Lizzie had been forced to let her small sister tag along. And if, by giving it, Sybil could win some praise from her beloved elder brother and her adored father . . . Her mind made up, Sybil pushed the doll into her knicker-leg, lifted the big iron latch on the back door and pulled. The door creaked open and she slipped inside, into the warm, steamy kitchen where it was already dusk, for the tiny windows, their sills crammed with jars and bottles and plants, let in the minimum of light.

'About time too! Lay the table when you've had a wash, Sybs.'

That was Mum, stirring something over the fire. A vegetable stew with scrag-end of mutton, Sybil's nose informed her authoritatively. They usually had something nice for the meal on Mum's day at home, for on a Friday, if he and Georgie had not gone out in the boat, Dad sold fish in Beccles for Mum. The town was at the very outskirts of Mum's area and it meant an early start and no chance of cooking a meal, so Dad tried to be home on Fridays to do the Beccles trip. This morning Sybil had got breakfast, fed the hens and collected the eggs – not many, as hens lay best in summer – before hurrying off to school, since Lizzie's being poorly meant that she had two sets of chores. Sybil worked hard in class because Mum said it was the only way to better yourself if you were a fisherman's child, and Sybil was already determined to better herself. She was not pretty, like Lizzie, but plain as a boot, so she must get good results at school or learn to love selling fish. Lizzie nearly always managed to miss her turn on the fish cart, but Sybil was not so lucky and was often haled off to help. She hated it because fish smelt and was cold and slimy after its first day out of the sea, and boys called names and some of the snooty summer visitors drew aside their skirts and murmured things about the heat and the bad sanitation in country districts when Sybil walked by. Probably they did not mean to be unkind, but Sybil's cheeks burned with shame . . . and she studied more diligently than ever so that one day she might sit behind a desk in a blue frock and high-heeled shoes, and curl her lank hair and hide her boring light brown eyes behind beautiful tortoiseshell spectacles, and teach children their letters.

'All right, Mum,' Sybil said now. She smiled at Lizzie, who got languidly to her feet, glancing towards the damp treasures clutched in her sister's skirt. 'Here, Lizzie, take 'em!'

Lizzie gave a world-weary sigh but sat down again and made a scoop of her own skirt. She had been bored just sitting by the fire, and she looked much better already. Sybil tipped everything into Lizzie's lap – some pretty pebbles, the egg-cases, a couple of starfish, dry as tinder and hard as iron, and the bits of driftwood. It would have been wonderful to have added the doll, but that was for later, when Dad and Georgie were here to admire.

'Thanks, Sybs,' Lizzie said. Both children had collections of pebbles and shells in old cardboard boxes under their bed and she fingered the finds, as pleased with her small sister's offerings as though she herself had never played on the beach, never scoured the tidelines for the sea's gifts. She smiled at Sybil, turning the stones over one by one, admiring the colours of them, the shapes, never guessing that there was an even greater pleasure to come.

'It's mutton stew, isn't it, Mum?' Sybil said. She went over to the sink and washed in the water her mother had poured from the big enamel jug, then began putting the chipped grey and white plates and the bone-handled forks and spoons out on the scrubbed wood of the kitchen table. 'Anything for afters?'

'Apple pie,' Mum said. 'We'll give the spoons a wash in between, or you can use the pedlar's spoons if you'd rather.'

The pedlar's spoons were tin and according to the fastidious Cream family they 'tasted', so were rarely used. Dad said his mother had bought them for ordinary mealtimes, saving the good bone-handled cutlery for best, but Mum thought this was foolishness.

'How much wear does a knife and fork get?' she demanded. 'Little enough, for fish doesn't take much cutting! No, we'll use the decent stuff until it wears out and I'll put money by for a new set.'

Mum was always putting money by. A penny here, a halfpenny there, her Christmas boxes from the big houses on her fish round, all went into the battered tin teapot right at the back of the pantry. Sybil, whose clothes were all hand-me-downs from Lizzie, most of them bought at jumble sales, knew that one day she would have a real dress out of the money Mum saved so carefully. Mum had promised, and that meant it would happen. She would get a nice bit of material from the market stalls over in Lowestoft, and then, in the evenings, she would cut and shape and frown and finally stitch away, by hand, until the dress was made – and made just right for Sybil, furthermore.

'Don't use the pedlar's spoons,' Lizzie said now. 'I'll wash the good 'uns after the stew, Mum, me and Sybs will wash 'em.'

'Right.' Sybil put the bone-handled spoons and forks round the table, then got out the salt with the picture of a fleeing bird and a pursuing boy on the tin. She set the salt where she and Lizzie could see the picture, for though she thought the little boy was a stupid girlie any picture was better than none. Besides, there was writing as well as the picture and Sybil beguiled every spare moment by reading, so that even a tin of salt was better than sitting at the table for hours, just eating, whilst her library books waited for that quiet moment when she might delve into them once more.

'What's that, Mum?'

Lizzie, despite her colds and sore throats, still managed to have incredibly keen hearing. She reckoned she knew when the fish cart turned the corner up by the school, and she and Sybil often got the shed door open long before Mum – or on a Friday, Dad – had manoeuvred round the corner of the cottage and into the back yard.

Today, however, Dora Cream shook a reproving finger at her elder daughter.

'I've no doubt you're right, and it's the cart,' she said. 'But the wind's cruel, so don't you stir from that stool. Sybil, go and open the stable door, if you can manage it alone.'

Sybil saw Lizzie's expression change from excitement to annoyance and felt sorry. Poor Liz; she'd been condemned to indoors for at least a week, she had missed school, and now once more she was to be left out, to greet Dad and Georgie only after Sybil had done so, to wave to Beattie only through the window, not even the doorway. Impulsively Sybil fished the little doll out of her knicker-leg.

'Look, Liz! It's for you!'

It was worth the sacrifice of not showing off before Dad and Georgie to see the dawning delight on Lizzie's face. The large, sky-blue eyes lit up, the pale skin glowed, the faintest of rosy blushes stole across her cheeks.

'For *me*? Oh, oh, a real doll! Mum, a baby doll, and Sybs says it's for me!' Mum, piling the plates to warm on the back of the range, came over and examined the treasure.

'Well, Lizzie Cream, you *are* a lucky girl,' she said. 'That's the prettiest doll I ever did see – and you've got a kind sister too, and a kind sister is worth more than the crown jewels.'

Sybil, hand already on the latch, felt her own face glow. What a reward! Mum's commendation was worth more than anything to her . . . Mum said she was a kind sister . . . she would accept the praise, for she knew that it had been a close shave. She had never had a doll, and as she was the baby of the family it would have been understandable had she produced this one and said she wanted to keep it.

'I thought you might make it a dress, Mum,' she said, pushing the door open. 'Just a little one, out of a bit of sheet or something.'

'I don't see why not; close the door, love. I don't want to risk Lizzie getting another . . .'

The shutting door cut the sentence off and Sybil ran across the windy yard, struggled briefly with the shed doors, then got them back and wedged them with two hefty beach stones. She could see Beattie nosing carefully round the corner, bringing the fish cart home after its long day's work. Georgie was already down, running to the well to get a bucket of water. He would swill round the cart, though the big wooden boxes which held the fish would be carried down to the shore next day and given a good scrubbing. And now the equipage was before her, Beattie standing patiently whilst Dad undid the harness and backed the cart, and Sybil moved forward to give Beattie the handful of hay which she had snatched from the pile by the door when she first opened the shed.

'Have a good day, Dad?' Sybil said, coaxing Beattie into the stable. Not that the old horse needed much coaxing; she was eager for her sheltered stall and the hot mash which would presently be her lot, for Mum always had the great blackened kettle on the hob, steaming away.

'Aye, we done well,' Dad said, smiling down at her.

He was the tallest man Sybil knew as well as the biggest, and he was bright, too. His auburn hair was streaked with gold in summer as the sun lightened it, his complexion was tanned and ruddy from his outdoor life, and because he was so large Mum had to make all his clothes specially – no hand-me-downs for Dad – so that they, too, tended to be brighter than the dull stuff Dora Cream made do with for the rest of the family.

It always seemed odd to Sybil that Dad had passed his strange eyes only to herself, who was so different from her leonine sire. But the light eyes, more gold than brown, with their thick, lightish lashes, were magnificent on Harry Cream while merely pale on his little daughter, and Dad's blaze of red-gold hair had somehow turned uninteresting on Sybil and merely hung, lank and lifeless, about her narrow face.

Georgie, swilling vigorously with the aid of the yard broom, was like Lizzie in colouring, and that meant like Dora. Georgie had fair hair, thick and curly, cut cruelly short. He longed to be darker and less conspicuous, and did not really appreciate his bright blue eyes, with the thick dark lashes fringing them, that made people exclaim, to Georgie's horror, 'Oh, what a handsome little boy!'

Sybil enjoyed the admiration excited by Lizzie's good looks, and tried not to regret her own plainness. She was too skinny, her head seeming slightly out of proportion to her body, her nose – hated feature – too beaky, her chin too firm and her hands and feet far too large for the thin little limbs attached to them. Beauty was supposed not to matter, but one glance at her mother convinced Sybil that beauty was very important indeed.

For Dora Cream, barely thirty, married for more than a dozen years and mother of three children, was very beautiful. Had Dad not chosen her from the hundreds of young ladies who languished after him? He said so, and his children believed every word of it. She had been the pick of them, he told them on winter evenings round the fire; his Dora had been head and shoulders above any other girl he had ever met.

Sybil knew a little of their romantic history; how Mum had come down to the village with an uncle and aunt, partly for a holiday but also to help look after her younger cousins. She had never been to the seaside before and had loved everything about it, from the Punch and Judy show on the pier to the theatrical entertainments – and the fisherman who came twice a week to the back door, selling his fresh fish from a great basket which he carried over one arm as though it contained half-a-dozen roses and not a couple of stone of cod and whiting.

Mum was a lady. Born Dora Elizabeth Maddeley, she had never dreamed of marrying a fisherman, living in a little cottage, selling fish from door to door – not until she met Henry Cream. One glance, Dad said dramatically, and they knew! One touch of the hand, and Mum had agreed to leave her uncle and aunt and her cousins, and to exchange her comfortable life in the big house just outside Norwich for the hand-to-mouth existence of a fisherman's wife in a rented cottage perched a few yards above the cold North Sea.

And wasn't it lucky for us that Mum decided to marry Dad? Sybil asked herself as she helped Georgie swing the shed doors shut. Dad had manhandled the cart into the shed, picked up the empty fish-boxes and carried them out as though they weighed nothing. But if Sybil and Georgie were detailed, next day, to do the cleaning, it would take two of them to a box to get them down to the waterline.

'Tea, kids,' Dad shouted presently. He breezed into the kitchen and over to the sink, Georgie staggering in his wake with a full bucket. Dad tipped the water into the big china basin and began to wash, though if he had waited Mum would have added some hot, for hauling the nets was dirty work. He splashed and soaped and rinsed, rubbed dry on the thin roller towel which hung behind the back door, then stepped aside whilst Georgie rather less enthusiastically followed suit. Only then, when her men were clean and turning expectantly towards the table, did Mum begin to dish up.

They all took their places, even Lizzie abandoning her fireside seat at a nod from Mum. She still clutched the little doll, and when they were seated Mum carried the big pot of stew over to the table and began to ladle it on to each plate. One ladle for Sybil, half for Lizzie who had to be persuaded to eat when she had a feverish cold, two for herself and Georgie and four for Dad.

Boiled potatoes from Dad's allotment, floury and bursting out of their skins, came next. Six for Dad, two for Georgie, and one each for the females. No grace was said since Dad kept such matters for Sunday, but they all waited until Mum picked up her spoon and fork before falling to, with Dad scattering salt and talking all the while, about the maidservant at the vicarage who had given him a bag of apples, and the scandalous price he had asked – and got – for a fine Dover sole as big as a Christmas turkey.

Lizzie's preoccupation with her new possession was noted, the little doll admired. Sybil was congratulated on her find and, again, on her kindness in making such a generous present to her sister. Georgie demonstrated, though Mum frowned, how he could now whistle an Irish jig even when joggling along in the fish cart. Potato sprayed the table and Dad laughed, boisterous as the blustering wind, whilst Mum scolded and hid her dimpling smile.

After tea, when the pots were washed up and put away and the hens and Beattie fed, the family settled round the fire for a while before the children were sent to bed. Mum knitted; Dad fetched out his pile of twine and went on with his net, his knots neat and his big fingers quick at the familiar task.

Georgie and Sybil sat on the rag rug in front of the softly humming range and Georgie worked on his model fishing boat. He made one or two every year and sold them before Christmas to get money for presents. Sybil hemmed dusters, a job she loathed and was extremely bad at, so that the dusters were always cobbled, blood-spotted and dirty. Still, as Mum said, the whole purpose of a duster was to collect dirt, so what mattered if it collected a bit first?

Lizzie sat with them, but though she was meant to hem dusters her needle moved even more slowly than Sybil's, and presently she stopped sewing, leaned against her father's broad thigh and pretended to read, by fire and smoky lamplight. Despite being the great age of twelve, Lizzie was not a keen scholar – too lazy, said their teacher, and too often poorly, said Mum. Now she had one of Sybil's old comics spread out on her knee and chuckled quietly to herself now and then. Sometimes Dad put his big hand across the pictures and said, 'Wait on, my woman,' and told them a story of something that had happened to him on the round to make them smile, and once or twice Mum capped a story with some experience of her own and they laughed aloud.

A nice autumn evening, Sybil thought contentedly, stabbing her needle into the thin cotton. Cold enough to make the kitchen cosy, to mean curtains drawn and the range opened up so that it roared and warmed the room delightfully. But later on, when winter really came, it would be too cold to sit on the floor, and Georgie, Lizzie and herself would shiver and long for bedtime. It was grand to slide on the ice and frolic in the snow when you were warmly clad, but darkness came early and the cold made the long evenings miserable. There was no fun in going to bed when you could feel the wind like icicles as you lay between the blankets and the water froze in the jug and Lizzie left you to sleep on a straw mattress set out in the kitchen as near to the range as Mum dared put her.

However, winter was still in the future and Lizzie, hugging her doll, would presently take her place in the big, sagging bed with kicking Georgie and snoring Sybil – so she claimed – to snort and snuffle all night herself, and pretend to be asleep in the morning no matter how zealously they tried to wake her, for dear, pretty Lizzie hated rising.

Posh people, like the Wintertons, were surprised that the girls should share a bed with their brother, but Dad said he'd slept with his sister until he got so big there was no room in the bed, so that was all right.

'Kids, they're like puppies; they thrive no matter what,' he said cheerfully. 'Don't you worry, gal Dora. Them littl'uns won't come to no manner of harm.'

But now, drowsing on the floor and watching Lizzie's golden head begin to droop, Sybil ignored the adult conversation going on over her head and wondered idly about the little doll. It occurred to her for the first time that her gain had been someone's loss. Further up the coast, perhaps, a child had laid the doll down on the sand for a few moments and then forgotten it, or perhaps someone on one of the big ships which plied up and down the North Sea had cast the toy down on the deck and it had been washed overboard in a storm. She knew that few local children possessed dolls.

It was even possible, she supposed, that the doll had come from the drowned village. There must be houses down there as well as the church, it stood to reason. One of Dad's stories concerned the night when the sea had come thundering in and the villagers had fled. It might be that the baby doll had been dropped in flight, or even left in one of the houses. Sybil often saw those houses in her mind, never looking like her own home but more like the illustrations in a book of Hans Andersen's fairy tales, with wavy tiles around which the fishes played, and gingerbread doors and window-frames. Now, for the first time, she allowed her mind to venture inside. She saw the quaint stove and the curly-armed chairs, the pictures, bright and glowing, the china set out on the dresser, all waving slightly as the water moved with the tides and the fishes investigated everything, as curious as Sybil herself. There were toys by the dresser: dolls, a spinning top, a big jigsaw. What misery, Sybil mourned, to lose such lovely playthings; how the children must have missed them . . . and yes, there was the baby doll, actually on the dresser . . . a big fish was nosing it, presently he would pick it up and swim out of the doorway with it. She saw the fish wriggle out into the underwater village street, complete with cobbles and quaint lamp-posts, every lamp lit. She followed, knowing the fish would be heading towards the coast, would drop the doll when someone threw stale bread from a boat into the surging, bobbing waves, and the sea would carry it . . .

'Come on, Sybs, no use pretending, you aren't asleep!'

Georgie's words were accompanied by a fierce tweak at her hair. For a moment Sybil was so confused that she held her breath, fearing that she might breathe water and drown, but then the dream receded and she recognized the firelit room, Dad's big fingers moving nimbly among the twine, Mum's slim hands placidly stitching a shirt. She must have been asleep and dreaming, just as Lizzie was at this minute.

Mum put down her work and leaned over to shake Lizzie's shoulder, but her daughter woke at the first touch and struggled to her feet.

'It's not fair. Sybil's the baby, not me. You should make her go up first!'

'She's a-goin', my woman, so just you get up them stairs,' Dad advised. 'How about a cuppa, Doe?'

'Kettle's boiling,' Dora said. 'You make it, I'll see the kids into bed. I think poor little Sybs is worn out tonight. We shouldn't have left them so late.'

Sybil could tell the clock. She read the hands . . . heavens, ten past nine! She and Lizzie were always upstairs by eight as a rule – and she, like an idiot, had gone to sleep and missed the extra evening!

'It's all right, Mum, I'm awake now,' she said, a trifle thickly. She put a hand on the wall to steady herself, for she was still dopy with sleep interrupted. 'Lizzie and me can put ourselves to bed.'

But Mum was leading Lizzie up the box-stairs, smiling, shaking her head.

'I'll see to her, she's still thick with cold,' she said. 'No school tomorrow, it being Saturday, so the three of you can have a bit of a lie-in.'

'I'm off early,' Georgie said importantly. 'I'm barrowing leaves up at the big houses. The Winterton place first – you like going there, don't you, Sybs? You could help me if you like; I'll give you a penny if you work hard.'

An extra penny! Cushies and comics! And best of all she would be spending time at the Winterton Place. The Wintertons had three children, a boy of Georgie's age and a girl who was ten, the same as Sybil, as well as a spoilt five-year-old, but she had a nanny and was rarely with the older children. Sybil hero-worshipped Ralph and thought baby Felicity pretty, but it was Chris who was her friend. Unfortunately, though, they had gone back to Norwich ages ago. They were summer visitors, spending the weeks from June to September in the big house with its beautiful garden and then returning to the city and their schools in time for the autumn term. It was wonderful to visit Malverns – that was what the house was called – during the summer when the Wintertons were in residence, but Sybil enjoyed being there at any time. It reminded her of Chris and the good times they had together.

'Thanks, Georgie; wake me when you get up, then.'

In their bedroom, Sybil began to undress as she had been taught, which meant slipping her voluminous nightie – a hand-me-down from Mum – over her clothes and then struggling out of everything else whilst the nightie heaved up and down like a ship at sea. She saw that Mum was busy with her sister, and wondered whether to cheat and leave her knickers and vest on. After all, it was very cold tonight, even though Mum would not consider October to be winter. She could pretend she had forgotten . . . but Mum was always liable to give her cast-off clothing the once over and the absence of underclothing would be immediately obvious.

Sybil began, wincingly, to slip out of her vest. It was shrunk from many washes but it was a good one, or had once been a good one, and Mum would be reluctant to pronounce it too small since there was no younger child to whom it might be passed on. Inside the underclothes she was warm, but her hands were like ice and she shrank from the prospect of touching her body.

'Mum saw her struggling and came over to give her a hand, having tumbled her elder daughter into bed where Lizzie lay snugly, the covers pulled up to her chin.

'Are you trying to get out of that vest? It's chilly up here; best leave it on,' she decided. 'I always say winter's here come November, but it seems to have arrived early this year, or perhaps it's just my bones growing older and feeling the cold more.'

'Then mine are growing older too,' Sybil said, picking up her shoes and putting them under the bedside chair, next to Lizzie's almost new pumps. Next, she brushed her hair until it crackled; Mum was strict about things like hair brushing and washing. 'Wish it was winter enough for a bottle.'

Mum smiled, but shook her head.

'No use growing up soft, Sybs,' she told her daughter, opening the bed invitingly. 'Just be glad we've not got enough money for sheets – now they really are cold of a night!'

'And Lizzie's like a hot bottle, only softer and nicer,' Sybil said, jumping into bed and putting both arms round her big sister, who squeaked at the sudden chill but cuddled close. 'Shout Georgie, will you, Mum?'

Georgie, who undressed in his parents' room, came through in his nightshirt. He brought his stump of candle with him, though Mum was even now pinching the girls' candle out between wetted finger and thumb.

'Into bed, Georgie,' Mum said cheerfully. 'Get a good night's sleep, all of you – you'll have a busy day tomorrow!'

She took Georgie's candle, watched him cuddle down and then made for the low doorway. Mum was taller than the children and had to bow her head to get out on to the tiny landing.

'No chattering, now. Goodnight.'

She went, her long shadow the last to leave the room. Sybil looked around her, as she did each night before she slept. The low, sloping ceiling was cracked and over the window rainwater had leaked through the roof tiles; the water made interesting faces on the plaster, only you couldn't see them at night, just the outline of the window, with the sky which had looked so dark by candlelight light now and freckled with stars.

Some nights, the round, enquiring face of the moon peered in at the three children in the sagging bed. But tonight Sybil could not see even a sliver, though it must be out there somewhere. If you could see the stars that meant a clear sky, and a clear sky meant a moon.

Sighing, Sybil curled a little lower in the bed and pulled a scratchy, comforting blanket up to rub it softly, hypnotically, against her cheek. As she moved she felt, in Lizzie's hand, the baby doll's head against her for a moment, warm and real-feeling from Lizzie's own warmth.

She remembered her dream suddenly, with affection. It was a beautiful thing, to dream about the village under the sea. Wouldn't it be strange if the doll really had come from one of those houses, cast ashore by a freak wave for Sybil Cream to find, for Lizzie Cream to cherish? But it could not possibly be so, things like that just didn't happen. No, the toy must have been dropped by a child. She just hoped it was not a poor child, like her and Lizzie, with no doll save for the one now sharing their bed.

But it was impossible to feel any real degree of sympathy for an unknown child who might or might not be missing the doll. We'll call her Jane Eyre, Sybil thought, after that book of Mum's. Well, Jane, anyway. I'll get Lizzie to knit a little wee blanket to wrap round her, like a shawl, and perhaps Georgie will make her a wooden pram!

Plans, dreams, wishes. Sybil lay curled close to Lizzie with Georgie's solid back against hers and let her mind stray until, at last, she slept.

2

Dora Cream left the children and made her way downstairs again. As she re-entered the kitchen Henry looked up and smiled at her and she felt again, as though it were only yesterday, the rush of warmth and love which that selfsame smile had conjured up in the young Dora more than fourteen years ago.

'All serene, gal?'

'Yes. Lizzie's settled, Sybs was half asleep and Georgie's head only has to touch the pillow for him to be off. He works hard, does that boy.'

'That he do.' Henry Cream stretched and yawned hugely, then heaved himself to his feet and rolled his work into a ball. Despite his size he was a neat man, but perhaps that was all part and parcel of his trade; there was no room for untidiness in a fishing boat, he always said. 'Well, old gal, I'm for a spot of kip; don't know about you.'

Dora glanced at the clock in the corner. A grandmother clock, its smiling face had watched every day of her marriage, for even when she had given birth to the children she had come downstairs to make her man his meals and see to his wants. Now, the hands announced that it was ten o'clock; plenty late enough when you had to pay for the oil in the lamp – had to be up early, too, day in, day out.

'Right; I'll just tidy round.'

Dora always saw Henry off to bed and then 'tidied round', as she called it. She damped down the range fire with ash and closed the doors across, and she pulled the rug away just in case the stove spat, though heaven knew how it could do so with the doors shut. Then she brushed through and checked that the water buckets were full for the morning. If she had used half a bucket she might refill it then and there or she might not, depending on how she felt. In winter she rarely bothered, in summer she usually did.

That done, she shot the big bolts, top and bottom, across the back door. She checked that the curtains were closed tight, she plumped up cushions, ran a duster over the dresser, laid the table for breakfast. Then she picked up the big, blackened kettle which was singing gently to itself on top of the stove and carried it with her up the stairs. Past experience told her that by the time she got up Henry would be snug in bed, and would watch her getting ready with bright, interested eyes.

'Don't you stare, you rude old devil,' she protested mildly tonight as she pulled her dress over her head, gasping as the chilly air touched her flesh. 'Just you close your eyes, Henry Cream!'

She began to wash, the water warm, the soap, though just cheap stuff, smelling sweet and fresh. It was a nightly ritual, this strip-down wash, carried out winter and summer alike, a left-over from her Maddeley life, when to go to bed unwashed would have been unimaginable unless one were ill.

'Why should I, gal, when you're such a pretty sight?' Henry said from the depths of the bed. 'Best thing I sin all day long, my missus in the raw!'

'After three kids and a dozen years of selling fish house to house, and cleaning and cooking . . .'

'It suits you,' Henry said.

He was grinning as she finished rubbing herself into a glow with the rough towel, still smiling when her head popped through the neck of her cotton nightdress. I'm the opposite of most women, Dora told herself, beginning to brush her long, wheat-coloured hair. Most women dress up to go out, and I wear my best to go to bed!

'Come on, my woman, don't hang around out there gettin' cold, do I'll simply hev to warm you up in th'only way I know.'

Dora shook a reproving head at him, then doused the candle, hearing the little hiss it made, smelling the cooling wax, with a familiar frisson of excitement running down her spine. Fourteen years married and still as daft for Henry Cream as she had been on that holiday in Pakeby when she had first seen him! Fourteen years married . . . eh, that it could come to this! Not that she regretted it, not really. Why, if it hadn't been for Henry, God knew what might have happened to her at the hands of her Uncle Ambrose.

She got into bed and immediately Henry's arms went round her. He gave her a hard hug and buried his head in her neck, inhaling deeply.

'Oh, littl'un, you smell so good! Oh, Doe, what you do to me!'

He was a strange man in some ways; despite her urgings he would never 'crack his jaw' as he called it and try to play down the rich

Suffolk accent he had grown up with. What was the point? he asked when she gently nagged him. But he was as quick as she to reprove the children, to see that they spoke a more standard English than that of their schoolfellows.

Not that it worked, or ever could. The kids spoke the dialect they heard all around them but calmed it down indoors, talking as their mother wished. And Dora did most urgently want more for her children than she wanted for herself. She had had her chance and thrown it away to go to Henry, and she had never regretted it nor ever would. The easy life held no attraction if it meant losing her man. She had decided that at sixteen, when . . .

Her mind went back to that long-ago day even as Henry, with the gentle deftness which was so much a part of him, began to take off the nightdress she had so recently put on.

It had been a hot summer. The war still raged in Europe and even Dora, who really knew very little about it, had grown depressed as the list of young men, wounded, dead or missing, lengthened in the newspapers. So she was doubly grateful to the Alsopp family for bringing her down to Pakeby, even though their altruism had been encouraged by the fact that Dora was 'so good with the little ones'. Uncle Ambrose, a heavy-set man in his early forties, had married Aunt Dulcie and proceeded to father what seemed to Dora like innumerable children upon her. Aunt Dulcie, never exactly robust, had shrunk from a pretty, nervous girl into a pale, nervous woman who, by the time she was thirty, could have been taken for fifty.

Of course they had a nursemaid, but because Ambrose was so tight-fisted they rarely kept anyone for long. The present incumbent, a child of fourteen – a mere four years older than the eldest Alsopp – had no chance of controlling her high-spirited brood. Indeed, it was all that Dora could do to keep them employed so that her aunt should have some peace and quiet.

Dora, however, was an only child and enjoyed the company of her young cousins. She was glad to give her aunt what help she could, and she loved the seaside and the less formal attitudes which prevailed in Pakeby. At barely sixteen she was still at boarding school, still officially a child, and therefore seldom allowed to take decisions for herself or do as she pleased. The Maddeley house was run by servants, who, though they were kind enough to the motherless little girl in their charge, still made her feel a nuisance at times. Her father, Giles Maddeley, was a diplomat in India, and treated his child like a stranger on his rare visits home. Dora was sure her father blamed her for her mother's death in childbirth; certainly he avoided her company, so it seemed wonderful when Uncle Ambrose not only agreed to take her to the seaside but actually paid her some attention, taking her for walks, accompanying her on shopping trips into Lowestoft and promising to hire a boat so that they might go a-rowing. Being not only young but also almost shamingly innocent, she had no idea that Uncle Ambrose intended anything but kindness towards his motherless niece.

So the stage was set. The rambling old house with its wild, unkempt garden, those trees that had survived the harsh winters bending sideways as though even in the warmth of summer the gales still blew. The worn-out mother, the hearty, too-attentive father, the boisterous children ... and Dora. Tall for her age, Dora had an hour-glass figure which drew admiring glances when she displayed it even in the decorous swimming costumes of the day, and her magnificent fall of wavy fair hair, deep blue eyes and milky complexion were much praised by Aunt Dulcie and much admired by Uncle Ambrose, who told her, thickly, when he had drunk his after-dinner port, that she was a little beauty, that she was!

And Henry Cream, strolling up the drive, tanned to a rich and even brown, his auburn hair gilded by the sun, his size, his strength, his laugh ... ah, they commanded attention. Even pale Aunt Dulcie smiled for him, but Dora, trembling at his mocking glance, had done more than smile. She had agreed to meet him at the beatster huts down on the beach one evening.

She was there. So was he. The Alsopps believed her to be visiting the girls at the vicarage. It was mid-week and Uncle Ambrose, who might have been suspicious considering what his own intentions towards her were, was home in Norwich, working. Dora tripped down to the beatster huts and was very soon inside one of them, examining the fishing gear, the nets, the floats, being shown how to bait a hook. Henry explained why he was not in the navy, not that she cared a jot for that – she was just glad. But he was the sole support of his widowed mother and had no intention of going off and leaving the old lady to starve, he told her seriously. Besides, he was only seventeen; there was plenty of time yet.

The two of them spent hours together, talking, tentatively kissing, and very soon Dora thought of little beside Henry Cream. She lived for the evenings, for the games the two of them played in the beatster huts when the light began to fade and Henry drew her down on to a soft couch of nets and blankets and taught her ... oh, all sorts of things.

She would never forget the evening when, in the midst of delight, she had noticed something about on a level with her head: boots, black and shiny, the laces neatly tied. Carried away by passion, she had barely registered that they were there, where they should not have been, before she forgot them. And next time she looked, lying sated and quiet, she saw that above the boots there were trousers. Dark grey, with a lighter grey stripe. Or were they black, with a grey stripe? And then she had looked up further . . . further . . . and seen Uncle Ambrose looming above her, knew that he had been there . . . too long. She had given a small, apologetic moan and tried to scramble to her feet, pushing Henry's strong shoulders aside, suddenly scarlet with embarrassment, speechless with terror.

There had been a scene between the three of them, but the purport of it had been lost on her at the time. Only much later did she understand why Henry had absolutely forbidden her to go with Uncle Ambrose, who intended, he said, to teach her the error of her ways. His eyes shone as though filled with tears and his lips were trembling and wet; a muscle twitched in his cheek and he kept trying to touch Dora's dishevelled hair and tear-streaked face, told her he would not be too hard on her if she came with him now . . .

And all the time, Henry. A hard arm round her, fingers gripping her shoulder, a firm young voice.

'We're a-goin' to get wed, her and me,' he repeated. 'Don't want no errors . . . we're a-goin' to get wed!'

He had walked with her up to the rented house, insisted on speaking to Aunt Dulcie, would have taken her up to the room she shared with the nursery maid and two small cousins, save that even Dora had been shocked by that.

And next day, very early, he had come to the house. 'I've hed words wi' Vicar, told him we want the knot tied,' he said. What did the Alsopps intend to do about it?

They would have carried her home to Norwich, but Dora warned them she would simply run back to Henry. They reminded her she was under age, that her father would never agree. She said – with truth as it turned out – that she was going to have a baby and her father would be only too happy to see her married to the man of her choice. As it happened he never did see her married, since even after his final return to England he never came near nor by his daughter. But he sent a long letter saying that he washed his hands of her, and it would be as if she had never lived.

Only it wasn't, not quite. Henry knew the Maddeleys were a proud family and he wrung some concessions out of them. The house, for instance. When they first married he and Dora had moved into the small house on The Street with Henry's mother, but this had not been a satisfactory arrangement at all. So Henry put on his best suit, tilted a rakish trilby over his glorious auburn hair, and set out on the bus for Norwich. He did not take Dora, but when he came back he had worked it all out, he said. They were to rent the end cottage on Beach Road, nearest the sea. It would be cheap as it was in poor condition, having been 'let go' by the old man who had lived there for the past eighty-odd years.

The babies came. First Georgie, then Lizzie, finally Sybil. Times were hard; the depression was making itself felt. Henry's small boat would not support his growing family, so a share in a larger boat was indicated.

Once more Henry put on his best suit, now very shiny at the elbows and more than a trifle tight across the shoulders, for Henry seemed to get larger and stronger and . . . and warmer, somehow, with each passing year. This time he was gone longer, but when he came back he was smiling. A share in a bigger boat had been negotiated, and, what was more, a little cart!

'I told 'em if I caught more fish I wouldn't want you trying to carry a heavy basket door to door,' Henry murmured in bed that night. 'Said with a little cart we'd be able to git further afield, do more trade. Said that waren't no manner of use them turnin' up their snouts at us, do we'd hev to come up the city, let folk see what you'd come to.'

'Oh, Hal, that's blackmail,' Dora protested, snuggling into his arms. 'And I never would shame them so . . . though it would serve Father right if I did!'

'He've married himself a fine sorta woman,' Henry remarked presently. 'That's her we'll want to keep our eyes on, gal – holds herself to be suffin' special, she do.'

Dora sat up.

'Married? My father, married again?'

'That's right. Never a word to us, what should've been at the weddin'. Did he ax our littl'uns to be bridesmaids? That he didn't! Still, that's a rare good little cart.'

It was. And the mare, Beattie, was a sturdy beast and reliable, not given to histrionics when she found herself pulling a fish cart nor making a fuss when cars came too close or rude boys shouted after them as they plied along the village streets.

And Dora Cream, née Maddeley? The young lady who had gone

to one of the country's foremost boarding schools? Who had had her own personal maid and a staff of servants who, if they did not rush to cater for her every whim, at least fed, clothed and pampered her? How did she take the change in her circumstances? She had never boiled a kettle, let alone an egg; couldn't even make up a fire, never mind lay and light one. She could sew, true, and knit as well, since boarding school girls were expected to make blankets for the poor and awful little vests and socks for the heathen. Now, she *was* the poor, though she did not immediately realize it. At first she just watched Henry's sharp-tongued mother doing the work; then she began to copy her. She carted heavy buckets of water for old Mrs Cream and cut thick wedges of bread and buttered them, peeled potatoes, sliced cabbage. She left gutting fish and scrubbing floors to her unwilling hostess, until the day, twelve weeks after their marriage, when Henry came in and told her about the house.

It should have been easier, despite the thickening at her waist which was shortly to be Georgie, to work in one's own home. But it was not. She found she resented the hard, back-breaking toil, the unremitting labour from early morning until late at night. She hated the fish-round, trying to cope with the heavy basket, feeling ashamed to be asking the maidservants who came to the kitchen doors to buy her fish, swearing it was fresh that day, sometimes being disbelieved, sometimes turned away.

But she had a strong back and a strong mind too, did Dora Cream. She bore her son without much fuss – a few harsh screams were torn from her, screams of pain and surprise, because no one had told her how much it hurt to give birth – and then she began the business of being Henry's wife in earnest.

She took in washing in the summer, and went up to the big houses to clean for the visitors. The Alsopps never came again, thank heaven, for Henry had told her what Ambrose had intended to do to her, and why he, Henry, had talked to Aunt Dulcie so earnestly and long. She carried her baby on one hip and the basket of fish on the other, and trudged all round Pakeby and even Lowestoft in the summer, so that Henry could be out with the boat from dawn to dusk and not have to come home early to sell his catch.

She scrubbed and cleaned her little house, whitewashed the walls and painted the doors and window frames. She dug a strip of garden and planted potatoes and peas and winter cabbage. She bought hens and a cockerel and reared their chicks, then sold eggs, bought flour and fruit and sold the rich and heavy cakes she made in her awkward old open-fronted oven. The years ought to have taken their toll of her, robbed her of her youthful bloom, but somehow they had not. She remained tall and slim, heavy-breasted, her hips round and firm, her skin white and smooth and her hair thick and shining, soft to the touch and smelling of roses. She kept herself scrupulously clean and saw that her children were clean too, and although she was often tired and sometimes cross she was also deeply happy.

But she knew what she had missed, and even though she did not want it for herself she wanted it for her children, particularly for her daughters. Georgie was a good boy; he would take to the fishing like a duck to water, follow in Henry's footsteps and perhaps even do better. But Lizzie was going to be a beauty, and since there were not likely to be two men like Henry in one century the girl must not stay here in the village and find herself scrubbing floors and selling fish for the rest of her life. She must have the chances that Dora Maddeley had so blithely spurned, begin the scramble upwards towards the favoured position which Dora had taken such delight in leaving behind her.

And Sybil? Well, she was not beautiful, but she was bright and hardworking and if she did well at school she might at least earn a good living. Besides, she had Henry's colouring, though she was a stringy little thing. If only she had his charm as well . . .

What was that saying? You can't make a silk purse out of a sow's ear. Ah, but my girls *are* silk, Dora reminded herself. Pure silk. They're worth more than this, and they're going to get it if I have my way. What does it matter if Sybil's plain? She's got brains and character; that will be sufficient. So Dora encouraged Sybil to read everything she could lay hands on, to study hard so that school became a pleasure and not a penance. She made sure, too, that Sybil could clean and cook and make do and mend, because her younger daughter might well find herself wed to a fisherman and needing such skills more than the bright intelligence which Dora saw in the child's plain little face.

Lizzie must be taught the importance of a good education too, of course. Lizzie was lazy, but she had a good brain and must be taught to use it, if only to further herself. Dora had always impressed on her children the importance of cleanliness, of decent clothing, and above all of clear, self-confident speech. She knew they must mix with the village children and understood that they would speak dialect amongst their peers, but she encouraged them to play with the summer visitors whenever possible and was delighted when Georgie and Sybil took to the Wintertons as they had.

It was lucky, really, that the Wintertons had the house whose land came all the way down to the coast. They were very well-to-do and had ponies which, in summer, grazed right up to the Creams' back yard. Dora had fed those ponies over the fence when her own stock were going short – she felt ashamed, but knew she was doing the right thing when the kids began to chatter to each other, when Christina Winterton swung, side by side with Sybil, on the five-barred gate leading out into the lane.

Dora would have preferred Christina to have become friendly with Lizzie, but like goes to like; Sybil and Christina were the same age and both crazy about ponies. Lizzie did not like horses and was just beginning, her mother noticed, to take some interest in boys. Her appearance was becoming increasingly important to Lizzie, even at the tender age of twelve.

Christina, who had no interest in her appearance whatsoever so far as Dora could see, had lovely dresses and smart bathing costumes and rode in real jodhpurs and shiny brown leather riding boots. She had a bicycle which Sybil had learned to ride, her kite was the envy of all Pakeby, and she had pocket-money and heaps of beach-toys and a French cricket set. But she was a tomboy, a plain girl with protruding teeth which were being straightened by means of a wire brace. Her hair was well cut, but it was a very ordinary brown. Nevertheless, Dora knew that doors which would open wide for Christina would never creak even an inch apart for Sybil. That was birth for you – and money, of course. Birth and money would mean more, in the end, even than the beauty which Dora could clearly see in Lizzie and hoped, rather despairingly, might miraculously appear in plain little Sybil.

But if Christina was plain, Ralph was handsome. He was Georgie's age – thirteen – and his golden-brown hair curled. He was tall and straight-backed, though he wore his nice clothes with an air of indifference and as often as not his bicycle was slung down in the Creams' front garden whilst Ralph hung around the beatster huts with Georgie or begged a trip in the fishing boat from Henry.

He'd do nicely for Sybil, if only she was pretty, Dora found herself thinking, sometimes. He's got a kind heart, he gets on well with the kids, he'll make a grand husband . . . but he'll not want plain little Sybs. Lizzie, then? Yes, Lizzie could do a lot worse. It didn't do to plan too much, but Dora could not help thinking what a nice couple they would make, Elizabeth Cream and Ralph.

Kids usually went against what you wanted, of course, but Lizzie would be sensible. Anyway, the last thing she intended to do was get stuck in Pakeby. She had announced only a few days ago that she would have to work harder in class because she wanted to win a scholarship to the grammar school in the port, so she could visit the shops. That was sensible talk, Dora considered, and she hoped that, in the fullness of time, Lizzie would not just talk about working harder at her lessons, but would actually do so. Right now, Sybil was the one with ambition. She said she wanted to be a teacher, but though teaching would suit her youngest, Dora did not believe in pretty girls' wasting their time on careers; they married well. Sybil should teach, but she saw no need for lovely Lizzie to squander her talents in the classroom.

Henry guessed that Dora had plans for the kids, but he didn't mind, so long as she didn't give them ideas above their station or make them look down on their own parents. As if they would! Henry hoped that one day he and Georgie would own a trawler; now that really was thinking big!

Dora smiled and sighed to herself, turning over in bed. Good heavens, if she did not get to sleep soon it would be morning and then how would she tackle the day? She cuddled up to Henry, clinging warmly. Oh, God, how she loved him!

Soon, she slept.

3

'Miss Christina, what are you rootin' in that cupboard for? Just you come outer there this minute!'

Chris backed out of the cupboard and smiled placatingly at Norah, who had been the family nurse and was now what her mother described as 'a sort of housekeeper'. Whatever she was, Chris had more sense than to cheek her – Norah could land you a clout over the side of the ear which could send you halfway across the room, no error!

'I'm trying to find Pheenie,' she said soothingly. 'Don't fuss, Norah, I won't make a mess. But Felicity hates going to bed without her, you know.'

'She've only just remembered she've lost the bloomin' creature,' Norah said. 'What's the use of goin' through all that there truck? She left that at Pakeby, as well you know, miss!'

'She thinks Pheenie might have been brought back and then mislaid here,' Chris explained. 'Of course she wasn't, but you know what Flicky is; if I can go back to the nursery and say I searched the whole toy-cupboard and Pheenie wasn't there, then she'll calm down, but if I say she knows jolly well the doll's in Pakeby she'll have a blue fit.'

'That child's spoiled rotten,' Norah grumbled. She came over and stirred with a contemptuous foot the piles of toys, dolls and books which Chris had already removed from the deep, walk-in closet. 'All this stuff and come Christmas she'll have a pile more. You didn't ought to give way to her, miss, do she'll be downright nasty by the time she's your age.'

'She can be pretty nasty already,' Chris observed from the depths of the cupboard. She came out, backwards, with her arms full of rag picture books. 'There! That's the lot. And no Pheenie. Do you know, Norah, I often feel sorry for Flicky, even though she can be horrid. She's awfully lonely . . . Mummy won't even let her start school!'

'Your mum think the sun shine out of that little madam just because she've got curly hair and blue eyes,' Norah remarked. 'No, don't put that stuff back – I'll give that cupboard a brush through now it's empty.' She hurried out of the room and Chris smiled affectionately at her back view, the tight little bun of greying hair, the starched pinafore, the navy and white striped dress, the thick black stockings wrinkling down to her ankles. She loved Norah, knowing that the slaps and the discipline hid a very soft heart, and that Norah would probably have died for herself or Ralph. Norah, despite her gruff ways, was fond of all her nurslings, though Flicky tried her patience sorely.

'Here we are,' she said triumphantly now, returning with a long-handled broom. 'Soon have that nasty dust outer there.' Norah had a round, countrified face, a snub nose which shone as though polished and a big mouth overfull of yellowy teeth. But despite her looks, all the Wintertons, from the oldest to the youngest, valued her enormously. Chris watched as she proceeded to brush with great enthusiasm, guiding out on to the linoleum floor a number of wax crayons, pencil sharpenings, crumpled paper and other debris as well as a good deal of the despised dust. Then Norah picked up the little brass shovel which hung by the grate, scooped up the dirt and flung it on to the dying fire, finishing it off for good and all, Chris suspected. 'There! Now I'll give you a hand to tidy up, my woman.'

'Thanks, Norah, you're a brick,' Chris said with real gratitude. 'I'm sorry we didn't find Pheenie, but knowing Flicky, she'll have forgotten all about her in a day or so. Uncle Dan brought her a teddy bear from London with a little red jacket and a lovely growl when you press its tummy. It should have been a Christmas present, but Mummy said she might have it right away. She'll soon stop grizzling for Pheenie.'

'I don't see how she can say she miss the doll, when we're bin back from Pakeby weeks and no word till now,' Norah observed, picking up the piles of toys and replacing them in the cupboard in orderly rows. 'That in't like Felicity not to air a grievance.'

Chris, staggering into the cupboard with her arms full of soft toys, chuckled breathlessly.

'She hasn't given Pheenie a thought since we left,' she admitted. 'It was Uncle Dan's teddy – she was parading round with it and happened to say she'd take it to bed with her and Mummy, never thinking, said, "My goodness, darling, so Teddy is to replace Pheenie!" and of course that just about did it.'

'I can imagine,' Norah said grimly. 'Set up a squall, did she?'

'You could've heard her on Castle Meadow,' Chris said with a trace of pride in her voice. The Winterton family lived halfway up St Giles, so a holler which could be heard clear across the city was something to boast about. 'She threw the teddy smack into the big vase of chrysanthemums by the window, and Mummy had to ring for Ena.'

Ena was Mrs Winterton's maid, a starchy, disapproving woman who had been with her mistress before her marriage to Frederick Winterton and whose devotion was a by-word amongst the family. Norah sniffed.

'Your mum oughter give that child a good smack round the chops,' she said uncompromisingly. 'She'll find she've reared a monster if she give Felicity her own way over and over.'

'Oh, Flicky will be all right. After all, Ralph and me aren't so bad, are we? And she's a Winterton, like us.'

'I dare say. But you had me to keep you on the straight and narrer. Who've Felicity got, hey? A tottie-head like that Elsie in't goin' to do her much good.'

Norah had resented being told, at the age of forty-one, that she was 'too old' to take care of the latest addition to the Winterton nursery, though mollified by being kept on as a sort of general factotum. And she was right about Flicky, Chris considered, as she finished tidying the things away. Elsie was no match for her spoilt little charge, much preferring to give in to her rather than face tantrums and tale-bearings. But quite soon now school would be Felicity's lot and that, Chris knew, would be a salutary lesson for her small sister.

'Have you done? Then you'd best be gettin' downstairs,' Norah said, as Chris emerged from the cupboard for the last time. 'Oh, you'll want to nip into the night-nursery to tell Felicity you in't found Pheenie.'

'I'll do that on my way down,' Chris said. 'Thanks a lot for your help, Norah. Nightie-night.'

'Goodnight, my woman,' Norah said gruffly as Chris gave her a hug and then kissed her resoundingly on the cheek. 'You're a good gal, you are! Now off with you; I've got work to do even if you han't.'

Chris turned to leave the nursery, seeing that Norah was about to make up the fire with coal dust to keep it in till morning. It was Elsie's job to do things like that but she hardly ever remembered and Norah, though she grumbled about the younger girl, would not have dreamed of letting poor Elsie face a chilly nursery in the morning. Of course the fire was allowed to go out every Sunday night and one of the housemaids laid and lit it anew each Monday morning, but during the week Elsie was meant to keep the fire in or lay and light it herself.

The entire top floor of the house in St Giles was given over to the three children and their various attendants. There was the day-nursery, from which Chris had just emerged, and the night-nursery, where Felicity lay, no doubt still snivelling, with Elsie's bed opposite her own. Between the two there was Norah's small bedroom and the sewing room, where Norah and Elsie did quantities of ironing and darning besides a good deal of what Mummy called light dressmaking but which, in practice, more often meant making up curtains, chair-covers and other household items. Mummy adored what she called interior decorating and was always changing her colour schemes.

On the other side of the landing was Chris's own neat room and Ralph's larger – and untidier – domain, and then came the schoolroom where, in the evenings, Ralph and Chris sat to do their homework and afterwards amused themselves with jigsaws or books or squabbled amicably over draughts or card games.

At least, that was what their parents thought they did. In fact, released from both the routine of the nursery and the discipline of school, they usually managed to fog the waters by letting Norah think they were downstairs with their parents whilst Mr and Mrs Winterton believed in the myth of the schoolroom. Chris and Ralph had led secret – and fascinating – double lives for several years. They were in the habit, when the weather was sufficiently clement, of leaving the house via the rooftops and visiting the less salubrious but more interesting parts of the city, where they met the sort of children whose mere appearance would have raised their parents' eyebrows.

The door of the night-nursery was ajar; Chris popped her head round it and opened her mouth, then closed it and backed out as quietly as she could, gently pulling the door to behind her. Her small sister was asleep, clasping the despised teddy.

What a blessing, Chris thought to herself as she made for the schoolroom. It's awful to dread your own sister's tantrums, but I definitely dread Flicky's. Thank heavens she's too small to be with me and Ralph much, or I'm sure I don't know what we'd do.

Ralph was sitting in the schoolroom, a maths book open in front of him, but as his sister entered he slammed it shut.

'Finished!' he said triumphantly. 'Thank God tomorrow's Saturday – no more homework for two whole days now I've finished that lot. Any luck with Pheenie?'

'Nope. It's at Pakeby all right,' Chris said. 'Isn't it cold, Ralph? I was going to suggest a trip to the market to look for presents, but the roof can be dangerous when it's frosty. I know it's a while since we went off and we've not seen Snatch or Fuzzy for ages, but it'll probably be all right to climb down tomorrow or the day after. What'll we do instead now?'

'Talk about Pakeby,' Ralph said nostalgically. 'I know it isn't always sunny when we're there, but somehow, when I remember it, the sun's always shining. And even when it isn't, there's always something to do.'

'I know; and someone nice to do it with,' Chris agreed. 'I do miss Sybil. Do you miss Georgie?'

'Ye-es, but I've got Bland minor at school and Eddie Crisp over the road to muck about with, and Snatch and Fuzzy in the evenings. The thing is, at Pakeby we aren't kept an eye on all the time, so it's easier.'

'Yes, that's what I mean,' Chris said, collapsing on to a faded, ink-spattered chair. 'In Pakeby Sybs and me can do almost anything, but here it's always *Why do you want to do that?* I can't go anywhere without someone saying nice girls wouldn't. And then there's that awful kid' – she jerked a thumb towards the night-nursery – 'following me round in the house, and when she isn't there Delia is.'

Ralph grinned. Delia was a prim little girl who lived up the road and bored Chris to tears. 'Tell Delia to get lost,' he said, standing up and coming over to make up the fire, which meant moving the fireguard, selecting two suitable logs and standing them, wigwam style, amidst the embers. When both logs had caught he dusted his hands, put the guard back and slumped into the chair opposite his sister.

'Yes, it's harder on you,' he agreed. 'You aren't the type to play nice quiet games with the other kids out in Chapel Field. You'd rather be with us.'

'Yes I would. Only *nice* girls . . .'

'And you're three years younger than me,' Ralph pointed out. 'It's a good thing you're so keen on cricket and so on. Some of the fellows wonder why I let my kid sister tag along with me the way you do.'

'Kid sister? Oh, come on, your kid sister's Flicky. Besides, when Georgie's out on the boat you're often quite happy to hang around with me and Sybs.'

'Well, there isn't much alternative in Pakeby,' Ralph pointed out unkindly. 'Besides, age and that doesn't matter so much as whether you all get on together. Which we do, by and large.'

'There's Lizzie,' Chris said. 'You could go around with Lizzie.'

'What, little blondie-curls? Little look-at-me-how-blue-my-eyes-are?' Ralph said jeeringly. 'All she thinks about is herself, that one. She doesn't ride or help get the hay in or play on the beach . . .'

'She's probably too busy in the house,' Chris said defensively. 'Sybil works ever so hard, so perhaps Lizzie does, too.'

'Not her. She came out once when we were mucking about on Beach Road and I asked her whether she'd like to play Rescue and she looked at me out of those great big silly saucer eyes and said, "No thank you. I don't like playing games."' Ralph snorted. 'Silly fool!'

'Yes, she is silly,' Chris acknowledged. 'But Sybil thinks she's really nice, so I suppose she can't be all bad.' She leaned forward as one of the logs toppled and flames, azure and gold, roared up the chimney. 'I wish it was summer and we were in Pakeby! I wish I knew what Sybs was doing this very minute!'

'So you and me's going off to Norwich on the bus, first thing, and we're goin' to git Mum a dress – me paying, you choosing.' Georgie was talking quickly, anxious to get the message out before Lizzie emerged from the wooden two-seater petty. 'Not a word to a soul, because this is a secret and you know what Lizzie's like.'

The two children were standing shivering on the dark garden path whilst a few lazy snowflakes drifted on the chilly wind. It was the first opportunity George had had to get his younger sister on her own and he had to make the most of it, Sybil quite realized that. Lizzie, she knew, would not tell a secret deliberately, but she might give it away. And furthermore, if she knew Georgie was paying for a trip to Norwich to choose a dress, Lizzie would want to go on it, not Sybil. Which would be fair enough, except that lately Lizzie had become rather remote from the other two children. She had a friend in the village who was also at the secondary school, a girl called Linda Poole, and the two of them always seemed to have their heads together over the silliest things – old fashion magazines, knitting patterns, odds and ends of make-up. Georgie resented his sister suddenly going off with someone else, but that was the way of it, Mum said. Everyone has to grow up, and Lizzie had taken her first step away from them all.

'Well?' Georgie hissed impatiently. 'You coming? You on?'

'Oh yes, please,' Sybil said fervently. 'But what'll we say to Mum and Dad?'

Mum didn't sell fish on Saturdays and Dad didn't take the boat out. Saturday was their day for gardening, cooking, whitewashing the sheds, just as Sunday was their day for church morning and evening, a vast midday meal and cards after supper.

'Dad knows. I've been saving up for ages,' Georgie muttered. 'Mum thinks I'm going up to Malverns to muck out the ponies, and she'll think you're giving me a hand.'

'Right.' A stirring sound, as of paper rustling, came from the two-seater. 'What time's the bus?'

'Eight-fifteen. We'll go up together, as if we're . . .' The door swung and Georgie hastily spoke at full volume. 'Oh, go on then. You can go next if you're desperate!'

Sybil, perched on the seat with her eyes pressed tightly shut so that she might not see, in the faint light of the lamp which Lizzie had passed to her as she came out of the lavatory, anything horrible, like an outsize spider or one of the bloated slugs which favoured indoors in cold weather, had all sorts of questions for Georgie which she was dying to ask. What should she wear? She did not have much choice, but there was her Sunday coat . . . if she could smuggle it out right under Mum's nose. Likewise, her Sunday dress and shoes should surely be worn on an expedition of such importance, but how to get into them without Mum smelling a rat?

Lizzie had scurried indoors as soon as her own visit was paid, however, and now Georgie came and stood just the other side of the door so that Sybil could see the dark shape of him through the gap where she had left it ajar. Not for worlds would Sybil have shut herself in with all the insect life!

'Sybs? It's all right, she's gone in. Look, I've put my best things in a sack and hidden it in Dad's beatster hut. If you put your good coat and shoes out I'll make some excuse and take them down there too. We'll change in the hut, then walk along a bit and get to the bus stop that way. All right?'

'Which way? Towards the ruined cottages or the port?'

Georgie snorted. 'Towards the port, of course. Put your coat and shoes in the sack under your side of the bed and I'll say I have to pay a visit in the night and nip down there.'

'But how'll you get them? You don't sleep in our room any more.'

'No, but if you were to leave your door unlatched . . .'

'You'll sneak in? Oh, you'd wake Lizzie and she'd scream . . . no, tell you what, I'll say I've got to pay a visit and take them to the hut.' Sybil rustled paper on her own account, then slid off the seat. Her heart gave a cheerful little bound of relief as she dragged her drawers up. There was a small hole and a larger one in the long wooden seat, both touchingly heart-shaped, and she had recently taken to using the larger one despite a dreadful inner conviction that one day she would fall into the nauseous contents and die, whether of suffocation or drowning she did not like to contemplate.

'Right, if you're sure,' Georgie said, taking the lamp from her. 'You'd best go up right away, Sybs; you don't want to oversleep.'

Sybil made her way back along the path between the winter cabbages and the sprout plants. A hen gave a sleepy cackle as she passed the wooden fowl-house and Sybil thought of the warm, feathery bodies crowded close and quickened her step. Bed was not a bad idea when the currant bushes were thickly rimed with frost which brushed off as you passed and an occasional cold snowflake kissed your cheek. Especially when you had to be up early, for a trip to the city!

It was chilly on the bus at first, but gradually it grew warmer as more passengers piled aboard. Sybil and Georgie were not the only people going up to Norwich to do their Christmas shopping and the bus was full of excitement as they neared their destination.

'We want to go to the market place, on The Walk,' Georgie said authoritatively. Compared to Sybil he was much travelled, for he had been to the city several times before with Henry. 'Saturday's a good day, because all the stallholders will be there. We'll take a look round before we start on the shops.'

'Do the stalls sell dresses?' Sybil enquired as the bus lumbered along the city streets. 'I thought we'd go to a shop.'

'So we shall, but we'll look at the stalls first; they're cheaper, you see,' Georgie told her. 'Dad writ out the measurements so's I'd know, but you can tell them to the woman – I dare say it'll be a woman who sells women's dresses?'

'Sure to be,' Sybil said confidently. 'Oh, isn't that pretty?'

'It's the market,' Georgie said agitatedly. For all his visits he had clearly been unaware that they had reached their destination. 'Quick, Sybs!'

But there was no real need to hurry because others beside themselves wanted this stop. They simply joined the patient line of passengers waiting their turn to get down and then ... oh, the joy of it! They were on the market pushing their way through the crowds, hand in hand so they didn't lose each other, and Sybil's eyes were round with wonder at all the stalls, piled with every imaginable luxury, or so it seemed to a small girl from a small seaside village.

'There's someone selling hot potatoes. I'll get us a couple,' Georgie said presently. 'I say, look at those – aren't they grand?'

'They're beautiful,' Sybil said, scarcely able to drag her eyes away from the tinsel and the gold, scarlet and blue of the decorations Georgie had indicated. She saw birds with gleaming silver bodies and tails made out of dyed feathers, little Santa Clauses with tiny sacks across their miniature shoulders, stars, cradles, blue-shawled babies, all supplied with clips to attach them to your Christmas tree.

'Come on, don't gawp,' Georgie said, tugging on her hand, but he did not speak unkindly. He, too, must have marvelled at the sight, Sybil thought, turning her head to stare even as she was pulled away. She and Lizzie spent happy hours popping corn in the big black pan, dipping it into raspberry syrup to turn it pink and then stringing it on cotton so that it could be hung on their small tree. They cut pictures out of the comics and magazines which came their way, sticking them together with flour and water paste so that there was colour on both sides.

And our tree is beautiful, Sybil thought loyally. I expect even the smallest of those decorations would cost a penny!

They reached the baked potato man, who proved to be selling roast chestnuts too. Georgie bought them both a ha'penny bag as well as the potatoes, and then he and Sybil made their way to the steps which led up from the market to the street above and sat there and ate until they had finished all the food. It was still extremely cold and snowflakes still drifted down out of the cloudy sky but somehow, Sybil thought, you didn't notice the weather when you had so much to look at and marvel over.

'We'll go to the shops now,' Georgie decided. He sighed deeply. 'You get really hungry when it's cold . . . that spud was huge, but I could eat it all over again!'

'I couldn't,' Sybil said, getting to her feet. 'But I am thirsty.'

'There's a drinking fountain somewhere.' George frowned round him. 'Oh, I remember. It's near the fish stalls.'

The smell led them to the fish stalls. Sybil looked at the cod, the haddock, the plaice and the whiting, all beautifully laid out on the nearest stall with parsley in between, and felt sorry for the fat red-faced woman and the black-clad, weaselly man behind the stall. If we had a stall I'd never get free, she thought uneasily. I'm glad we've only got the cart!

'There we are – you drink first.'

Sybil eyed the fountain cautiously. It was the first one she had come across and it didn't look much, just a little round porcelain basin with a silver knob in the middle.

'No, you. Then I can copy what you do,' she urged.

Georgie, laughing, bent over and showed her how to press the button to make the water rise. Once she'd seen how it was done Sybil would have been quite happy to play with it all afternoon; she had several drinks, deciding that the water was very much nicer than that which gushed from the Pakeby pump even though it numbed her mouth and made her teeth ache, but Georgie was getting impatient.

'Come on, Sybs, you can't possibly still be thirsty! We'll go down that way, I think. There are lots of shops down there.'

There were, but they were, Sybil saw at once, way out of their class. Mum would never wear a dress like those displayed in the windows; each one must cost shillings!

'Let's ask,' she begged, but Georgie was unwilling to admit to anyone that he was not a native of the city and dragged her round until she got quite hot and bothered and began to wonder if they would ever get home.

Finally, she broke free of him and went over to where a woman and a small child were staring into a window.

'Excuse me . . . my brother and I want a dress for our mum . . . not too expensive. Can you tell us where we should try?'

The woman turned and smiled at her. She had a round, pale face with rather thick lips and her hair was greasy and set in little rolls. But the smile was bright enough and her eyes looked kindly down at Sybil.

'Well now, dear, you'll want to try down Magdalen Street, or maybe St Benedict's . . . yes, that's nearer. Now go down London Street . . . that one, there, with the big shop on the corner . . . and take the second alley on your left . . . Swan Lane, that is. Cross over Bedford Street, go down Bridewell Alley and at the bottom there y'are, St Benedict's! You'll find a coupla shops down there which may suit.'

'Thanks very much,' Georgie said rather stiffly. 'Come on, Sybs, we'd better be getting along.'

Carefully following the directions they had been given they reached St Benedict's, found a shop which had dresses on display and went in. There was a long counter, a couple of shop assistants, and several customers being served. Those still waiting were wandering round the shop examining the goods on display.

'This is much better,' Georgie whispered. 'People here don't look so rich.'

'No; they look nicer, too,' Sybil hissed back. 'Oh look, Georgie . . . that blue one!'

The blue one was the dress of her dreams; she could imagine with perfect clarity just how pretty her mother would look in it. She clutched Georgie's hand hard. 'It costs four and tenpence. Do you have enough money?'

'Will it fit Mum?' Georgie wondered. 'I like that stuff round the neck, though. I reckon you've hit it, Sybs; that's the dress all right.'

And it proved to be the dress indeed, for Sybil read out the measurements her father had written down to a sympathetic shop assistant, the young lady disappeared to check the stock and came back wreathed in smiles and carrying a blue dress as like to the one on the stand as two peas in the same pod.

'That's a sturdy warm wool,' she announced, spreading the dress out on the counter. 'That'll last years, given careful washing. Is that for a present, then?'

And upon Georgie producing his money and admitting that it was a present for his mother, she wrapped it in a beautiful piece of blue and silver paper and said there was no extra charge and she hoped they would be satisfied.

Outside the shop once more, they saw that it was now snowing in earnest, though Georgie, wise in the ways of weather, doubted that it would lay.

'Be gone by morning,' he said, stepping out. 'Best get the next bus though, Sybs, in case.'

Sybil was willing and the two of them hurried along through the softly falling snow which, despite Georgie's confident prediction, continued to build up on rooftops and gates and windowsills.

'There's a bus!' Georgie cried as they regained The Walk and saw the market temptingly spread out before them. 'Oh, damn . . . we ought to get it, but I thought we might buy some wool for Lizzie, so's she can knit herself a jumper. Did you see the wool stall? Their wool was cheaper by far than the stuff in the village shop.'

'Perhaps it isn't our bus,' Sybil said hopefully but, tugged by Georgie, she broke into a trot.

And that was her undoing. The pavements were icy, the ice dusted with snow was treacherous, and Georgie was pulling at one hand whilst the other was encumbered with the precious dress. She slipped, tried to right herself, couldn't, and then Georgie tugged again and she

45

was down, falling awkwardly, one arm trapped beneath her whilst the parcel slid across the snowy paving stones.

'I'd better carry the dress,' Georgie said, scooping it up and examining it closely. 'It's all right, the paper isn't damaged . . . jump up, you aren't hurt!'

Sybil wanted nothing more than to jump up, but the fall had shaken her more than she realized, for as she started to move she began to feel swimmy and stupid. She got to her knees, however, with the arm which had been underneath her hurting like toothache, and then she collapsed, straight on to her face. She felt the pain of the paving stone's clout on her brow and then darkness rushed up at her.

She came round to find herself in bed. She could not think, for a moment, how she came to be here, and then she remembered. She had slipped on the icy pavement, had tried to get up too quickly, and had knocked herself out. But why was she in bed? And where was she? This was certainly not the Pakeby cottage . . .

'Nurse! She've come round, nurse!'

A small figure in what looked like a long blue coat had appeared by Sybil's bed, grinned, and disappeared again. After a moment a rustling announced the arrival of the summoned nurse. A big woman with a hard, hatchet face, she materialized beside the bed, stared at Sybil, sniffed, and then asked in a rough, creaking voice, 'All right, are you?'

'Umm . . . I think so. Where am I, though? And where's my brother? He was with me when I fell.'

'I'll get 'im,' the woman said, and went away. Sybil now saw that she was in fact in a small curtained-off area which contained just her bed, a cupboard and a hard wooden chair.

After a few moments Georgie appeared. He was pale, and beads of sweat stood out on his forehead, but he gave a great, relieved grin when Sybil smiled at him and took hold of her hand in a gentle grasp.

'Sybs, I nearly died when you didn't come round! Someone got an ambulance and they brought us both here . . . are you really better? I asked, but they won't let you out tonight, said you might have concussion, whatever that is. Look, I've got to go home, but you'll be all right here till tomorrow, won't you? The doctor said you'd got a badly bruised arm and a bump on the head . . . Sybs, I *must* go, you know that, don't you? They'll be mad with worry if I'm not back before dusk. I'll come back tomorrow and fetch you.'

'Don't . . . oh, you're right, you've got to go,' Sybil gulped. 'But I'm

46

scared of this place. Wait a sec, Georgie, and I'll get dressed and sneak out with you. They can't really keep me, can they?'

'They've taken your clothes,' Georgie said worriedly. 'You'll have to stay.'

Sybil sat up a bit further in the bed. She was wearing a horrible calico bed-gown with no sleeves and her left arm was badly bruised, the wrist swollen and shiny-looking. But other than that I'm fine, she told herself. Aloud, she agreed that Georgie must go, but inside she was determined not to be far behind him. Hospitals cost money, and the Creams had none to spare. Besides, there was nothing wrong with her. That nasty, cross-looking nurse was just keeping her here out of an urge to bully someone smaller than herself. She would not stay! She would wait until the other people she could hear outside her curtains were asleep and then she would jolly well find her clothes and make her own way home!

She was caught, of course. Making her way, slowly and fumblingly, across the icy linoleum, barefoot and shivering, she was haled back to bed by a fat and friendly night nurse, as different from the nasty, uninterested Sister as chalk from cheese. And the night nurse had been understanding and kind. She had given Sybil a cup of hot tea and a biscuit – the Sister had refused to allow her to eat or drink in case she vomited and messed up the bed – and promised to make sure she was released next day.

'Your brother and your dad, they'll fetch you,' she said. 'But if suffin' go wrong and they don't, do you have any friends in the city?'

'Yes; the Wintertons,' Sybil said shakily. 'They'd help me, I'm sure.'

It was in her mind that her parents might not be able to pay the bill, which might mean the hospital would hang on to her – she thought she would die if she was here another day. But the Wintertons were rich, everyone knew that!

'The Wintertons. Where do they live, my woman?'

'St Giles,' Sybil said promptly. Chris often talked about their house. 'It's opposite the church.'

'Right. Then if suffin' go wrong and your parents don't get, I'll go round to the Wintertons meself.'

'But what might go wrong?' Sybil wailed softly. The night nurse put a finger to her lips. She was sitting on the end of Sybil's bed, smoking a cigarette and looking pretty and raffish. 'Aren't there buses on a Sunday?'

'Yes, but . . . han't you noticed the weather, littl'un?'

She gestured to the window. Sybil pulled herself up and looked out. She could see snowflakes whirling but not much else.

'The snow, d'you mean? But Georgie said it wouldn't lay.'

'Then Georgie was wrong,' her new friend said emphatically. 'Ask me, we're in for a white Christmas!'

4

When Chris drew her curtains on Sunday morning and saw the snow on the rooftops below her, her first thought was sledging and her second was what a blessing that the school holidays had begun.

Mummy and Daddy always insisted that their older offspring go to the morning service, though Daddy hardly ever went with them. But Norah went, Elsie sometimes took Flicky, and Mummy hardly ever missed. However, once church was over the children were fairly free to please themselves, and Chris had no doubt that her parents would be only too delighted if she and Ralph took themselves off to Chapel Field gardens with the sledge and their warm coats on.

After that, though, the snow would put a stop to rooftop excursions for a while . . . in fact she and Ralph might find themselves confined until spring!

A year or so ago a friend of their mother's, being taken around the house, had looked out of the schoolroom window and said gaily how lucky the children were to have such a view and had added that when she was young she would have been out of the window, down over the rooftops and away before you could say Jack Robinson.

There had been an embarrassed silence from the Winterton children, though Mummy had smiled and murmured conventionally enough. Chris and Ralph had been using the rooftop route for after-hours excursions into the city ever since Chris had been old enough to climb back up on to the water butt in the yard. Ralph always tried to give the impression that he had been sneaking down over the roofs since he was in nappies, but he had certainly been doing it for quite a while.

But they were not foolish, and it would have been foolish beyond belief to have attempted the climb in any but excellent weather. Rain, ice or snow made the tiles a death trap, though they had gone out once in a thick pea-souper which had nearly proved fatal. Ralph had not

49

realized that the foggy damp would have slicked the tiles as effectively as rain until he was halfway down, and sliding fast.

Chris, poised above him, watched in helpless horror as her brother glissaded down the steeply slanting roof. But he had managed to wedge his boots in the gutter, pausing just long enough to make a collected jump on to the rainwater barrel rather than the horrendous, bone-snapping crash which might so easily have ended his slide. Chris herself had climbed cautiously back into the schoolroom and gone downstairs to let Ralph in through a side door.

So now, with the snow thick on the tiles and the sky overhead dark with more falls to come, she turned back into her room. Oh well, no one could have everything; they might lose their chance of any more trips into the city after dark, but they would have the snow!

Later in the morning they walked through whirling flakes down St Giles, past the town hall to St Peter Mancroft. The market stalls were just snow-covered humps on an icy desert and the roads showed no sign of tarmac. Few car owners had ventured out, preferring to wait until the streets had been cleared, and even cyclists, wobbling unsteadily over the squeaking white blanket, were not making sufficient impression on the snow to allow the black surface to appear.

'Isn't it great, Ralph?' Chris said, scooping a mittenful of snow off a wall as she passed. 'Sledging later!'

Daddy had already said that he would drive them out to Ringland Hills when the roads were clear, but when would that be? So Ralph, Eddie Crisp and herself were going to take the sledge into Chapel Field gardens, and then they would probably sneak off to Grapes Hill and get a good fast pace going from top to bottom if the road was still snow-covered. Being sensible young people, however, they certainly did not intend to let their parents have an inkling of that particular plan. It would come under the heading of 'things nice children don't do', so better to say nothing and bide their time.

They reached the tall iron railings which surrounded the church and Chris ran an experimental mitten along them, causing snow to cascade down on her.

'You'll get soaked,' Ralph said warningly. 'Wonder how deep it'll get?'

'Tremendously deep! By the time the service is over it'll be up to my knees, over the tops of my boots,' Chris said happily. 'Gosh, suppose the Rev. hasn't made it? He comes by car quite often, doesn't he?'

'Then young Mr Evans will take the service,' her mother said, overhearing. 'Come along, dears, don't loiter.'

Chris, who enjoyed church, hurried whilst Ralph, who thought he could be better employed, lagged, but even so they all reached the porch at the same time, where Mummy brushed herself down and then did the same for Chris, knocking the flakes briskly off the little round red velvet hat which was required wearing for morning service and whisking the unwanted snow from her daughter's matching coat.

Daddy took his coat off, shook it and put it on again and then they all went into the church, greeted at the door, as always, by old Mr Spalding and even older Mr Douglass, offering them Hymns Ancient & Modern and the Prayer Book respectively.

It was warm inside after the cold; Chris could see hot air rising from the big banks of black-painted radiators and felt snug, even though common sense told her that most of that gloriously warm air simply went on rising until it nestled beneath the beautiful timbered roof high, high above.

Despite the weather the church already contained a fair congregation. Chris cast a friendly glance to her right at the sand-coloured memorial stone sacred to the memory of Nathaniel Roe, whose career in Norwich politics was succinctly set out below his name. Sheriff of this City 1766, Alderman 1767, Mayor 1777. It always gave Chris a warm glow to think that nearly two hundred years ago Mr Roe might have sat where Daddy sat, and cast occasional admonitory glances at a little girl just like herself, sitting by his side.

They walked to their aisle over shiny black slate gravestones set into the floor so that you had no choice but to tread on someone. Clara Alice Tipple had a brass memorial; you could avoid that one all right, but it was very difficult to avoid Frances, Nathaniel Roe's wife, and Lloyd Hurst who had died in 1781, aged nineteen. Chris always looked very hard at Lloyd Hurst, because it was such an elderly, settled sort of name for such a very young man, but of course his parents would scarcely have expected him to die so young when they christened him.

Down their aisle, treading lightly, apologizing inwardly, on the honey-coloured stone belonging to Mary Page, 1802, and into the fourth pew down, beside the gravestone with a skull and crossbones on it sacred to dear Jacobi Skipper, whose taste in art kept the Winterton young happy throughout the longest services. Ralph, his sister supposed rather uncharitably, probably thought about pirates, imagined Jacobi a skipper, not only in name, of some speedy, black-sailed sloop.

51

For her part, Chris mused on who had drawn the skull and crossbones, because it had an amateurish look, as though a child had lain on the stone with a pocket-knife, industriously chipping away.

The family filed into their pew, Mummy first, then Daddy, then Ralph and finally Chris. Usually Flicky would be there too, by Mummy's side, but today it was deemed too cold for her and Flicky had been left in the nursery with Elsie to keep her company and promises of later treats, when the snow had eased up a bit.

Everyone went down on their knees and Chris had a quiet word with God, hands over her face, to see if she could persuade Him to clear the roads whilst allowing the snow to remain thick, but this seemed a trifle unreasonable, so she suggested instead that He might see His way clear to arranging that they go to Pakeby for Easter. Or at least for Whit, she added, not wanting to embarrass Him with what must seem like an impossible demand, for they never went near Pakeby until Whitsun, and then only if it was exceptionally mild.

Next to her, Ralph slid up on to the seat with a sigh just as she heard the preliminary shuffling of the choirboys being led from the vestry up the aisle, the smallest and probably the naughtiest of them bearing the cross, the rest singing as they came, mouths rounded, eyelids lowered, so that they looked impossibly charming, impossibly sweet. Chris, who knew several of the choir for the rogues they were, always marvelled that they could put on such a good show, but that was boys for you. Born to deceive.

That was one of Norah's favourite expressions; she had been in love once, many years ago, with a handsome young man who worked on the farm near her mother's cottage at Blofield. Reg kept ferrets which he took rabbiting in other people's woods, and he fished for trout anywhere a fish was rising. He told Norah he poached for the excitement of it, but it seemed that he needed even more stimulus than that, for one summer day Norah, visiting her mother from her job in Norwich, had gone for a stroll in the hay meadows, picking wild flowers as she went. In a sheltered corner by a newly built haystack she had come upon her young man and a flighty piece from the neighbouring village of Brundall, rolling in the hay.

'What were they doing?' Chris always asked, and always received the same reply.

'None of your business, my woman! They was doing wrong, that's what they was doing, and him promised to me!'

How fatally easy it is to let your mind wander in church, Chris was thinking sorrowfully as the sermon started. It was the Rev. himself, a man who seldom managed to get Chris's attention let alone hold it, so she sat back on the shiny wooden pew and gazed up at the sparkling beauty of the East window. Ralph liked the massacre of the innocents best, with soldiers flourishing swords thrust through distraught, doll-like figures which were the best the artist could do, it appeared, to represent children, but she liked the birth of Baby Jesus, with the shepherds playing their pipes to please the mother and her child, angels hovering, the animals watching and Joseph, bored by the whole thing, staring glumly down at the black and white tiles on the floor.

Black and white tiles in a *stable*? Chris asked herself for the hundredth time. But Daddy had explained that the window was very old indeed, as much as five hundred years, and in those far-off days an artist with no experience of an oriental stable might well imagine that there would be a tiled floor, for coolness, per-haps.

'Let us pray.'

Everyone reached for the embroidered hassocks and Chris, kneeling obediently, wondered if it was still snowing, and whether the Rev. had come on a bicycle instead of in his huffing, puffing baby Austin, and if so whether he had put it in the porch or would go outside, presently, and find it just a snowy hump resting against the ash-coloured church wall. Does he bicycle in his robes? Chris wondered. Oh, if the bicycle is wet he'll get a wet bottom . . . I wonder what he wears under his cassock?

'We will now sing hymn number fifty-one: Lo he comes with clouds descending.'

Chris emerged from her comfortable chrysalis of conjecture and opened her hymn book. She began to sing with all her might, competing with the choir, enjoying both the pleasure of singing at the top of her voice and the equal pleasure of knowing that the service was almost over and the snow waited outside. Perhaps it was up to the windowsills already, perhaps they would be unable to open the door of the church for the weight of snow upon it!

Chris's mind careered off on yet another wild goose chase, though she continued to sing vigorously.

They got out of church despite the fact that the heavy flakes had continued to fall throughout the service. The members of the congregation clustered briefly in the porch, exclaiming over the depth of the snow and the apparent inability of the authorities to clear it on a Sunday; then everyone began to wrap themselves in scarves and button up their coats and pull on their gloves.

Daddy went to the front of the porch, looked out and then came back, turning his collar up.

'Right. Where's my umbrella? And which of you two prayed for more snow, may I enquire?'

Ralph grinned but Chris immediately felt conscience-stricken. How had he known? Not that it could have anything to do with her prayers, not really, but trust Daddy to guess!

Daddy took the big black umbrella and erected it over Mummy's head, gestured to the children to follow and set off. The snow had thickened both on the ground and in the air during the course of the service and now the children only had to drop a couple of yards behind their parents to lose sight of them completely. Ralph bent and picked up a double handful as soon as his parents were far enough ahead, then began to squeeze it into the sort of dangerous, rock-hard snowball with which schoolboys like to pelt one another.

'This is prime, this is! We'll eat dinner quickly and then we can have longer to play out.'

'In this? They won't let us out if it carries on,' Chris said indistinctly. It was so cold that she had ducked her head into the fur collar of her coat as a tortoise does, and pulled the hated hat far down over her eyes. 'You know what Mum's like about our getting wet through . . . anyone would think snow or rain melted us!'

'I shall go out,' Ralph muttered crossly. He aimed his snowball at the thickness of the falling snow and hurled it viciously. Someone yelped, a startled sound, and Ralph grinned at his sister's reproachful face. 'Oh, come on, Chris, we'll ask if we can go round to the Crisps'. Then we'll tell Eddie to say he's coming back to ours for tea, and we'll sneak off.'

'They won't let us; they'll guess,' Chris insisted. 'But it can't go on snowing like this much longer . . . it'll stop by the time we've had dinner.'

Dinner was at midday on a Sunday, though in the evening on other days of the week, and the evening meal was called Sunday supper and was much prized by the children for its informality. Daddy had decreed long ago that, since it was a day of rest for the servants as well as for everyone else, supper on a Sunday should be buffet style. Food, all cold, was set out on the long table in the dining room and everyone helped themselves. In summer there were usually salads, cold meats, fruit and jellies. In winter it was often open sandwiches with as many different fillings as Cook could think of, a meat pie to slice, a brawn, trembling and savoury, and a big apple tart for pudding, with thick cream to pour over it and soft brown sugar if you had a sweet tooth.

Chris began to feel hungry. Suddenly it no longer seemed quite so important that the snow might continue to fall throughout the afternoon and spoil their chance of playing out. Following Ralph's lead, she began to collect snow and pack it into a hard ball. Presently, she saw a gatepost looming ahead and hurled the snowball hard at it; it burst gloriously, not like Ralph's icy missiles which scarcely burst at all. What's the fun of an iceball? Chris thought contemptuously. Just like a boy!

Daddy was halfway through carving the Sunday joint – a great, golden-brown saddle of lamb with mint sauce or redcurrant jelly, whichever you preferred – when the front door bell rang. Daddy cocked his head to one side, glancing at Mummy.

'Who on earth can that be, right in the middle of Sunday dinner?' he said impatiently. Out in the hall, they heard the quick footsteps of Mavis, the maid, then the front door opened. 'Oh well, I dare say we'll know soon enough.'

He bent to the carving again and Mummy continued to spoon vegetables from the big tureens on to everyone's plate. There were bright green sprouts, discs of orange carrot, golden swede mashed with butter and black pepper, long creamy-coloured parsnips, and Chris's favourites: potatoes cut up small and roasted in the oven round the joint until they were a glorious golden brown on top and soft beneath with the meat's juices.

Daddy handed the next plate to Mummy for vegetables and Chris, knowing it was for her, inspected it critically. Three big, thick slices of pink lamb with a frill of crispy brown fat around each slice. She would help herself to mint sauce and redcurrant jelly and then, when everyone was served, Daddy would come round with the gravy jug – you could have as much as you liked and Chris would have a good deal.

Her mind was still on her dinner when there was a little scuffle at the door and it shot open. Mavis had once told Chris that she wouldn't knock properly on an internal door because she was a communist, but though Chris had made 'oh, now I understand' noises, this was not strictly true. In fact she had no idea what difference being a communist made to one's ability to knock at the dining room door.

'It's a bit of a girl, ma'am,' Mavis said, addressing her mistress. She was a pretty girl despite, or perhaps because of, her communism, but she very rarely addressed a word or even a look at Daddy. Perhaps communists didn't like men, Chris thought.

'A girl? Oh, had I better come . . .'

But her daughter, peering into the darkness of the hallway, was before her. Chris had seen a familiar little face and straggly fair hair . . . and had she not prayed, that very morning, for a visit to Pakeby soon? Well, God had gone one better – God had sent Pakeby to her in the form of Sybil Cream! Gosh, thought Chris as she tore into the hall, all thoughts of her dinner forgotten, two prayers answered! I'd better be careful what I ask for in future!

Sybil had been near despair that morning when she looked out on the snow, deep and crisp and even as in the carol, but to her at that moment a barrier between her and home, her and freedom! The horrible Sister was on again, too, and had been as mean to Sybil as though Sybil had brought the snow down deliberately, so that she could not be called for and taken away from the place.

'Han't you got no relatives here?' Sister demanded, when the doctor had been round and pronounced Sybil fit to leave. 'There in't no point in you hangin' around here, fit as a fiddle, when a sick kiddie could need that bed.'

Sybil, poor fish, had been about to burst into tears and say that she would catch the first available bus back to Pakeby, when she remembered her talk to the night nurse. There was a way out, if only she had the courage to take it!

'Yes, I've got an aunt and uncle and three cousins living in St Giles,' she said firmly. 'They'll be glad to have me to stay there until my parents can fetch me home.'

'Oh. Well, that's all right, then,' Sister said grumpily, foiled of her grudge. 'Snow's thick, though . . . how can we git a message to 'em to come an' fetch you?'

'No need, I'll make my own way there,' Sybil said airily. 'I've got a thick coat and good shoes . . .'

'Can't let you go alone,' Sister said. 'There in't no buses today, so it'll be a walking job. Here, let me think.'

She thought whilst Sybil all but held her breath, agonizing over the woman's supreme power. As long as she held Sybil's clothes in some far off, hidden cupboard Sybil was completely at her mercy.

'Sally Andrews!' Sister said suddenly. 'Oh ah, Sally live up Unthank Road. She can go down St Stephens with you and then up Theatre

Street and through. You'll be with your aunt before you know it!'

It seemed she was to be saddled with this Sally Andrews, but once she was out of the hospital Sybil was sure she would be as good as back in Pakeby. She would go to the Wintertons' house, of course, but she could not possibly ask if she could stay with them. No, she would just explain the situation and borrow the bus fare home.

Sally proved to be a plump little student nurse of no more than fifteen or sixteen. She did not have a smart uniform like Sister, with her cap, her collar and her cuffs, but she worked twice as hard and was at least twice as cheerful.

'Thass a nice coat,' were almost her first words to Sybil. 'Cor, you'll be rare warm an' snug in that!'

She chatted as they went, too, slowing her pace to match Sybil's, for Sybil found walking in such deep snow very tiring and was aware, for the first time, that the fall had bruised her all over and her enforced bed-rest had weakened her. So the journey through the snowy city, which would normally have interested her immensely, just seemed strange and tiring and far longer than she had expected. She and Sally slogged along through the snowstorm until she, at least, was soaked and aching. When Sally said, 'Here we are, then – St Giles. Where's your auntie live?' she was so relieved she could have wept.

'Opposite the church,' she said instead. 'Thank you ever so much, Sally, for bringing me, but I can find my own way now.'

'I in't a-goin' to leave you till I've seen you taken in,' Sally said firmly, however. 'Opposite the church? Tha's a posh sorta place, then?'

'Yes, I suppose . . . yes, it is,' Sybil mumbled. 'It's . . . er . . . it's ages since I was here. I'm not sure which one . . .'

Vague descriptions from Chris were not quite enough until, suddenly, she remembered the tunnel which Chris had told her led under the house from the roadway to the yard at the back. She stared at the row of houses and saw that only one had such a feature. Greatly relieved, she pointed.

'I remember! It's that one!'

They went to the front door because Sally said it was the thing to do. With her heart in her mouth, except that it was leaping and bounding away under cover of her best coat, Sybil put a faltering finger on the bell. She pressed and heard the peal echoing all round the house, from the sound of it. Cringing, she removed her finger from the button. Please, GGod, she prayed fervently, please let Chris come!

*　　*　　*

That evening, Sybil lay in a soft bed, between warmed sheets, in a small bedroom on the top floor of the Wintertons' house and thought about the day which was just ending. It had been a wonderful day, perhaps the best part of it the way the Wintertons had accepted her at once as a welcome guest, with never a suggestion that she was either uninvited or unwanted. Mr Winterton had telephoned the post office in Pakeby and the postmaster, grumbling mightily, sent his son round to the cottage on Beach Road, telling the lad to pass on to Henry Cream that a postmaster in't no messenger boy, nor he in't paid to gad around the village passin' on information, especially on a Sunday. Henry had hurried up to the public call box on the post office forecourt and telephoned the Wintertons to thank them for looking after his girl, so Mr Winterton was able to assure Sybil that her parents were happy for her to stay in St Giles until the snow cleared.

She had been lent a nightgown by Chris and a clean flannel and a bar of soap had been provided, besides a fluffy, pale pink towel so beautiful that she hardly dared touch it, let alone wipe her hands on it. She had been shown to Chris's small bedroom and told that the spare bed, the very one in which she now lay, was hers until she left the house. She had been given food the like of which she had never eaten before – roast lamb with some lovely sort of jelly, mint sauce and vegetables, followed by a pudding that was all yellow, lemony sweetness below and fluffy sugary white above, which Ralph, seeing her trying it with care, informed her was 'nothing special, just Cook's lemon meringue pie'.

Nothing special! It tasted, Sybil decided dreamily, the way clouds looked. She had her meal in the dining room, just she and Chris and Mrs Winterton, since the others had eaten whilst Sybil was settled in, and no sooner had she finished the last of that delectable pudding than Chris and Ralph had haled her off to ride on a sledge, first in Chapel Field gardens and then down Grapes Hill, where they had careered dangerously down the very centre of the carriageway, whooping and shrieking and tumbling into the gutter whenever the sledge was steered awry.

Home in St Giles again, it was time for more party food. Unable to stop herself, Sybil had stared at the long table piled with delicious things and known that this must be meant to last the rest of the week. Certainly her own family could have managed comfortably on it for at least as long.

But no. Plates were heaped, more food was produced, and despite the fact that the Winterton family, even with Sybil's help, had scarcely made a dint in it, the pies, salads and puddings were carried out again. Would the same food return next day, and the next, until it was all gone? But Chris thought not, mentioned vaguely that the servants would probably clear up what was left – was she mad? There were several servants, but it would need an army to eat that lot!

After supper, as they called it, she and Chris and Ralph played 'Snap' with Flicky, and then Flicky was taken off to have a bath whilst the older three were left with books. Sybil was so enchanted by the choice available that she sat on the floor in the midst of a motley collection, picking a sentence here, a paragraph there, unable to select just one from so many.

No one told them to go to bed, but because they were trusted perhaps, or because they were as tired as she after the games in the snow, they put their books away at half past eight and headed for their rooms. There was a tray in the schoolroom bearing a jug of hot cocoa and three mugs with kittens disporting themselves on their china sides, and an oval platter set out with chocolate, shortbread and currant biscuits from which they were apparently meant to help themselves. Chocolate biscuits! One each was the rule in the Cream household, and then only on high days and holidays. Yet here she was, plain little Sybil, the baby of the family, allowed to take as many as she liked . . . and inhibited, by shyness and natural good manners, from taking the lot, stuffing her pockets with them so that Georgie and Lizzie might share the treat!

Then bed. Mum had said sheets were cold, but these were gloriously warm and smooth and they smelt wonderful and not at all like the Cream blankets, which were washed in spring and autumn and in between smelt of the three little Creams. There were stone bottles in the bed, one for her feet, one to cuddle. The bottles wore neat little jackets, a flannel one for the foot bottle, a knitted pink one for the cuddly. The house was lit by electric light, another marvel, and Chris had been apologetic because she had a little pink-shaded lamp by her bed whilst Sybil had to make do with the main light, whose switch was by the door.

'But if you want to get up in the night, just lean out of bed and give me a poke,' Chris said kindly. 'Then I'll switch my bedside light on for you.'

They were allowed to read for ten minutes, Chris explained, but they did not bother. There was too much to talk about, and Chris did most of the talking since Sybil was still stunned by the strangeness

59

and speed of the events which had brought her to this cosy bed in this warm and welcoming house.

'What fun it is to have you here, Sybs,' Chris declared. 'I wish you could stay for always.'

Sybil thought about the food, and the rooms with fires all lit and lights blazing. She thought about the city and its shops and the fact that Chris did not just have one nightgown but at least two, for how, otherwise, could she have loaned one to Sybil? Henry Cream thought nightgowns for children a luxury, but Dora had insisted, so the girls wore Dora's old nightdresses cut down, and Georgie had homemade nightshirts. Dad grumbled that when he was a lad he was sewn into his vests and drawers in October and snipped out of them in April, but Mum just said each generation had its own ways and Dad grinned and went along with it.

'If you were here for Christmas we could go carol singing with the choir . . . Ralph and I always go . . . and then there's the pantomime, and . . .'

The clothes in Chris's wardrobe! All the time we've known each other, I've never really thought about her clothes, Sybil thought now. Besides, it was mainly summer frocks and sandals, though the riding clothes were always special, I knew *that*. But now she had seen for herself the dresses, skirts, kilts, blouses, jumpers, cardigans. Chris had a chest of drawers packed with underwear – knickers, liberty bodices, vests, socks and stockings – each garment soft and new and either white as driven snow or gaily coloured. Sybil had stared at the rows of strap shoes, button shoes, little boots, sandals, slippers, not so much with envy, for she would never have found the time to wear the half of them, but with wonder that two girls, of similar ages and interests, could be so different.

A dress and a skirt for winter, a dress and a skirt for summer. Underclothes which had been worn until they were harsh and tickly to the skin, their original white greyish yellow with age, and shoes which were either too big and slipped so that you got raw heels or so tight your toes were cramped into a bunch. Clogs for yardwork which were heavy and ugly and rubber boots which had once been Georgie's and let water in through cracked soles.

'Sybs? Lucky it's school holidays. We'll be able to go up the city, look at the shops, muck about round the market. Did you buy your Christmas presents, you and Georgie? If not, you can help me buy mine and I'll help with yours. Have you written your Christmas present list? I have, but we don't send them up the chimney until

Christmas Eve, that's the rule. Not that we believe in Santa Claus, haven't for absolutely thousands of years, but it's what you do. You could start yours tomorrow, I'll help you. Have you ever been to the museum at the castle? There's Egyptian mummies and butterflies and stuffed birds . . . rooms made up to look like countryside, and a lovely seashore room . . . Sybs?'

'I'm too tired to talk any more,' Sybil muttered. She shrugged the covers up over her shoulders and cuddled her bottle defensively.

Chris sighed and then snuggled down herself. Sybil felt a trifle guilty, but she simply could not cope with the flood of questions her friend was shooting at her. Christmas present lists? Sending them up the chimney? Egyptian mummies and butterflies? Had Chris run mad or were their lives so far apart that even language had a different meaning?

Christmas presents, though – that made sense. Not that she could do any buying now even if she had wanted to, because she had no money, but her presents were already bought and hidden. She had saved up her pennies and bought Lizzie the most beautiful length of blue satin ribbon to match her eyes. Georgie was to have a pair of woollen socks – she had paid for the wool, Lizzie had knitted them – and a big bag of toffee which Lizzie and Sybil had made in the kitchen a week ago, and cracked into crazy-paving pieces with Dad's lump hammer. Georgie would give Mum the blue dress, and the girls would give her a pretty hanky and two Fry's chocolate bars between them. Dad, renowned for his enormous frame and sweet tooth, would also get chocolate bars, with a muffler which all three children had coveted for him and contributed towards to the best of their ability.

I wonder what it will be like here at Christmas? Sybil asked herself drowsily just before she fell asleep. It will be wonderful, I'm sure. Chris will probably have a pile of presents, and they'll eat a turkey or a goose each, I shouldn't wonder, and they'll have a tree like in books, with little coloured candles on the branch-tips and a fairy on the topmost twig. I wish we could have things like that – but I wouldn't like to be away from Beach Road at Christmas, no matter what.

Her thoughts wandered home, to the tree which Dad and Georgie acquired from somewhere every year, to the way the warmth of the kitchen brought out the resiny pine-scent from the uprooted fir to mingle with the good smells of the goose cooking and the pudding boiling in its square of white cloth. They unwrapped their presents after breakfast and oh, the excitement! It was grand. Everyone exclaiming, everyone getting what they most wanted . . . even Lizzie flushed and happy, for all she thought herself a young woman and pretended to despise childish things, like unwrapping presents. And then there was morning service, rigged out in your best, and Vicar full of smiles and the good smell of cooking everywhere . . .

It probably would not compare with a St Giles Christmas; but everyone has their own place, Sybil thought. And the good thing was, as Mum kept trying to tell them, that no one was forced to stay in their own place. Sybil might never have what Chris had – the big house, the rich parents, the servants to do the work – but she could do better than the cottage on Beach Road. She could do well at school and go away to teaching college, and one day she could have a dear little house of her own, with a cat by the fire, food in the cupboard and shelves and shelves of books. She would never sell fish or hem dusters again, because she would be a teacher, like Miss Elliot at school, with neat grey skirts and white blouses, navy cardigans and flat brown brogues.

She wondered what Chris wanted to do when she grew up. Stay in this beautiful house and become her mother's helper, or get married? Wouldn't it be lovely if Chris wanted to be a teacher as well? But rich girls didn't teach, they married.

I wonder what Mum wanted to be when she grew up? Sybil thought drowsily, on the very brink of sleep now. Lizzie wanted to work in a big shop, Georgie wanted to have his own fishing boat, but what had Mum wanted? On the ladder which Sybil sometimes saw in her head, with Chris at the top and herself and Lizzie grimly scrambling up halfway, poor Mum was always down at the very bottom. But she likes selling fish so long as she's got Dad and us, Sybil told herself, just before she slept. And she's going to be so happy when she sees the dress we bought, me and Georgie!

5

Fenn had been awake since dawn, listening to the wind. It howled around the tall chimney pots and along the narrow streets of the Cheetham Hill district in Manchester, now and again sending a roof-tile spinning into the street below, trundling a dustbin lid briskly along the cracked and patched tarmac, or snatching the sound of an early-morning tram from its route and bringing its clatter almost into the room with Fenn.

Fenn's mother, Rachael, hated the wind. She was frightened of it, as she was of so many things. Of her Uncle Joseph, who had taken her in when her father died; of her cousin Jessica, who was clever and impatient as well as beautiful, though to Fenn's twelve-year-old eyes Rachel was beautiful too, with her shiny, midnight-dark hair which she brushed out by candlelight every night before climbing into the little trundle-bed in the attic she shared with Fenn.

Mother and son did not have the attic to themselves, of course. Not in the hungry thirties, with Great-Grandpa and his son Joseph having to keep the whole family, now that Fenn's beloved Gamps, as he had called Rachael's father, was dead. Jessica slept in the bed nearest the window with her older, plainer sister Sarah, and Leah, who was Uncle Joseph's child, and her small son Charles shared the remaining couch. Charles's father was dead, as Fenn's own father was, so Fenn was interested in the small boy, though the age difference, as well as Uncle Joseph's attitude, precluded real friendship.

Charles and I will be friends one day, when he's bigger, Fenn told himself sometimes. But most of the time he resented the pretty, curly-haired little boy who seemed to get all the affection and admiration for which Fenn craved but which seemed, unaccountably, to pass him by. Great-Grandpa positively hated him. Fenn never quite knew why, but often felt that he could have known, had he allowed himself to analyse the various remarks passed by others. It was something to do with his father . . . and perhaps something to do with Rachel too, though his parent was so meek, so eager to please, that Fenn could not understand Great-Grandpa's attitude towards her at all.

Uncle Joseph, who was his great-uncle really, didn't like him much, either. But Gamps had loved him and had never been ashamed to show it. He had never seen the many faults in Fenn which Great-Grandpa and Uncle Joseph seldom failed to mention daily, and had even criticized his three nieces, Jessica, Sarah and Leah, when they made slighting remarks about his Rachael.

Gamps had loved Rachael, had known her worth and appreciated everything about her. Not just her looks, but her patience, her kindness, the hard work she put in both at home and at the shop where she worked. To help her, but also because he liked it, he had played with Fenn, taught him, teased him . . . until Fenn was almost six, when Gamps had been taken off to the hospital with what had started as bronchitis and ended as pneumonia.

That winter had been a bitterly cold one, yet somehow Gamps soldiered on despite it. Fenn could vividly remember the treks through the streets, the little presents Rachael had saved so hard to buy or to make for Gamps. The hospital was Jewish owned and run so all the food was kosher, but even so Rachael cooked chicken soup and made dumplings for the kind-hearted nurses to warm through on the spirit stove in Sister's office and feed to her father, grown suddenly old as his helplessness increased.

Not that Gamps had ever seemed old to Fenn, not until that terrible winter when he saw his grandfather getting thinner and more breathless every day, saw the flesh drop away until the bones showed through. But even then, Gamps loved him and was not afraid to show it.

'Where's my boychik, then? Ah, but he's a little princeling, this one, he's going to be the brightest kid in school when he goes there . . . he can read already! You want a piece cake? That's right, Gamps has saved a piece cake for Fenn. Who gives an old man cake?' The chuckle, thin now and wheezing, the eye bright with the water of weakness, but the smile still v-shaped, mischievous and sweet. 'Every pretty nurse-lady bring the old man cake, Fenn, when I make them to laugh!'

It was true that the nurses loved him, that the doctors lingered longer by Gamps's bed than any other. They tried, Fenn gave them that. But in vain. Gamps kept going all through that harsh winter, when the small Fenn, clad in a cut-down man's jacket and a pair of rubber boots two sizes too large, came daily to the hospital through storm and rain, snow and wind. But then sweet spring came, with the scent of blossom on the gentle wind, and Fenn stole money from his aunt's purse and bought daffodils in the street market for his Gamps and took them to the hospital.

Gamps loved the daffodils; he said so, though not with his voice. With his sad, dark eyes, scarcely open in his skeletal face, and with the trembling hands which touched first the blooms, then Fenn's cheek.

'Next time I'll take him vi'lets; vi'lets smell so good,' Fenn said to Rachael as they walked home. But there never was a next time, and the violets, clutched and crushed in Fenn's small hand, were carried home again and in due course laid on the fresh-turned earth of Gamps's grave in the lordly cemetery where the Jews of Manchester had been buried . . . oh, for ever, Rachael said, when her small son asked.

Gamps had lived in a little house which Fenn had always assumed was his own. But after he died it appeared that he had rented it, and Rachael, unable to keep herself and her small son on the tiny wage she was paid for her part-time work, had been forced to move in with her only relatives, old Moishe Kitzmann and his son Joseph.

That had been the end of any happy family life for Fenn. He knew Rachael loved him, but she was too tired, too frightened, to stand up for him when the others mocked. Because they had been so good to Gamps, she got a job at the Jewish hospital as a cleaner. She had wanted to train as a nurse but that would have meant living in, and she could not bring herself, Fenn knew, to leave him to the far from tender mercies of Great-Grandpa and Uncle Joseph.

Great-Grandpa, a terrible old patriarch with white hair, a hooked nose and a stick which he used to good effect when Fenn annoyed him, made no secret of his dislike for his son's erring daughter and her child. In his view they were living in the house on sufferance, particularly Fenn, who was just another mouth to feed.

He said that often, did Great-Grandpa.

'What is the boy but another mouth to feed? A liar who sits on his *tochis* and eats me out of house and home, is shameless, learns nothing, gives nothing. Only to take he was born.' And sometimes, when he thought no one but Fenn was listening, 'A *gonif*, like his father; ay-yi-yi, a *gonif* who is also *goyim*; my granddaughter Rachael should have been strangled when she gave birth and the brat with her. Her wickedness killed my son; killed him!'

Uncle Joseph despised Rachael because she wept so much and wrung her hands and sometimes spoiled the food she cooked through

65

inattention, but he hated Fenn. He said Fenn was a liar just because Fenn sometimes told people what they wanted to hear, and a cheat because Fenn skipped school and then came above Uncle Joseph's own son, Saul, in class. Uncle Joseph tried to beat the devil out of Fenn, but usually Fenn was a match for him. He kept out of the way, he ran very fast, he ducked behind his mother, or Jessica, or Leah, and even descended, at times, to using little Charles as a shield. Charles admired Fenn and wept dolorously when tempers were lost and voices raised – he was worth a king's ransom to Fenn when his great-uncle or Great-Grandpa was on the warpath.

There was his mother, of course. He knew she did her best by him, but he often felt angry and sore with her. If only they had been able to keep Gamps's little house! If only she had forbidden Uncle Joseph to touch him instead of pleading softly, or even turning away, telling him that if he would tell stories she could not defend him!

Now, he felt her close to him, warm and soft in the narrow bed, sleeping. Fenn turned over and stared at her face, willing her to wakefulness. She had a small, unformed nose, dark eyes which were tightly closed at present, and a soft, anxious mouth. She worked terribly hard, Fenn knew, but he rather despised her for it. It got her nowhere! Look at Jessica, teaching at a school for young ladies; she always had money, she had lots of boyfriends, she wore pretty clothes and smelt of flowers and sunshine.

Rachael, on the other hand, made no attempt to use her brains or better herself. She had been forced to leave the little shop on Cheetham Hill when times were hard, and now she was just a servant whether she was at the Jewish hospital, in this house, or in that of her second employers, a rich Jewish family by the name of Levett for whom she cleaned three afternoons a week. At the hospital she scrubbed floors, cleaned windows, washed down walls and worked in both kitchens, milky and meaty. When she was at the Levetts' she also lit fires, humped scuttles full of coal up to the drawing room and hods of coke to the kitchen. She did some cooking for them and kept Benjamin's mother clean and tidy so that Mrs Levett, who was thin and sharp-nosed but a grand old lady, told her she really ought to be trained as a nurse. And when she came home to the house in Belstrode Street, worn out, she let the family bully her into starting all over again! Where was the sense in that?

What was more, Fenn had not failed to notice that those who bullied his mother did very well out of it. Great-Grandpa had the biggest helping of meat and Uncle Joseph got almost as much, whereas

Fenn and Charles, who was too little to bully anyone, went short. And Jessica's clothes were ironed so scrupulously that folk thought they were laundered professionally, while Fenn's own trousers and shirts were always ironed last, when Rachael was too tired to do a proper job.

There was dim light coming in through the attic window now. Fenn put his hands stealthily out of the covers and when they were icy drew them in again. Then he pushed both fists inside Rachael's thin old nightdress and grabbed at the warm softness of her breasts; she gave a muffled scream and her eyelids flew open. Her eyes, dark with terror, stared into his, and she pulled away from him, colour suffusing her face, the too-ready tears rising to her eyes.

'Don't be so cruel, *bubeleh*. I was asleep and dreaming. How could you hurt me like that?'

'It's time you got up and went to your skivvying. Besides, I want my breakfast before I go to school,' Fenn said, too loudly. From the other bed he heard Jessica's even breathing pause as her sleep was disturbed. She seemed to settle again just as Rachael sat up on one elbow and peered at the curtains, then with real reluctance swung herself round and out of the bed. She sat with her feet cringing away from the cold linoleum, plainly reluctant to start the day.

'Up!' Fenn said, but very quietly this time. He had decided months ago that the only way to treat his mother was to copy Uncle Joseph and Great-Grandpa and it certainly seemed to work. Accordingly he put both his feet in the small of his mother's back, above the curve of her buttocks, and pushed as hard as he could. Rachael gave another little cry and stumbled to her feet. She looked sheepishly at him as she scooped her clothes up from the floor where they had lain all night.

'All right, all right, I'll hurry. But you're a big boy now, Fennish; too big to give trouble to your mother the way you do. Just try, there's a good fellow, to be nice today. I do my best for you, my little son who is now so big and strong.'

'All right,' Fenn growled, cuddling down the bed again. He felt no shame over his bad behaviour, having realized years ago that in a peculiar way his mother liked to be treated badly, that she thought a man should be masterful. He just hoped that now he was being unkind to her he would no longer have to see Uncle Joseph getting the best meat when Rachael dished up the chicken pie, nor have to notice, with watering mouth, that the biggest, most sugary cakes went to the adult men. Still, it was early days. When he was bigger and stronger he would make sure that Rachael gave him the best – or regretted it. Yet even thinking such thoughts gave him a pain inside, because Gamps would have been so distressed, so very angry with him. A woman, to Gamps, was a gentle creature, to be protected, not punished. How, then, had this present state of affairs come about? If Gamps was to be believed, those who bullied the weak would suffer for it, but a fool could see that Great-Grandpa and Uncle Joseph simply went from strength to strength. It was only common sense then, Fenn told himself now, that having tried the path of righteousness and found it miserably wanting, he should see whether the opposite way would pay off.

Because, despite what Uncle Joseph frequently said, Fenn knew himself to be clever; he could certainly draw conclusions! The first time he had hit his mother, his helping of soup with matzo ball dumplings had actually contained a couple of dumplings instead of being all liquid. Inside himself, he had shrugged at the strangeness of women, but he could not forget it. Sometimes, remembering Gamps, he was sweet to Rachael, brought her little gifts, teased her, played games with her. But mostly he pushed her around, shouted at her, hit her in her soft, womanly places . . . and saw himself regarded with a sort of shamed admiration as a result.

Sometimes Leah or Sarah or even Jessica would remonstrate with him, and then Rachael always took his part. It occurred to Fenn that it was the only time Rachael stood up for him against anyone, which was crazy, because she was standing up for him against her own interests.

'The boy's right, I'm too slow,' she would mumble. Or, 'He's careful of me in his own way. It's right that he must tell me when I do wrong.'

'You're a stupid jellyfish, Rachael,' Jessica would snap. 'Never should you allow a child to correct you, a grown woman!'

'He'll turn into a real bully-boy,' Leah's soft voice complained. 'Poppa won't have little Charles mixing with him if he gets worse.'

Much I care, Fenn told himself, stung that Leah should threaten him with the removal of her spoilt pretty-boy. I'm on my own, I am . . . I hate them all as much as they hate me!

But he didn't, of course. He wanted to love them, to be accepted by them, to hear Great-Grandpa's voice praising him when he ran down to the corner shop for a newspaper or some pipe tobacco, to see Uncle Joseph's eyes light up when he and Saul, neck and neck, were top of the class. Instead, he saw Saul go off to Shul on a Saturday without him, 'because Saul's a good Jewish boy, who's learning Hebrew and can recite the Talmud. Not like that by-blow of Rachael's . . . Yankee

navvy who runs back to his heathen country at the first sign of trouble
. . . Outlandish names . . .'

By-blow? More Yiddish, no doubt, Fenn thought philosophically.
And what was wrong with a good name like Fennimore Kitzmann?
A part of Fenn knew very well that he should not bear his mother's
surname, since it meant his parents had not married, even that his
father had skipped sooner than marry, but he pushed such useless
knowledge to the back of his mind. And Great-Grandpa and Great
Uncle Joseph were Kitzmanns as well, so it had to be Fennimore
which they considered outlandish. They were just jealous because it
was his father's name, that was it. His poor dead father.

Not that he knew his father was dead; in fact, a part of Fennimore's
mind – for that devious organ was divided into many parts, and
Fennimore was perfectly capable of shutting one part off and
pretending it did not exist – was fairly sure his father was not
dead. That he had simply left on learning that Rachael was expecting
a child.

Still; death, Fenn had realized, was more respectable than departure, and because every week since Gamps's death he and his
mother had visited the cemetery in Crumpsall where, amidst the
tall tombstones with their Hebraic and English writing, Gamps was
buried, it was only sensible to tell those children who were interested
that he visited his father's grave.

Fiction, Fenn soon discovered, was a strange thing. Say it often
enough and even those who ought to know better begin to believe it.
Saul, for instance. Of course Saul was only a year older than Fenn,
so his recollections of Fenn's father must be non-existent, but he had
ears. He listened as Fenn did and must, surely, have realized that
Fenn's father was not respectably beneath the sod up at the cemetery
but unrespectably gone, having legged it like a thief in the night at
the mere mention of parental responsibilities.

Yet Fenn had heard Saul – and there was no love lost between
the two of them – confirming Fenn's story of the heroic dead father.
Perhaps fortunately though, Saul had not been present when Fenn
had led Becky Mossman, the prettiest girl in the school, up to the
graveyard one day last May.

Fenn liked Becky and had been trying to impress her for some
time, for though he sometimes supplied her with answers to sums or
with a neat essay which she only had to copy out, these were favours
which she took for granted, tossing her jetty plaits and smiling at him,
but then going off with her gaggle of girlfriends, or even worse, with

Solomon Reifer, who was another of those 'pretty' boys that Fenn despised, save that Solomon had, in addition to curls and melting dark eyes, muscles which made one a little shy of jeering at him.

And then, quite by chance, he mentioned his father's grave, and Becky, it appeared, had been taken to the cemetery by an aunt the previous week and had been much impressed by the stones with their elaborate topknots and beautiful script.

'Which one is your father's?' she asked eagerly, her big eyes sparkling. 'Can I come up with you at the weekend and see it?'

What choice had he but a bashful acceptance of her company? What choice but to embark on another lie? And, since he must lie, it should be a good one, he decided, as they walked up the long hill, past the pond with its weeping trees, its grassy banks, and into the graveyard itself. Only the best was good enough for his father!

He got over the difficulty of the name by explaining that although, as she could see from the magnificent tombstone, his father's name had been Joseph Sleutenastein, after his father had passed on it had been agreed that Fenn should take his mother's name of Kitzmann to make things easier.

Becky nodded sagely; she could see that it would make things very much easier, particularly in the spelling department. She had found Mossman difficult as a small child, she confided; lucky Fenn not to have to worry about a mouthful like Sleutenastein!

Fortunately she did not notice that the Sleutenastein who slept beneath the imposing black marble stone, with its inscription in gold and the topknot, so like an intricately tied turban, towering over all, had died in 1916, quite two years before Fenn's own birth. Becky, Fenn saw thankfully, was a bit of a *schlemiel* despite her pretty looks and taking ways, but what did it matter, after all? She believed, admired him, and later they sat by the pond, with the rhododendrons just coming into bloom and the scent of grass and leaves sweet in their nostrils, and Fenn told her how his father had won medals in the War, how he had owned a huge house in London and another in the country, and how very much he had loved Rachael and his small son.

It was, perhaps, a pity his embroidery led him to the lengths of claiming his father has been a great scholar and a famous pianist to boot, since when Becky relayed this information to her friends there was more than one pair of eyebrows disappearing into hairlines. But he dealt smartly and totally with Isadore Davissohn, who queried the date as being more than a trifle unlikely.

'So how come he and your mother had you three years after he'd gone to his rest?' Izzy said sarcastically. 'How come it happens, eh, or are you claiming your father was the Holy Ghost, like Jesus of Nazareth?'

'Oh, you noticed, did you?' Fenn said offhandedly. 'I suppose you didn't bother to check with the Hebrew, you *golem*? The stone-mason got the English wrong, but it's right in Hebrew, if you like to check.'

'I'm no idiot, and you can't read Hebrew any more than I can . . . less, I dare say, since you never come to classes after Shul on a Saturday.'

'No. But my grandfather could; he read it to me when he was teaching me my letters; I was just a kid then, but I remember he told me that it should say 1919 and a six is only a nine upside down, so since replacing a stone is an expensive business they left it as it was.' Izzy snorted but walked off, clearly beaten, and Becky took Fenn's small, grubby paw in her own.

'Never mind him, Fenn,' she whispered. 'I never believed you were telling stories – who'd tell stories about their dead father? Besides, your cousin Saul says it is so, and he's older than us . . . he probably knows even more about it.'

But right now, lying in his bed, Fenn thought about Rachael, toiling in the kitchen far below. She would light the fire, boil a kettle for tea and for hot water, then she would start to get breakfast. When all was prepared she would take a cup of tea and a breakfast roll up to Great-Grandpa's room and that would be the signal for everyone to get up and go into the kitchen for their own meal. Weak tea and hot rolls, but never enough rolls to fill you, so you made up with tea and tightened your belt and spent most of the day longing for the evening meal – at least Fenn did. He and Saul both took sandwiches to school but somehow Fenn's bread was always thin, the margarine scraped on, the cheese the hard little bits nearest the rind. If he had an apple it was a withered one, not like the red-cheeked beauties which Saul enjoyed. But then Aunt Anna had thought her child-bearing days were over when Saul had put in an appearance, so Saul was coddled in a way which Fenn deeply envied.

In the other bed, Leah stirred. Charles was all she had now that Samuel was dead, so when it was time to get up she dressed herself and then dealt lovingly with Charles, but Fenn, for as long as he could remember, had always been despatched down the attic stairs and into the freezing cold bathroom to dress himself. Sinful as he was, he had been judged far too naughty to watch the women dress and undress – except for Rachael who, it seemed, did not count.

71

Now, Jessica stretched and sat up on her elbow to peer at her little gold wrist-watch. Immediately, Fenn slid out of bed, trying to ignore the cold of the linoleum but sympathizing with his mother's earlier toe-curling. He picked up his clothes, just a ragged jersey and trousers since he slept in his shirt, and made for the door, not waiting for Jessica to shout at him that he was supposed to get up when Rachael did and what did he think he was doing, lying in bed like a lord until almost eight o'clock?

Never mind, Fenn comforted himself. What does it matter? In April I'll be thirteen, a man! I'll have a *barmitzvah*, like Saul did last year, and Great-Grandpa or Uncle Joseph will give me a *tallis*, and I'll go to Shul with the menfolk and quite soon after that I'll get a job and begin to earn money of my own – real money, gelt, mazooma, not just the pennies and ha'pennies I pick up here and there.

He wondered what would happen about sleeping arrangements, though. At thirteen, surely he would no longer sleep in the attic with the women and baby Charles? Perhaps he could share Saul's bed? Not that he wanted to share with his cousin, since Saul slept in solitary splendour on a trundle bed which pulled out from under Great-Grandpa's creaking old four-poster . . . there would be room for two in it, though, so it would be a solution of a sort, since he and Rachael were already unbearably cramped.

Fenn, padding down the uncarpeted wooden stairs, reached the bathroom and pushed the door open. It was empty, but certain sounds from Great-Grandpa's room told him that Saul would be hurrying in quite soon. Fenn always had to wash in cold water but Rachael began carting hot up for everyone else as soon as the kettle boiled, and once the family heard her footsteps toiling up the stairs they would all make a rush for the bathroom. It behoved Fenn to be well clear of the room by then.

Accordingly, he washed skimpily, dragged on his clothes and was halfway down the stairs when his mother, carrying the big iron kettle, began to mount them. She smiled at him.

'Get some food; there's porridge,' she whispered. 'You can eat and leave before the others are down. Go on, get to school early for once.'

It was good advice and Fenn knew it. Eat and run, get out of the way before the rest of the family noticed that Fenn had had porridge, grab whatever Aunt Anna had left in his bit of greaseproof paper and go. Once he had taken the contents of Saul's neat sandwich tin and put his own food in its place, but only once. Uncle Joseph had seen to it that Fenn had not been able to sit down for a week – almost worth it for salt-beef sandwiches, two bagels with cream cheese and the honey-cake which Aunt Anna baked specially for her precious Saul. Almost, but not quite, because Uncle Joseph had not only laid into him until Fenn had nearly passed out, he had forbidden him the evening meal, laying ceremoniously in his place at the kitchen table for a whole week a thin slice of bread and a mug of weak tea without sugar or milk.

'I'll cure him of thieving,' he had said grimly, and Fenn, making his way down the stairs and plunging thankfully into the comparative warmth of the kitchen, had to conclude that, in a way, Uncle Joseph had succeeded. He no longer took anything which could be directly blamed on him. Now, he was careful when stealing food; he took one cake from a tinful, or a handful of raisins from the blue paper bag, a couple of bagels when Rachael had made a couple of score, or a spoonful of honey from a full jar, and even then, only when no one was about to see.

Like now. The fire was roaring up the chimney, heating the kitchen and baking the breakfast rolls. A bowl of porridge stood on the side of the stove and Fenn, gobbling it down, was thankful for its warmth even though he knew that by dinner-time it would be forgotten, gone as though it had never been, and his hunger would gnaw as strongly as ever.

But still. Rachael had sliced the loaf; he took a slice and folded it into his pocket to eat on the way to school, his eyes darting round the room; anything else? But already he could hear his mother's footsteps descending the stairs. He had better cut his losses and get going . . . pity he'd not had time for a cup of tea, but there was a drinking fountain in the school playground so he could have some water before classes started.

He got his old coat down from the hooks by the front door and slid out into Belstrode Street. The front door led straight on to the pavement without any garden or even a strip of cement you could call your own, but it was a good neighbourhood and they were nice houses. Once, they had been 'smart', with their arched doorways, ornamental brickwork and whitened front steps, but now they were overcrowded, crammed to the eyebrows as the Depression deepened and made it necessary for father to move in with son, son to bring cousins home. And they were neglected, too. Paintwork peeled and blistered, unpolished door knockers hung awry, windows, once neatly curtained with white net, showed little furniture, now, between the skimpy, faded drapes.

But Fenn, hurrying down the road with the wind slicing to the bone despite his cut-down greatcoat, and the rain soaking everything and flattening his hair to his skull, cared nothing for the bygone grandeur of Belstrode Street. He wanted somewhere dry to eat his bread and wait until school opened. If he went right along to Cheetham Hill Road he would find small shops, some already open, but it was off his route. It would be easier to see if he could get someone to invite him in; it was not unknown for his friend Cecil's mother, a homely soul with an ingenuous appetite for tall stories, to give him some breakfast. Sometimes they had a sort of pancake called a waffle, spread with butter and honey. It was one of the most delicious things ever to have come Fenn's way.

He quickened his pace, reminding himself that whether or not Mrs Finagler took him in, he would be in school in less than an hour. School was warmer than the street, and in his way he enjoyed lessons. Saul tried hard, yet his brain was not quick, like Fenn's. He scowled and frowned and reasoned and added up on his fingers, whereas Fenn seemed to have an affinity for sums and could not understand why his cousin made such heavy weather of addition, subtraction and multiplication, let alone the writing of essays, which were only stories when all was said and done. As for the committing to memory of poems and prose and the digestion of facts, historical, geographical or literary, these things seemed to Fenn the simplest tasks of all.

Still, Saul wasn't bad. They might have got along together if only Uncle Joseph had been a decent sort, if only he had treated Fenn fairly and not encouraged Saul to tell tales and despise his young relative. Fenn would have counted himself fortunate if he could have been as happy at home as he was at school with his teacher, old Bizznizz, thus called because he had once asked a boy what bizznizz he had in the stationery cupboard.

But facts were facts and Uncle Joseph was as hateful as Great-Grandpa, always seizing any excuse to haul Fenn off by the ear to the backyard in summer and the icy bathroom in winter, there to thrash him until someone interfered or Fenn, with the black wings beating closer and closer round his head, dropped almost senseless to the ground.

Almost. Fenn's ingenious brain had long since realized that once he pretended to swoon Uncle Joseph took fright and stopped hitting him. Now, a wily oldster of almost thirteen, he was stronger than he had been and less willing to allow himself to be savagely attacked. He

74

fought back, wriggled, screamed the place down and only 'swooned' in a dire emergency, when Uncle Joseph's zeal overcame caution and he armed himself with some implement which could do Fenn real damage.

'You'll kill him one day,' Rachael moaned, scooping her son off the floor and clasping him to her soft bosom. 'That's what you'll do, Joseph, you'll kill my boy.'

But Joseph, breathing heavily, with the bloodlust still there to see in his mean little eyes, would only say that a hiding never hurt a boy and if it taught Fenn his place . . .

I wonder what my place is? Fenn asked himself now, fighting the breathless wind. No one has ever said, not even Uncle Joseph, unless you count him telling me all the time that I'm a devil and expecting me to be a saint! But he won't take me to Shul on the Sabbath when the rest of the family go, I can't go with the women because that wouldn't be right, and I don't go to classes to study the Talmud either. He says it's not fit. So if I *was* bad, which I'm not, you couldn't really wonder at it.

He passed Cecil's house in the next street and went down the side alley. It was bricked with neat red bricks but grass and weeds flourished between them and the drain in the middle was choked with rubbish so that when it rained the alley flooded. It was flooded now. Fenn picked his way carefully along to the back of Cecil's house, pushed open the leaning wooden door and slipped into the tiny yard where Mrs Finagler kept four hens in a battered run and hung her washing above the cracked and crazy concrete. The hens crowded the wire netting at the sight of Fenn, clucking and purring hopefully; he thought about his slice of bread but decided his need was greater than theirs – they were probably better fed than he since Mrs Finagler was fattening them up for Cecil's *barmitzvah*. She was going to have a big party, and not just in her own home, either. The Finaglers were hiring a hall, and the hens would, by the time April came, make a noble contribution to the feast.

Reaching the battered back door, Fenn knocked politely, waited a moment, then popped his head round the door. Mrs Finagler was at the stove, cooking something in a big black pan; drops of water hissed and spat on the hot iron and there was a nice smell of food. Mr Finagler and Cecil sat at the kitchen table, eating; opposite them were Constance and Cassandra, Cecil's older sisters, and at the head of the table sat a stranger, a man in clerical black with a spade-shaped beard. He looked up and winked at Fenn as the boy came hesitantly into the room.

75

'Ah, Fenn . . . want some grub?' Mr Finagler was a tailor but he looked more like one of the red-faced countrymen who sold vegetables in the market on Saturdays. He had a round, ingenuous face, pale blue eyes and a fringe of blond, greying hair. He worked at home, making suits for one of the big shops on Deansgate, and Mrs Finagler and her two daughters worked with him. Between the four of them they produced, so Fenn had heard it said, more first-class work than any other family in the city.

Right now, however, it was not of Mr Finagler's expertise with his sewing machine that Fenn thought, but of the contents of the big pot his wife was stirring. Porridge? Soup? Something hot for such a day would be really nice, for his own breakfast was already history to Fenn's eager stomach.

'It's vegetable soup, because it's cold out,' Cecil ventured. He pulled out the chair next to his own, gesturing hospitably towards Fenn. 'Come and sit down, there's tons of time before the bell.'

'Ah, Rabbi, this is Fenn Kitzmann, the son of a neighbour and a friend of Cecil's,' Mr Finagler said as Fenn took his seat. Fenn hastily stood up again and offered a hand, which the rabbi shook heartily.

'Hello, Fenn,' he said. 'Unusual name.' He did not wait for Fenn to explain, however, but launched into a discussion which Fenn soon realized was about Cecil's coming *barmitzvah*. He listened eagerly, spooning in the thick vegetable soup, envying Cecil not only his delightful parents and their generous cuisine but the easy assumption that his thirteenth birthday was the most important event to have occurred in their family for some time.

'An expensive business, though,' the rabbi sighed at length, unashamedly wiping his soup bowl out with half a white and fluffy roll. 'A pity you cannot expenses share with another . . . not unknown it is to see two boys, good friends, get their *tallis* together. What about this fellow here – Fenn? Any good? He looks near the right age, to me.'

'I am,' Fenn said eagerly. 'I'll be thirteen two days after Cecil, won't I, Mrs Finagler?'

Mrs Finagler looked uncomfortable.

'Ye-es . . . but you'd have to ask your great-grandfather,' she muttered. 'I don't know . . . there's been some talk . . .'

'I'm sure Great-Grandpa would be glad to share expenses,' Fenn said eagerly. 'Saul's *barmitzvah* nearly broke the bank, he said. He won't want to spend so much on me, either, seeing as I'm . . .'

'Time you two were off,' Mr Finagler interrupted. 'Don't want no

76

bad marks for being late, eh, lads? Off with you, off with you! Got your grub, young Cecil?'

Cecil flourished his bag, pushed the last remnants of roll into his mouth and made for the back door.

'C'mon, Kitzmann,' he said thickly. 'Don't want old Bizznizz buzzing round our ears.'

But Fenn, dragging his feet, still managed to hear the whisper from the rabbi to his host.

'Kitzmann? There's nothing down for a Kitzmann in April, only young Saul last October. Are you sure . . . ?'

'The girl married out,' Mrs Finagler muttered. 'A strange old man, the great-grandfather . . . sends the boy to school with no good breakfast inside him, gives him more kicks than kisses . . . they won't *barmitzvah* that one; too mean.'

All the way to school Fenn was quieter than usual, because he was thinking. Thinking back, mostly. There had been constant talk of Saul's *barmitzvah*; the adults, even his mother, even Leah who was not much interested in her younger brother, had gone on and on about it. The party had been large though not lavish, the ceremony sufficiently striking to stay in Fenn's memory as a grand and auspicious occasion.

Soon, he had kept thinking, it will be *my* turn. Soon it will be me who has to recite the *barmitzvah* prayer; Great-Grandpa will teach me and be really pleased when he finds I know the words already . . . *O my God and God of my fathers, on this solemn and sacred day which marks my passage from boyhood to manhood* . . .

It was a long prayer. They had started teaching Saul his part many weeks before the great day and even then he had not got it by heart in time, but had stumbled over some of the longer words. And Cecil had gone to special classes, had known the prayer now for weeks. But he, Fenn, had learned it just by listening to Saul stumbling through it. He had hoped to please and surprise them all – could it be true what Mrs Finagler had said? That the Kitzmanns were too mean to give him a *barmitzvah*? If so, how would he ever be a man?

6

A week later, on just such another wild day, Fenn was running at a stumbling gallop down Belstrode Street and out across Cheetham Hill Road, scarcely able to see the traffic for the driving rain and wind.

Or was it the tears? Because Fenn Kitzmann, who never cried, not even when Uncle Joseph beat him until his arm was too tired to move, was crying now. Crying because at long last he had plucked up his courage and had the final show-down and it was all true – true! Uncle Joseph had said that Fenn Kitzmann was no true Jew, that he did not intend to *barmitzvah* the bastard son of a *goy*, and furthermore unless Fenn went down on his knees and begged pardon for his impudence in even expecting such a thing it would be bread and water for him until well past the thirteenth birthday he seemed to think such an important family matter.

Rachael had wept. Naturally she had wept. She was like a great sponge; every time anyone squeezed her there was water everywhere, but of course she didn't really care or she'd have fought to have her son treated right. She had tried to interfere, tried to save him from the beating, but she had not tried hard enough. And he'd hit Uncle Joseph when he'd called him the bastard son of a *goy* because he was insulting Fenn's heroic father as well as his weak, pathetic mother. Fenn knew now what a bastard was and he resented being called one, resented, all of a sudden, the treatment he had received at the Kitzmanns' hands all these long years.

And even through his tears, Fenn had to smile as he remembered the look on Uncle Joseph's face when the wooden rolling pin cracked across his kneecaps, swung by Fenn's vigorous hand. Pain, yes, and incredulity and even, for a second, a sort of stunned respect.

'Take that back, you old pig,' Fenn had shouted at the top of his voice. To a Jew, to be called a pig was an insult indeed, though the Kitzmanns were not a particularly religious family and were certainly not orthodox in their habits. Nevertheless, though they had been known to stew beef and even eat shrimps – though never on the Sabbath – not one of them would have touched bacon, ham or any other pork product.

The whack across the knees with the rolling pin had been followed by Fenn rebounding off the kitchen floor and butting Uncle Joseph very hard, with his head, in the middle. Uncle Joseph had folded up whilst Great-Grandpa, sitting in his chair, had laid about him with his stick, hoping to catch Fenn a nasty blow yet clearly far less anxious to bring Fenn's swinging rolling pin into action once more – or not directed at himself, at any rate. And Fenn hadn't touched the old man, though he had told him a thing or two.

So why was he crying? Crying and running along the streets which he knew so well? Boo-hooing, furthermore, rubbing at his eyes with his dirty fists and not caring who saw? Shouting to the indifferent wind that he would never go back; he would die first?

Because of Great-Grandpa's last shrieked remark, that was why. Because he had said the one thing that could truly hurt Fenn, had been like a dagger through the heart.

'If Aaron hadn't died . . .' Aaron was Gamps, to Fenn. 'If Aaron hadn't died when he did you'd have killed him by now, you filth! I'm glad Aaron's dead, glad he's not here to be hurt by your lies and your cheating, your evil ways! Glad, glad, glad!'

Rachael, weeping, telling him he was a bad boy – Rachael, his mother, who was supposed to love him! Oh, she had tried to make Uncle Joseph shut up, had told him that he had gone too far, but when he had defended himself, hit back, to accuse him of being a bad boy was wickedly unfair. Then there was Aunt Anna, screaming curses down on his head because he had dared to strike big, bullying Uncle Joseph – one act of rebellion after a lifetime of kicks and curses – and Leah telling him she'd never let him speak a word to Charles because he was cursed by God for raising his hand against her father.

Fenn had been running, seeing the houses whip by out of his tear-filled eyes, but now he slowed, sniffing. Where was he running *to*? Where did one go when one's family had cast one out? He was, after all, still a couple of weeks short of his thirteenth birthday. He had friends . . . Cecil, Becky, even Izzy . . . but they would all be in school now, with Bizznizz standing before the class, chalk in hand, expounding maths.

Fenn looked around him, and half-admired his own crazed flight. He was on Crescent Road, a long way from Cheetham Hill, school, and friends. He was almost in Crumpsall, not far from the cemetery. He straightened his shoulders and then wiped his nose on the sleeve of his ragged black coat. He would go and see someone who really did care for him – Gamps. Gamps slept beneath black marble and cold earth, but he still had more warmth and love in his heart than all the rest of the Kitzmanns put together. I wish to God I wasn't a Kitzmann, Fenn told himself furiously, lengthening his stride now that he knew where he was going. I wish I was anything but a Kitzmann because it's a name to be ashamed of since I share it with cowards, bullies and braggarts.

But Rachael loved him. He had always known it and now it comforted him a little, that she had threatened Uncle Joseph, frightened though she was of him. She had screamed at one stage that she and her son would both leave the house and who would cook for them, clean for them, skivvy for them then? Yet . . . she had not followed him when he ran out, had remained behind with the Kitzmanns.

He reached the cemetery gates, black and imposing, with their complex pattern in wrought iron which he had wondered over weekly for as long as he could remember. He began to walk up the hill, the rough cinders of the track grinding beneath his boots, giving the pond, the rhododendrons, the lashing trees around it no more than a passing glance. He was here for a purpose . . . he would tell Gamps what had been going on. If there was a God in heaven, which he was beginning to doubt, Gamps's influence would surely have some effect? Uncle Joseph ought to be struck dumb or something and Great-Grandpa, in Fenn's opinion, had troubled the world quite long enough and ought now to be out of it. He was well over eighty – fair's fair, Fenn told himself rather obscurely, and what was more the old bugger had said he was glad his own son was dead! It's time the old pig got off my back, Fenn told himself, and tried to whip up his fury once more so that he could curse Great-Grandpa properly, with bell, book and candle, so to speak.

But the angry words, the curses, would only come when the blood was hot and now he was beginning to cool down in every sense of the word. Less angry, more resigned, and of course cold to the marrow of his bones as soon as the heat engendered by fury had left him. He stomped along, head bent, and felt a shudder shake him. Perhaps a graveyard was no place for harbouring grudges; perhaps he should not have come up here on such a wild afternoon, with no one else around. But be that as it may, he was here now so he would at least visit Gamps. He knew the way blindfold between the tall gravestones and gradually, as he reached the summit, his chilly misery began to recede and a sort of peace flowed into him.

Gradually, the place itself calmed him, because it was here he had come to think about Gamps, to remember. The very tombstones seemed to smile at him, to understand. Lazarus and Fanny Mistovski, 1887, Joseph Davis, 1886, Julius Samter, glorying in four stone pillars, a wrought-iron gate and an urn, born 1852, died 1910, an important man with a memorial which could be seen even from the little red-brick building where the services were held, with its doors fore and aft so that the coffin went in one door but came out the other, carried by its solemn, black-clad acolytes.

And Gamps. A good tombstone, one of the best, tall and grave, the Hebraic characters picked out in gold, the English writing in white. It had cost Rachael all of her small inheritance, but she thought it worth it and Fenn agreed. All of Gamps's life should have been here – some stones had whole family histories engraved on them, beloved wives, dear departeds, lists of grieving relatives, sadly missed, deeply mourned – but that had been more than Rachael could manage so it said, plainly, in English and Hebrew, that Aaron Kitzmann lay here, sadly missed by daughter Rachael and grandson Fennimore.

And Gamps was there, of course – what choice had he? Fenn was sure he listened, as, in a breathy mutter, he unburdened himself of his sorrows. But Gamps wasn't altogether on Fenn's side, because he reminded Fenn that he had lied in the past, and cheated, and stolen, too.

'A pity, but not past remedy,' he seemed to be saying as Fenn sat with his back against a beloved wife, staring at Gamps's simple inscription. 'You're young, you'll grow. Let them have their *barmitzvah* and keep it all to themselves; you'll be a man despite them, Fennimore my *bubeleh*, worth ten of them! As for your father, there was a man!'

It was exactly what Fenn wanted to hear and he basked in it, even though, inside his devious head, he knew that Gamps could only say, now, what he, Fenn, allowed him to say. Well, something like that, anyway. And then, in the middle of some more sonorous words, Gamps's voice faded right away, leaving Fenn sitting there gazing at the view, for the wind, though still rough, had blown the rainclouds away and the pale blue sky, sparkling clean after its storm, was suddenly clear from horizon to horizon as the gentle gold of the spring sunshine washed everything with colour.

Fenn stood up and looked outwards, past where the old, old graves tumbled down the hillside, over to where he could see a great factory, flat fields, little streets begin.

That was his home, all of that. What did it matter, really, whether Uncle Joseph and Great-Grandpa allowed him to go to the synagogue and wear a *tallis* round his neck and a little skullcap pinned to his hair? Saul only wore his cap for services, and since it was clear that Fenn would not be allowed to attend services, why should he care about these things?

And, gazing over the countryside stretched out below him, Fenn found that he did not care, that he was going to be a man despite them, not because of them, and that he would go home now for his mother's sake, not for any other reason, and would brazen it out somehow until he was old enough to leave and earn his own living. He had blamed his mother for not supporting him; he knew he had been unfair. She had done what she could as a mere woman. If he was to be the man he wanted to be, then it was his job to take care of her, see that she came to no harm, and he would start at once, as soon as he got home that night.

Satisfied that he would be taking the right action, he began to ponder what he should do when he was a man. He rolled ideas around, liking the taste of one, discarding another. A teacher? No; he'd had enough of people telling him things, had no desire to become the teller. A lawyer, then? A tailor, like Mr Finagler? You had to have talent to be a tailor, if you wanted to make money. He quite liked the thought of working in a bank; all that lovely cash! What else did grown-ups do, then? Uncle Joseph had a warehouse and bought and sold things, that was about all Fenn knew, and his mother was a sort of general cleaner. He supposed, doubtfully, that he could be a manservant, perhaps a butler – and dismissed the idea at once. No! Worse than being a school-teacher, worse than working in a warehouse, to take orders all day long and be polite to someone you possibly disliked, certainly despised.

He was thinking about going down the hill again to take up once more the life being lived in the streets below when, behind him, someone cleared his throat. Startled, he spun round.

A man stood there. He was of medium height and balding, but such hair as he had was tightly curled like a lamb's fleece, and his smooth, slightly shiny skin looked almost golden in the afternoon sun. He was clad in the oddest coat Fenn had ever seen – it was made of some substance which was as tightly curled and black as his own hair, save for the collar and cuffs which were of softer, smoother, lighter stuff.

Around his neck he wore a silk scarf with tassels and fine leather gloves covered his hands. He smiled at Fenn, revealing square white teeth.

'Good afternoon. I wonder, could you tell me where I might find the tombstone of Aloysius Kertzer?'

'Born 1848, died 1915?' Fenn said automatically.

If the truth were known, there was scarcely a gravestone in the cemetery he was not familiar with, but the stranger could not possibly know that. He raised both eyebrows and stared, looking very taken aback yet somehow pleased, too.

'Phew! Well, there's a thing . . . you must have known the Kertzer family kinda well to put dates to the name like that! Though come to think of it you're only a kid, so there's no way . . . me and my sister Dobie, we're all that's left so far's I know. I come to pay my respects to my family whilst I'm in the old country and there's no one left; they've either died out or moved on.'

Funny accent, Fenn mused whilst admitting that he did not, in fact, know any of the Kertzers personally. And then, being Fenn, he added that it was, however, a respected name hereabouts.

'My great-grandfather knew them well,' he persisted. 'He's still alive, though very frail. Moishe Kitzmann . . . he's been a powerful man in this city in his time.'

'Now that's fascinating . . . but how old would he be?'

'Just ninety,' Fenn said, automatically adding a decade. 'Of course, his mind's going,' he added hastily, in case his new friend decided to visit the wicked old man. 'Not much he can tell you now, though only a few years back he was sharp as a needle.'

'Hmm. I'd like to go to Shul and meet some of the old'uns,' the man said. 'But it's too late this time, at any rate. I'm sailing tomorrow.'

'Sailing?' Fenn was all this time leading the way through the cemetery; now he stopped in the middle of a crowded row and pointed. 'There he is; and his good lady beside him.'

The man was not wearing a hat, but had he been doing so Fenn just knew he would have pulled it off. As it was he bent his head, read the inscription very slowly and carefully, and then took a couple of steps back.

'Excuse me,' he said. 'Gee, this cemetery's sure full, you can't get back a decent pace without treading on another grave. Just going to have a picture for the folk back home.'

Fenn stared as the stranger produced from the pocket of his exotic coat a small black box. A camera! Great-Grandpa had paid a photographer to take a picture of Saul at his *barmitzvah* – and was still grumbling at the price. This man must be very rich!

The man clicked his camera several times, insisting that Fenn stood beside the gravestone once, so that 'the folk back home' would see what a noble monument it was, then with another of his shy smiles he handed the small box to Fenn.

'Ever used one before? No? Well, see that little square of glass there? What you see in that is what you'll see in the photograph, when it's developed. Now this here's the button to press when you want to take the photograph . . . got it? Then try to get me in with the stone, eh?' He walked away and stood, in sorrowful profile, looking at the stone as though reading the writing on it. Fenn had to smother a giggle because the man looked so cheerful and square and lively that the expression of grief did not sit well on his rubicund countenance.

'Got it? Good, good. Aw, gee, I never told you my name. I'm James Kertzer; my friends call me Jim. So now you'll be able to tell your folks you've met a dam' Yankee!'

He laughed, taking the box back, fitting it into the capacious pocket of his odd coat, but Fenn was struck by wonder and excitement. A Yankee, just like his vanished father! Fenn's mobile mind gave a little wiggle, and was sure at last that his father was not dead. His father was alive, in America, where this man had come from, and for respectability's sake Fenn now lent him his own surname, to make up for the elder Fennimore's strange lack.

'How do you do, Mr Kertzer,' he said formally, shaking his new friend vigorously by the hand. 'I'm Fennimore Kitzmann, named for my father, who is a dam' Yankee, just like you!'

'No!' The round, golden-brown eyes stared, then Jim Kertzer beamed at Fenn. 'Well, if that ain't the durndest thing!'

'I'm going to the States one day, to see my father,' Fenn confided as the two of them walked slowly back the way they had come. 'He left me with my great-uncle Joseph and Aunt Anna after my mother died, God rest her. I suppose he couldn't very well take a small child away from the only home it had ever known but now . . . well, I'm being *barmitzvahed* quite soon, and after that I'll probably write to my father and suggest I join him.'

'Wonderful!' Jim Kertzer said enthusiastically. 'It's a great country, the land of opportunity for Jews, I can tell you. I hail from New York now, Lower East Side, and I've done well enough for myself to have this trip just as a little holiday, to satisfy my desire to see the old country. Whilst I'm away the store will still tick over and the dollars will still roll in. Oh, you couldn't do better than come over to the *golda medina*, the golden land, Fennimore.'

'Tell me about it,' Fenn breathed as they skirted the graveyard and began the descent on to Crescent Road once more. 'Tell me all about it!'

Fenn might never have run away had he not met Saul as he was making his way back to Belstrode Street in the late afternoon. He was mooching along, dreading his return to the house, planning what to say to his mother and to Aunt Anna. But he would never speak to Great-Grandpa again, dreadful old man, nor to Uncle Joseph.

He had skipped school, of course, but he could not go home until classes were over for the day or they would guess. He thought he might go along to the Levett house where his mother worked, and find out from her just what sort of reception he was likely to get from the Kitzmanns when he returned to Belstrode Street.

He was walking in that direction when he saw Saul ahead of him. Saul was eating something and immediately water rose to Fenn's mouth. He hurried alongside his cousin and pulled at his elbow. After all, his quarrel, if you could call it that, was with Saul's parents, not with the boy himself.

'Saul . . . what happened after I left? Will it be all right when I go home, do you think?' Fenn said urgently. 'Did my mother go to work as usual? She's at the Levetts' place this afternoon, I think.'

Saul turned and stared at him. There was chocolate round his mouth and for the first time Fenn noticed that Saul had eyes just like Uncle Joseph's and would look exactly like his father when he grew up. The eyes were small and glittering and they looked spitefully at Fenn out of Saul's pale, chocolate smeared face.

'Oh, it's you. Haven't you heard?'

'Heard? Heard what?'

'Your precious mother went to work all right, but she never got there. Crossing Cheetham Hill Road she was knocked down by a tram; an ambulance came and took her off to hospital, but it wouldn't be no good. Flattened, she was, deader'n a doornail I bet . . . and it'll serve you right, Fennimore Kitzmann, for hitting my good father, to say nothing of the language you used.'

Shock held Fenn rigid whilst a numbing chill crept over his body. He stood on the pavement as if turned to marble whilst Saul stared at him, half-gloating, half-uneasy.

'Did you hear what I said, Fenn? *Rachael's been run over!*'

'It's a lie,' Fenn said slowly. His voice was very small and seemed to come from a long distance away.

'No it's not! It's you that tells lies, Fenn, not me. Where are you going?'

For Fenn had turned blindly away from Saul and plunged across the busy road, dodging the cars and buses and bicycles more by luck than any judgement since he certainly did not see where he was going.

Mother, dead. So that was what happened when you doubted God, hit your great-uncle, swore at your great-grandfather! God turned round and struck your mother dead.

Fenn found that he was heading for the hospital where Gamps had died, where Rachael worked four days a week, the Jewish hospital in Elizabeth Street. But he did not reach it. He stopped halfway and thought.

This was it, then. He was really on his own now. Rachael, his only defender in the house, was gone, so he could never go back to Belstrode Street. But where should he go? He could scarcely make himself up a bed in the cemetery, near Gamps's tomb, and the Finaglers, delightful though they were, would not hide him from the family.

I am truly alone now, Fenn told himself, trudging unseeingly up the street, pushing past children returning from school and parents out shopping. Now I am truly alone, without a relative in the world, for Uncle Joseph and Great-Grandpa were just waiting for a chance to cast me off and disown me and now they've got it. Mother's dead.

Which is what you told that Jim Kertzer earlier this afternoon – God thought it was what you wanted, the small inner voice which occasionally made pointed and unpleasant remarks to him said coldly. You've done it now, haven't you? God has decided to make you a teller of truth, so it was *your* fault that your mother died, as it is undoubtedly your fault that your family will cast you off.

So if it's true that my mother's dead, then it's also true that my father's alive, Fenn reminded himself. My father's in America and Jim Kertzer's going back there tomorrow . . . I could go as well!

Without money? the little inner voice jeered. Without a bean to your name? But that meant nothing because Jim Kertzer, bidden to tell Fenn everything, had made him a present of one very interesting bit of information – that as a young man he had stowed away aboard a ship plying between Liverpool and New York, when he had first decided to go to America twenty years ago.

At once, Fenn's fertile brain started making plans. Trains went all over the place; he could surely steal a ride on a train? Many a time he had got on and off buses without paying a fare. A train would probably be easier, if anything. And once he reached Liverpool it would be simple enough to find the docks. He would ask around until he discovered a ship bound for New York and then he would get himself aboard somehow.

Dusk comes early in March and Fenn had no intention of going anywhere near Belstrode Street, not even to see his mother's body laid out for burial. There was no point in it, for he had made up his mind to go no matter what. He would hide up some-where . . . there were plenty of places a smallish boy could sleep rough in the city . . . and he would catch an early train the next day.

Fenn found some nice area steps with sacks piled up underneath them quite near Victoria station. He settled for the night and fell asleep very quickly, almost as if his mother's death was a matter of no importance to him which, in a way, was true.

Because once again, Fenn's devious brain was playing its useful little tricks. With one part of his mind Fenn knew that Saul had been lying when he said Rachael was dead. Knowing his cousin as he did he guessed that Rachael must indeed have been slightly injured, or perhaps was staying overnight at the Levetts' place to look after the old lady, so would not be around should he return to the house in Belstrode Street. But right now the sensible part of his mind which acknowledged that Saul was just being spiteful was being completely over-ruled by the other part, which mourned her – rather inadequately – as dead and gone. He did not want to go home to more reproaches – for Uncle Joseph and Great-Grandpa would undoubtedly find a way to blame him for whatever had happened to his mother – so it was easier to accept Saul's story, have a good cry, and then run away.

And presently, despite the chill and the strangeness, Fenn fell quite happily asleep, warmed by a thought which had just occurred to him.

He would write a letter to Great-Grandpa and send it as soon as he could lay hands on an envelope, to say nothing of a ha'penny stamp. He would explain that he had met Saul and been told of his mother's sad demise, and realized that the family would not want him, so he had gone off to seek his fortune.

And just in case Great-Grandpa and Uncle Joseph, between them, decided to suppress such a letter, he would send a copy of it to the Finaglers with a little note asking them to see that all the right things were done for his mother, since his Kitzmann relatives were unlikely to do anything, and promising to pay them back one day, when he had made his fortune.

What a cat that would put amongst the pigeons, Fenn thought contentedly, just before he fell asleep.

7

It was a fine April day when Fenn scuttled ashore at New York.

He had done it! He had smuggled himself aboard a ship, kept well hidden during the voyage, tagged on to this one and that one, and finally arrived in the great city of New York which looked, even to Fenn's inexperienced eyes, quite a bit larger than Manchester.

At least upwards, he told himself, gazing awestruck at the skyscrapers which reared on all sides. To say nothing of the traffic – cars, buses, vans, lorries, they all thundered along the streets which were really wide but looked narrow because of the height of the surrounding buildings, as though each and every driver was desperate to reach his destination.

Fenn was the only one who sauntered, partly because he did not know exactly where he was going and partly because he had learned long ago – it seemed a lifetime ago – that a truant should never hurry and never look furtive. A brisk walk was good but so was a slow, enjoyable saunter.

So now, Fenn sauntered. Financially, he was all right for a little while. He had soon realized that the ship on which he had stowed away was so overcrowded with refugees from the Depression which was hitting the whole of Europe that he had little fear of being picked out as illegally aboard. So he had cheerfully run errands, played games, made friends even, and managed one way and another to collect a small store of coins . . . American coins, too . . . which would at least enable him to eat for a few days.

And though he sauntered, he did know, more or less, where he was going. Lower East Side! It had a magic ring to it, an enchanted sound. And he told himself he would be glad to get out of this particular part of the city anyway, for despite his dreams and the promises of Jim Kertzer, New York was a bit of a blow. It was large, but it was also dirty. Beggars hung about subway stations, on corners, outside theatres and restaurants. Voices were raucous, accents so different that at times Fenn had the greatest difficulty in understanding what was being said. Furthermore, life here was clearly dangerous. There were gangs of youths, some of them black, and Fenn had not previously encountered anyone black other than an old man selling roast chestnuts who had a brazier in a doorway on Market Street. Seeing so many black faces worried him.

His first night in New York was spent in a huge park, curled up under a bench on which lay a dirty, unshaven old man wrapped in several thin blankets topped off with newspapers. He did not object to Fenn sliding under the seat with his own blanket – filched, of course, from the ship before he left her – but he was not a talkative man. Having ascertained that Fenn was not Irish he seemed to lose all interest in him, and Fenn, who had grown adept at sleeping in strange places, settled down quite happily beneath the bench. The ground, to be sure, was cold, but he had always been adaptable. Now he shivered and snoozed and shivered and woke, and then he just lay there, savouring one of his favourite fantasies – the arrival of his letter at the Kitzmann house.

I bet they were stunned, Fenn told himself for the hundredth time. I bet they were knocked over!

It took Fenn three days to run Lower East Side to earth, largely because he became so fascinated with the great city. A warm spring was bringing people out, giving even the hungry hope, and one way and another Fenn did quite well. People were generous, and what was more, they took Fenn for granted. No sideways looks because he wasn't in school; half the polyglot kids of the slum areas simply didn't bother with school. And he had always been willing to work or indeed to pick pockets, provided he could also eat.

It could have been argued, of course, that at home in Manchester Fenn had no need to pick pockets and nor he had. But here a sharp-faced Armenian taught him the trick and Fenn used it, though only on a drunk and then only because Hepo, the Armenian, assured him that if they failed to take the wallet sticking noticeably out of the drunk's hip pocket, someone else would.

He didn't need to pick other pockets because a bright kid could always earn a few dimes running errands, delivering a parcel, or minding a small child whilst its mother went into one of the city's numerous big stores.

So Fenn got by; and gradually found his niche. In fact he found

Barnard Street before he realized that this, at last, was the Lower East Side for which he had searched.

He found Barnard Street through the good offices of a street gang. He had been wandering along one of the side streets leading off Broadway, wanting to make his way down to the piers which he had visited the day before and found a rich hunting ground, when he saw the group of boys coming towards him. He could almost feel the predatory heat of their gaze, yet what had he got which they could covet, he reasoned, walking on. He was penniless, ragged, homeless. He had nothing anyone else would want.

After fifty yards or so, he glanced back. Dusk was falling but even through the evening greyness he could see the boys, clustered like a wolf-pack, definitely following him. He wondered whether to pause, to challenge, but it seemed foolhardy. He knew enough about gangs from home to realize that this could be serious trouble. A broken head, far from home, was no light matter and though he had seen a hospital the previous day he knew that such things cost money, more than he was ever likely to lay hands on.

Accordingly he continued to walk along the pavement, which the boys behind him would call a sidewalk; he was learning the language, he thought with some pride, and they wouldn't say 'boys', either, they'd say 'guys'. But the soft slither of footsteps behind him did not cease; they seemed to be coming closer, in fact. Casting bravery to the winds he dodged into a doorway. It was a narrow doorway with stairs leading up from the tiny foyer crammed with overflowing garbage bins which smelt strong and terrible, but it was unlit and the stairs were of iron. If he was careful he could get halfway up and pause, listening for the sound of pursuit. He guessed that this was one of the tenement blocks he had seen, overcrowded with people who could no longer afford to live even in family groups in small flats but huddled, eight or ten of them to a small room, with no running water or proper heating.

He heard the boys come nosing in, approach the stairs, cluster to discuss. He was halfway up, just a shadow crouching against the wall, when he heard footsteps coming, not up, but down the stairs. Quite a number of footsteps.

Fenn shrank against the wall and stared as round the corner came a group of lads ranging in age from ten to fifteen. Even in the dimness he could see that they were all dark-haired, and there was something about them which made him stand up, creakily, it is true, and smile uncertainly as the leader of the group drew level with him.

'Hello! What's this? What're you doin' in this block? You don't live here!'

Fenn shook his head.

'No. I'm hiding. Some b— guys are following me.'

The leader grinned, a flash of white teeth in a dark face.

'Micks?'

A great rush of relief almost overpowered Fenn; these were yids, as the Jewish gangs were called. He would be all right with them.

'Yup, sure were,' he confirmed. He stuck out a grimy paw. 'I'm Kitzmann.'

The name was his password or his undoing, he had realized, as soon as he had worked out that the gangs were not formed by schools or friends, but strictly by race or creed. The leader, after only a slight hesitation, gripped his hand.

'Schulman. Where're the Micks now?'

They were speaking in very low tones. Above the sound of their voices, Fenn heard what he had been dreading, the scrape of careful feet mounting the iron stairs. He did not speak, but gestured with a quick jerk of the head, a pointing finger.

The other nodded, signalled the gang's imminent approach to his followers with the very same head jerk that Fenn had used.

The group of boys clustered, then sprang down the stairs. Fenn found himself in the midst of them, happy, his blood up. As they whooped down the last flight someone pushed a weapon into his hands; it felt like a big old cabbage stalk and that, it turned out, was exactly what it was, but though not the most conventional of weapons it was presently doing yeoman service amongst the bunched heads of the enemy.

The Schulman gang had, of course, all the advantage of surprise. The Micks, fallen on from above by a group of fighters when they had expected to corner one small, lonely boy, very soon broke and fled, but not without causing something of a riot in the tiny foyer. Garbage bins, already overpiled, tipped their stinking contents out on to the concrete floor, a stumbling block to friend and enemy alike as they skidded and slipped in the rich, reeking stuff.

But the battle was short-lived. The Micks scattered, many nursing wounds, and in the semi-darkness it was easier just to let them go, some bawling and clutching, others threatening reprisals. Soon the victors were sitting in rows on the iron stairs, comparing injuries and gloating at their own brilliance.

'We owe you one, Kitz, for leading Whalley and his buncha mothers into our hands,' Schulman said at last, addressing Fenn for the first time since the fight had started. 'Live near?'

'Don't live anywhere,' Fenn admitted. 'My mother died so I came to the city to find my father, but . . .'

'Noo York's sure a big city,' someone else observed sagely. 'Where's your fader work?'

Fenn shrugged eloquently.

'An' where d'you come *from*?' enquired a small, bright-eyed boy of about Fenn's own age. 'What para the state?'

Fenn's mind was always giving him sound advice about lying or not lying, but this time it hesitated. To lie or not to lie? Tell the truth, Fenn, where's the harm? it counselled at last.

'I'm from England. A city called Manchester,' Fenn said slowly.

Afterwards, when he had been taken in by the Kopinski family and shared a pile of rags and newspapers in a corner with Sammy, Fenn often wondered what he would have done had the gang not believed him. It was impossible to prove, for they had simply accepted his Mancunian accent as something strange to them without ever suspecting that it was a relative of that Oxford English which they occasionally heard in the cinema or on the lips of music-hall artists.

But the question never arose, because belief was instantaneous.

'English! Howja get here?'

Fenn hardly had to exaggerate at all, so strange were the events leading up to his arrival. His mother's death brought sympathy but no disbelief, his own flight was regarded as the most sensible thing he could have done under the circumstances, though the gang were sceptical about his ability to find his father.

'Don't waste your time searchin',' Schulman advised at length. 'There's no point wastin' time. Jest keep your eyes open and we'll put the word around . . . Fennimore Kitzmann, that's the moniker, same as yourn? But you're thirteen and you've never met him . . . thirteen years is a long time, kid. He could've passed on.'

'Yeah,' Fenn agreed. 'He could've. But I'll keep looking.'

He would not look at all, of course. Fenn was no fool and he knew that his father's last name could not possibly be the same as Rachael's. But it was a good story, and besides, you could never tell. Miracles did happen. His father might miraculously appear and know him.

That had been the first night. Sammy had taken him home when at length the gang split up, because he felt they had a lot in common. Sammy's mother was dead and his father was struggling to get work from time to time so that he could keep his son and himself. Sammy knew his father would not object to someone else bringing in a few dimes, and so it proved. You could not have described the elder Kopinski's attitude to the new lodger as exactly welcoming at first, but he soon grew to appreciate Fenn's abilities as a provider.

'I don't wanna know where you got it,' he would say quickly, accepting the potatoes, the loaf of bread, even the odd handful of tobacco. 'Why not try for a little nip of spirit next time, just to keep out the cold?'

But Fenn and Sammy had more sense. Working as a team they could earn, beg or steal odds and ends of food, but Fenn soon realized that it was better not to give Mr Kopinski money since he was violent when drunk. Fenn remembered violence all too well and had no intention of bringing it down on his head again. After all, Uncle Joseph had a sort of right to beat Fenn when the fancy took him, but Mr Kopinski wasn't even a relative. What was more, despite the fact that he only worked a couple of days a week he was still a big husky chap and the first time he came singing up the street after a skinful, Sammy advised Fenn that they should make themselves scarce.

But such bouts were a rarity and since a lifetime of experience had taught Sammy that his father was a gentle soul save when in his cups, it was easier to see that Mr Kopinski was well fed but fairly short of cash than have to live in fear of a man who was essentially gentle, but had no head for alcohol.

So with Sammy and Fenn holding the purse strings, life began to improve for Fenn's adopted family. Mr Kopinski delighted Fenn with stories of his old life in a tiny village in the Ukraine, where the Jews and the Ukrainians had lived in harmony, both oppressed by the State, until Orthodox Russian priests had organized a terrible thing called a pogrom, a word which would fill Fenn with dread for the rest of his life. A pogrom, Mr Kopinski explained, was just another name for a massacre, when the priests got the innocent villagers fighting drunk on vodka and then told them that the Jews were usurping their rights and their country, and that the village could only be cleansed by fire and slaughter.

The priests had come to Mr Kopinski's village followed by a long line of peasants, all filled with drink and lusting for violence. The priests broke down the doors of the little houses with axes, letting in the drunken peasants who killed anyone they could find, burnt the houses to the ground, destroyed the crops growing in the fields outside and slaughtered livestock, dogs, even the innocent cage-birds fluttering against their bamboo bars. Then they moved on, having destroyed every living thing in sight, declaring that the village was free of Jews – though it stank of death and destruction for ever after, Mr Kopinski declared.

'And you want to know how I escaped?' Mr Kopinski beamed at the boys, hanging on his every word. 'I and my little sister Devorah were pushed, by my good mother, into a pile of logs in the yard. Strange, that they burned the house but left the logs, yet had it not been so, I would not be here today.' Mr Kopinski nodded at the boys. 'We stayed there for days, Devorah and me, not daring to move, smelling the smell of blood and burning, faint with fear and hunger. And then we heard soft voices near the log pile, and crawled out of the little den my mother had made until we could see our yard. And we saw an uncle from a nearby village, come to see if he could find us. It was with Uncle Dava and Aunt Tasia that we came to America all those long years ago.'

That was the best story, but there were others which Fenn liked almost as well. Stories of life in that village before the pogrom came, when the small Yacob Kopinski had stood on a stool in his father's store to sell tea, candy, tobacco, dried meat – anything and everything, in fact.

The village was set in beautiful countryside in the province of Poltava. Young Yacob loved to watch the birdlife, fish the streams, roam the meadows and woodland. Summers were warm, winters harsh. Yacob learned to skate and to walk in snowshoes on top of the drifts. He and his small friends sledged, taking it in turns to swoop down the long, gentle inclines. In summer he swam in the streams and played on the swing his father had erected in the orchard, dreaming beneath the apple trees. He had a fleet of little wooden boats carved by an uncle to sail on the pond, and he went with his father and uncles to the synagogue where he enjoyed the fine singing and tried to learn his letters as his father whispered the words from the holy book.

'What was it like in England, Fenn?' Sammy would ask when Mr Kopinski ran out of stories of his homeland and sat back in his chair, puffing on an empty pipe or reading the newspaper. 'Tell me about England; what's the synagogue like? We don't often go, now, but sometimes we do, the old man an' me.'

But Fenn did not intend to waste his powers of description on the synagogue. He had gone there with Great-Grandpa and Uncle Joseph and consequently tried not to remember it. Instead, he told

Sammy all about the cemetery in Crumpsall, the school, the house in Belstrode Street and the hospital on Elizabeth Street where his mother had worked and Gamps had died. The hospital, according to Fenn, was the biggest and most advanced in all England, the house was a mansion, the school a grand one with a fancy uniform, but the cemetery was so wonderful that, in Fenn's eyes, it needed no exaggeration to make it perfect. Only he had to remember that his father's tomb, which had done so much for his image in Manchester, would only serve to make him a liar here. So he described Gamps's tomb, claiming that his maternal family had been laid to rest in that cemetery for generations past, and Sammy listened, enjoyed and asked for more.

And between selling newspapers, stealing from street markets, running errands and diligently refusing to go to school, Fenn's life was good. He enjoyed being a street kid, liked living on his wits. He learned to be charming, to deal with violence, to fight his own battles in such a way that, regardless of whether his opponent was large or small, right or wrong, Fenn always won. He had always had a certain amount of low cunning but now he grew devious. He was fighting to survive in a hard world, for as the Depression deepened so Fenn had to struggle harder simply to stay alive, and that meant he had, at times, to be all things to all men. When with *goyim*, be they Micks or just non-Jews, he called himself Fennimore Kitson. He announced that his mother had been a Peroni when he was with Italians and claimed to have coloured blood in his veins – and he was very dark – when with black Americans. He would have boasted kinship with Attila the Hun or Lloyd George had it paid him to do so, without feeling one stab of conscience. Indeed, as time went on, he believed his own fantasies more and more, particularly when he was telling them.

'You don't know fact from fiction,' Sammy grumbled sometimes, but it was said admiringly. 'One of these days you'll be caught out!'

But the day had not yet come, and Fenn was content to wait for its arrival whilst he strove to keep body and soul together and remain in the arms of his only love – New York City.

Rachael Kitzmann had left the house after the great fight truly worried for her son. She had not realized it was so important to him to be *barmitzvahed*. Not a particularly religious woman herself, she had hardly registered that Fenn was left out of the male, Shul-going parties more often than not. Even had she done so, she would merely have thought, philosophically, that Joseph was at it again – trying to get her excluded.

She had been mad to go out with Michael Fennimore, of course. An Irish-American, he had come back to Manchester from the States to see his older sister, and had spotted Rachael in the park. He had had all the boldness, the sweetness, which Rachael's other admirers had lacked and he had introduced himself, smiled at her, and simply swept her off her feet. She knew she was being foolish even to walk with him, yet nothing could have stopped her. Rachael was totally enamoured of a twenty-five-year-old Irish-American who told her he was an orthodox Jew because he sensed that this would forward his cause: the quick courtship of one of the prettiest and most desirable girls he had seen for a long time.

It had been less a courtship than a seduction, in fact, for Michael Fennimore, with his intriguing American accent and his considerable supply of Irish charm, had never intended – or pretended – marriage. How could he, with the child of a strongly Jewish family who would have gone mad had they even known he was seeing their daughter, let alone . . . well, let alone holding her in his arms in the sweet hay which grew in the meadows beyond the cemetery?

So Michael had kissed and cuddled and taken all she had so innocently offered, and then he had gone and she had been left to bear not only the shame and the reproaches, but the child, too.

Rachael had been motherless by the time she was six, but her father's love had transcended even the shame of her illegitimate pregnancy. He had taken care of her, rejoiced with her when the baby was born whole and strong, and told her to love her son even more since she was his only parent. For the first two years of Fenn's life she had been extremely happy, not even missing the games she and Michael had played, for though she was now sexually awake she was also of a placid and easy-going disposition. Provided she was loved and could give love she asked little more, and soon learned to subdue the itch of desire.

Indeed, it was not until her father died and she was forced to move in with her uncle that she realized the extent of what she had lost, and then, deeply though she loved Fenn, she began to have her first misgivings.

Within two years, she knew it would have been wiser and kinder to have given him up for adoption, as some had suggested. But how could she have known that Gamps would die and leave her to the totally untender mercies of Joseph and her grandfather? And how could she have foretold that her courage would drain away under their constant battering until Fenn had to fight his own battles whilst she wept on the sidelines?

When Fenn was six or so, it quite simply got too much for her. She had enjoyed her job at the Jewish hospital but she needed more money so began to work for the Levett family, too. They were nice people, but the work was hard and without ever realizing quite how it had happened she found herself on a treadmill. Her life had become all work from the moment she woke in the morning until late at night, when all she had strength for was to drop into bed. The Levetts would have liked her to live in and work for them full-time, but that was impossible. Benjamin Levett and his wife Rebecca were in their sixties and set in their ways, and old Mrs Levett, who was confined to either her bed or a wheelchair, was well into her eighties. Fenn would have turned the house upside down, Rachael supposed, and accepted that, for her son's sake, she must simply soldier on.

There were compensations, of course. Days when she had time off from the Levetts and could actually get away from the Kitzmanns too. She insisted that on Sundays she should simply make one meal, in the evening, which gave her most of the day with her son.

But as Fenn grew up it became more and more obvious that they must get away. Somehow or other, she had to escape from her prison, free herself from her treadmill.

The snag was that Joseph charged her for her keep and her son's, which meant that the money she earned at the Levetts was barely enough to clothe her and the boy and pay for things like shoes, books for school and birthday presents once a year. Fenn was resourceful, she knew that, but she could scarcely confide in him that they must save to escape from Uncle Joseph and Great-Grandpa. She told herself that they were not strict with Fenn for no reason, that he was a little liar and a handful. But in her heart she knew that this was not the sort of parental strictness which would have been resented perhaps but also accepted by the boy. This was deliberate harassment, and the beatings Fenn endured were cruel. She had seen the marks on his body and wept silently into her pillow on many a night.

But she had done nothing constructive until today, when she had screamed at Joseph that she would leave his house and take the boy with her.

'You should have gone years ago, you pair of no-goods,' he had growled, eyes spitting venom, saliva dribbling from the corners of his cruel, turned-down mouth. 'Take, take, take, that's all you and that *schlemiel* ever do.'

She had left the house, still hot with hatred for the two men who had used their strength to hurt a woman and a child, and gone straight to the Jewish hospital. She knocked on the door of matron's office, afraid of nothing and nobody for once, and entered. Matron was sitting behind her desk, writing on a large sheet of paper. She looked up when the door opened, then smiled.

'Yes, Mrs Kitzmann?' she said pleasantly. 'Can I be of help, my dear?'

'Oh, matron, things at my uncle's house are becoming quite impossible. I'm afraid I'm going to have to hand in my notice and see if the Levett family can give me full-time work and let me and my son live in. They find it very difficult now that old Mrs Levett is so dependent, but if they don't need me I shall have to look elsewhere for a live-in place where they can take my son as well. Fenn's thirteen soon, old enough not to make a nuisance of himself.'

'We shall miss you sadly,' matron observed. 'I used to talk to your father when he was a patient with us, and I know it was his wish that, one day, you might train with us as a nurse. But clearly you must get your son settled before that can happen. Only don't forget us, my dear. Just put your future in abeyance for the time being and concentrate on your boy. The time will come, believe me, when he'll want his independence, and then you can come back to us.'

'Oh, matron, thank you,' Rachael said breathlessly, fighting tears. 'If it had been possible nothing would have given me greater pleasure than to train here, and I'll miss my work . . . the staff . . . but one day . . .'

She left the hospital and went round to the Levett place. Mrs Levett had cooked breakfast and was waiting for Rachael in the kitchen.

'Good morning,' she greeted her. 'Trouble at home?'

No doubt she could tell something from Rachael's white face and red-rimmed eyes, and on this occasion Rachael had no intention of pretending it had been nothing much. So the Levetts knew Joseph and Anna and respected them. So she had gone to pains, before, to see that this respect was not tarnished by the truth. Not any more; not now that Joseph had done his best to kill her son!

Carefully, almost neutrally, she told Mrs Levett what had happened and made the first independent statement she had voiced since Gamps's death.

'I'm very sorry, Mrs Levett, but I shall have to change my job. I shall have to get live-in work where they will let me take Fenn with me. I dare not leave the boy with Joseph . . . and no matter what you may hear Fenn isn't a bad boy. He does his best and his best is getting beaten out of him by a jealous man, because that's what annoys Joseph most – that Fenn is cleverer than Saul.'

Half an hour later she knew herself truly valued, wished she had had the courage to make that statement years ago.

'We'll have you both,' Mrs Levett told her. 'The boy's old enough to understand that old people need a certain amount of peace and quiet. Bring him back with you after school this evening . . . and no need to get your things from Joseph's house. I dare say you've got little enough anyway. We'll see you right.'

Rachael could only stare and smile, tears filling her eyes. She examined the little attic room which she and Fenn would share – with a screen for decency and two separate truckle beds – and then she made her way to the school to tell Fenn the good news.

He had gone. Joseph destroyed the letter, of course, but when Rachael had visited the Finaglers' house Mrs Finagler had promised to let her know if Cecil heard any news of Fenn, and three days later she visited the Levett house with the copy in one hand.

'It's that wicked boy of Joseph's,' she said. 'Oh, he should be well whipped for this! How can we tell poor Fenn that it was all a wicked lie? How can we bring him back?'

Rachael, reading the note through her tears, felt a sudden stab of doubt. She loved her boy, but she was a realist at heart. Fenn frequently told lies himself so how could he possibly have believed what his cousin had said? But he had plainly gone, and the note said he intended to search for his father, though where she had no idea. Not in America, that was certain. Fenn had no money and it would take him months, if not years, to earn enough for a passage across the ocean. Of course the poor kid had no idea that her lover was in the United States, even though she must have said, at some time, that he was an American. No, Fenn would search nearer at hand and surely, when his pain and hurt had lessened, he would come home?

She took the note to school and showed it to the head teacher, who promised to speak to Saul Kitzmann and to do what he could to trace Fenn.

Everyone assumed he was still in Manchester somewhere and would turn up quite soon – everyone except Cecil.

'If Fenn wants to, he'll get to America,' he told anyone who would listen. 'There isn't much Fenn can't do if he puts his mind to it.'

So Rachael charged Joseph, Anna, Saul and the old man to say not one unpleasant or derogatory word when Fenn appeared on the doorstep but to send him straight round to her, at the Levett house. Yet the days turned to weeks and the weeks to months, and Fenn did not come.

A letter from him finally arrived in late summer, addressed to Cecil Finagler but clearly, Rachael thought, meant for her. It said he was alive and happy and might come back some day. She missed him, but she was happy enough in her new life, putting money aside, beginning to take an interest in her appearance again. She had been a pretty girl and could still be, she realized, a pretty woman. She had her black hair fashionably cut, eschewed fattening foods and took exercise for pleasure, now that she was no longer working twenty hours out of the twenty-four. Her complexion improved, her cheeks were pink and her dark eyes shone. Men began to notice her again – approvingly, what was more. Rachael exchanged smiles, nods, the odd remark with neighbours and acquaintances.

That autumn old Mrs Levett died peacefully in her sleep and Rachael went round to the Jewish hospital and talked to matron. The two women discussed ways and means and an hour later Rachael walked out of the hospital with a big smile on her face and went round to the Levetts' place to fetch her belongings. She was to move into the nurses' home that very day and start work at the beginning of the next week.

Rachael had often meant to visit the Kitzmann women but had somehow never done so, and today seemed like a good opportunity. Telling herself that she was only doing her duty and should not feel nervous or ill-at-ease, she set off, the frail autumn sunshine warming her shoulders through the cream wool of her jacket and her small feet in their fashionable shoes click-clacking briskly along the pavement. She reached Belstrode Street and very nearly turned into the alley, then remembered that she was now a visitor and continued along the pavement until she reached the three steps leading to No. 18. They had not been whitened since she left, she saw disapprovingly. She had felt, not proud precisely, but pleased with the snowy whiteness of those steps. However, it was none of her business now, thank God, so she knocked on the door and waited.

Anna opened the door and stared, eyes widening. Then they

narrowed and she smiled coldly, though the smile did not reach her eyes. She stood back so that Rachael could enter the house.

'Hello, Rachael. D'you want to come in?'

Anna could no more be friendly than fly, Rachael told herself, following the older woman into the once-familiar kitchen. She accepted a cup of tea and sat down in one of the fireside chairs to drink it. Sneaking a crafty look around her she saw that the room was no longer clean and shining, that the floor was not polished nor the wooden table scrubbed. When she had worked here, this room had looked like any other Jewish woman's kitchen, with the two sets of pans, the fire roaring, the oven gleaming black and the hearth brassily shining. There had been the good warm smell of baking bread, of bagels and stewing chicken. The windowsill had jostled with herbs, spices, tattered cookery books. Now the place was cold and neglected; unloved.

'I don't like to cook,' Anna said, sitting down opposite her visitor. 'Jessica's too busy, Sarah don't live at home no more, Leah's lazy. We miss you.'

'I'm sorry,' Rachael said sincerely. She remembered how the men liked their food, how Saul tucked into anything going, how her girl cousins had eaten every meal without a word of thanks and had left her to wash up and clear away without a thought. But she was sorry, because Anna was getting on and was married to the detestable Joseph; punishment enough, Rachael felt, without adding the hated chore of cooking to her lot.

'You wouldn't come back? We'd do our share, treat you good. After all, the boy's gone, and he was the main cause . . .'

Rachael put down her teacup, still only half-empty, and got to her feet. She knew colour had flooded her face and felt righteous rage welling up in her. But poor Anna looked grey and cross and very tired; better go gently with her.

'No, I wouldn't come back even if I could, and I can't,' she said quietly. 'That was what I came to tell you – I've been accepted for nursing training at the Jewish hospital. From next week I'll be living in at the nurses' home.'

'Oh. Well, I suppose I must say *mazel tov*,' Anna said grudgingly. 'Not that I'd want to do such a thing . . . laying out dead bodies, putting your hands where you'd rather not.'

Rachael laughed.

'Oh dear, Anna, if you only knew! Now I must go, I've got rather a lot to do before the weekend.'

Walking back down the street, humming a song, seeing her reflection in the window-glass of the houses she passed, Rachael felt ten feet tall, as though she had just slain a dragon. Fancy being afraid of that sour little grey woman and her stupid, selfish husband! She had dreaded seeing Anna or one of the others at the shops in case they either cut her or abused her verbally, but now she had no such fear. She would speak to them politely, they would do the same to her, and she would know herself to be the better person whether it was plain Sarah, beautiful Jessica or pretty Leah, because none of them could run the house now that she was gone, and were letting the place degenerate into somewhere they went back to at night, after work. It was no longer a home, a refuge, it was just a lodging house.

I bet they haven't cleaned the bath for weeks; I bet there's a ring round it an inch thick and the lavatory will be *disgusting*, Rachael thought happily. Oh, aren't I glad it won't be me, on my hands and knees, scrubbing and rubbing away at the sticky stains old men leave around lavatory pedestals!

And tomorrow she would get her uniforms – neat dresses and aprons, caps and cuffs and collars – and although her room was attractively furnished she would bring some of her own things, pictures and books and cushions, to make her feel more at home.

She wondered, as she walked along Cheetham Hill Road, threading her way between the shoppers and the idlers, the well dressed and the shabby, whether the other nurses would remember that she had been a cleaner at the hospital only a few months before and despise her for it. But the thought merely crossed her mind; it did not bother her. Ever since seeing Anna and her old home, Rachael had realized she was on the up and up. Dear Fenn, she thought affectionately now, had done her more good than she had thought possible by running away, though at the time she had not realized it. After all, she was no age – she was not even thirty yet, had all her life before her.

And I'll have a profession in a few years, she reminded herself. She saw a cake shop owned by Jewish friends and lingered by the window, wondering whether to buy herself a celebratory meringue or two. After all, she had lost a lot of weight and looked good in the black and white checked skirt and the little black jacket that went with it. A cake would do her no harm and nursing was hard work, both mentally and physically. She would study in the evenings ... the very word study made her think of her schooldays, when Gamps had been alive, when no man had touched her ... and she would pass all her exams because she loved her books and had done very well at the school she had attended in Waterloo Road.

I'll not be a fool this time round, she told herself as she came out of the shop with two meringues in one brown paper bag and a slice of cold bread pudding in another. I'll go to dances and join a whist club and enjoy myself, but I won't let any man take advantage because I'm going to be a nurse first, then a sister and then, perhaps, a matron!

The heady thought made her give a little skip, brought a smile to her face and turned her cheeks pink. A great many people, passing Rachael on that sunny autumn afternoon, thought her a very pretty girl and envied her her innocent enjoyment of the day, her bright eyes and sweet, placid smile. Few would have thought her the mother of a son, far less a son now well past his thirteenth birthday.

8

'It's the post!'

Sybil's shriek brought the entire family up from the breakfast table through to the front door. Sure enough, down the road came the postman, his sack on his shoulder, whistling.

Whistling as though today were just an ordinary day, Sybil thought, scandalized at such a patent lack of feeling. Today was Results Day. Today she would know, at last, whether she was one of the lucky scholarship winners or whether she was doomed to spend the next year at the local school, prior to selling fish.

She had slogged for the scholarship. From the very moment that Miss Boydell had told Dora her daughter had a good chance of winning a scholarship Sybil had worked all the hours God sent. And one of the reasons she had worked so hard was that wonderful snowy week just before Christmas when she had been the unexpected guest of the Winterton family, in St Giles.

It had been a magic week from start to finish, the sort of week that had confirmed Sybil's strong feeling that there must be a life more suited to her than selling fish. Mum talked about it constantly, of course, when Dad wasn't around, but even so, seeing at first-hand how a rich family lived had ensured that Sybil would work, and work hard, to get the education Mum considered so essential.

'Is he coming here, gal?'

That was Georgie, grown tall and handsome, working full time on the fishing boat now and enjoying every minute of it. He was sixteen, and signing on for a trawler when autumn came because Dad thought it best. Distant-water trawling was an art which had to be learned, Dad said, and since he had every intention of investing in a share of a trawler as soon as the kitty could run to it, Georgie had best get what experience he could.

'Yes . . . no . . . I'm not sure,' Sybil said, in an agony of expectation.
'Oh, Mum, what'll I do if I've not got it?'

'You'll get suffin',' Dad said comfortably. 'All my kids are bright.
You'll get a place somewhere, never you fear.'

'Oh, but I want St Leonard's! They're the best – they have higher
pass rates than . . .'

'I did all right at the secondary,' Lizzie pointed out. 'Not that I'm
clever, like you, Sybs. But I did all right.'

'You could still do all right, only you're set on being a shop-girl,'
Dora said rather sadly. Their mother still hoped for better things for
Lizzie, Sybil knew, but Sybil was old enough, now, to realize that
Lizzie, who was pretty as a picture, would probably get the better
things their mother wanted for her whether she worked behind a
counter or taught in school. She also guessed, as her mother must,
that Lizzie would not return to school when the autumn term started
in September. She would be off to the port for a job as soon as summer
began to fade into autumn.

'Oh, I know, and Pakeby Secondary would be fine. I'll go there if
I don't get a scholarship, but if I could choose . . .'

The postman was delivering up the road. He was chatting on the
doorstep, laughing at something Mrs Biggs had said. Sybil tried to
take her mind off the waiting, tried to think back to what had first
determined her to be a teacher. Had it really been that week with
the Wintertons? If so, taking the examination for the scholarship had
reawoken those old feelings, made her aware, all over again, of the
two different sorts of lives lived by Creams and Wintertons.

And then there had been Chris's own interest in the future which
Sybil had outlined.

'It would be grand if we were both teachers,' she said when Sybil
had admitted her great ambition. 'I'd like a career, and though I'm
not clever perhaps I might manage to teach very little children.'

'Why don't you work together, then?' beautiful Mrs Winterton had
suggested the previous Easter. Craftily, perhaps, Sybil realized, but
still very kindly. 'You're very welcome to bring your books up here,
Sybil, and if there's any way either Chris's daddy or I can help you
we'd be only too happy.'

Dora Cream, appealed to for her agreement to the plan, had been
willing that Sybil should go but uncertain whether Chris would
actually stick to swotting.

'She doesn't need to get a scholarship, and you do,' she told her
daughter. 'Her parents are rich – how many girls of thirteen or so

have two homes, just for a start? – and what she can't get for herself they'll buy her. Which means, love, that she may easily grow bored with studying and wander off down to the beach. And if she does that, bang goes your invitation to work up at the Winterton place.'

Nevertheless Sybil set off each morning with her books in an old linen shoebag and the two girls spread their work out on the playroom table and helped each other. They did sums together, appealing for parental aid when they got hopelessly stuck but usually managing to work things out. They learned by rote – poetry, chunks of Shakespeare, rules of grammar, history dates – and 'heard' each other until both were word-perfect. And to Chris's openly expressed amazement they both enjoyed it and both found themselves very much more at ease with their work by the end of the Easter holiday than they had been at the beginning.

As Dora had said, Chris was not taking a scholarship, but she had what she called end-of-term exams. Her results had come before Sybil's, of course, and, she informed Sybil by letter, she had never done better. Everyone was most awfully pleased with her.

Sybil had gone up to Norwich to sit the scholarship examination. She and sixty other girls had sat at big desks in an old church hall with an elderly schoolmistress on the dais at the end of the room and four or five younger teachers wandering up and down the aisles between the desks, keeping an eye on the contestants to make sure there was no cheating.

Sybil loved the examination, which was a two-day affair. She stayed with Chris in St Giles overnight and saw again the beautiful house which Ralph and Chris took so for granted that they thought Sybil's rhapsodies quite amusing and totally unnecessary.

'It *is* quite old, I suppose,' Chris said, when Sybil pointed out that plastered ceilings with such a richness of fruit, such a plethora of decoration, were almost worthy of a place in a museum. 'Daddy said something once about the observatory being very old . . . want to take a look at it?'

Sybil had not visited the observatory before but now she was escorted up three flights of stairs and then up a little metal ladder into a tiny round room made entirely of glass which afforded panoramic views of the city. She had never been so high in her life, nor seen so much sky, and clutching Chris she declared she felt quite giddy. Chris said it was nothing really, not compared with the view from the top of Norwich Castle, but Sybil was truly impressed. Such a patchwork of rooftops, gardens, green trees! Such a vastness of echoing, deep blue sky flooded with sunshine as gold as poured honey! It was enough to make the most unimaginative child think, and Sybil was far from unimaginative – quite the opposite.

Back in the examination hall, bidden to write an essay covering at least five sides of paper on a subject of her own choosing, she at once launched into an enthusiastic description of the wonders of an old house in a fine old city, and knew at the end of an hour that she had produced some of her best work.

The examination ended at four o'clock on the second day and Mr Winterton, who had been as kind as his wife to the little Pakeby lass, suggested that Sybil stay with them for one more night and be escorted home by his wife next day, after luncheon.

But it was impossible; Dora needed sensible Sybil at home. Lizzie had one of her headaches and Henry had brought home a record catch. What they could not sell Dora wanted to salt down and she badly needed Sybil.

Chris was deeply disappointed but Mr Winterton put them both in the car and hurried them round on a brief tour of the city. Sybil saw the Norman castle on its great grassy mound, the beautiful public parks where bright young things played tennis, the girls in brief white skirts and the young men in long white trousers. The cattle market, its pens empty now, the cathedral with its lofty spire, and the two rivers, the Bure and the Wensum, where holiday boats moored for the night by the tow-path whilst further down the timber yards and docks added their bustle to the scene.

'Tomorrow we could have gone to Stranger's Hall and the Bridewell Museum . . . and round the shops as well,' Chris said wistfully. 'Still, you're needed at home. I'll ask Mummy if you can come to stay in the summer hols for a whole week – that would be so jolly!'

But though she had gone home on the last bus that night, Sybil did not repine because she had seen so much and enjoyed every minute. She felt sorry for Lizzie, who only knew Norwich as a day-shopper, but Lizzie just smiled her enigmatic smile and said not to worry, one day she would know Norwich better than any of them.

Now, with her hand on the latch, waiting impatiently for the postman's approach, Sybil remembered the pleasures of the examination hall – perfect peace, the sort of questions she enjoyed answering and plenty of time to get her ideas down on paper, with no one calling her to lay the table, or fetch Lizzie up from the shore this minute or peel a pan of spuds, there's a good girl – and the short but wonderful stay in St Giles.

The Wintertons had all been so kind, from Chris's parents to Chris herself, and Ralph, and dear Norah, who had petted Sybil and ordered her about just as she had when they were all on Pakeby beach and Norah in charge of the party. Everything had been perfect. In bed that night she had thanked God passionately for his kindness to her, and had told him that if she failed to get the scholarship she would not grumble, not even inside her head, because at least she had had the fun of taking it, and spending the night with Chris.

But now that the moment had come, now that the postman was whistling down the shingle road towards the cottage, Sybil could only hang on to the windowsill and jump up and down and finally fling the window wide and lean out. Useless to pretend indifference, with Georgie grinning from the doorway, Lizzie, her newly washed hair brushing Sybil's cheek, at her elbow, and Mum and Dad trying to pretend that it was a matter of indifference whether she passed or failed, because she would still be their beloved daughter.

'Marnin'!' the postman said brightly. 'Noice one an' all.'

'Lovely. Is there . . . ?'

'. . . A letter? That there is!'

The postman held up a cream-coloured envelope with Sybil's own handwriting on the front. When the examination was over they had all been given an envelope and told to address it to themselves if they lived too far out to come in to Norwich to get the results personally. Everyone filled out the envelopes, Sybil had noticed. Even if you lived next door to the examination hall you would not want to walk bold-faced up to a board and read that you had failed.

The letter changed hands. For a moment Sybil just held it, staring down at her familiar handwriting. She saw again the desk with its scarred surface, her own hand neatly writing whilst sunlight poured down on to the envelope. She tried to recapture the feelings of pleasure and confidence she had known at that moment, when the exams were over and her official 'visit' with the Wintertons about to begin. She had been so *sure*, then, that she had done her best and that she would be one of the lucky ones, but right now . . .

'Open it,' Lizzie commanded, her lovely eyes bright with excitement. 'Go on, Sybs, open it!'

'Git it over with, my woman,' Henry advised, smiling at her. Normally at this hour he would have been out in his boat but he had lingered to wait for the post, today. 'Let's know the wust!'

'She'll have done right well,' Georgie said stoutly. 'She's clever, is our Sybs; got plenty of the brains in her head.'

Sybil took a deep breath and poked a thumb into the corner of the envelope. It was thick, heavy paper, what they called 'cream-laid', and it tore slowly, as though reluctant to give up its secrets. The sheet of paper was folded in three so that not one word was visible through it. Sybil went to unfold it, then hesitated.

'You do it,' she said, holding the sheet out to her father. 'I can't bear to know I've failed!'

'You haven't failed,' Lizzie said impatiently. 'You haven't ever failed a school test, Sybs, so why should you fail this one?'

Unsaid, the words 'But just passing isn't good enough; we can't afford the school unless I get a scholarship' seemed to hang in the air between Sybil and her family.

Henry smoothed the letter out flat. He read, eyes lowered, then turned and grinned at his daughter.

'Well, well, well! Who'd 'a thought? Hev she passed, then? Not only hev she passed, she've passed out top for this area! She've got her place at St Leonard's School for Girls and a very handy grant for uniform, equipment and such. Come here, Sybil Cream . . . you're a heroine, you are!'

Dora rushed forward and enveloped Sybil in a giant hug. Lizzie clutched at her hand, Georgie smote her between the shoulder blades. Henry read the letter aloud, his face shining with love and pride.

'Well, Sybs? What about that, then? Didn't I tell you you'd do it?' Dora smoothed a hand across Sybil's hot face. 'Now go you off and tell Chris, because I'm sure you're itching to do so and they were so good over the studying and having you to stay and everything . . . then come back and we'll talk.'

Sybil, following her father and Georgie out of the front room and across the kitchen – for no Cream would dream of using the front door unless they were entertaining the vicar or the doctor – stopped and turned.

'Talk? What about? Oh, Mum, don't say we can't afford for me to go . . . I'll work ever so hard, holidays, and I'll do my chores after school . . . only . . .'

'What nonsense is this, then? We don't have to pay a penny, not now you've got the scholarship with a full grant. And you're a good girl. You'll help out as much as you can, I'm sure of it.'

'That she will; she've never been an idle one,' Henry said heartily. He picked up his packet of food from the draining board as he passed and Georgie followed suit. 'See you tea-time, then.'

The men went out, slamming the door behind them. The three

Cream women looked at one another a little ruefully in the sudden silence.

'I do my bit already,' Lizzie said untruthfully. At fifteen she had lived up to her early promise of beauty and her health had improved out of all recognition, but she was incurably lazy and had to a large extent already turned away from her family. For her own sake Dora insisted that she stay on at the secondary school in the village to try for her school certificate, but she was a reluctant scholar and was desperate to leave and start work. She giggled and whispered with the other village girls, she spent hours trying to improve her already flawless complexion, and since she knew very well she was Dora's favourite she always had an excuse ready to get herself out of selling fish, scrubbing floors and doing most of her chores. She was bright enough but disliked the discipline the teachers enforced, hence her determination to get work in a shop or office as soon as she was able.

'We'll both work hard, me and Lizzie,' Sybil said now. 'Mum, can Chris come to dinner?'

'Yes, if she wants to. But you know what a family the Wintertons are for plans, love. Don't expect them to change their lives just because you've got your exam results, will you?'

Sybil pushed open the heavy kitchen door and paused in the doorway. Henry and Georgie were already out of sight. She longed to run wildly across the yard, but she must curb her excitement. There was still a long way to go before she became a teacher.

'No, but they won't go out until they hear, Mrs Winterton said. See you later, then.'

She flew out of the house and across the yard, skidding round the side of the cottage and into the road. It was August so the sunshine was a rare treat – Henry was always grumbling over school holidays being in August when, he reckoned, this part of the coast got most of its annual rainfall – and Sybil hurried along, the letter clutched in one hand, wondering whether she would have to say a word to the Wintertons or whether the expression on her face would be read from afar.

She reached the end of the drive and began to try to compose herself. She would look sad, dejected, as if failure had to be confessed – then imagine their surprise and delight when she showed them the letter!

It was a good idea, but doomed to failure. She was only halfway up the drive when around the bend came Chris and Felicity. They were in light summer dresses with rolled-up towels under their arms. Clearly, they intended to make the most of the fine weather. Chris saw Sybil and began to run.

'Oh, Sybs, I'm so happy for you! Did you get the full grant? Oh, come back to the house and tell Mummy, she's been so anxious.'

'But how did you know I'd got it?' Sybil asked, rather aggrieved, as the three of them turned back towards the house. 'I was going to tell you I hadn't. I was going to look sad and disappointed and all that, only you never gave me a chance!'

Felicity laughed.

'Just one look at your face was enough, Sybs! And you were running as if you could hardly stay on the ground.'

'That's how I feel,' Sybil panted, as they hurled themselves in through the front door – no back door exits and entrances here – and went to look for Mrs Winterton. 'And it's the school I wanted, too – St Leonard's!'

'Scrumptious! Mummee! Mummeee!'

'Darling, do stop bawling.' Mrs Winterton, glasses perched on her nose and a notebook in one hand, appeared in the kitchen doorway. 'I was just about to . . . Sybil! Well?'

'She's got the full scholarship to St Leonard's,' Chris announced. She had taken the letter and perused it as they flew up the drive. 'Isn't she a clever girl, Mummy? So when September comes I won't be the only one shopping for new school uniform!'

'Sybil darling, I'm so happy for you,' Mrs Winterton said. And she looked it, too, Sybil saw. 'Heaven knows you worked hard enough . . . now you must keep it up, my sweet, and work just as hard at your new school, and before we know it you'll be going to college and becoming something very grand indeed.'

'A teacher,' Sybil said yearningly.

Mrs Winterton laughed but shook her head.

'You may not believe me now, but there are more interesting jobs for girls these days,' she declared. 'Just wait – perhaps you'll be a member of parliament, or a famous journalist, or . . . or . . .'

'If I can just get to be a teacher,' Sybil said. 'A nice warm classroom, books to mark, books to read, too . . . and all the school holidays off!'

'Well, that sounds nice, I suppose, but first catch your hare, as Mrs Beeton says! Now, are we going down to the beach, or shall we let Sybil choose what we should do today?'

'I'll come to the shore,' Sybil said eagerly. 'But my mother asked if Chris could come to lunch with us, please? It won't be much, but she'd be very welcome.'

'Of course she may,' Mrs Winterton said at once. 'And perhaps Mrs Cream would spare you to us tomorrow, Sybil. We're going cockling at Wells and could do with your help.'

'Wells! Oh, I'm sure Mum will let me,' Sybil said eagerly, if not quite truthfully. Dora could never see why the Wintertons bothered to get into the car and drive miles just to sit on a different beach and dig for different cockles, but for Sybil such a trip was a wonderful treat. The miles of countryside which skimmed past the car windows, the unrivalled opportunities for her and Chris to giggle and chatter, the magnificent picnic lunches eaten out of a big hamper on strange sands and then, usually, the bought high-teas, sitting at a restaurant overlooking the broads or the promenade, or sometimes in a cottage garden with apple trees all around and a fat and kindly countrywoman bringing out her homebaked scones and strawberry jam.

'Very well, then. I'll see you later. Felicity, darling, I'll send Norah down to the beach to fetch you home at noon.'

'I'm sure Mum would be glad . . .' began Sybil, uncomfortably aware that she should have asked Dora for Felicity as well, but was firmly interrupted.

'It's very kind of you, dear, but Felicity and I are going visiting this afternoon. I'm going to see Aunt Cynthia, and her two little girls would be most disappointed if their big cousin didn't spend some time with them.'

How tactful she is, Sybil mused as the three of them set off once more for the shore. How tactful and kind. Felicity, who might have sulked over being left out, was now cock-a-hoop at the idea of being a favourite older cousin; she and Chris could have the whole afternoon to themselves, and even Mum would be relieved of a guest she had not expected. But that was Mrs Winterton all over – she always saw the other person's point of view.

'I'll have to nip in and get my costume,' Sybil reminded her friends as they reached the cottage. 'You go on down, I shan't be two seconds.'

She ran indoors, bounded up the stairs two at a time, and lugged her drawer in the chest open. It was crammed with patched and faded garments, a good few of them too small for her, but the bathing suit, a discarded one of Chris's, was right on the top. She grabbed it with the usual little pang of pride – it was navy blue and had a red anchor embroidered on the chest – and added a thin towel, then ran down the stairs again.

'We're going swimming . . . you don't mind, Mum? We'll be in for dinner at twelve.'

'Good girl. Enjoy yourself.'

Having a meal with the Creams was always enjoyable, Chris thought, once you got over the smell of fish. The trouble was the smell wasn't easy to get over. It impregnated everything, the cottage, the furnishings, the hair and clothing of the Creams.

And it was a poor place, the cottage. No carpets, skimpy curtains, cheap furniture which looked as though Henry had knocked it up himself on a Sunday afternoon – some of it he had – and no modern equipment.

So it was odd that she liked the place so much – loved to be there, with Sybil and Lizzie, Dora and Henry. And with Georgie, of course.

Georgie was so good-looking! Not that looks mattered, but he was kind too, and indulgent towards his little sisters' friends. He was only sixteen, the same age as Ralph, but he seemed like a grown man. Perhaps it was because Ralph was still at school, whereas Georgie had been working on the fishing boats for two years. Now that he was old enough he had put in for a berth on a trawler which, in the autumn, would set out on distant-water fishing right up in the Arctic. Not many would go up there of their own accord, but Georgie would.

'Money's good,' he said briefly, when Chris had asked him whatever possessed him to undertake such a dangerous voyage. 'We can do with the extra, especially now.'

He might have meant now that the girls were growing up, needing more, or he might have meant now that fish, like everything else, wasn't fetching the price it once did. He might even have meant now that he himself was older and needed things, though Chris doubted that. One thing all the Creams had in common, she decided, was that they seldom thought of themselves but always about other Creams. Even Lizzie, who was a very self-centred girl, would be more likely to ask for a treat for her sister than for herself.

I wish we were like that, Chris found herself thinking, as she took her place round the scrubbed wooden table in the kitchen. They were going to have crab salad and bread and butter, followed by a rhubarb tart. Henry Cream's crab pots had provided the crabs, the lettuce, tomatoes and radishes had come from Georgie's allotment, and the rhubarb was a present from the Wintertons' gardener, who had sent down a bunch of sticks a couple of days ago.

114

Henry and Georgie having gone to sea it was just Dora, Sybil, Lizzie and Chris who sat down to the meal. And how good it was! The Wintertons ate very well, but somehow there was an additional pleasure in Dora's simple cookery. The crabs had been scuttling on the sand the previous day, the salad had been in the earth, and even the custard which went with the rhubarb tart was made with milk drawn from the cow that morning. The Creams had no refrigerator, no electric stove, no tinned goods. They did not use 'bought bread' because it was expensive, so Dora baked three times a week, great big untidy cottage loaves, and bought farm butter from the market when she could afford it and margarine when she could not. And of course, Chris reminded herself, Dora bakes for old Mrs Cream as well, in her cramped little cottage on Pakeby Street. The two women could never be described as friends, but an uneasy truce existed between them and Sybil, Georgie and Lizzie took turns to visit their grandmother and to help her with her chores. Chris, who went with Sybil sometimes, rather liked the fierce old lady and her home cluttered with ugly furniture and ornaments. There was never a leaf in sight – she called her daughter-in-law's plants 'them old dust-gatherers' – yet somehow the place was welcoming, even though it was so different from the Beach Road Cottage.

'Isn't it strange how different people's lives are!' Chris exclaimed when she and Sybil were washing up for Dora after lunch. 'At home I hardly ever go near the kitchen but I love doing the dishes here and at your gran's house. You probably think it's boring, but for me it's fun.'

'It's not too bad when there are no saucepans,' Sybil said. 'But scraping the bottoms clean with sand sets my teeth on edge. And I do know what you mean, because for me it's more fun at Gran's than it is here. But I pity whoever does your washing up – you must have scores of pans, all the different meals that get ate in your house.'

'Never thought about it,' Chris confessed. 'Had we better rinse our swimsuits next? Oh, and are you going to tell your Gran? She'll be pretty pleased, won't she? And as it's a special day, with you getting the scholarship, do you think Mrs Cream would let you come and exercise Dandy and Trotter? We could go inland, along the lanes.'

'Today she'll let me,' Sybil said blissfully. 'Today I reckon she'd let me do anything. As for Gran, you can never tell what will please her; she'll probably say Pakeby was good enough for my father and it ought to be good enough for me – but that doesn't mean she won't be pleased inside.'

'That's good, then. We'll nip to old Mrs Cream's first and then go right up to the common where the gorse grows and the larks nest. And we'll come back by the deep lane, and see if the tadpoles in the pond are frogs yet. But we'd best ask your mum first.'

Chris liked Mrs Cream but was secretly a little afraid of her. Sometimes she caught Sybil's mother giving her looks which were almost cross, as though she wondered why it was that Chris had so much and her own daughters so little. It was natural that a mother should want the best for her children, Chris knew, but she always tried to show Dora Cream that she was well aware of Sybil's worth, knew herself lucky to be the other girl's chosen friend.

'It'll be all right,' Sybil said, swishing the swimsuits round and round in the clean well-water. 'We'll take a loaf and some fish to Gran, that'll save Mum a trip later. Don't worry, Chris, we can please ourselves today!'

The midsummer beach bonfire was Ralph's idea. He was growing up, Sybil could sense it, growing away from the simple pleasures which he had shared with Chris. Sybil took his place most of the time on Trotter, because all of a sudden Ralph found riding boring, besides being too tall for the ponies. He felt silly, he said; all legs.

He and Georgie, being three years older than Sybil and Chris, had always held themselves a bit aloof from them and Sybil was flattered to find that Ralph was actually pleased about her results.

'Well done, kid,' he said languidly, when Chris had explained why her friend was allowed a holiday from her household chores. 'You'll like St Leonard's; Chris says you're good at maths, like me.'

'Well, I'm not too bad,' Sybil muttered, knowing her cheeks were scarlet but scarcely caring, so proud was she to hear that she was discussed when the Wintertons were *en famille*.

'Georgie is first-rate at figures,' Ralph continued. The three of them were in the stable, Ralph leaning against the wall and watching whilst his sister and her friend groomed the ponies, currycombing the rough coats, oiling hooves, plaiting manes. 'I dare say it runs in your family – lucky Creams! Poor Chris has her work cut out to get past long div., don't you, old girl?'

'Well, I hate sums,' Chris said equably. She straightened from her task of unmatting the thick hair under Dandy's round little stomach and blew at her fringe, making it stand away from her hot forehead. 'Phew, I'm sweating! Pass me the rug, Ralph.'

'Which one? Oh, it's the red checks for Dandy, of course.' Ralph made a long arm, reached the rug down from the partition where it hung, and handed it to his sister. 'What are you doing to celebrate your success, then, Sybs? Having a party?'

'Nope. Can't afford parties.'

It was dim in the stable, though the yard outside was flooded with late sunlight. A slanting ray of it, coming through the doorway, lit Ralph up whilst leaving the rest of them in shadow. Sybil, ducking under Trotter's belly and coming up the other side, thought how beautiful he looked with the sun gilding his hair and making his profile as pure and clean-cut as some young Greek god's. But I like Chris best, she reminded herself loyally. She's much nicer, even if she's not so good-looking.

'No, of course you can't. Silly of me. Tell you what, Sybs, suppose us Wintertons give you a party? Sort of like buying you a bike or something to celebrate? I mean, my father gave me a bike when I was confirmed and they bought me my first pony for learning all my tables backwards and dodging, so I don't see why we can't give you a party, which our family would enjoy as much as yours. More, probably.'

'What sort of a party?' Chris said. She fastened the blanket under Dandy's stomach and stood back. She was wearing a white Aertex shirt and riding jodhpurs and her hair was plaited and neat for once. Sybil thought she looked reliable and nice, like a school prefect in a Girl's Own paper. 'The sort with balloons and fizzy drinks and crackers?'

She sounded pleased with the idea but Ralph made one of the rude and scornful noises which boys are so good at.

'Balloons and fizzy drinks? My dear girl, try to be a bit sensible for once! That's kids' stuff, and Sybil has just proved she isn't a kid at all, she's . . . she's some girl! No, *not* that sort of party, stupid. What about a midsummer bonfire party on the beach? After dark, of course, with potatoes in their jackets and sausages – we could cook our own, all the more fun – and games and someone telling ghost-stories because midsummer is spooky . . . we could dress up as druids and pretend to sacrifice Dandy, he'd enjoy that.'

There was an outcry at this but the girls were enchanted by the idea, particularly when Ralph pointed out that it was just about the cheapest party anyone could hold, that grown-ups as well as small kids would love it, and that it would be the best sort of celebration anyway since keeping the bonfire going would give the fathers plenty to do and overseeing the little kids would keep the mothers busy.

'Leaving us older ones to please ourselves,' he said. 'Look, Sybs, are you on? Will you sound out your people this evening, if I speak to ours?'

'Yes, and I'm sure they'll think it's a marvellous idea,' Sybil said eagerly. 'We could share what it cost, and we'd all find old wood and that for the fire. Dad could cook fish, if he's had a good day – he often says there's nothing like the taste of fish cooked over an open fire.'

'Nothing like the smell, either,' Ralph said, then laughed and apologized. 'It's a grand idea; your father's absolutely right. If he could get some herring . . .'

'I'll talk to him,' Sybil promised. 'I'm sure he'll manage something.'

9

Although Sybil had spoken confidently to the Wintertons, she was by no means certain what reaction she would meet with when she mentioned the proposed party after tea that evening, but to her delight everyone, from Dad to Lizzie, thought it a very good idea.

'I'll bake extra bread and we'll dig a few extra spuds,' Dora said, as she cleared the table and poured hot water from the kettle into the sink. 'There's a mound of driftwood behind the shed and we can scour the beach for anything burnable – dried seaweed's good. We can use the big old fish-kettle to boil water for a cup of tea . . . and do we still have that old grill, Henry?'

When they were newly married the heat in the cottage had been too much for Dora, who was expecting her first child and frequently felt queasy. When she became unable to eat meals which she had been forced to cook over the range in the stuffy little kitchen, Henry had found from somewhere an old cast-iron grill, made it sturdy legs with cement and big beach pebbles and put it down by the shore. Then he had lit a fire beneath it and he and Dora had cooked and feasted out of doors like two savages on a desert island, or a pair of runaway lovers. Henry had often told the children about it and Sybil had always thought it the epitome of romance to eat cooked food outdoors. Now, she looked expectantly at her father.

'That old grill?' Henry's contribution to clearing the tea consisted of removing his large frame from his wooden kitchen chair to the chintz fireside one. He did this now and stretched out, reaching automatically for his string and netting-needle. 'Oh ah, that's in the shed, under a pile of suffin'. I can fetch that out easy as easy.'

'There we are, then. We can boil water on half of it and grill herring on the other half. That leaves the bonfire for the spuds and sausages and things,' Dora said. 'Who shall we ask?'

'Everyone,' Henry said largely. ''Twon't cost much, not a foo fish and a foo spuds. Tell 'em to bring a pinch of tea or a bottle of beer . . . that in't no use you a-frownin', my woman . . .' this to his wife, who shook her head indulgently at him, '. . . for that wouldn't be a party without ale, not for the boys.'

'Boys aren't supposed to drink ale,' Lizzie observed. 'You mean boys like you I suppose!'

Henry roared with laughter and pretended to smack Lizzie, who grinned and dodged.

'Tha's right, my woman, boys like me . . . roaring boys! Let's have a chorus, eh, Georgie?'

Georgie was stacking kindling by the stove so that it would be dry by the following morning. He grinned at Dad, got to his feet and filled his lungs with air.

'Right you are, Dad! Here we go then, one, two, three!'

They began to sing, or rather to roar, whilst Lizzie joined in and Dora tapped time with a spoon on the nearest plate and Sybil, drying the dishes, hummed the rousing tune.

> 'The roaring boys of Pakeby
> They didn't know how to contrive,
> They only had two parsons,
> And one they buried alive!'

The song was a long one, with dozens of verses, but fortunately Dad always ran out after the first five or six and went on to other songs with familiar tunes. Sybil sometimes suspected that verses seven and eight, probably to verse one hundred, were rather rude, not the sort of thing that men sang to their children. Anyway, soon enough they were on to Negro spirituals, swinging low sweet chariot, and then to the Ash Grove, which Mum loved, and finally to the best of all, fishermen's hymns, the sort they sang in the little church opposite the cottage on a Sunday morning, when the men wore creaking blue suits and unaccustomed ties and the Rev. Fulthorpe told them that strong drink had been the cause of many a good man's death, and that with the sea thundering only yards away from the building he had no need to remind them how terrible could be the vengeance of the Lord, nor how cruel the perils of the deep.

So now the family sang and sang, and every now and then Dad broke off to throw some other party suggestion at them, or Mum remembered someone they must certainly invite.

'It's our first party,' Lizzie said later that night, as she and Sybil settled down in bed. 'Think of that, Sybs – I'm fifteen and I've never had a party!'

'You have! Christmas parties at the Wintertons, and at the church hall, and the parties the school gives . . . you must have been to lots.'

'Oh, them . . . but I mean the first party *we've* had, Sybs. Other girls have parties, even at the village school, but not us Creams. I wonder who I should ask? Ralph will be coming, of course.'

'Of course he will. But why should that matter? You wouldn't have asked him to a party at our house, surely?'

'Don't see why not.'

'You've got a cheek, then. You hardly know the fellow. Come to that, Lizzie, you hardly know any of the Wintertons really.'

'So what?' Lizzie moved restlessly in bed. 'I'll tell you something, one of these days Ralph will wish he knew me better.'

'If Ralph wants to know you better he's only got to walk down the road and lean over the wall for a chat, or come in and ask you to go for a walk on the beach,' Sybil said a little coolly. Lizzie was getting awfully conceited!

'He doesn't know what he wants, not yet,' Lizzie said. 'But he'll learn – fellows always do, in the end. And you must have noticed, little sister, that he's easily the best-looking fellow in Pakeby.' She propped herself on her elbow in the dark; Sybil could see her shape suddenly rearing up. 'I wonder if I ought to pray for fine weather?' she said consideringly. 'After all, it is our first party.'

Prayers were said kneeling beside the bed in summer and between the sheets in winter. Now Lizzie made to struggle out of the blankets again but Sybil seized her by the shoulder and held her back.

'Don't get out, Liz. You're only adding a post-script, like you get on the end of letters. It's all right to do that in bed even if it is summer, and besides, there's time left before the party to pray for good weather.'

'You're probably right,' Lizzie said, lying down again. 'Please God let it be fine for our party and let everyone who matters come and let the house not smell of fish and let Sybs and me be the belles of the ball because the Wintertons have lots of parties but we'll probably only get the one. Can you think of anything else, Sybs?' she added, for all the world, Sybil thought, as if she were making out a shopping list.

'That sounded a bit like nagging, and Mum always says don't nag God,' Sybil said tentatively. 'All I want is fine weather.'

'Little goody-goody! Sunshine and a warm evening for the party if you please God, and give Sybs a cheer for being clever and working hard and getting us the party in the first place. Amen.'

'Oh, Lizzie!' Sybil said. She put her arms round her sister's slender and supple body and gave her a hug. 'I think we ought to pray for clear skies and no rain each night until the party day from now on, though. That really is important – imagine a beach bonfire in the rain!'

'Right,' Lizzie said practically. 'Every night we'll both pray for the same things. And on our knees, not in bed. Just to be on the safe side.'

Perhaps the prayers really worked or perhaps they were just lucky, but whatever the reason the day of the midsummer party dawned fresh and clear, with the sky in the east barred alternately a pale apple green and glowing gold. Sybil, who woke with the sun, sat on the end of her bed and rapturously watched the light strengthen.

'So long as it isn't a red sky,' she said to Lizzie, as that young lady woke and peered anxiously out of the window. 'Now a red sunset, like we had yesterday, is fine: red sky at night, fisher's delight. But red sky in the morning, fisher's warning. So you see, all the omens are good. It should be fine all day!'

'I thought they were old wives' tales and not to be taken seriously,' Lizzie said. 'My, but that is a beautiful sight. I almost wish I woke every morning to see the sun rise.' She leaned back on the thin bolster and looked hopefully at her younger sister. 'Now you're up, a cup of tea in bed would be a real treat.'

'You're awful,' Sybil said, but comfortably and with resignation. She had learned early in life that if she wanted a contented, good-tempered Lizzie, then it was best to indulge her a little. 'Well, it looks as if we're off to a good start. I don't mind bringing you up a cup of tea, but you'll have to get up quite soon. It's going to be an awfully busy day.'

'You're probably right,' Lizzie said, staying where she was and looking adorably pretty with her golden curls spread out on the pillow. 'But a cuppa will help me get started, and anyway all I'm doing is helping Mum bake bread – *you've* got to gut herring!'

But not even the truth of this could damp Sybil's enjoyment on such a day. She ran down to the kitchen and brought Lizzie up her cup of tea, and then they both dressed in their oldest clothes and hurried downstairs. Dad, who had gone out long before sunrise, came in with a huge sack of herring so fresh that they were still stiff, curved into the painful shapes from which Sybil always had to turn her eyes. Too well could she imagine the burning agony of air in little water-lungs, the cruelty of such suffocation. But Dad said herring died quicker than any other fish and she wasn't to make excuses about gutting them.

'Mornin', gal-Sybil,' Dad greeted her. 'No guttin' for you today; your mum say I'm to let you orf.' He guffawed. 'Like a rocket . . . let you orf . . . get it?'

'Yes, very funny,' Sybil said, smiling at him. She stood on tiptoe and kissed Henry's smooth, fresh-smelling cheek. 'Oh, Dad, today's the day! The midsummer party starts at six this evening!'

'Why you had to call it a midsummer party, when everyone know midsummer's in June and we're in August, I'll never understand,' Dad said, but he lifted her off her feet and gave her a bear hug nevertheless. 'Them Wintertons are on the beach . . . you get yourself over there, ask 'em back to breakfast. There's nothin' nicer than fresh herrin' with your mum's new-baked bread.'

Breakfast was a success, far more so than Sybil, rather cringingly handing on Dad's open invitation, could have guessed. Mr Winterton said he would breakfast later, but came into the kitchen to thank Henry and smelt the freshly fried fish and the new bread and somehow there he was, seated at the table with a plate of herring before him and a couple of thick slices of bread sparingly buttered. Ralph, sitting beside him, was tucking in, and Chris was eating heartily. Even Flicky, known to be a fussy feeder, was putting away a slice of toast thickly spread with last year's bramble jelly and taking a drag, now and then, from a mug of tea so strong that her brother and sister eyed her with covert amazement. Flicky, who whined at being made to drink warm milk, positively revelling in Dora's dark brown, bitter brew!

And Lizzie behaved beautifully, rather to Sybil's surprise. She had thought her elder sister would sit down at the table and expect to be waited on, but instead Lizzie bustled about, very quiet, very efficient, and helped with the meal, not putting herself forward or trying to boss anyone. Chris smiled and chatted and ate and took no more and no less notice of Lizzie than anyone else, but Ralph watched her quite a bit – Sybil saw his eyes on her several times, though she could not read the expression in their depths.

Not that it mattered. Nothing mattered but that apparently a breakfast served in a cottage kitchen, with simple food and strong tea and good humour, could be such an enjoyable occasion.

After a start like that, the day could only go well. And it did. Mr Winterton directed the boys piling the fire, Mrs Winterton came down and chatted to Dora about the food, the maids came giggling and nudging across, carrying two long trestle tables which they had borrowed from the church hall, and the gardener brought a box of fireworks which Mr Winterton had purchased at Ralph's instigation.

'We never have a bonfire night in St Giles, because you say it's dangerous with so many houses so close,' Ralph had been heard to remark pensively. 'And we never see the Pakeby fire because we're in school. But with all that empty beach, we could at least have a few fireworks of our own.'

They looked more than a few, Sybil considered, eyeing the box every time she passed it, carrying loaves of bread, sharply pointed sticks to toast sausages on and buckets of water down to where the food was going to be served. Mrs Winterton had provided a lot of little cakes which she said might be eaten by the workers – they had coloured icing and cherries. Sybil had seen Flicky, cheeks bulging, handing out cakes to favoured friends, the boys kept wandering over to the box and helping themselves, yet there were always more. Sybil decided that if she had been younger she would have thought it was a magic box, then scolded herself for a flight of fancy unworthy of a thirteen-year-old scholarship winner. But still. It was marvellous how those cakes fed everyone and stopped them dipping into the party food before the fire was lit.

Darkness falls earlier in August than on the real midsummer's day, but it could not come soon enough for the assembled company. They went to their own homes at five, changed into decent things and returned just as Henry and Mr Winterton lit the fire.

How it roared, once the flames took hold! How the sparks flew upward, a golden stream against the darkening sky, making the stars look faint and foolish! Sybil stared and gasped, and ran about like one of the really little ones, pushing potatoes into the embers, passing the gutted herring to Dad, helping Mrs Winterton to stab the sausages so that each guest could toast his or her own food.

It was, furthermore, a marvellous night. A slight breeze, mild and balmy, scarcely stirred the flames and the moon rocked in the sky, benign and indulgent, enjoying the frolics going on below.

Everyone came. The vicar, Mrs Fulthorpe, their maids Tess and Phyllis, and the entire Winterton contingent from the boy who did the boots and helped weed to Mrs Winterton's personal maid, Ena. And more than half the village, of course. Friends, acquaintances, shopkeepers, churchgoers, they all seemed to find the thought of a party to celebrate young Sybil's success irresistible, and a bonfire on the beach the most sensible way to please everyone.

As it grew darker the moon and stars came into their own and Sybil, having a wonderful time with Chris, Ralph and his friend Peter, who had come all the way from Norwich on the bus to enjoy the party, thought that never again would there be a night so lovely or so exciting. The smell of the fire, the flickering flames, the orange glow . . . and the food . . . all combined to make it a night she would never forget.

Mr and Mrs Winterton left at ten-thirty with a very cross Flicky between them. They were going to have a nightcap, they explained, with Dora and Henry Cream, who had gone in to put the kettle on. After that they would make their way home. They trusted Ralph, who was sixteen after all, to bring Chris indoors well before midnight.

The fireworks had been lit earlier; everyone had watched them soaring into the night sky, the rockets seemingly bent on reaching the moon or even on passing it by. Afterwards, a sleepy satisfaction seemed to descend on the grown-ups. Whilst the younger children chased and shrieked and the sensible thirteen and fourteen-year-olds ate piping hot sausages and glorious, floury jacket potatoes, the older ones sneaked off into the darkness.

'Where's Ralph?' Sybil asked Chris, who shrugged and said she was going to get some more lemonade and went off up the beach.

Earlier, the four of them had retreated into the gentle sand-dunes, giggling when the marram grass scratched their legs and when the sand, suddenly ice-cold after the warmth of the day, slithered into socks and sandals, invading even their food. But then Ralph and Peter had muttered something about finding a friend and wandered off; now Chris, in search of lemonade, had also gone, leaving Sybil happily alone.

It was still a wonderful night. The warm little wind caressed Sybil's cheek, the wonderful smell of burning driftwood and sausages, of seaweed piled on the tideline and a whiff of gunpowder from the spent rockets, came to her on that same breeze. The sky burned with stars, brilliant pinpricks of white light in the blue velvet of the dark, and she was far enough away from the fire now to hear the talk and laughter as a musical background to her thoughts, to feel pleasantly detached yet to know that she had only to stand up and walk a few yards and she would be solitary no longer, part of the crowd once more.

When she saw the boyish figure silhouetted against the dying flames she sat up, however, for she had been sprawled very inelegantly against the nearest dune and wanted Ralph – for it was he – to consider her as almost a grown-up now that she was to go to the grammar school.

'Did you find your friend?' she said shyly as Ralph cast himself on to the sand beside her. 'Where's Peter?'

'Oh, *Peter*'s doing all right,' came the strangely embittered reply. 'Oh yes, *Peter*'s doing very nicely, thank you!'

'Oh,' Sybil said inadequately. 'Are you having a nice time, Ralph?'

Something had annoyed him, that was clear, but she still felt she did not know him well enough to ask what it was. Chris said Ralph was the best brother in the world, but he always seemed awfully old and clever to Sybil, and not a bit easy to talk to.

'Well, I was, until . . . your sister's awfully nice, isn't she?'

'Lizzie, you mean?' Sybil said, as though she had a dozen sisters. 'Yes, she's nice. And she's pretty, too.'

It was a statement, not a question, but Ralph answered her anyway.

'Yes, she's pretty enough . . . Peter seems to think so, anyhow!'

'Well, he would,' Sybil said vaguely. 'I mean, she is. I expect lots of boys like her. She's not giggly like Tess at the vicarage, and Tess is pretty too, wouldn't you say?'

Ralph snorted.

'Oh, Tess! I'd sooner . . . I mean, Peter's supposed to be my *friend* yet he thinks nothing of simply dumping me and going off with Lizzie.'

'He doesn't mean anything by it,' Sybil said unhappily. 'You must be wrong, Ralph. Peter's far too nice to dump you, and besides, Lizzie's sitting up at the top of the beach with Tess and some other girls, or she was just now.'

She put a tentative hand on Ralph's arm; it was warm and it was also hairy, which surprised her. She had not thought of Ralph as being hairy, like her father. Georgie wasn't, or at least she didn't think he was. Since she was not in the habit of stroking her brother's arm, though, she supposed she would not have noticed whether Georgie was hairy as a badger or bald as a coot.

The thought surprised a giggle out of her and Ralph, who had been lying beside her, leaning against the dune, half turned towards her. In the moonlight he looked quite different. His blue eyes looked very dark, his fair hair glinted like silver and when he grinned at her his teeth flashed very white in his deeply tanned face.

'So he may be, but . . . but there are other fish in the sea, as your dad would say, Sybs. And you're one of them.'

She had opened her mouth to ask him what he meant, when his hand slid smoothly along her leg. It was just a sort of stroke, his fingers were gentle enough, yet for some reason all the soft down on her skin prickled erect and she felt her breathing quicken.

'What? I'm not a . . .'

The hand slithered up her leg and on to the white skin of her inner thigh. Immediately she felt horribly hot and embarrassed. Ralph was just being friendly; he didn't realize he was right up by her knicker elastic. She had better get to her feet at once or he'd feel the most awful fool!

But she didn't move. She just lay there, scarcely daring to breathe, whilst the hand caressed, rubbed, moved on her skin. And then, just when she felt she might easily scream from the most peculiar mixture of tension, pleasure and downright fear, the hand removed itself abruptly from its dangerous proximity to her knickers and landed innocently at waist level.

The deep breath of relief she took naturally caused her rib-cage to rise. Afterwards, she wondered whether this had inadvertently led to what followed. Ralph's hand, accompanied by the other one, began to move upwards. The hand on her back patted consolingly up her spine until it rested between her shoulder blades, which seemed rather nice and cuddly, a bit like the way Mum had held Suzie next door when she was a baby. But the other hand proceeded to slide smoothly inside the gap where a button must have come undone on the front of her frock . . . heavens, there were fingers on her bare skin, warmly clasping one of her tiny budding breasts!

'Ralph . . . don't, you shouldn't,' she said breathlessly. But the trouble was, she liked it. It was really strange how her small breast seemed to fit neatly into the palm of his hand, as though the two had been made for one another. He squeezed gently and she gave a fluttering sigh; her heart was banging like a trip-hammer. Surely he would hear and realize that even though she liked what he was doing she was really very worried by it all.

'Shouldn't I? Are you sure?'

She laughed. It came out squeakily, too high. It made her sound like a frightened five-year-old. She waited a moment, for her heart to calm down, for the little pink nipple on her breast to behave itself and stop going all hard and tight as though it wanted to encourage Ralph to cuddle it some more. She took a deep breath; more rib-cage movement made Ralph squeeze again, and pull her against him. She could feel his leg in its grey flannel trouser sneaking over hers whilst his weight pinned her neatly to the dune. Sand slithered from above them, channelling down the neck of her dress. She shivered violently and tried to escape, which had the effect of drawing them closer still.

'Ye-es, I think I'm sure. What would Chris say?'

It was his turn to laugh now. His laugh was deep but quiet. It sounded like a man's laugh, not a boy's.

'Oh, come on, you like it too – they all do! You'll like this even more.'

Fingers left her breast, fumbled at her buttons. She felt the cool night air caress her skin, then his face was sliding down, he was kissing the hollow at her throat, his mouth moving downwards, hot and exciting, pushing aside her print shirt-waister dress, burning on the tender skin directly above her breasts.

And suddenly she felt threatened by him; his skin was rough against hers, his hands were gripping her upper arms too tightly for comfort. She no longer felt wanted, she felt victim rather than partner in this strange, one-sided cuddling.

'Get off!' she squeaked. She kicked, nothing happened, so she drew her knee up to kick again . . . and felt it sink into some part of Ralph she preferred not to think about too closely. 'Get off,' she said again, but nicely; quite pleasantly, really.

He obeyed. She was surprised, perhaps even a little disappointed, but he rolled away from her, releasing her arms. He rubbed at his face with both hands, then adjusted his clothing and sat up beside her again, as though butter wouldn't melt in his mouth.

'Hi, Chris,' he said in a perfectly normal voice. 'We're over here . . . did you bag us some sausages?'

Chris loomed. Sybil could only hope that in the darkness her own state of semi-undress – well, unbuttoning – was not immediately apparent. She half turned away from her friend and, with hot and sandy fingers, desperately re-buttoned.

'I didn't know you'd come back,' Chris said with all her usual good-humour. 'But I got Sybs and me two each, so you can have one of mine.' She sat down next to Sybil and handed over a sausage wrapped in a thick slice of Dora's homemade bread. 'I couldn't carry the lemonade back, so I just had a drink up by the tables, I'm afraid. But I bagged some ripe greengages – they're in my frock pocket, if you can reach one out.'

Normality had returned. By the time the three of them had eaten the food and told each other that this was the best party ever, Sybil's breasts had stopped tingling and her breathing had returned to normal. Even her frantic heartbeat had slowed. She began to think she had over-reacted, that Ralph's actions had been no more than casually friendly. Certainly there was nothing embarrassed or embarrassing about him any more. He talked naturally to her, teased her, gave her a shove . . . then ambled to his feet saying that he must look for Peter.

'Ralph likes you,' Chris said in her direct way when her brother was out of earshot. 'I know he teases us and says we're just a couple of kids, but he really does like you. I'm most awfully glad.'

'Yes, so am I,' Sybil said dutifully. 'He's very nice, Ralph. And Peter too, of course.'

'Oh, yes, Peter's most *awfully* nice,' Chris said dreamily. 'I thought there might be trouble earlier, though. Ralph and Peter were both buzzing round the girls at the top of the beach . . . I don't know all of them . . . but it obviously didn't lead to anything since Ralph came back here and sat with you and Peter went off with Georgie to see if shrimps were phos . . . phos . . . oh, to see if they showed up at night.' She got laboriously to her feet, stretching and yawning. 'I'm so tired. Isn't it lovely to be so tired? Shall we go down to the sea and have a paddle with the boys, Sybs? I'd quite like to see the shrimps glowing, if it's true that's what they do!'

Sybil followed her friend down to the edge of the waves and watched the little breakers creaming against the shore, but she no longer wanted to be with the boys or to play on the moonlit beach. What she wanted was to cuddle up in her own warm bed and dream about Ralph and ask herself a million questions, most of which concerned the degree of liking Ralph felt for her and her degree of response.

When Henry emerged from the shadows presently, to upbraid his daughter affectionately and carry her off to her mother, she was quite glad to go. It had been the most wonderful night in the whole world, she agreed ecstatically, as she and Chris trudged across the sand. But she knew it had been too much for her, too exciting, too stirring. What she wanted right now was to be thirteen again, little Sybil who had won a scholarship to the best school in Lowestoft, who badly wanted her bed!

Lizzie had seen Ralph go off into the darkness and chuckled to herself. So he didn't like her flirting with Peter! Well, if he didn't like it, at least it proved something. He must like Lizzie Cream rather more than he appeared to. So she flirted with Peter and let him kiss her and bided her time and then, as she had known he would, Ralph reappeared.

He told Peter quite curtly that Norah was dispensing little dishes

129

of trifle and Peter looked at him, went a bit red, and walked off towards the long table of food. And Ralph grabbed Lizzie's hand.

'Quick, Lizzie Cream! Let's scram whilst the going's good!'

Lizzie smiled to herself; more kisses, and what was more, the kisses she had been after all along. It just went to show that nothing was impossible if you played your cards right.

With her hand warm in Ralph's, she walked beside him up the beach towards the ruined cottages.

It had been a marvellous summer. September arrived, the days scarcely less golden, scarcely less warm, than July and August. Sybil went with her mother on the bus to Tuttles and bought the navy skirt, white blouse and navy cardigan which was the basic school uniform. There were other things to buy as well: a length of navy ribbon to tie back her hair, for Dora had decreed that it should be worn in a plait for the new school; underwear – navy bloomers, woollen vests and liberty bodices – a hockey stick and a short, pleated skirt for gymnastics and games, indoor shoes which were soft-soled and fastened with a strap, outdoor ones which had laces and stout soles. A shoebag with her initials on, which Dora made from a piece of canvas, a brown satchel for her books and homework, and a navy blue blazer for Assembly. A wooden pencil-box with a sliding lid and the pencils to go inside it. A fountain pen with a lovely silver nib and a bottle of ink, though Dora told her to leave the bottle at home and fill her pen before school each day rather than risk a spillage.

Every time Sybil said, 'So that's the lot, then?' it seemed that Dora would wrinkle her nose, consult her list, and remember something else. A big soft rubber for mistakes, a purse on a ribbon to be worn under her clothing which would contain her dinner money and bus-fare, white linen hankies which Dora would initial for her and, last but not least, the name tapes.

They went into an awfully smart shop for the tapes and they saw lots of different ones on a card and Sybil chose the one she liked best – they all cost the same – and the lady promised to have the tapes ready in a fortnight.

'Is *that* the lot?' Sybil asked despairingly, and was really pleased when Dora said yes, it was, and suggested that they go into Wallers for a nice cup of tea before catching the bus home.

'I never thought I'd get tired of shopping,' Sybil admitted as they sat at a little round table in the window, sipping tea and eating doughnuts. 'But I'm quite glad it's over. Will the grant really cover all that, Mum?'

'Well, not quite. It's a great help, but they don't realize that people in our position don't usually dress properly from the skin up.' Dora leaned back in her chair and laughed. 'Good thing I've got a decent memory or you'd have arrived on your first day without half this stuff.'

'Then if the grant didn't stretch . . . ?'

'I've saved a bit from the moment I saw where you were heading,' Dora said simply. 'Your dad knows, but there's no need to say anything to the others. Lizzie's a pretty girl and I'm sure she'll do well, and Georgie is a good lad, but they aren't ambitious. I wanted you to have . . .'

'To have what you didn't? But Mum, you could have!'

'Oh, yes, no one forced me to marry your dad and turn into a wife and mother. I wouldn't have it any different, either. But at least I had the *choice*, Sybs. That's all I want for you – the ability to choose.'

'And no one will go short because I'm at the grammar?' Sybil asked anxiously. 'Lizzie won't suffer?'

Dora smiled and picked up her cup.

'Lizzie had her chance two years ahead of you. She could have had just what you've got. But she's made up her mind to work in a shop or a hotel or something and although she seems so pretty and biddable, Lizzie's got a will of iron in some things. So she'll probably be earning by the time you start at St Leonard's. Besides, I told you, I've been hoarding bits of money for a long time, and one day you'll repay me. Not in money or anything like that, but by becoming someone special. Do you see what I'm getting at, Sybs?'

'Ye-es, but I want to be happy, as well,' Sybil said. 'It 'ud be better to sell fish and be happy than to be Queen and unhappy, wouldn't it, Mum?'

'So they say, love. So they say. But at times, when the customers aren't buying and the basket's heavy, I'm not so sure.'

A few weeks after Sybil started at St Leonard's, Lizzie left home. She had been threatening to do so for a while, but then one morning she made an excuse to leave home late and went off to the job she had found herself in the port, and when evening came she did not return.

But a small boy came to the door with a letter, having been paid a threepenny joe to deliver it.

The letter was from Lizzie. She had got a job in Norwich, she said, and was going to stay with a friend. Nothing else. No address, no clue as to what the job was, no word as to when she would be home.

And after that for a long while, silence. The occasional postcard, usually addressed to Sybil, simply stating that she was doing well and would be in touch. Sybil and Georgie were both sure Lizzie would have landed on her feet, but they knew their parents worried terribly, and could have smacked Lizzie for such seeming selfishness.

Meanwhile, Sybil began to settle down at her new school. Her best friend was Myrtle, who had been a paying pupil at the school for years. Her father was a crossing-keeper for the London and North Eastern Railway. He had once been a train-driver, but he had lost an arm in a rail accident, when his train had rammed the buffers due to a faulty braking system, and had been given the job of crossing-keeper once it was realized that he would no longer be able to control a steam engine. Myrtle was a lively girl with frizzy dark hair, straight white teeth with gaps in between which, according to Myrtle, meant that she would one day marry money, and dark eyes which saw everything. She was kind-hearted, energetic, did not suffer fools at all, let alone gladly, and she hated what she called 'side'. What was better, she took to Sybil on sight and the two of them spent all their spare time at school together, gossiping about the other pupils, the teachers, and Life.

Myrtle was intrigued by Sybil's stories of fishing and a life lived within a few feet of the seashore; Sybil was equally intrigued by Myrtle's stories of her father's poaching abilities and the romance of living beside a railway line, of seeing trains with snow-ploughs on the front in winter and laden with holidaymakers in summer. People waving, a driver slowing his train to shout a message to Mr Saunders, free rail trips to places as far away as Devonshire or Scotland when the Saunders decided on a holiday.

Being Myrtle's best friend made life a good deal easier for Sybil, since Myrtle took her working-class status for granted and was, if anything, proud of it.

'There's a lot of snobs at this school,' she was prone to announce loudly. 'Toffee-nosed kids who think they're special just 'cos their mums and dads are rollin' in it. Well, I'm here to tell you that we're not all like that! Some of us – and that means me and Sybs – don't have to keep tellin' everyone how bloody marvellous our homes are, nor how much money our big brothers spend at the race track, because we know what we're worth and we don't have to boast about it. See?'

By and large, they did see. The other girls in Sybil's class were an easy-going lot. Some children were bullied because they were different, but it is doubtful whether the bullies would have picked Sybil out even without Myrtle's championship. Her speaking voice was low with the merest trace of a local accent. She was polite, she had the right clothes, the right equipment and above all the right attitude. Now that she was going to 'the big school', her hair was washed weekly and her person every night. Georgie had been moved out of the girls' room a while back and had a fold-away bed in the kitchen. He gloated over Sybil in winter, when he could snuggle down in front of the dying fire, but he would be too hot in summer and would, Sybil knew, envy her the cool room under the eaves with the window open to let in the fresh grey breeze at dawn.

The Cream family were delighted that Sybil had settled down so well at school, and, when they met Myrtle, delighted with her as well. Within twelve months, Myrtle had stayed for a couple of long weekends in Pakeby and Sybil had slept at the crossing-keeper's small wooden house and listened, in the dark, to the exciting roar of a passing train, seen the driver's face lit by the orange glow and the fireman's muscles gleaming as he fed the fire.

Chris Winterton was still Sybil's dearest friend, of course, but although the two girls wrote regularly, when Malverns was reopened for the summer only Flicky, Norah and the servants appeared on the beach and in the village.

'Chris and Ralph ha' gone wi' their ma and pa to France. Seems they'll need languages for whatever fancy course they're havin',' Norah told Sybil when they met in the local shop. 'Thass a pity, to my way of thinkin', but Mr Winterton, he want them two to see Europe – France this summer, Germany next and so on – and he say mebbe in a coupla years they won't be able to waltz about the continong like they could when he was young.'

'Why not?' Sybil asked, only half attending. She was wishing that she could just nip over to France for the summer to practise her French.

'Oh, he think there's goin' to be a war,' Norah said rather scornfully.

'No, that there in't, I told him, not after that last lot. But did he listen? Not he! Just said he wisht I was right with all his heart and went on wi' his plans. That's men for you!'

'That's men all right,' Sybil echoed. War? She bought a daily paper now to keep up with current affairs and knew a great deal more than Norah. She knew about Mussolini, the Italian dictator, knew that Japan and Germany had left the League of Nations and that a small, dark-haired man with a pencil moustache called Adolf Hitler had become Führer and Supreme Commander of Germany. But these were things which happened on the other side of the world, things which could not possibly *mean* anything, or not anything like war, anyway. People wouldn't go to war any more, Norah was certainly right about that. Why, though the papers had voiced outrage over an attack on the Jews in Germany, no one had done anything, and even the murder of Chancellor Dollfuss by the Nazis had called forth nothing but protests from various governments. If they sat back and did nothing whilst Jews were murdered and an important man like Dollfuss, Chancellor of Austria, was gunned down by Nazi thugs, it did not seem likely that Britain would go to war unless she was actually attacked. And Britain was an island and these Nazis and Fascists and Storm Troopers were foreigners when all was said and done, so probably they were safe enough, Sybil thought.

She missed Chris, though, and spent a lot of her pocket money on letters to her friend which Chris did not get until her return to Norwich in the autumn. By then Sybil was back in school and working hard and Chris was already looking forward to her next trip abroad.

When she had time, Sybil visited Gran and gave her a hand, dug her little garden when Georgie was too busy, did her shopping and walked her down to the beach. There she was rewarded by hearing the stories she loved, of when Pakeby had been a very much bigger village and the church had not been poised a-tiptoe no more than ten yards above the sea but had been well inland, surrounded by meadows and little lanes, by brambly hedges and lush, overgrown ditches. It seemed strange, almost impossible, to look at the calm and smiling face of the sea and realize that it hid, not a romantic drowned village with gingerbread houses, but a real village, her village.

It was Gran who told her about the rocks you could see some yards from the shore, too.

'They in't rocks, my woman,' Gran told her. 'They're all what's left of Mr Hubbard's bathing chalets, what he built to mek his fortune. Only the sea took 'em, along with his fine house.'

Gran made old Pakeby come to life with her stories, some alarming, some just strange. Houses which simply slid quietly over the cliffs as erosion worked its insidious way beneath their foundations, others which were overwhelmed far more dramatically by heavy seas thundering in and snatching their prey – acres and acres of good farming land as well – never to release their grip on it.

'I hope our house never slides into the sea,' Sybil said rather apprehensively. 'Wouldn't it be awful, Gran?'

But Gran thought they were safe enough, because the sea had taken enough of the village. Surely it would leave them the church and the Beach Road cottages?

Sometimes Gran asked about Lizzie, but there was little Sybil could tell her, save that Lizzie wrote sometimes.

'She'll come back one day, Gran, large as life, and tell us all she's been up to,' she said cheerfully. 'You know Lizzie; she won't come back until she's doing really well.'

'Hmm. Well, I in't getting no younger, gal-Sybil, so let's hope she don't leave it too late,' was the enigmatic reply. 'Mind, she do write to me, from time to time. Just a card like. To let me know there's no ill-feeling. So she's not all bad.'

And since Sybil had no idea what she was talking about they generally left it at that.

Sybil missed her sister, though, and was often lonely, a feeling which was foreign to her. Once there had been Lizzie all the time and Chris all through the summer; now there was just Myrtle during school-time and Georgie when he was home.

She missed Ralph too, though her feelings regarding him were still a trifle ambivalent. He had been easy with her at Easter, when Mrs Winterton had come down with him and Chris to make sure the house was all right after the winter gales and the three of them had met, but Mrs Winterton had seemed to need the children by her and their meeting had been brief and hurried.

But what with studying and doing as much as she could for Dora and Gran, Sybil's days were pretty full, so she should not repine. She wrote long letters to Chris and got rather shorter ones back, and sometimes Ralph added a postscript to say he was well and hoped she was the same. Chris was working hard and hoped to get to teacher training college with Sybil, and Ralph was destined for great things, probably in his father's firm.

I'm destined for great things too, Sybil told herself, scrubbing the quarry tiles in the kitchen with a scrub-brush which was worn almost down to the wood. In a few years I'll be living in my own place, like Lizzie, and only visiting Pakeby on a Sunday.

10

The family thought Lizzie's departure sudden, the result of a whim, but in fact she had planned it for a couple of weeks. On that last morning she stood in the road outside the cottage and looked around her, stared in fact at the familiar scene. She had been born here, brought up here, knew every blade of grass, every brick and tile, every grain of sand on the beach, or so it seemed. She looked straight ahead of her to the church with its surrounding grass and gravestones, with the shingled causeway leading off to the centre of the village, then she glanced to the right towards the gap where the sea, today, was a distant line of silver, the sand pale gold in the early rays of the winter sun. To the left, just visible, was Malverns, where a few short weeks ago the person responsible for it all would have been sleeping the sleep if not of the innocent, at least of the unaware, though now he was far away in Norwich.

That midsummer party! Not that she could possibly blame the party, except that it had been the start of all the trouble, the reason why she was saying farewell to Beach Road and Pakeby. Ralph had shown interest in her before the party, it was true, but she'd never been at the centre of his attention, always on the periphery. There had been other girls, easier, more willing, or so he had apparently thought, even if none lovelier – Lizzie never underrated her charms.

And then, after their initial beach-kisses at that party, he and Lizzie had got together – a trip to the Grand, a cuddle when the lights went out, a comforting arm when the film was frightening was the extent of it at first – and things had begun to happen. Lizzie learned what the vicar meant when he referred to the sins of the flesh, and she loved them, thought them no sin but marvellous pleasure. Even the affair of Phyllis, the maid at the vicarage, which caused a lot of head-shaking, did not stop Lizzie's joyful indulgence in this new pastime. So it could be dangerous — so could almost every type of fun. She would just have to be careful.

She wasn't, of course. She simply purred her way further and deeper into Ralph's affections until they reached a point when they absolutely had to make love every day. They were only young, she thought defensively now, Ralph as innocent, in his way, as she, yet here she was, definitely in trouble having missed two of the dreaded monthlies and unable to think of any way out which did not involve leaving home and telling lies.

Not that she didn't long to leave home; she really did. But not like this, not sneaking off as though to work and simply not coming back. She had left a note, of course, telling her mother that she'd got a job in Norwich, a wonderful chance, and would be in touch again from the city once she'd settled in.

There were places for girls like her, who were going to have babies but didn't want the world to know. Some girls had their babies adopted, but there was another way. Gran had told her about it, though she didn't know she had. She'd been talking about pretty Phyllis at the vicarage, who had got herself in the family way and not managed to keep it quiet. There had been all sorts of rumours but not many people knew for sure who the father was.

Lizzie did. The same as her baby's. Ralph. Mr Winterton had paid for Phyllis to go away to have her baby and then have it adopted. Everyone knew someone had shelled out but not who, though Lizzie thought there would be some pretty shrewd guesses. But even if they found out it was the summer visitor from Malverns, that didn't necessarily mean the father was Ralph. It could have been his cousin Rupert, or his friend Tod Upton, or even Mr Winterton himself. Only a couple of Phyllis's closest friends knew who was really the father, and Lizzie was one of them.

But Gran had said that if Phyllis had played her cards right she needn't have gone around looking like a dumpling for weeks. There was an old woman who lived down an alley at the back of the Free Library in Norwich, who'd see you right. Quite cheaply, too; no need to go begging to the feller's father. Get the baby born before it was ready, so you wouldn't have no worry about it. Of course, when she'd said it she hadn't known a thing about Lizzie's predicament, hadn't meant Lizzie to go there — had she? Sometimes Lizzie wondered about Gran. She'd said it in a thoughtful sort of way, told Lizzie the address and the woman's name — Nellie Stick — even given her some money from the old sock under her mattress, though she'd said it was towards the journey to London because Lizzie had made out she was after a job there.

Lizzie had told Gran about London a couple of days ago; preparing the ground, so to speak. Gran admired Mum but didn't exactly like her, so there was little chance of her tittle-tattling about Lizzie's sudden interest in the great city.

And at least I'm not far along, Lizzie told herself comfortingly, remembering where she was and shutting the gate carefully behind her before setting off along Beach Road towards the bus stop. I've only missed a couple of monthlies, so there shouldn't be any trouble . . . it was not as if the baby were alive and putting her in the soup.

She'd prepared the ground a bit with Sybil, too, saying she was sick to the teeth of the job in Tuttles, that it would never lead anywhere, they didn't think enough of her. Which was an awful lie and very sad to have to pretend, since Lizzie was the apple of the chief saleslady's eye and was thought to have a great future in gowns ahead of her.

It was a cold day, but Lizzie was warm as toast, due to having two jerseys on and two skirts as well. She had packed a case slyly, the previous weekend, hoping against hope that Mum wouldn't go ferreting around amongst her things, and now she had lingered well past her usual time for leaving so that the house would be empty. Sybs had gone off to school, Georgie and Dad to the fishing, Mum with yesterday's catch in the cart. Lizzie had feigned a cold in the head, said she was on a promise to start at ten instead of eight-thirty, so she had a reason for being last out of the house. But she didn't want any nosy-parkering, anyone asking why she was lugging all her worldly goods around with her, so her bag was not a large one and she had doubled her clothing instead. Since she had already given in her notice at Tuttle's she intended to go straight to the station and thence to Norwich. There she would visit Nellie Stick and get rid of her unwanted burden, and then she would find some sort of work in the city until she decided to return home.

She reached the bus stop in plenty of time and climbed aboard in company with a couple of shift workers heading for the port and some women off on a shopping trip. She sat and watched the passing scene and planned what she would have to eat when the old woman had finished with her – should she treat herself to fish and chips, or would it be better to buy a huge and sticky cream cake and eat it all by herself?

And presently the leafless trees jogging past the bus and the verges knee-high in wet grass and the little houses sheltering behind their winter-bare hedges began to blur together. Lizzie Cream was crying.

'You're all right now, my love, you're all right now. Lie still and don't move do you'll start yourself a-bleedin' again. Now what did you say your name was?'

'Linda Miller,' Lizzie moaned, trying to open her eyes to see who was bending over her. 'I'm Linda Miller and I come from Galloway.'

'Are you sure, now? Where do you live in Galloway?'

'Twenty-four, Cream Lane,' Lizzie muttered. She still felt ill, but not as bad as she had felt earlier when she had found out for herself why Nellie Stick was so named. Fear and pain had caused screams shrill enough to call down curses on her head, to bring harsh, calloused hands to clamp her mouth shut, almost stopping her breathing, and then she had passed out, plunging thankfully into the dark pit of unconsciousness where the pain no longer tore her apart and the cruel sensation of being impaled on the horns of a mad bull no longer haunted her. But she had been unable to prevent herself from coming round once or twice to the same apparently unending pain, whilst someone gripped her wrists to hold her still and someone else pulled her knees painfully apart and announced defensively that she was a strong little bugger and would come through it all right, same's they all did, and prodded at her until she shrieked and shrieked again, her cries growing fainter as her weakness increased.

But now at last there was stillness and quiet, and although her body hurt dreadfully no one was doing anything to her, unless you counted the quiet voice and the relentless questions which, even in her muddled state, she knew she must answer only with lies.

'Twenty-four, Cream Lane,' the voice repeated gently. 'And your name again?'

'Linda Galloway,' droned Lizzie. 'Can I go to sleep now?'

She still had not opened her eyes but she heard the smile in the voice which answered her.

'Sure you can, you poor little sod! And if I could get hold of the feller that started all this wouldn't I tie a knot in his john william which wouldn't come undone for a month of Sundays? And as for old Nellie Stick, she should be nibbled to deat' by ducks, for I'll be bound this is her work. Are you thirsty, now?'

Lizzie ran a dry tongue over her dry lips and discovered that she would give a small fortune for a mouthful of water. She tried to open her eyes and half-succeeded, but the lids were as heavy as though they had been weighted with lead. Instead of speaking, she nodded, and saw, through the slit in her lids, a figure clad in blue and white sitting near her.

'You've had a little bit of an operation, just to clean you up, like,' the gentle voice continued. 'You were in a poor way when they brought you in – said they'd found you lyin' in the road, they did, and Mr Samuels operated at once, probably saved your life. Now, just a mouthful, that's all.'

An arm slipped under her shoulders, raising her, and Lizzie felt the rim of a cup against her lips. She opened her mouth like a nestling and felt the cool sweetness of water touch her tongue, deliciously moisten her mouth. She made a purring sound of satisfaction and took a second sip, then felt herself gently laid down on the pillow again as the cup was removed.

'What a good, grateful child,' the kind voice said. 'Now you may sleep, Miss Linda Galloway – or was it Miller?'

But this time Lizzie could not answer; huge waves of sleep were breaking over her unresisting head. For the second time that day – she thought it was only a day – she plunged thankfully into unconsciousness.

She was in hospital three days but they never did find out who she really was. She settled for Linda Smith in the end, of 24 Green Lane ('Cream? You must have misunderstood,' she said, wide-eyed), Aylesbury, Buckinghamshire. She knew nothing about any baby, had been suffering from some sort of haemorrhage, she supposed.

They knew she lied, of course, but they had other things on their minds. Whilst she was there a lorry and an omnibus collided. There was a rush of casualties, two nurses were off sick so they were short-staffed – what did it matter, after all, if she preferred to keep her name and address to herself?

She emerged on a cold and sunny day, shaky-legged, pale, her hair stringy and unappetizing, her body aching all over, all her small personal possessions gone, no doubt taken by Nellie Stick. All she now owned were a few pence in her coat pocket, the packet of sanitary towels the sister had given her to deal with the bleeding and a towering sense of injustice which she remedied by going, with cold determination, round to the small house behind the Free Library where Nellie Stick reigned.

She banged on the door and Nellie's sharp-nosed little face peered round it, made as if to withdraw and then, it seemed, recognized her erstwhile patient.

'Oh, it's you,' she said grudgingly. 'All right, are you? That give us a scare that did, you passin' out like that. Good thing Freda come by – she got you into the 'orspital, see.'

'I'm all right now,' Lizzie said grimly. 'Where's my case? And my blue handbag with my money in?'

'I've got 'em,' Nellie said, bristling a bit. 'I in't never took nothin' what weren't mine to take, but I thought you'd not want 'em in 'orspital . . . better come in, then.'

She had charged Lizzie in advance for her services and Lizzie, snatching up her handbag and checking her purse, was so glad that it still contained the rest of her money, so pleased that her small case was apparently unopened, that she did not grumble over Nellie's cavalier treatment. Indeed, all she wanted now was to escape, because the very smell of the kitchen made her shudder to the depths of her soul, made her feel small and raw and easily bruised. She turned on her heel.

'Everything seems to be here,' she said crisply. 'I won't trouble you further.'

'Not a word of thanks,' Nellie muttered behind her as Lizzie marched up the hall; she would have run, but pride would not allow it. Nevertheless she walked fast. There was a horrible creepy feeling on the back of her neck, a coldness in the pit of her stomach, which could only be assuaged by escape.

Once outside again in the winter sunshine, the first real doubts hit her. She had done it; she was Lizzie Cream again, just Lizzie. But where should she go? Not home – they would take one look at her and know her shameful secret. It would be weeks, perhaps, before the bleeding stopped; sharing a room with Sybil as she did it would be impossible to conceal her condition.

She suddenly realized that she hated her family, the smug Creams. If he ever knew, Henry would have her hide . . . but she knew things about her father which she could have told had she so wished. And Georgie, so smug, such a wonderful son – well, he'd always preferred Sybil to Lizzie, never hidden the fact. He wouldn't be pleased if he found out that she'd had an abortion. It wasn't the sort of thing brothers wanted to know about their sisters. Mum of course had always loved her – but not enough to realize I was in bad trouble and to help me out of it, Lizzie thought now. As for Sybil, what sort of a girl would let her sister go through what Lizzie had just suffered without any support at all? The Cream family had let Lizzie down in the worst possible way, and Lizzie knew, in a weird and painful way, that she had let them down too. They did not love her enough to take on board what she had done and forgive her for it, and yet they knew her well enough to guess about the abortion as soon as they laid eyes on her. And anyway, what about the tears? Even as she walked, telling herself how pleased she was that it was all over, she found that she was crying. Tears brimmed over, ran down her cheeks and plopped off her chin, whilst her mouth pulled itself into ugly shapes and her nose needed blowing.

So she could not go home – did not want to go home. She had told them she had got a job in Norwich and that was just what she would do. There were hostels . . . she would find somewhere, somehow.

She found a place, booking a bed in a long dormitory on the promise of payment as soon as she got work. That night she struck up a friendship with Moira Hawkins, the girl in the next bed, who was only a couple of years older than Lizzie. Moira said that since she was so young they probably wouldn't want her in a factory, which was where Moira herself worked, but why not apply to one of the big stores? Get yourself really clean, speak nice, dress neat, look them straight in the eye whilst you tell 'em whatever you think they want to know and you'll be okay, was Moira's advice, and Lizzie conscientiously took it. Next morning she washed her hair, scrubbed herself in the four inches of tepid bath-water which was all the hostel allowed, dressed in her navy skirt and striped blouse and set off to tour the department stores.

She struck lucky in Curls, where the very elderly woman on gowns told her that she needed a young pair of legs to go up and down to the stockroom for her. Lizzie, whose recent experiences had left her feeling at least a hundred and who could not, to save her life, have run up a flight of stairs that day, assured Miss Trent that nothing would give her greater pleasure than replacing stock.

'I start Monday,' she told Moira jubilantly when she got back to the hostel. 'The money's not bad, either, for shop work. But I'm not staying here once I can afford a room of my own.'

Soon she had money put by and began to look for a place of her own. At first she had a tatty little room above a shop on St Benedict's, which seemed extremely cheap until she had spent her first night there, when she realized that the noise from the brewery was enough to put off most would-be lodgers. Not that it put Lizzie off; her head only had to touch the pillow and she was asleep until the alarm clock went off next morning. The brewery, so far as a sleeping Lizzie was concerned, might just as well not have existed, and though the fumes sometimes caused her to slam her window shut and use language, it was not enough to put her off her room. After the hostel just to be alone was bliss, and besides, she found suddenly that she was taking a pride in her tiny domain.

She bought water-damaged material from a warehouse which had suffered a bad fire and, with great care and loving attention to detail, made herself very pretty curtains with ruffled hems. She found an old rug in a secondhand shop and bargained briskly for it, and persuaded a woman at work to sell her a brass coalscuttle and a set of fire-tools. She began to haunt jumble sales and auctions and to drag her purchases triumphantly home. Dora would have been amazed to see how carefully her once-lazy daughter restored her finds, how meticulously she cleaned and polished and tidied her room. Even Lizzie, notorious for her skill in getting others to do her work for her, sometimes wondered at her own change of attitude.

But she did not go home. Instead, she concentrated all her energy on making her new room as like a home as it could be. She even taught herself to cook – in a manner of speaking, since she only had a primus stove to cook upon and a very tiny open fire in a little black basket-grate – and she learned to sew straight seams and to knit quite expertly.

She was not happy, exactly. Deep down inside her she yearned for something, some warmth which was missing from her life. But she was certainly not unhappy. She sometimes thought that she was poised on the brink of life, waiting, though she could not have said for what. Time passed pleasantly enough; she went to the pictures regularly, had a meal out once or twice a week, walked by the river as the weather improved and spring began to bring daffodils out to dance on the Castle Mound and starred the trees in the Castle Gardens with blossom.

She wrote short letters home and Dora and Sybil wrote much longer ones back. Sybil was doing well at school, she was still desperate to be a teacher, she had a friend called Myrtle who was a card. Dora was putting a bit by and would love to see Lizzie . . . should she come into the city and visit the room in St Benedict's?

But Lizzie put her off. She said she wasn't ready yet, that as soon as she could she would come home, that she often thought of them.

Grandma didn't write.

She wouldn't, thought Lizzie viciously. She no longer had any doubt that Grandma, smug old bitch, had intended Lizzie to visit Nellie

144

Stick, had not cared that Lizzie might die under the old woman's vile ministrations. Yet . . . you had to give Gran her due; she'd not breathed a word to Mum or Dad, nor to her adored Sybil.

And all this time Lizzie never thought about boys, or Ralph, or anything like that, and she was helped in her indifference by the fact that few men worked in Curls anyway, and none in the gowns department. Which was as well, because since her time in hospital Lizzie found herself hating men, shying away from them almost fearfully, as though if she exchanged a word or a look she would find herself re-living the nightmare of Nellie Stick.

Then one wet day in July Lizzie was scuttling along London Street, hurrying past Boots the chemist and Coe the photographer, making for the Maypole which wasn't really in London Street at all but just on the corner as you turned into the Back-of-the-Inns, when she walked slap-bang into a young man studying the big studio portrait of a very beautiful debutante, feathers and all, which graced the main window of Coe's.

'I'm awfully . . .' Lizzie began, meaning to apologize and hurry on, desperate to get to the Maypole and buy half a pound of broken biscuits before they shut, when the young man looked up at her, started to speak, then grabbed her by the shoulders and smiled into her face.

'Lizzie Cream, by all that's wonderful! What on earth are you doing in the city? Come up for a shopping trip?'

It was Ralph and not a young man at all, for Ralph was, as she very well knew, only a year or so older than herself. She tried to pull free of him but he held on tight, then manoeuvred her into Coe's doorway.

'Lizzie? What's up?'

'Nothing's up. I'm trying to get to the Maypole before they close. What are *you* doing here, anyway? You should be in Pakeby.'

'I'm not allowed. There was a bit of trouble . . . can't you guess?'

Lizzie thought in a painful little rush of Nellie Stick and shook her head, trying to look wooden and uninterested.

'No idea. Look, I must go . . .'

'Hang on . . . no, I'll come with you. Where are you going? The Maypole? Well, for goodness sake, girl, it's only just round the corner. Come on.'

They set off together, both heads down against the rain. Lizzie barely had time to think thankfully that at least they were unlikely to be recognized before they were bundling into the Maypole, where she made straight for the biscuit counter.

The broken biscuits were a fraction of the cost of whole ones, so Lizzie usually treated herself to a half-pound or so for the weekend. She liked to spoil herself on a Sunday with a cup of tea in bed and a selection of biscuits, carefully picking out the chocolate ones and the little round ones with pink, white or blue icing. But now she was so confused by Ralph's sudden eruption into her life that she just let the girl's little trowel dig at random into the pieces, not bothering to point out that there was half a brandy-snap and quite a good chunk of chocolate crumbles which might easily be included.

'Let me,' Ralph said as she was about to pay for them, but Lizzie ignored the offer and handed over her own threepence. If he wants to buy me something it can be a whopping box of chocolates and not a few broken biscuits, she thought crossly. But by far the best thing would be for him to go away and leave me alone; that's what I really want.

He walked along beside her as she scuttled back across London Street and down Swan Lane. He actually took her arm crossing the road, which was busy with cars and bicycles all hurrying to get out of the wet. Cheek, thought Lizzie, trying to jerk her arm free, trying to ignore the little spark of warmth which lit within her at his touch.

'Liz? Why are we going down here? Did you come in by bus or by train? Look, let's go and grab a bite to eat somewhere . . . we can go to Lyons, on the Walk, if you like . . . it's a good place. Or there's the Castle Tea-Rooms, further down London Street, or . . .'

'I live here now,' Lizzie said impatiently, still hurrying along. 'I'm going home. Why don't you go home as well?'

It was unfriendly to the point of rudeness but Ralph did not seem to notice. He continued to walk beside her, his long legs making short work of her attempts to out-pace him. He bent over, though, so that he could look into her face.

'You *live* here? Does your father work in the city now, then? Did you sell up in Pakeby? Lizzie, do explain!'

'There's no reason why I should, but . . .' Lizzie thought wistfully of Lyons, of the delicious food they served, of the nippies in their smart uniforms hurrying between the round, marble-topped tables. Ralph came from a rich family, everyone in Pakeby knew that, so why shouldn't he treat her to high tea? She might as well make some use of him after what he'd done to her! 'All right, you've convinced me. You can buy me a high tea at Lyons.'

'Smashing. I told Mummy I was going to the flicks with Steve, but she won't check up. Or we could go after we've eaten, if you like – have you been to the Haymarket this week? There's a Mae West on, I believe, or there's a Western with Tom Mix at the Theatre de Luxe.'

'I . . . I wouldn't mind,' Lizzie said cautiously. Suddenly, all in a moment, she realized how lonely she was, how she missed Sybil and their occasional trips to the port, the lemonade drunk and the buns eaten, giggling, in the milk bar on Pier Terrace, as well as all the rich conglomeration of family life. Even Tom Mix, who had seemed to the sophisticated Lizzie to lack sex appeal, suddenly seemed desirable, if only for his entertainment value and the pleasant familiarity of his dark, square-jowled face.

'Here we go, then,' Ralph said exuberantly. He swung her round, his hand now firm on her upper arm, and again she felt that treacherous warmth. Once she had revelled in this young man's touch, once she had enjoyed . . . oh, very much more than the feeling of his fingers through her waterproof!

They reached Lyons without incident, unless you counted wading through the increasingly deep puddles, and Ralph led her inside. Lizzie took off her wet mac and shed her soaked headscarf, then pushed both hands up through her flattened hair to give it back a bit of bounce. She wished, despite being indifferent to Ralph, that she was looking her best, but at least she looked healthy now, not pale and sickly. They found a table easily, ordered tomato soup and a crusty roll followed by fish and chips, then settled down to talk. The soup was lovely, really hot and tasty, the roll the sort that has a shell-like outer crust and a soft white interior. Lizzie would have liked a pot of tea, but knew it was not the done thing to drink tea with soup, so bided her time. Ralph ordered butter with the rolls though he told her that his mother would have a fit and, smiling at her, he spread his roll thickly and then, unasked, did the same for hers.

'Now!' he said at last, spooning soup. 'Tell me everything!'

'I got a job at Curls, in gowns, and I booked into a hostel until I could afford a place of my own,' Lizzie said, telling the truth but arranging the order of events to suit herself. 'I moved into my new place before Christmas, and I'm doing well in the store. I actually do some modelling; if you ever come in there with your mother for a coffee you'll see me walking up and down, ever so elegant, in lovely tweed suits and things and gorgeous shoes. I get paid extra for it.'

'I see,' Ralph said. 'There wasn't – anything else you wanted to tell me? Was there?'

Lizzie looked superciliously across at him, raising her plucked, perfectly shaped brows. She just wished the rain hadn't flattened her hair and probably washed most of her make-up off at the same time. It would have been nice to have impressed Ralph with how very grown-up and independent she was whilst she was about it.

'Anything more? Like what?'

'We-ell . . . what's everyone at Pakeby saying about me, for instance?'

Lizzie was so cross that she had to force herself to take another mouthful of soup and a piece of bread before replying. How typical of the male attitude that he was more interested in what people thought of him than in the real reason why she had fled! However, by the time she had slowly and carefully eaten the bread she had thought better of making a comment to that effect.

'About you? Why, whatever do you mean?'

Ralph made an impatient noise in the back of his throat and stared across the table at her. He had the sort of face which was simply a pleasure to look at, Lizzie realized rather crossly. A pair of intensely blue eyes, a broad, unlined brow, a mouth whose sculpted shape made her think . . . oh, the sort of thoughts she never wanted to think again, and though his thick crop of golden-brown hair was soaked and slicked flat with rain in the warmth of the restaurant it was already beginning to curl again. She had always admired his straight nose, too, and his firm, square chin. But she tried not to show any of these feelings as he sought for a reply to her rather contemptuous question.

'Oh, Liz, for God's sake! Why do you think I'm not going to Pakeby this summer? There was enough fuss, God knows – that girl from the vicarage, what's her name . . .'

'Phyllis,' Lizzie said dryly. How could he pretend to forget someone he'd – with whom he'd – he'd . . . oh damn it, he'd got her pregnant, hadn't he, put her in the club? So the least he could do was remember her name, for God's sake!

'That's right, Phyllis. Nice kid – well, not a kid, nearly as old as me, but nice anyhow.' He shot a quick sideways look at Lizzie across the marble table-top. 'They say . . . I believe she's had a baby. A boy, it was. She had it adopted.'

'True,' Lizzie murmured. She was enjoying his evident discomfiture too much to let him off the hook. 'So?'

'We-ell . . .' Another sly glance, this time half hang-dog, half pleased with himself. 'It could be mine – the baby. I'm not saying it is, but it could be. So the parents want me away from Pakeby this summer. Out of temptation, it seems.'

'Rubbish! No parent could be so stupid,' Lizzie said roundly. 'Unless they sent you to – to Siberia, there's bound to be temptation as you call it. You're a feller, you've only got to *see* a girl who's halfway pretty and all you can think about . . . well, if your parents don't know they're sillier than I give them credit for.'

'Go on . . . all I can think about when I see a pretty girl . . . ?' Ralph said provocatively, grinning at her. But Lizzie would not rise to such bait and gave a disdainful sniff, putting her soup spoon back into her now empty dish with a clatter.

'We both know what you think about – we should,' she said briefly. 'Here come our fish and chips.'

The waitress was slim and pretty with rich chestnut hair cut in a pageboy bob. She smiled at Lizzie but gave Ralph the eye. Lizzie had no difficulty in interpreting what the girl was offering nor the half speculative, half quizzical glance which Ralph gave her in return. Once she would have minded, but not now. If the nippy wanted what she, Lizzie, had suffered then let her go ahead. So long as it isn't me, Lizzie thought with a shiver; so long as it's never me again.

After they had been served, Ralph took up the conversation where it had left off.

'So there'll be no Pakeby this summer in case people stare and talk, and in case Phyllis tries to make claims,' he said. 'Not that she would; that was all part of the bargain.'

'What bargain?'

'My father paid for her to have the baby in a nursing home somewhere. He reckoned no one would know if she left Pakeby before she was too far gone, but Mummy said folk talk. Anyway, she had the baby and went back to the vicarage, but I suppose it's best if I stay away for a bit.'

'Phyllis is going with Jimmy Cartwright; they'll probably get married next spring,' Lizzie said, popping a chip into her mouth. The food was awfully good, and if Ralph offered her a pudding she would have the treacle sponge – with custard, of course.

'Is she? Well, the parents simply wouldn't believe that any girl who had a chance of marrying their son and heir would pass it up for a village yokel,' Ralph said cheerfully. 'Anyway, with you not in Pakeby any more, I can't say I'm much worried. Where's your room? I'll walk you back there after, if you like.'

'After the flicks?' Lizzie said nastily. She did not intend to be cheated of her evening out, especially as Ralph had intentions, she was sure, of picking up their relationship just where it had left off. It would be rather fun to watch him slope off with his tail between his legs after her refusal to allow him even a kiss, but she wanted a trip to the cinema first.

'Oh, sure, if that's what you want.' Ralph finished his last chip and glanced across at her. 'Room for a pudding?'

It would have been nice to have said no, she never ate puddings, or to have suggested a cream-ice, but the treacle sponge beckoned; it might not be as good as Dora's, but it was a great deal better than Lizzie's, since there was no way a decent treacle pudding could be cooked over a primus stove. Lizzie picked up the menu card and pretended to consider.

'That was very nice, but I do have a little space left so I'll have the treacle sponge and custard, please,' she said just as a nippy arrived, a different one this time with yellow hair permed so stiffly that it stuck out like a wig at the sides. 'And a pot of tea.'

Ralph nodded carelessly up at the girl.

'Twice,' he said laconically, and Lizzie had to admire such *sangfroid*. It was plain that Ralph was well used to eating out. 'And can I have the bill, please?'

The treacle pudding was as good as she had hoped, the tea came in a large pot and they drank two cups each, and then Ralph went up to the woman at the cash desk and paid whilst Lizzie struggled into her damp mac and felt her headscarf suspiciously. It was still damp and a glance through the window showed her that if the rain had not actually stopped at least it had eased up a bit. She stuffed the scarf into her pocket, therefore, and was ready when Ralph, pocketing his change, turned away from the cash desk.

'All right? Let's go, then.'

They set off down the stairs, across the floor of the shop and out of the swing doors. Outside, the sky still threatened rain and the city hall clock said that it had taken them almost an hour to eat their meal. But the Haymarket was only just up the road . . . Ralph took Lizzie's arm and began to hurry and she trotted alongside, still not in a good mood with him but definitely feeling less antagonistic.

They reached the cinema and Ralph paused outside, where the still photographs of the films were displayed.

'We're halfway through the big picture,' he said. 'Sure you want to go in? Mind, we can see it round.'

'I always see it round,' Lizzie said. Why not, after all? It cost the same even if you sat there all evening and someone else was paying the heating bills.

'Oh. Right. Circle seats do you?'

'Yes, all right,' Lizzie said grudgingly. Circle seats were the most expensive, especially balcony seats, but he'd probably want to sit in the back row, as they always did.

'Balcony?'

There was a short queue, nothing much. Most people would have gone in at the beginning of the film rather than halfway through. Lizzie nodded.

'Chocolates? Or you could have some salted peanuts.'

'Chocolates,' Lizzie said definitely, deciding on the spur of the moment to have an ice-cream in the interval and peanuts as well, if the fancy took her. 'Soft centres, please.'

They fumbled their way into the cinema, the usherette shining her torch behind her and then, cruelly, across the seated audience. Girls huddled into their escorts' shoulders, young men turned their eyes away from the light as the torch passed across them. Lizzie and Ralph sat down and began to make themselves comfortable, rolling their wet coats up and stuffing them unceremoniously under their seats, getting out the chocolates, giggling a bit as they tried to open the box without too much noise or fuss.

Up on the screen Mae West was curving across a dance floor, holding a microphone, singing sultrily. Lizzie took Ralph's hand, more with the intention of holding it still, she told herself, than as a gesture of affection, and settled back to enjoy herself.

They came blinking out into the summer night to find that the rain had ceased and the clouds had cleared. Above them the darkening sky was pricked by stars, and a moon, round and bright as a silver penny, shone down on the city.

'I'll walk you home,' Ralph said, and Lizzie did not demur because the film had made her feel romantic and anyway she knew she could handle Ralph. Presently, as they crossed the Walk and cut down Exchange Street, he put his arm round her waist and in Bedford Street, turning into Bridewell Alley, she slid her own arm around him. For convenience, of course, because it made walking easier. Down Bridewell Alley they went, their sides pressed warmly close, with the bulk of the church black yet not at all sinister on their right and the small shops on their left. They swung into St Benedict's, crossed over opposite Jordan's, the tobacconist's, and wandered along the pavement until they reached Lizzie's door.

It was painted green but it looked black in the moonlight, the lock twinkling with polish. She inserted her key, turned it, then carefully freed herself from Ralph's arm.

'Thanks, Ralph. Goodnight.'

'Oh, Lizzie, I've got a long walk back to St Giles. Why don't you ask me up for a nightcap?'

She should have said no, turned him away. She knew it; perhaps they both knew it.

'Well . . . just for a moment, then.'

He followed her up the stairs and into her room. His admiration of her little domain was genuine. He particularly liked the matching bedspread and curtains, and thought she had made a real little palace from unpromising material. He said he felt comfortable here, and completely at home.

There was only one armchair so he lay on the bed whilst she made two cups of cocoa and tipped the broken biscuits on to a plate.

'Dear me, you've broken the biscuits, but I'm sure they'll still taste every bit as delicious,' Ralph said in the very voice of Miss Bertha Higgins, who played the organ at Pakeby church and helped at church bazaars. 'What a *kind* girl you are, Elizabeth!'

'I'm not all that kind,' Lizzie said repressively, but she could not help giggling over his cruelly accurate imitation both of Miss Higgins's voice and of the exact words she would have used. 'Do sit up, Ralph . . . behave!'

'I will, I will. For cocoa and bickies I'll behave like a real little gentleman,' Ralph said, sitting up. He drank his cocoa too hot and made her laugh by chasing to the jug of water and pouring a trickle over his extended tongue. Then he sat on the bed again and coaxed her to sit by him so he could give her a nice, cuddly hug.

Before, their clandestine meetings had taken place on the floor of a beatster hut, or amongst the sand dunes, or even in the woods at the back of the village. Now they had a whole beautiful, soft bed to play on. And Ralph was kind and careful – and very clever, Lizzie thought afterwards. He undressed her gently, laying her back on the pillows, admiring the smooth roundness, the silkiness, of her breasts with their tight little red berries, so much plumper and shapelier than they had been last summer, he marvelled.

She had meant to repulse him but found herself quite unable to do so, because with his very first kiss – and he kissed her with a thoroughness and an intimacy which she had never known before – she wanted him. All the terrors of Nellie Stick, all the pain and the horror of it, should have risen up to help Lizzie give Ralph his marching orders, but it did not happen. Instead, strange, hot longings arose in her; she wanted his hands to play with her breasts, wanted them to stray lower, was eager for an invasion of her body which she knew, not from memory but from a strange new instinct, would bring her deeper and more marvellous pleasure than she had ever known before – a pleasure which Ralph would share.

She did murmur a protest about babies when he first began to unbutton her cotton dress, but he produced a condom, swore she would be safe as houses, that he had found out a thing or two since last summer.

'I'll see you right, little Liz,' he murmured as their bodies fused after such tantalizing and delicious love-play that she scarcely cared any more about the consequences. 'Oh, Lizzie, Lizzie, there's no one like you!'

II

1940

'Well, that's it, I reckon. France has gone, and them little countries
. . . Holland and Belgium an' that. And now the krauts are knockin'
hell outa London, blitzin' it wi' bombs every night, killin' little kids
. . . They got Buckn'am Palace last night, it said on the wireless.
D'you reckon they're after the King an' Queen? Is that what you
think, Fenn?'

'Yup.'

'Is that all you kin say?'

'Yup.'

'Fenn, you're an aggravatin' guy. Don't you feel *nothin'* now your
country's gettin' beat up at the deep end?'

Fenn and Sammy were sitting on a park bench, eating. It was a cold
December morning and they usually ate outside at midday since the
garage where they worked as mechanics was noisy and smelly, not at
all the sort of place in which to enjoy a meal. They liked the work and
the money was good, but every morning fresh stories of the London
blitz came over the airways whilst they were eating their breakfast
and though Fenn would have indignantly denied it, Sammy believed
his friend was beginning to get depressed and restless as the outlook
for Britain seemed to get gloomier and gloomier. Yet despite this,
Sammy concluded, looking sideways at Fenn, the other man did not
seem over-eager to discuss it. He was eating a peanut butter sandwich
and scowling over a day-old newspaper which some bum had left on
the bench.

Sammy gave Fenn a nudge which Fenn stoically ignored.

'Fenn? Didja hear me?'

Fenn looked up at last. He still didn't look the way a Britisher should
look, Sammy thought with wry affection. Fenn was powerfully built
and of only medium height, with thickly curling dark hair, navy-blue
eyes and a squarish, aggressive face. His body was strong rather than

athletic and the thick eyebrows which barred his forehead made him look bad-tempered, which he certainly was not. In fact, he had a cheerful and optimistic temperament, was clever in a way which Sammy knew he himself could never aspire to emulate, and although his temper flared up to white heat when he was roused, by and large he kept it well in check.

'Fenn?'

Fenn put down the paper and shook his head sadly at Sammy.

'Honest, Sammy, I jest don't know *how* I feel! Guess I don't feel as British as I ought, for a start. Not any more. Bin here too long, I reckon. Yet there's times . . . I dunno.'

'Then you ain't burnin' to go back, to join in?'

Fenn shook his head again, but in puzzlement, not negation. Sammy could tell because he and Fenn had shared homes and jobs and thoughts for so long now . . . more than nine years, Sammy realized, awed. Gee, fancy knowing a guy for nine years. That must make them good as brothers, just about!

'I dunno. Guess I'd kinda like to go back . . . in a way. But I'm an American, mostly. It's jest there's a bit of me still remembers, still feels mighty proud of the way ordinary folk turned out to rescue th'army . . . last May, when there was that Dunkirk stuff . . . and when I think of them Nazis dropping bombs on Cheetham Hill . . .'

He ground his teeth; Sammy heard the sound and recognized it.

'Cheetham Hill? That where you lived?'

Fenn was one of those guys who could talk and talk and yet never repeat himself and somehow contrive to tell you nothing of a particularly personal nature, either. Sammy knew it was because truth didn't mean much to his friend, but it didn't matter. He loved the stories, revelled in Fenn's powers of invention, though occasionally he would remonstrate. Sometimes Fenn's stories were powerful like lies and Sammy's dad, dead and gone these three years past, had not approved of lies. But Dad had understood Fenn, understood that the stories were more like romancing than lies, more like wishful thinking than either, perhaps. Guess folk like Fenn make up what they can't have, Sammy decided, and why should I moan? Gee, I love Fenn's stories!

'Uh-huh. Well, jest off of the Hill. D'ya think they will? Drop bombs on my place, I mean.'

'I guess they will,' Sammy said ruefully. 'Guess it won't take long, neither, 'fore ole England gives 'em best. Them Huns know what they're doin', I reckon. Say what you like, they took over ole France and no messin'. Yes, I reckon they'll jest keep on a-goin'.'

There was a pregnant silence. Fenn's navy-blue eyes stared unseeingly ahead of him, while his surprisingly long and sensitive fingers first tapped the seat at his side, then curled themselves into workmanlike fists. Then he stood up.

'C'mon,' he said curtly. 'I gotta think.'

Sammy trotted along beside his friend, doing some thinking himself. War! It was exciting, sure, but only exciting as a cowboys and Indians film was exciting. It had nothing to do with real life, not when you lived in New York. He had half-wondered whether he might lose his pal, whether Fenn might quit, go back home, but it was clear that the thought had not crossed that bright but devious mind until his own words had put it there. No, Fenn wouldn't act on impulse and against his own interests. He might talk a bit wild, but he usually behaved right sensible.

They reached the turning which led back to their place of work – and passed it. Sammy caught Fenn's elbow.

'Hi . . . where we goin'?'

'Oh . . . you still there? Wanna go back? No need to tag along, Sammy.'

Tag along! Sammy felt the blood rush to his cheeks. He had no intention of 'tagging along', he was walking with a friend. He said as much through gritted teeth. Fenn slowed his pace for a moment to grin down at him.

'Sure, sure. But I'm goin' to join the army, see. You won't want to lose an hour's pay to see me do that.'

'The army? Hell, the *British* army?'

Fenn laughed, a short bark. When he laughed like that a long crease appeared beside his mouth. It gave him a piratical look and right now, with the dangerous twinkle lurking in those eyes and the whiteness of his grin, Sammy would have believed his friend quite capable of joining anything – the Foreign Legion, the Ku Klux Klan!

'No, Sammy, not the British army. I wouldn't know how to start. The good old United States Army. You mark my words, we'll get drawn in, sooner or later. Guess I want it to be sooner, but if it is or if it ain't, I want to know how to fight them Nazi bastards. Guess I better get trainin', eh?'

'But Fenn, we've got jobs!' Sammy gasped, shocked yet fascinated. Fenn usually had that effect on him. 'We can't chuck up our jobs, can we?'

'Watch me,' Fenn recommended. 'See how easy it is!'

'We-ell, I guess we could, all right. Prob'ly a fine life, the army, eh, Fenn? They feed you good, I guess. And dames like a guy in a uniform.'

'Yup. I'll be fightin' off them chicks,' Fenn said, striding along the sidewalk. 'I'll write you from trainin' camp, Sammy, and tell you all about it.'

'*Tell* me?' Sammy gasped, affronted. 'Tell *me*? Fenn Kitzmann, when didja have to tell me *anythin'*? I'm comin', ain't I?'

Fenn slowed again and grinned down at Sammy. His eyes were dancing with amusement and the thrill of adventure.

'I ain't suggestin' you join up, or tryin' to persuade you,' he remarked. ''Course, I can't *stop* you, if your mind's set on it.'

'My mind's set,' Sammy said firmly. 'Jeez, as if I'd let you join the army without me – keepin' all the fun to yourself, as well as all the dames.'

Fenn's pace picked up; he nodded thoughtfully and began to hum beneath his breath. Sammy, trotting again, picked up the tune and when they reached the chorus they both burst into song.

There was a scattering of snow on the sidewalks and more in the grey clouds overhead, and Sammy was none too warm in the torn and stained overalls which were his working clothes. New York in winter was cold and uncomfortable; the snow could keep you off work for days with no money coming in. And Fenn was off to join the army, to have adventures, to be somebody – what more could a guy ask?

The United States Army! Jeez!

They did not join the army, however. They joined the Air Corps, not because they preferred it but because they saw an advertisement saying that the Air Corps was short of experienced mechanics.

Fenn swung into the recruiting centre, Sammy following, and lauded them to the skies to the guy behind the counter. In the end, the guy was glad to start them in signing papers, Fenn could tell, because the queue at his desk was growing longer and longer whilst Fenn fished up from the recesses of his fertile mind all sorts of imaginary expertise garnered by himself and Sammy in their lives. He even falsified their ages to make them sound more respectable – then forgot and put his true date of birth on the forms.

Not that it mattered. The Air Corps, for some unfathomable reason – for Fenn's enthusiasm, no matter how self-imposed, always convinced him, amongst others, that he was doing the right thing – was not appealing to quite enough people right now. Or not people with mechanical engineering skills, at any rate. Probably, Fenn thought as he tried to fill in forms without getting engine-oil on everything, everyone wanted to fly, which would leave the Corps short on mechanics.

'Okay; we'll let you know,' the guy behind the desk said, when Fenn pushed over their completed forms.

'Let us know? But I thought . . .'

'You'll hev a physical,' the man drawled, bored by the whole thing. 'P'raps a written 'xamination fer all I know. It all takes time, fellers.'

Fenn led Sammy out again, fuming.

'When I wanna do something, I wanna do it *now*,' he said forcibly. 'Don't that feller know nothin' about the heat of the moment?'

They returned, disconsolate, to their place of employment. But less than a week later they were lining up once more, this time for the physical examination which, if it was satisfactory, would ensure their acceptance into the Army Air Corps.

Neither had much doubt that they would be found to be in good physical shape and so they were. The only surprise came on their receiving their assignments two weeks later.

Fenn was to go to Lincoln, Nebraska, for primary flying school. And Sammy was to go to another training centre for airplane mechanics.

'But I thought we'd go together,' he wailed, on opening his letter. 'This ain't good enough, Fenn – you wanted to service engines, you said you did!'

'We'll sort it out,' Fenn said comfortingly. 'Musta been a mistake . . . I ain't never flown an airplane in my life, but I've sure put right a lot of engines!'

Fenn made some 'phone calls and visited some addresses that day, then came home to the apartment in the evening with a frowning face.

'It seems my math is good enough for a flyer; likewise the results of the physical,' he said slowly. 'Guess we've gotta bite on the bullet, Sammy. And we won't be apart for long, you see – you'll be my mechanic when I'm a flyer. Wouldn't trust my life to no one else!'

The sky above was a deep, glowing blue, the sunshine fell on to the yellow wings of the Stearman trainer airplane and on to Fenn's helmeted head. In normal circumstances, which meant yesterday and for many days before it, there would have been another helmeted head in front of his own – his instructor, Jack Neave. But today the seat was empty. Today Fenn was going solo for the first time.

There had been days of theoretical training, then days of the practical sort, flying the airplane with Jack there to take over at once should something go wrong. And from the very first moment that he had found himself in the air, Fenn had known that this was it – his reason for living, what he wanted to do for the rest of his life.

There was, quite simply, nothing like it. He compared it, in his mind, to all the other things he had tried and found them wanting. Eating, sleeping, swimming, reading ... no, they didn't compare. Making love? Well, that was good, all right, but it was over so quick and it involved girls who seemed, to Fenn, to need more commitment than he was ever likely to offer.

He remembered how thrilled he had been when he'd driven for the first time. That feeling of power, of *being* someone. When he'd taken his boss's new Ford out on to a straight stretch and put his foot down ... that had been a thrill, all right. The roar of the engine, the knowledge that he was in command and that he could master the intricacies not only of the driving itself but of the workings of the engine pumping away under the hood.

But flying! There was no road beneath your wheels – no wheels, either, whilst you were in the air. You could not only go forward, you could go up, down, round, you could turn somersaults, though they called it looping the loop, you could dive like a fish, or roar up like a rocket ... sometimes he thought there was nothing that he and his bi-plane could not do, between them.

That was the crunch, of course. He was one with his ship. When he slipped into the pilot's seat he felt he almost put her on, became a part of her. Yet when he was finished here, at Primary Flying School, he would go happily on to Basic School, then to Advanced. He would fly airplanes of increasing power and sophistication. And right now, although he knew it wouldn't last, he felt surge after surge of happiness and confidence. He would be all right! All flying cadets lived in fear of being 'washed out', sent to train as gunners or navigators because they were not deemed competent flyers. But it wouldn't happen to Fenn Kitzmann! No sir, Fenn Kitzmann was a natural!

One's first solo flight was carefully laid down and Fenn's urge to throw the plane into a loop or a figure eight had to be severely damped down and sat upon. It would never do to fail just out of a silly urge to show off, to prove that he knew what he was doing. Instead, he climbed to two hundred feet, made a turn, climbed again, turned, until he had completed his square and was lined up for his final approach.

It went like a dream. Johnny Flavell had dug a wing into the ground on landing, Andy Cox had lost his nerve at the last minute and circled half-a-dozen times before finally putting her down in a neatish way, Simmonds had ground-looped. Kitzmann would be perfect, Fenn vowed, gritting his teeth. He was going on to Basic school and then Advanced; he could not, would not, even think about defeat!

There was a crosswind; he judged it carefully, slowed, glided in to land knowing that it had all gone well so far and could still go disastrously wrong. Seconds before the wheels touched down he pulled back firmly on the stick, watching the nose for any deviation, correcting with the rudder so that the wheels kissed the runway and clung, and then, with the landing accomplished without so much as a quiver, he taxied into line.

He climbed stiffly out of the cockpit; he could feel a silly grin spreading right across his face, saw his instructor grinning too. It was always a personal business with one's instructor, it had to be. Jack had four cadets to teach. He was with them for the entire duration of the course, and he was like a dog with two tails when one of them did well.

'Was it okay, Jack?'

Jack stopped grinning and tried to frown but he didn't fool Fenn for one moment. He was all the more pleased, probably, because of what had happened to Flavell and Simmonds, though everyone knew that going solo was a tricky business and they would not wash you out for that. No, the four of them would probably go on to Basic together, if the others forgot what had happened to them this afternoon and did better in future.

'You're doin' okay,' Jack said at last. 'I'll write up you did okay.'

It might not have sounded like enthusiasm, but Fenn knew that from Jack it was high praise indeed. He gave the instructor an exuberant thumbs up and hurried off. He suppressed an urge to spread his arms out like wings and make engine-noises. That was how he felt, though – flying, even without a 'plane, might well be possible to one so exalted as he. And what was more he felt he had proved himself, that very soon now he would be well worth boasting about. And because he loved the world he decided on the spur of the moment to write to Rachael; a real letter, with a real address, so she could write back to him.

But she's dead, a voice in his head said half-heartedly; for years you thought she was dead.

Aw, grow up, Fenn told the voice affectionately. That was just one of Saul's lies and didn't I always know it? But now I've really got something to tell her – now I'll write!

'Sister . . . can you come here a minute, luv?'

Rachael, in her navy dress with the stiff white collar and cuffs, her hair strained back from her face and coiled into a French pleat, walked quickly up Laski ward. It was a long ward, dealing with surgical or orthopaedic patients, which meant a fair amount of heavy nursing. Not that Rachael minded that; a dedicated nurse, she loved her work and even managed to enjoy nights which was as well because ever since the outbreak of war the shortage of nurses and the over-abundance of patients meant that she frequently had to work a double shift. As she went she checked, with her eye, that all was as it should be. Down the far end of the ward a figure in the short-sleeved grey dress and white apron of a staff nurse was helping a patient into a wheelchair and in the bed against the far wall the small figure of Edgar Jonas, one leg in traction for a fractured hip, was waggling wildly as he attempted to get his neighbour's attention through the glass partition.

The patient who had called her was Ernest Watts, a cheerful young man with a fractured tibia caused by coming off his motorbike when the machine hit an icy patch. He would be here for at least another ten weeks but was taking his enforced incarceration cheerfully and even said he liked the food, which Rachael thought touching. Ernest was not a Jew, but since this was the Jewish hospital he had to eat kosher and like it, so on Christmas Day his turkey would not be accompanied by bread sauce, nor his Sunday beef by a slice of Yorkshire pudding.

'Yes, Mr Watts?'

'Oh, sister . . .' Ernest blushed. 'Umm . . . my young lady visited me this afternoon. Did you see her? Ever such nice red hair she's got, warm your hands at it, you could! I give her some chocolates, but I was wondering . . . it's nearly Christmas and me mam's ever so busy, I give her so much to do one way and another . . . There's no visiting tonight, I suppose?'

'That's right. But you'll get your supper in a minute, that'll help to pass the time. Did you fill in a menu card yesterday?'

The hospital had been the first to introduce menu cards and they were a great success with both patients and staff, particularly those working down in Milky and Meaty, the kosher kitchens. Life was so much easier when you were producing food which you knew would be eaten, rather than having to make a gallon of tapioca and another gallon of stewed apple, knowing that large quantities of one or the other would be left.

The young man grinned.

''Course I did, Sister – I do like me grub! But I was wondering . . . me young lady's coming up from Wales again to see me come Christmas Day and I was wondering . . .'

'Come along, Mr Watts, don't be bashful,' Rachael said briskly, and wondered at her own cheery tones. Once, she had been the bashful one, the one who stammered and blushed. Even as a staff nurse she had known times when she had nursed a terminally ill patient almost without a word, too afraid of an emotional outburst from the patient or even herself to speak. But all the shyness and lack of faith in herself had ended when she had perched on her smooth hair the ruffled cap of a fully fledged sister. Once that happened she could no longer doubt her own abilities – she knew she was worthy of trust. 'Now, Ernest, what can I do to help you?'

'Well, sister, I was wondering if you could get an orderly to nip out some time before Christmas to buy me a few flowers? You see, I wanted to get me young lady something nice for Christmas, a little ring to wear on her finger mebbe, but she knows I can't do that yet, not laid up here, like. Only she does like chrysanthemums and I thought it would make up for not getting a real present. You know how it is, sister; flowers mean something to you ladies!'

'I'll go myself when I come off duty tomorrow and choose you a really nice bunch,' Rachael said at once. 'I'll not leave it till Christmas Eve because prices will probably soar then. How much do you want to spend?'

'Tuppence,' the young man said, grinning. 'But I dare say it'll cost a bob. Will this do?' He held out a handful of small change which Rachael could see at a glance contained more than the shilling he had suggested.

'That will be fine. A nice bunch of "mums" as they say. Any particular colour?'

'Well, I'd rather yellow or tawny,' Ernest said. 'But white if there's nowt else, I suppose. It's the smell, you know, sister. It's all autumn and bonfires . . . a right good smell.'

'Yes, I love chrysanthemums myself,' Rachael agreed, slipping the money, hot from Ernest's hand, into the pocket of her skirt. 'Well, if that's all, Mr Watts, I'll go back to the office and make a note in my diary so I don't forget your bouquet.'

'You are good, sister,' Ernest Watts said fervently. 'Everyone here's been good to me. Even old Wheezy-guts has his good points.'

Old Wheezy-guts was what the irreverent Ernest Watts called one of the surgeons, an elderly man who had been called out of retirement when younger doctors had been conscripted into the forces. Mr Cargill was in his late seventies and Rachael worried that one day he might fall dead across a patient whilst operating, but somehow he soldiered on, wheezing whenever he had to climb the stairs to the operating theatre, constantly losing swabs, instruments or his glasses, yet well liked, and trusted within the limitations which age had imposed upon him.

'Be more respectful, Mr Watts,' Rachael said therefore, though with a twitching lip. 'Mr Cargill is a brilliant man. He's saved many lives.'

'Oh ah,' the irrepressible Ernest agreed. 'They stopped him amputating Harry Marple's leg and taking out Fred Green's appendix 'stead of the other way round, I believe?'

There was just enough truth in this remark to make Rachael turn away from the bedside to hide her smile. Poor old chap. He had been an excellent surgeon in his day and even now, doddering and slow, he had undoubtedly done as good a job as conditions allowed. Trust the hospital grapevine to pick on that awful, or almost awful, incident when Mr Cargill had bent over the unconscious Harry Marples, remarking, 'The leg doesn't look too bad – great shame it must come off; great shame.'

According to Theatre Sister Agnes, there had been a moment of stupefied silence before a houseman had leapt into the breach.

'You mean out, Mr Cargill,' he said respectfully. 'This one is to come out . . . the appendix, sir.'

'Ah yes, of course. Silly of me. Amputation's on the list somewhere, though . . . later, is it? Ah well, best get started.'

'Good job we don't deliver babies; the mind boggles at what he might do . . . absentmindedly sew 'em back in, or try a forceps delivery on a haemorrhoidectomy,' the orthopaedic surgeon was rumoured to have remarked on hearing of Cargill's latest feat. 'God save me or mine from general surgery for a few months.'

Now, walking back down the ward, Rachael reminded herself that she must speak to Sister Agnes before she left work. Jewish hospital or not, Christmas Day was special here as it was all over Britain. There would be a Father Christmas, presents, an especially fine Christmas dinner with turkey and all the kosher trimmings, and each ward would have its decorated tree in position. They never put the trees on to the wards until Christmas Eve because the heat was not good for pine needles, so the trees were a short-lived treat, being erected on the twenty-fourth and taken down again on Boxing evening.

Sister Agnes would only be on duty for an emergency operation, so she usually acted as Father Christmas's righthand woman and took the presents round to those patients unable to leave their beds. Everyone always did their best to see that suitable gifts were purchased and this year was no exception, though shortages meant that Theatre Sister's homemade toffees and fudges were in much demand. Rachael had gone without sweets herself for a year and stopped taking sugar in her tea which had helped, but even so they were going to be hard-pressed for something attractive to put into the gaily wrapped parcels when Christmas Day dawned.

Re-entering her office, Rachael sat down behind her desk to try to think what they should give young Ernest Watt. A book? He didn't read much, though he was a keen wireless listener and boasted that he had never missed a performance of ITMA, even listening when he was barely conscious after the operation to realign his fractured leg. She had wondered whether there were books available about his favourite programmes but so far enquiries had failed to run such things to earth. He would have some nut fudge and some toffee, but the balaclavas, the knitted mufflers and the fingerless mittens which the staff had been busy making in their spare time were scarcely appropriate for someone who would still be in his hospital bed when the first day of spring dawned.

A rattling announced that suppers were coming up in the lift from the kitchens. Since all staff were fed – and well fed, too – on the premises, Rachael looked hopefully towards the trolley. The blue-uniformed orderly pushing it saw her and turned to smile. She was a fat and jolly woman in her sixties called Katie, a great favourite with patients and staff alike.

'Evenin', sister,' she said warmly. 'There's a lovely fish pie tonight, you'll enjoy that. And milk jelly for afters!'

'Lovely. I'm off duty in two hours, so I'll probably eat later,' Rachael said. 'Any chance of a cup of tea, Katie?'

''Course! Want to wait till the patients get theirs, or shall I bring you one up when I've handed these dinners out?'

'I'll have one when you bring the urn up for the patients,' Rachael said. 'How lovely, something to look forward to! And now

I must put my thinking cap on and dream up a sensible gift for Ernest Watts.'

'A new flannel; his looks like he's been a-cleaning that motorbike with it,' Katie said promptly. 'And a book on engines; talks of nothing else, young Ernest. Says when he gets out, he's joining t'air-force, seeing to all them airy-engines.'

'Kate, you're a genius!' Rachael said. 'Now why didn't I think of that? Bless you, you clever old thing!'

Katie, beaming, shuffled on up the corridor pushing her trolley and Rachael, having made a note to herself to buy the boy's flowers, put down her pen, yawned, stretched, and decided she would just nip back on to the ward for a moment to make sure that Nurse Brenner, a dedicated girl who got so involved with her work that she quite forgot mundane things like food, did not miss her supper break.

I'll take over for her if necessary, Rachael decided, rustling down the corridor. I keep meaning to tell Brenner that a rested and well fed nurse is a good nurse, but somehow there's never time!

She was back on the ward, walking down its length to where Nurse Brenner was helping her patient back into bed, when she remembered Amos Balonokov. He had been suffering from stomach ulcers and Mr Cargill had done a partial gastrectomy two days before. Rachael had been watching the patient closely since he had run a temperature the day following the operation and had been in a lot of pain, but today he seemed better, more collected, and earlier in the day had actually got out of bed and taken a few wobbly steps to his bedside chair and then gently, and with her assistance, walked around the bed itself. He had been cheerful, pleased to have pleased her, for as she had explained it was important that he walk to avoid a thrombosis forming, but he had fallen asleep as soon as he got back into bed and had slept deeply for several hours.

Now, she saw that he was awake though still drowsy. She smiled at him and went softly over to the bedside, automatically checking the saline drip to make sure it was running freely.

'Mr Balonokov? How do you feel?'

He was in his fifties, she supposed, with very thick white hair and a thin, intelligent face. His dark eyes were still pain-filled but they fixed on her face with humour in their depths.

'I feel like hell, sister,' he said hoarsely. 'What do you expect? Half my stomach's missing!' He ran a dry tongue over dry lips. 'Oh well, it could be worse, I suppose. Did Staff tell you I ate a spoonful of rice pudding at lunchtime?'

'Well done! And though half your stomach *is* missing, it was the ulcerated half,' Rachael said consolingly. 'Is your mouth dry? I can let you have a piece of ice to suck if that would help.'

His face lit up.

'Ice! That would be good, especially since I was only allowed a measly half-cup of tea. Many thanks, sister.'

'I'll fetch it right away,' Rachael was beginning, when she heard the sirens begin to wail. Oh damn, a raid, though it might well be that the aircraft were just passing overhead, on their way to some other target.

'What now?' Mr Balonokov said, grinning as she turned to glance towards the blacked-out windows. 'Shall I get under my bed?'

Rachael was smiling too, about to say he was in the safest place, when there was a peculiar whistling and then a very odd sort of sound, as though a giant fist had slammed down on to a large, hollow box. The reverberations went on for several seconds.

'What . . . ?' Rachael began, to find herself abruptly seized. Mr Balonokov, drip and all, was pushing her down on to all fours, pointing to the window, shouting something which she could not make out for the noise all about her.

'Get *down*, sister,' he was saying as she collapsed on to the shiny linoleum. 'Stay there!'

There was an earsplitting crash, and outside someone shone a light on the blacked out window. It was an odd reversal, to see the window illuminated from without, tiny lines of light appearing, for an instant, round the edges of the blinds.

It was a bomb, that sound had been a bomb exploding . . . and even as she realized it there was another of those whooshing *whump* sounds and the tall, narrow window just up the ward slowly, very slowly, began to collapse inwards. It bowed towards them, bulging like a huge stomach, and then the fragments of glass came darting down, each shard dagger-shaped and bright.

Without even having to think about it, Rachael knelt up and grabbed Mr Balonokov and in a violent, frantic movement, the two of them, clasped in each other's arms, slid under the bed. Mr Balonokov's drip-stand crashed over and the bottle bounced on the floor but did not shatter and Rachael leaned over and straightened out the tubing so that the saline would continue to flow. She reached for the bottle and stood it upright, then another crash had her shuddering back under the shelter of the bed.

'Are you all right, Mr Balonokov?' she said presently, when the roar of another bomb exploding, or a building collapsing, they could not tell which, had subsided. 'Am I squashing you?'

Rachael tried to move away from her patient but somehow it was impossible; what with the bed above and the drip-stand and their own closeness it was better just to lie there quietly and wait until the raid was over. The dim lights which illumined the ward had all gone out and only the vivid flashes which showed round the edges of the blinds relieved the darkness.

'No, you aren't squashing me; I feel quite comfortable, considering,' Mr Balonokov said. 'I suppose you couldn't get a blanket? There's a draught round my back where my pyjama jacket's come adrift.'

Rachael tried, but could not get the blanket off without disturbing the saline bottle, and this she was reluctant to do. It was more important that a partial gastrectomy should not dehydrate than that he should be kept warm. She said as much and then tried to tuck the pyjama jacket back into Mr Balonokov's trousers, which meant that she had to put both arms round him . . . and suddenly, without warning, a picture appeared in her mind.

The last time she had lain with a man in her arms, like this, she had given birth to Fenn! And the man had been Michael, her one and only lover.

She thought of Michael, so strong and handsome, with his appealing ways and teasing grin. And then she thought of poor Mr Balonokov, with the huge, unhealed scar from the gastrectomy, the drip attached to his arm, his dry mouth . . . and her hands fumbling with his pyjamas whilst they lay in each other's arms under a hospital bed and bombs rained down on the city.

It was absurd . . . trust Rachael Kitzmann to happen upon the absurd rather than the romantic! She began to giggle. She tried to stifle her laughter because Mr Balonokov would imagine himself stranded in the dark with a lunatic, but there was just no stopping it. How silly they must look . . . oh, poor Mr Balonokov. Of all the nurses to dive under the bed with him, it had to be Kitzmann, not pretty Nurse Brenner or sophisticated Nurse Adler but the plain, thirty-eight-year-old sister of Laski ward!

Mr Balonokov felt her shaking and he began to laugh as well.

'Oh, sister,' he gasped out at last. 'Laughing kills . . . it kills! But of all the things to happen! Many times I've wished to get you into my bed ever since I first noticed you at synagogue, looking so pretty in your blue coat and hat, but I never dreamed of getting you *under* the bed . . . and you're in my arms and laughing, thinking it all very amusing, when I would much rather you were serious, listening whilst I tell you how much I admire you, how much I want to get to know you as a person, not as my nurse!'

It stopped her in her tracks and it stopped the giggles, too. She knew in a moment that he was serious. He had watched her at synagogue and she had never even noticed him because she never noticed the men, never even glanced across at them, not since Michael.

'Sister? Are you offended? I'm sorry, I never would have said . . . far too much in awe of you, only somehow right now, when we're all in the same boat, could be dead any moment if a bomb has our name on it . . . sister?'

'I'm not offended,' Rachael said, very low. 'Indeed, I'm flattered that . . . that you noticed me. And I wasn't laughing at you, it was just so absurd, the pair of us under the bed . . .'

Another echoing whistle and thump announced the arrival of yet more bombs. With the glass gone the blast blew the blind straight out and for a moment Rachael could see the brilliant orange and gold light of what looked like a thousand fires, directly outside. She gave a little moan of distress and felt her patient's arms go round her again, and this time there was warmth and tenderness in the embrace and she cradled him too, murmuring words of comfort.

'Rachael? May I call you Rachael?' He must have felt her speechless nod, and a hand came up and caressed her cheek. 'Good, that is good. When this is over, Rachael, if we both survive, I shall ask something of you. You won't mind?'

Rachael sighed deeply, and, very gently, stroked down his back.

'No, Amos, I shan't mind,' she whispered.

A month after the big raid on the city, Amos Balonokov and Rachael Kitzmann walked up Elizabeth Street and turned down Waterloo Road. Ahead of them was the school where, long ago, Fenn and his cousin Saul had been pupils, and Rachael's heart began to beat harder. She could see the Belstrode Street turning ahead – any minute now!

A lot has happened in this last month, Rachael thought as they walked, hand in hand, past the recreation ground where Fenn and Cecil had played on the weary, dog-abused grass. Since the memorable night of the city's first raid she and Amos had fallen in love, he had asked her to marry him, and she had agreed to do so. Amos was fifty-one to her thirty-eight, but he had been widowed many years ago and had never, until now, met a woman he liked enough to contemplate spending the rest of his life with.

And he thought Rachael very beautiful. It seemed that he loved everything about her, her gleaming cap of dark hair, her creamy complexion, her big dark eyes. Even her figure, too cushiony to be fashionable, seemed to meet with his approval. 'I like a woman with big breasts and a proper bum,' he had said last night as they cuddled on the sofa in her rented room. The nurses' home had been flattened and all the nurses had hastily found themselves alternative accommodation. 'I like a *womanly* woman, my dearest girl.'

She had told him everything, of course. All about Michael and Fenn, all about her grandfather and Uncle Joseph and Fenn's flight. And oddly enough, as though to reward her for her honesty, a week ago she had received a letter from Fenn, with a return address.

Her boy was a flyer in the United States Army Air Force! He was proud of himself, anxious to explain what had happened to him, why he had only sent postcards before, and those to the Finagler family.

She had been so eager to write back and tell him her wonderful news that she had not paused to think what effect it might have on him, to hear that his mother was marrying and would soon be Mrs Amos Balonokov. But Amos had assured her that a young man who had fled almost ten years ago was unlikely to suffer pangs of jealousy – he could have come home any time, he reminded her, and now that he was settled enough to write no more misunderstandings should arise.

Amos was so sensible! And so handsome, and so loving! She could hardly wait to marry him. She had tried to give in her notice at work, but since they were lamentably short of competent staff they had asked her to stay on.

So now she had taken her courage in both hands and they were going round to see Joseph to tell him of her changed circumstances. Her uncle and his father went to a different synagogue, lived different lives, and until now she had never tried to get in touch. She had passed the time of day with Anna and with her girl-cousins, but had no desire to get back on to any sort of terms with the Kitzmann males.

Now, though, she was so happy that it seemed foolish to bear a grudge. Better go round there, tell them she was to be married, invite them to Shul for the wedding, and suggest that bygones be bygones. Amos agreed so here they were, on this quiet Sunday morning, turning into Belstrode Street, the place where she and Fenn had known much unhappiness to be sure but, occasionally, bouts of real fondness for one another, a fellow-feeling in adversity similar to that spirit which pervaded air-raid shelters during an enemy attack. She could almost see Fenn, whistling down the pavement towards her, turning into the back alley with its grassy brickwork, bulging, rundown walls and lopsided wooden doors. Unconsciously she clutched Amos's arm harder; not only Fenn was a ghost here, but Gamps, also. The dark eyes which lit with pride whenever his gaze fell on either her or Fenn, the strong hand holding hers when things had been hard, his humour, the depth of his understanding when she had had to tell him she was expecting a baby and her lover was long gone.

That brought back Michael, of course, another ghost in this street. The laughing face above her own, the deep blue of his eyes, the touch of his hands . . .

Guilt would have banished the picture quickly enough, but something else was quicker. Shock. They could see the whole street now, the neat houses, the whitened steps, the variety of doorknockers, some polished until they looked like new-minted gold, others allowed to dull into obscurity. Rachael recognized the bit of pavement outside No. 12 which was always scrubbed by the woman of the house when she scrubbed her steps and so looked unnaturally new and clean. She remembered the aspidistra in the window of No. 14 and the pink net curtains in No. 16, which made the place look, according to Great-Grandpa, like a house of ill-repute, though God knew Mrs Abraams, poor soul, was eighty if she was a day and lame in one leg. That hadn't stopped Great-Grandpa talking about her, though. If anything it made him worse, knowing that Mrs Abraams was alone all day once her daughter had married and moved away. He had grumbled, Rachael remembered, at every mortal thing the poor old lady did – how she must have hated him!

It was odd how, at times of crisis, you remembered the little things. The feud between Mrs Abraams and old Mr Kitzmann had been a one-sided affair but Great-Grandpa had attacked her with zest, putting out stories of what he had to put up with, the noise she was supposed to create by playing her wireless at top register, the dust which landed on his steps because of her incessant brushing of hers. And now there was No. 16, still with the pink net at the windows, though you could see dust thick on the window panes and on the three once-white steps. And No. 18? No. 18 where she and Fenn had suffered and gone without and been derided? But where they had laughed, sometimes, stuffing the pillow into their mouths at night to muffle the sound, nudging each other like children, sharing the odd treat, the odd grumble?

No. 18 wasn't there. It was strangely neat, too. Just a pile of bricks and beams and odds and ends of furniture which, had Rachael examined them closely, she would undoubtedly have recognized, having polished them for so long.

Amos put his arm round her. They walked very slowly up to No. 16 and then lingered to stare at what had once been her home. At first glance it had seemed as though No. 18 had just fallen down somehow, but now they were closer they could see the great crater into which most of the house had collapsed. Rachael found that she was shivering, her teeth chattering like castanets. Why should this be? She had been all but killed in her own hospital a month before but she hadn't felt like this. She turned her head into Amos's shoulder, shuddering uncontrollably.

'What is it?' she muttered. 'Oh my love, what's the matter with me? I'm going to faint . . . I feel so funny, so very odd!'

'Shock,' Amos said briefly. 'Come away. We'll go to the nearest . . .'

The door of No. 16 creaked open. Mrs Abraams stood there, a broom in her hand. She looked down at her step, tutting at the coating of red-brown brick dust liberally speckled with soot. When Amos moved she looked up but did not at once recognize Rachael.

'Vat a mess, vat a mess,' she said fussily, beginning to sweep. 'Not only is dere bengs unt danger most dretful, but dirt also, vich I must sveep before I cen set foot outside my own door.'

Rachael tried to speak.

'C-can you tell us wha-wha-wha . . . ?'

'What happened to the Kitzmanns?' Amos said baldly. 'Were they at home?'

The old lady stopped brushing for a moment.

'A bomb heppened, that's vat heppened. Anna unt her boy vere in the country somevere, but the old feller and Joseph Kitzmann bought it.' She chucked wheezily, beginning to brush once more. 'My son, he's in the plane-flyink game and that's vat he says – they've bought it!' She peered at them curiously. 'Ain't you the Kitzmann girl, the one they treated bad? Well, they treated me bad too, *faygeler*, and two nights ago they're gone, pouf, wit' the only bomb on the street, and I shed no tears. I'm no hypocrit.' She brought out the big word triumphantly, then her brush began on the second step, filling the air with dust. 'Anna, she's not so bed, a good enough voman, but the boy – ay-yi-yi, vot a no-goodnik! Does he fight for his country? Does he hell! Gets himself into a reserved occupation . . . made sure he'd see it out, vun vay or anodder.'

171

'Thank you,' Amos said courteously, seeing that Rachael was still too overcome to speak. 'Where is Anna, did you say?'

Mrs Abraams shrugged, swept the second step clear and was about to start on the bottom one when she suddenly seemed to think of something.

'They vas bad to you, too . . . but you've come to see, eh?' she said, half to herself. 'Vell, there's an address somevere . . . wait!'

She was gone no more than two minutes and came back with a pair of tiny pince-nez glasses perched on her sizeable nose and a card in her hand.

'Here ve are! Sent me a card saying they vas settled in,' she announced. She peered, then gave a little exclamation of disgust and held the card out to Rachael.

'My eyes ain't vot they vere,' she admitted. 'Go on, read . . . the postman probably did!'

Rachael read the card aloud.

'We are living in a nice house just outside the town, address as under,' the card said in Anna's small, cramped hand. 'Saul goes off to work each day and I keep house for him – quite like old times. Hope you are well; Joseph will keep an eye on you. All the best, Anna.' And then, below that, in even more cramped writing, 'No. 22, Church Lane, Rhostyllen, Denbighshire.'

'Denbighshire's in Wales,' Amos said thoughtfully. 'What sort of work's he doing, Mrs Abraams?'

Mrs Abraams gave a chuckle.

'Vell now, this is rich! Little Saul, the apple of their eye, is down a coalmine! Won't fight, so they said he must dig for coal . . . heh, heh, heh!'

'And that'll be why Anna went with him and Joseph wouldn't,' Amos said thoughtfully, as they made their way back down the street after thanking Mrs Abraams for her help. 'I dare say they might have expected Joseph to work if he'd gone there – they say they've called back quite elderly miners to work the pits for coal. Well, I wonder how Saul likes that? Some might think he'd be better off in the forces.'

'I shouldn't think he likes it at all, since he was very work-shy as a boy,' Rachael said thoughtfully. She was still shivering but the awful shudders of shock were subsiding. 'I'll write to Anna; perhaps she'll come back for our wedding, but I doubt it. What does it matter, after all? It's us that matter, Amos, and we'll be there. Let's go home.'

The short winter afternoon was already fading into evening. Street lamps could not be lit, curtains had to be kept securely drawn so as not to breach the black-out, but the sky above their heads was pricked with stars.

12

1941

'Well, who'd have thought it?' Chris surveyed the emptiness of the enormous ploughed field spread out before her with distaste. 'All that training, gal-Sybil, all those lovely hopes, and what's come of it?'

'Adolf-bloody-Hitler's come of it,' Sybil said ruefully. 'You have to laugh, though, Chris. There was me, wanting to better myself, thinking I could work hard and have a good life using my brains and sitting on a chair all day telling other people what to do, and now look at us!'

'The Land Army's grand in some ways, though,' Chris observed. The two girls had gone through a year at teacher training college together, had emerged, had actually got themselves jobs – Sybil at a big primary school in Norwich, Chris at a boarding school just outside Ipswich, and then Hitler had invaded Poland.

For the first few weeks they had stayed where they were, enjoying their first taste of teaching combined as it was with fire practice, rushes to the shelter, gas-mask drill and helping to cope with evacuees, but they knew it couldn't last, and soon enough they had been given a choice of war work. They had both opted for the Women's Land Army, whilst older and less fit women took over their classes.

'Come along then, gals, let's be havin' you!'

Mr Franklyn wasn't a bad boss, but you couldn't just stand in the lightly falling drizzle and admire the clean land. They were here to plant sprouts and sprouts they must plant. Sighing, Chris pushed her sou'wester off her eyes and opened the gate. She led the way into the field and on to the soggy earth.

'Right; where are the plants? Let's see who can get the most in before the rain really starts!'

Sybil and the half-dozen or so other girls stooped to their work. Ahead of them, Chris began to shuffle along the row, setting out the tiny plantlets with the neat, methodical movements which typified her work. Following suit, Sybil thought ruefully of what Lizzie had said when she had been forced to leave her comfortable position in the gowns department and do war work.

'Be a *landgirl*?' she had exclaimed incredulously. 'Have you seen the uniform?'

It was not flattering, though the girls did not wear their brown jodhpurs and green jerseys to work in, nor the brown leather boots and gaiters or the wide, floppy hats. In the fields they wore brown overalls and gum boots, with an oilskin and sou'wester on a day like today, though they sweated under the oilskin and got almost as wet as though they had been standing out in the pouring rain.

But Lizzie had opted for war work in a factory – making wireless parts on a long bench in the warm, with no uniform to worry about and no farmer at her heels, she said, though she moaned about canteen meals and had a female supervisor who hated her.

Lizzie lived in Norwich still, in her little flat, but Sybil and Chris lived at home in Pakeby. Malverns had been closed down, the garden allowed to go wild, the drive which had once been so neatly gravelled all but invisible beneath a carpet of weeds, but the Creams' cottage had Lizzie's share of the bed going spare, and with Henry away most of the time, his boss's trawler having been converted into a minesweeper, Dora was glad of their company as well as their ration books.

And although the landgirls grumbled, for they came from all walks of life, had had all sorts of different occupations in peacetime, Sybil thought that they had a pretty good time of it really. It was the hardest work most of them had ever done, but there was satisfaction in it. She and Chris could both drive and maintain a tractor, plough a field, lay a hedge and, in theory only so far, cope with gassed or shell-shocked farm stock. Mr Franklyn had taught them both to drive his old truck so that they could take stock to market, and they had the satisfaction of knowing they were helping to feed Britain at a time when food was woefully short.

In fact, I ploughed this field five months ago, then Chris harrowed it, Sybil remembered. She stuck her dibbler into the sticky soil and inserted another plantlet, filled in the hole, firmed the soil down. As they worked she thought back to last year.

She and Chris had been harvesting whilst the Battle of Britain raged overhead. At one point, with spent shells splattering around them like hail, they had considered running for the shelter of the hedge, but there had been no point in it really. The planes above were far too busy with their own affairs to worry about girls cutting corn, so they had continued with their work, both all too aware that one of the Spitfires angling across the wide blue sky might easily be Ralph's.

They did not see much of Ralph now, though. He had been sent to East Africa just before Christmas 1940 and had not been home since, though Chris had said that his secondment might well be finishing soon.

The friendship between Ralph and Sybil, therefore, which had seemed to flower at the bonfire party, had never come to anything. Ralph had not returned to Malverns for the summer holidays again and though Sybil heard about his doings from Chris, even hero-worship such as hers needed more than that to feed it. Now Ralph was just someone she hoped to catch up with one day and not the close friend she had once thought he might become.

As for Lizzie – well, Lizzie came home to Pakeby now and then, but never for long, and somehow the sisters' early friendship had not survived their enforced separation. It was odd, Sybil thought, trying to forget that her feet were rapidly becoming as numbed with cold as her hands, how she and Chris had remained the best of friends despite separation, yet she and Lizzie had let it change their relationship. But Lizzie was such a sophisticated young lady – even when Sybil had been in Norwich, at the teacher training college, Lizzie had tended to avoid her. Sad, but just one of those things, Sybil supposed philosophically, reaching the next little bundle of plantlets which Mr Franklyn, on the tractor, had dropped earlier in the day. She picked them up and continued, doggedly, to plant.

'Well, girls? Have a good day? I suppose you were working indoors on a day like this,' Dora said cheerfully when the two girls came in, having dumped their bikes in the shed where Beattie still lived. 'You must be hungry – macaroni cheese and jacket spuds tonight.'

'Wonderful. And we weren't indoors, we've spent the day planting out sprouts and getting rheumatism,' Chris said bitterly, heading for the sink. 'Oh, bless you, Auntie Dora, hot water!'

'Well, I did wonder if you'd be out,' Dora admitted, as Sybil followed Chris, padding across the floor in her green ribbed socks. Both girls shed boots and oilskins outside the back door, then left them for Dora to deal with which she did by rinsing them in the sink and standing them, clean, by the stove to dry. 'Never mind, only another week and you'll be living it up in Norwich, or London . . . have you decided which, yet?'

'No, not yet. London's still being bombed quite heavily, though, so we might opt for Norwich.' Chris had stripped down to vest and knickers and now began to wash, a sudsy, splashy business which she seemed to enjoy.

'My turn,' Sybil said as Chris began to dry herself on the rough khaki towel which hung behind the kitchen door. The girls had been issued with two each when they entered the Land Army and Dora had quickly taken them into general use. 'What'll we do after supper, Chris? Want to go into Lowestoft for a flick?'

The port town had been badly bombed the previous year, and only a couple of months previously a single raider had dropped twenty bombs in an attempt to put the swing bridge out of action. Ten people had been killed and a great many injured, the bridge house had been destroyed and a good deal of damage done to surrounding houses, but the bridge was still usable if it was opened by hand, a slow process which meant long vehicle queues.

'No-oo, I don't think so,' Chris said, finishing with the towel and hanging it across the clothes horse which Dora had stood ready by the stove. 'After a day like today I really just want to sit and let my dinner go down, listen to the light programme on the radio and then go to bed early. Besides, remember last time we went to the flicks?'

Sybil laughed.

'The siren went three times,' she said. 'And we'd paid our money for nothing anyway, because the film kept breaking down. No, let's not bother. After all, next week we'll have a much wider choice of entertainment . . . we might even meet some nice fellers who'll take us dancing!'

'Fellers' were in short supply, though when the fleet came in Lowestoft was full of sailors, and there were airmen about too from time to time. But somehow Chris and Sybil were always too tired or too busy to find themselves permanent boyfriends, though they had been out with one or two.

'Blow fellers,' Chris said, heading for the stove. 'Shall I dish up, Auntie Dora?'

'What, in your knickers? Certainly not. Go and get yourself respectable and by the time you're ready so will the meal be,' Dora said. 'Hurry up, Sybs, you must be clean by now!'

Whilst the girls changed upstairs, Dora hurried round the kitchen, getting the table laid and the meal set out. She considered herself a lucky woman, for although her son was at sea on a frigate, Henry usually managed at least a couple of nights ashore every month or so and his mere presence was a comfort in the small house so perilously close to the sea. Not that the sea worried her; it was the aircraft, swooping low across it, coming to bomb and strafe, which Dora found unsettling. They came in low and fast and twice she had been machine-gunned whilst down on the beach, trying to pull in the heavy longshore net she and Henry put out when he was home.

It was a sort of keep-net really, since Henry fixed it in a half-circle and left her to harvest whatever swam into it, and a motley collection it was, sometimes. But it did not help when some sadistic young German pilot returning from a daylight raid thought it might be fun to machine-gun the shoreline.

But that hadn't happened lately and Dora was beginning to hope that this year would be a quieter one than last. After all, Russia was stirring; the Nazis would have to deal with Russia sooner or later.

The girls clattering down the stairs put an end to her musings. She began to serve the macaroni cheese and watched with pleasure as the girls helped themselves to potatoes and poured tea.

'Are you all right for spuds, Mum?' Sybil asked presently. 'These seem okay but there are a lot of bad ones about at this end of the season. Mr Franklyn's opened a clamp, though, and he says they've kept wonderfully well, considering.'

'I'm all right for a bit,' Dora said, passing the salt. 'When I begin to run short I'll let you know.'

They settled to their meal.

They went to bed early as they had planned, which was a good thing, as it turned out. At ten o'clock the sirens sounded in the port and the raiders swept in. Dora scrambled out of bed, threw on her coat and met the girls on the tiny half-landing.

'Better get down into the kitchen,' she said breathlessly. 'This sounds like a big 'un, but maybe they're all heading through.'

Even as she spoke the *crump* of an explosion proved this to be a vain hope, and the three of them scurried down the stairs and made for the kitchen. There was a Morrison shelter in the front room but no stove to keep them warm, so usually they sat under the kitchen table, pulled as near the stove as they could get it, and waited there for the all-clear to sound.

'We'd best get into the Morrison,' Dora said presently. The noises from outside were far too loud for comfort and through the uncurtained kitchen window they could see incendiaries dropping – lights to guide the following wave of bombers to the port. And when they reached the front room they knew at once that something had happened outside. The window was lit by an eerie glow.

'It's the thatch – the church thatch!' Dora gasped. 'Come on!'

They ran outside and saw for themselves the terrible destruction. Dora was right; the church roof was ablaze and already villagers were doing what they could, though it was a hopeless task. Even as the rector scrambled up a ladder and on to the roof more planes came over and more bombs were dropped, the explosions shaking the very ground on which the three women stood.

'Boots!' Sybil said briskly. 'We can get nearer in boots.'

They were all barefoot, Dora realized, but very soon, gum-booted and coated, they were struggling with everyone else to salvage what furniture they could from the doomed building.

As she carted water, Dora remembered that only the previous day she and the girls had worshipped here. And she only had to walk into the church to think at once of Henry, since so many of his stories were connected with it. He was fond of telling the children that it had been a sanctuary church, which was why the south door could be closed by dropping a great oaken bar across it – no fumbling with bolts or keys for the desperate fugitive from pursuit.

Later, as she shaded her face from the heat and pressed nearer to take the various objects being handed out by the fire-fighters, she saw the great painted east window and wondered painfully whether future generations would be told its story, as Henry had told it to the small Georgie, Lizzie and Sybil. As yet it seemed unaffected by the heat, which made Dora smile involuntarily, for as Henry told it the vicar at the time, a Welshman of the fire and brimstone school, was popular with some and much disliked by others, even, according to Henry, to the extent of his parishioners placing a guy on their bonfire which bore a marked resemblance to him. And as if the slight had given him the idea, the vicar then had the east window painted in honour of his ministry, ordering the artist to use his own face as a model for the figure of our Lord.

'Every time you look at our Lord in that there winder, you're looking at a likeness of that wicar,' Henry was prone to announce – and then shushed the children vigorously during services when they stared at the window and whispered.

She saw the flames through the pink and green window-glass, orange, brilliant yellow, fierce and blue; then the glass bowed out and out, there was a minor explosion, and the window-frame gaped empty.

The Fire Service poured gallons of water on to the thatch in vain, though by the time it collapsed most of the movable furniture and fittings had been brought out and taken to the nearest barn with a good roof.

Before dawn the raid petered out, thanks to a thick fog which rolled inland from the cold North Sea and completely hid the coastline from enemy bombers, and by breakfast time the fire was out, though it had not left much behind.

'There's no glass in our windows,' Dora said. 'And no paint at all on the window frames and the front door.'

But she stated it as a fact, not as a grumble. They had been lucky once again. With bombs dropping so close and the church destroyed it was little short of a miracle that the three cottages still stood.

The girls even went off to work as usual, though they were yawning and knuckling their eyes and Sybil declared that it would be another miracle if she didn't fall asleep on the way to Irewood and crash her bike. The bike was Georgie's and most uncomfortable, as Sybil had lost no time in telling Dora after her first five-mile ride to the farm.

'Mum, I didn't know boys were *that* different from girls,' she said. 'I mean, why should Georgie's bum and . . . and things . . . be comfortable on this saddle, which is like a bacon slicer on mine?'

The bike was a racing model and had been Georgie's pride and joy, but Dora had told Sybil that her brother was saving up for a motorbike – might even have bought one by now – and wouldn't want the bike when he came home, so she might as well sell it and buy herself a lady's model. This Sybil had refused to do until she had spoken to Georgie himself. Now she looked at Dora and raised her eyebrows enquiringly.

'Do you mean why do they *say* those saddles are comfy? I suspect it's to make us feel soft,' Dora observed. 'Your father was just the same. He rode round the yard when Georgie first got the bike and never said a word, just helped me on and grinned when I hopped off quick. It's all an act, I dare say.'

Now, seeing Sybil perched uncomfortably on the bicycle as the two girls cycled off, Dora thought of something.

'Sybs! If you go to Norwich, buy another saddle and swop them over, just whilst you're using the bike,' she called. 'Then if Georgie does want it later, he can simply change the saddles back again.'

'I might,' Sybil called back over her shoulder, wobbling down the road in Chris's wake. 'See you tonight, Mum!'

*   *   *

'Is this to your liking, darling Lizzie?'

Lizzie, lying in the big double bed, luxuriously cuddled beneath a cream-coloured silk counterpane, smiled down at the breakfast on the tray which Emil had just placed tenderly across her knees. A glass of orange juice, half a grapefruit, a small jug of coffee and two rounds of crisp buttered toast were carefully placed upon it, and a nice touch – a small crystal vase holding a spray of wallflowers – completed the picture. Lizzie blew a kiss to the tall young man bending deferentially over her.

'Emil, you're a marvel,' she declared. 'How glad I am that I'm not quite well this morning!'

Lizzie was an extremely well paid munitions worker at the moment, though she was going to have a nasty cold today to account for her absence. After all, Emil was fighting for freedom and he had five days off; who was she to deny him the pleasure of her company on his brief leave? So work could go hang today, then it was the weekend, and he'd have to amuse himself on Monday.

Emil smiled his slow, charming smile, and slipped into bed beside her. He got in very carefully but even so the orange juice tipped a little and Lizzie grabbed it and hastily drank down a couple of inches before wiping her mouth and starting on the grapefruit.

'Where do you get these lovely things, darling?' she chirruped. 'Go on, keep me company – have some toast and coffee.'

Emil took a piece of toast and began to eat but just as he turned to pour the coffee they both heard a clatter at the door.

'Oh, that's the post,' Lizzie said with a lift of the heart. 'Do be a pet and fetch it through, Emil!'

She always hoped for a letter from Ralph, for though she might share her bed with other men from time to time Ralph was her real, her only love. If he could have been with her . . . but he had been posted abroad after the Battle of Britain and she had not seen him for six months; too long for anyone of Lizzie's disposition to remain alone.

But she wrote to Ralph quite often and he wrote back and she adored his letters. They made him seem so near, as though it was possible that he might soon come home – and if he did, that would mean goodbye to Emil and all the others and she would not care one jot, not one scrap, if only she could be with Ralph.

Ralph had helped her to choose this flat, but he had not seen it in its newly decorated state. Lizzie looked fondly round the room whilst the obedient Emil padded out of the door and down the stairs to pick up the post. The flat was beautifully furnished, with some nice old stuff she had picked up cheap from the salerooms, though the carpet on the floor was almost new and had cost more than she liked to contemplate. That was another good reason for having men friends – they showed their appreciation quite often by little gifts . . . sometimes quite big gifts, depending of course on their circumstances. She had decorated the room herself, with help from various friends, and now it was just as she liked it, especially first thing on a Friday morning when she had decided to have a diplomatic cold, and the sun was kind enough to shine.

Emil came back into the room. The flat had two rooms and a shared bathroom, though because of restrictions a weekly bath with a measly five inches of water was the rule. That was another good reason for having a friend in – she and Emil had shared a bath last night, and it had been the greatest fun. She had felt quite justified both in filling the bath twice as full as she ought and in topping up with hot from time to time. After all, the geyser worked on a penny-in-the-slot system and Emil was quite happy to part with a great many pennies in order to be able to frolic in hot water with his little Lizzie!

'There are two letters for you, Lizzie,' he said in his careful, stilted English. 'One is in a blue envelope and comes from overseas, I think, and the other is in a white envelope and comes from your home. Would you like to read them now, whilst I shave?'

Dear Emil, he was so tactful, so understanding! He knew nothing about Ralph, of course, but he appreciated that one's letters were one's private business.

'Thank you, that would be nice,' Lizzie murmured. She waited until he had gone down the short corridor to the bathroom – everyone else would have left for work so they had it to themselves today – and then opened the white envelope first, because the blue one was from Ralph, and should be savoured. The letter was from Sybil. Lizzie scanned it briefly, frowned, then put the single sheet back into its envelope.

Sybil and Chris were coming to stay with the Wintertons for a few days and would probably pop in to see Lizzie at the flat some time. Lizzie knew about the attack on the church and assumed, rather unkindly, that the girls were escaping from the resultant mess. It was a nuisance because Sybil might see Emil, but she would just have to accept the fact that Lizzie had boyfriends, Lizzie decided crossly. She did not intend to let either Chris or Sybil suspect that Emil was anything more than a boyfriend, and a fairly casual one at that; she had no intention of her behaviour getting back, by some roundabout route, to Ralph. Sybil was all right, a nice kid really, but she knew nothing about life, or men. A landgirl! Lizzie thought with affectionate contempt. Working the most God-awful hours in God-awful conditions, wearing horrible clothes and being fed on potatoes and bread so your bum spread and your belly stuck out . . . and all for twenty-two and six a week, whereas Lizzie was paid three pounds fifteen shillings a week and more than four pounds when she did overtime.

Hers was pretty distasteful work, though. When she entered the factory she had to change into rubber-soled shoes, a fire-proof suit and a turban, and smother her face and hands in a special cream which stopped her skin from absorbing the materials with which she worked. All her own personal belongings, down to a box of matches or a nail file, were taken away from her, and she was only allowed to claim them back as she left the factory. This would have mattered to Lizzie had she been on public view, like Sybil and Chris, but in the confines of the factory, where everyone was dressed alike and no unauthorized person was allowed to enter, it did not matter so much.

But the money was good and the work, though you had to be careful, not onerous. Besides, Lizzie had done various jobs since she left school, and knew she could change again whenever she wanted. That was one thing: there was plenty of work now, with the war on; it was very different from when she had first joined Curls and had known herself to be very lucky just to have a job, let alone such a desirable one.

So Sybil and Chris were coming to stay in the city. All right, then. Lizzie put down the letter and picked up the blue airmail one, and immediately her heart began to pound. It was from Ralph, of course.

She opened it and read it avidly, seeing his face as she read, hearing his voice.

Darling Lizzie, it's damnably hot today and I'm not flying for once, so I'm lying beneath the shade of a jacaranda tree, thinking about you and wishing, desperately wishing, that I could grab you in my arms and cuddle you all up and take a great big bite out of my lovely peach of a sweetie.

There was a lot more, mostly in the same vein. Lizzie read the letter twice, then slid it into her bedside drawer. Not a word about coming home – he was 'somewhere in Africa' as they said – but you never knew. Pilots were desperately wanted here and he was only abroad on a tour of duty, though she had no idea how long an average tour lasted. She closed her eyes and prayed for Ralph, for his safety, comfort, and eventual return. Then she sat up in bed, pushed the tray out of harm's way and swung her legs on to the floor.

The sunny day waited, and she might as well make the best of it, for on Monday she would have to go back to work or there would be too many questions asked for comfort.

Lizzie reached for her cloudy negligee – a present from an American officer serving in some capacity in London – and entered the bathroom as a freshly shaved Emil left it. Bathsalts today, provided by Emil, and scented soap! Life, Lizzie concluded, as she sneakily ran herself a bath, is not all bad, even with Ralph away.

Sybil and Chris sat side by side on the top deck of the bus and watched the April countryside unfurl beneath them like a roll of delicately coloured silk. The trees in the woods hung out their catkins, the pussy willows were surrounded by a halo of yellow pollen, the very grass of the verges was a brighter, more hopeful green as though it, too, knew that spring had arrived at last.

The damage done to the church had been terrible, but one consequence of the destruction had been good. Mr Franklyn had offered to let the two girls go off a couple of days early for their leave.

'You were up all night trying to put fires out,' he said gruffly. 'Since then you've worked for me all day and gone home at night to a home with no glass in the windows and all the paintwork burned off, and you've been slaving like a couple of right'uns to get that put right. Well now, I don't want a pair of nervous wrecks on my hands, so go you off and get yourselves a bit of fun for a change.'

So now here they were, on the top deck of the bus, joggling towards the city. All Chris's best clothes were at home in St Giles but Sybil had a little case with clean undies and a dance frock in it and a bag bulging with food – two jars of potted shrimps, half-a-dozen brown eggs and a big piece of bacon – which was just about the best way you could pay someone back when you stayed with them. The Wintertons, Dora knew, did not keep hens in the heart of the city, nor did they have a fattener in a pen down the garden. Lately the Creams had taken to keeping geese on the beach and sandhills as well, and sometimes Dora, Sybil and Chris shared one of the huge, pale eggs, scrambling it and piling it on toast or making a vast omelette and filling it with wild mushrooms.

But you didn't give city folk goose-eggs because they wouldn't know what to do with 'em, Dora had decreed. And it wasn't the right time of year for mushrooms. So that left a nice chunk of poor Pig, a trusting creature with blond eyelashes and an appealing appetite, who had led a pampered – if short – life in the sty at the back of the shed and provided the Creams with their only real luxury: bacon, hams and various other piggy treats.

The shrimps will be a taste of old times, Sybil told herself as the bus slowed on the outskirts of the city. All the Wintertons loved sea-food, but although Chris still had plenty the rest of the family didn't get much now the house at Pakeby was closed.

Roll on the end of the war, people said hopefully. The Wintertons had been a rich source of income and a never-ending source of hand-outs, too, for never a gooseberry ripened on the Malverns bushes but the villagers were offered a share, never a hayfield was cut but their livestock, as well as the Winterton ponies, benefited.

Strange that now it's us who can give bits and bobs of food, Sybil thought cheerfully, eyeing her laden basket. How nice to be able to be a giver instead of a perpetual taker for a change! And despite working on the land all day, she and Chris helped Dora with the allotment too, so the vegetables she carried were just as much from them, really, as from Dora.

The bus drew up in Castle Meadow and Sybil and Chris got down. Sybil felt, proudly, that she knew the drill now as well as Chris – cross to the number eighty-nine stop and climb aboard the next one to arrive – but she was scarcely on the pavement before someone seized her suitcase and then turned to plonk a kiss on Chris's cheek.

'Hello, girls – lovely to see you. Mummy asked me to meet the bus so here I am, though you look quite capable of carrying your own bags, you great Land Army lasses, you! Well? Don't overwhelm me with your joy at seeing me back again – you can't have forgotten me, Chris! As for you, Sybs . . . my oh my, well indeedy!'

Sybil stared up at the young man holding her case and Chris's bag as though they weighed no more than a feather. He seemed, at first glance, to have nothing of the boy she had once known about him. It was a couple of years since she had seen him and in that time he had changed, seemed almost to have aged. His hair was still fair though it had darkened a good deal, the guileless blue eyes were more grey now and there was a detached look in them, almost a coldness. He had always been tall but he had not towered over her then, his shoulders had not been so broad nor his mouth so tightly set . . . nor had he developed lines of strain across his brow and beside his mouth which made his expression seem wary, guarded.

'Ralph! Well, I wouldn't have known you!'

He grinned. The guarded look fled whilst the smile lasted, then returned as it faded.

'Nor me you – you're a smasher, that's what you are! What I've been missing since that midsummer party – how could I have wasted my chances! My goodness, if I'd known you'd grow into a beauty I'd have come straight over to Pakeby and claimed you for my very own, instead of wasting my youth on inferior wenches!'

Sybil smiled too, feeling her cheeks burn; they had never had a chance to regain the easy comradeship of the early days at Pakeby but now, suddenly, she was glad of it. Her mirror told her that she had improved but now Ralph's eyes were telling her how much – a lot more than I would have believed, she thought, dazed. But she still retained enough common sense to answer him lightly, with a teasing smile.

'Nice of you to say so, Ralph, but you weren't around much, were you, after that party? We missed both you and Chris, but I dare say you had other fish to fry.'

'No, I wasn't around at all, in fact.' A curious smile, reminiscent, wicked, flickered across his face, even warmed those oddly cool eyes for a moment. 'I wasn't allowed. And then I was at university, working, and then the war came ... but I thought about Pakeby a lot. I always meant to come back and renew acquaintance, so to speak, only somehow I was always too busy. Then when you came out of teacher training Hitler interfered and since then my posting spoiled my chances.'

'It's nice of you to say so,' Sybil said, her tone polite but unbelieving. 'Now, are we going to walk, or shall we get the bus?'

'We'll walk,' Chris said. She linked arms with Sybil. 'Unless the bus journey has tired you so much, you poor thing, that you've no energy left?'

'It was very restful,' Sybil said primly, but with thumping heart. Five minutes ago she would have said she was over her childish pash on Ralph, as over as a girl could be, but now he had linked arms with her as his sister had, and how disturbing and delightful it was to have his arm in hers, the warmth of his body against her side! 'We're both used to working and cycling so hard that a bus journey is a real treat!' She turned to Ralph, trying to keep her voice friendly yet cool. 'How long are you home for, Ralph?'

'Five days, then I have to report to my airfield and meet up with my old buddies and a good few new ones. I was there before being seconded abroad, so it isn't exactly strange to me. I've got a share in a car and since I haven't taken my turn at it for six months I've got it for the duration of my leave, so we might go out for a run later in the week.' He leaned round Sybil and spoke directly to his sister. 'I came home with Toddy, if you're interested.'

Chris shrugged and tried to look indifferent but Sybil had seen the flush slowly rising to her cheeks.

'Oh, Sybil and I will make up a foursome, if that's what you mean. We intend to enjoy ourselves, this week.'

'Fine. We can go out daytimes, though in the evenings . . . But we'll cross that bridge when we come to it. I think I'm going to be busy over the weekend but we can go out on Monday. It's a bit early for picnics on the beach and anyway it's a bit coals to Newcastle for you, Sybs, but we could go off somewhere in the car, just the four of us.'

'I'd like that,' Sybil said cautiously. 'If Chris would.'

Chris said that was fine by her and Sybil looked around her as they walked, commenting on the warmth of the afternoon and the number of daffodils for sale on the market. But inside, very slowly, like a damped down fire which suddenly begins to break through, excitement was building. She was suddenly wise in a way she had never been before – she, who had never kissed any young man other than Ralph, let alone done anything more intimate. What had happened to her at the midsummer party had been new and strange to her. She had thought in her innocence that Ralph was just being rather over-polite, yet now she knew Ralph was making a play for her. He kept squeezing her arm and looking down at her, his eyes bright. His glance was affectionate and hopeful – no one had ever looked at her quite like that before, so she should have been at a loss to interpret his meaning, but she found, suddenly, a knowledge within her as deep and primitive as Eve's.

He liked her. He was interested in her. In short, he wanted her, though precisely what she meant by that phrase she could not have explained. But it was exciting, a bit frightening, it made her heart beat fast and her pulses race. It turned her all in a moment, with only the look in his eye and the pressure of his arm to go by, into someone who was serenely certain that she was not an ugly, scraggy little thing any longer. She was a desirable woman. And she, heaven help her, wanted Ralph, had wanted him without knowing it since that evening long ago when they had sat together on the beach, in the dark, and she had let him stroke her leg and tentatively fumble at her tiny breasts.

'Penny for your thoughts, Sybs.'

Ralph's deep tones sent a thrill right through Sybil, but she was older and wiser now than she had been ten minutes ago. Don't let him know how you feel, don't tell him you're every bit as keen as he is, the new, old-as-Eve knowledge warned her. Don't you remember how Ralph liked things that stretched him, difficult things? He only enjoyed riding until he had mastered it completely, then he wanted to do something else. As soon as he could row the little boat his father bought him he wanted to sail in the Creams' fishing boat, like Georgie. When he could crew the sailing boat he wanted to take the rudder. He rode his bicycle until he could ride faster and further than most other boys his age, then he wanted a motor bike, then a car. Play indifferent, Sybil Cream, play hard to get or he'll tire of the chase before he starts.

'My thoughts? Well, if you want the truth I was wondering what Mrs Winterton's getting for supper.'

He looked down at her. She read surprise in his gaze, even a little chagrin, then he smiled knowingly.

'Bet you weren't thinking any such thing! Bet you were wondering where we'd go on Monday.'

That evening, after their meal, they walked round to Lizzie's latest flat in Timber Hill, though in fact they almost did not reach it. Lizzie had changed her rooms several times, as indeed she had changed her jobs. Lizzie had made wireless parts, had worked in a forces canteen, had even stitched uniforms, though she had been very bad at it, she had told her sister cheerfully. But munitions, her present job, was so well paid that it looked as though she would stick it for a bit. And the new flat, according to Lizzie, was a dream, so perhaps she'd stay in Timber Hill for a bit, too.

Chris knew where Timber Hill was though not the exact location of the flat, so Ralph insisted that they walk three abreast, himself with a girl on each arm, all of them keeping an eye out for the shoe-mender's shop above which Lizzie lived.

But they had not even reached the street when Ralph pulled his two companions to a halt.

'Well, well, well! Look who's here!'

They looked, and coming along Orford Place towards them was a small girl in a swirly black chiffon dress. She had long, rippling ash-blonde hair and her face was delicately made up so that her lips were the colour of crushed roses and her lids faintly violet.

'Is it . . . it can't be . . . yes, it's Lizzie!' That was Sybil, almost shocked by her sister's appearance. Lizzie had always been pretty but this girl looked like a film star, like someone out of a book, and she was accompanied by the tallest, handsomest man Sybil had ever imagined. He was in RAF uniform and he dragged off his cap when he saw them smiling at his companion.

'Sybs!' Lizzie said, not sounding at all pleased to see her sister. 'Oh goodness, you're the last person I expected to see. I hardly recognized you . . . surely you can't *still* be growing?'

She could not have chosen a subject more likely to make Sybil want to disappear; Sybil was abruptly conscious of her slender height and wished she could sink through the pavement. Chris squeezed her fingers, whether in warning or support Sybil did not know.

'Hello, Lizzie,' she said. 'How are you? Do you remember Ralph?'

Lizzie started to speak, and Sybil noticed for the first time that her sister's cheeks were red and that her eyes were darting about from one to the other, though they seemed to be avoiding Ralph's altogether. But then she seemed suddenly to remember her manners. She gave a rather artificial little laugh and turned to her companion.

'There, the surprise made me forget you, Emil!' She turned to her sister. 'This is Emil Provinski; he's a Polish officer in our air force and speaks very good English. Emil, this is my sister Sybil and her friend Chris Winterton.' She had ignored Ralph completely but now she shot him a quick look out of her cornflower blue eyes. It was a rather shifty look, Sybil thought, and wondered what Ralph had done to make Lizzie regard him with what appeared to be dislike. 'And that's Ralph, Chris's brother,' she concluded.

Emil shook hands with everyone, clicking his heels and bending his head and being incredibly polite, but Sybil got the impression that he wished them anywhere but here.

'I've brought you a cake, Lizzie,' she said, when the introductions were over. 'Mum sent it – it's one of those carrot cakes you like. And a tiny jar of honey, because she remembers how much you love it.'

'Oh. Well, you'll just have to take them home again and bring them back tomorrow,' Lizzie said crossly. 'We're going dancing, and I can scarcely turn up at a dance clasping a carrot cake and a jar of honey to my bosom.'

Sybil could have cried. She hadn't meant to upset Lizzie but clearly she had done just that, and she knew how difficult her sister could be. But Ralph shook his head chidingly at Lizzie.

'Now now, Lizzie Cream, how ungracious you are! It won't take you five minutes to pop round the corner to your room and put the cake and the honey somewhere safe. In fact if you lend Sybs a key she could do it for you.'

'Oh! I didn't mean to seem ungracious, Sybs,' Lizzie said, her tone considerably friendlier. 'And Ralph's right. Emil and I can easily pop back for two minutes. I'm sorry we haven't really time to chat, we're going for a meal before the dance, but next time perhaps . . . See you around, then.'

'We'll walk back with you, so Sybil knows where you live,' Ralph said as Lizzie turned dismissively away. 'Are you working over the weekend?'

'I'm fully booked, I'm afraid,' Lizzie said over her shoulder. Even her back view somehow managed to look outraged, Sybil thought miserably. 'But some other time . . .'

She led the way back up Orford Place to Timber Hill where they spotted the shoe-mender's shop at once. Lizzie inserted her key in the green and cream painted door next to the shop and then turned to Sybil.

'The room's in a mess, so you needn't come up. Emil, stay and talk to them whilst I put the cake and things away.'

Sybil handed over the bag of foodstuffs but Ralph was clearly not keen to be pushed aside.

'Hang on, Lizzie – why can't we come up for a moment? What dark secret are you hiding?'

'The room's untidy; I want Sybil to have a good first impression,' Lizzie said at once. She shot through the door and closed it firmly behind her, finishing the conversation.

Ralph grinned and turned to Emil, who was looking supremely uncomfortable.

'Well, Emil? Talk to us!'

Emil, taking him literally, began slowly and carefully to explain that he was a flying officer based about forty miles away. Fortunately, however, Lizzie returned, breathless, before his conversation had quite run out.

'Here we are again,' she said gaily. 'Come on, Emil . . . sorry to rush off and leave you, but if I'd known you were coming . . . we're meeting friends . . . see you soon, Sybil . . . Chris!'

She seized the arm of the now silent Pole, who looked back at them, trying to wave and bow and smile all at the same time, and disappeared round the corner of the Bell Hotel and down towards Castle Meadow.

'Well I'm damned,' Chris said slowly as they, in their turn, crossed the road and headed for the Walk. 'I don't mean to be rude, Sybs, but your sister is a very odd girl!'

'It's my fault,' Sybil said uncomfortably. 'She wasn't expecting to see us. I am sorry! It was most awfully awkward, wasn't it?'

'Well, just the tiniest bit,' Ralph chimed in. 'However, let us not repine. At least it absolves us from feeling we ought to have asked Lizzie to come out in the car with us next week. She's obviously got her own social life nicely sorted out and doesn't need any outside interference.'

'Sybs wasn't interfering,' Chris said loyally. 'I suppose Lizzie felt awkward because she had that chap with her. Oh well, let's forget it, shall we?'

'I can't forget it,' Sybil said broodingly. 'When I think of it . . . why did she have to remind me how tall I am? She can be horrid, she really can.'

'For God's sake, girl! Forget it and let's go home and give Toddy a ring. He can catch a bus and be with us in half an hour and we can plan what we'll do for the rest of the week. We'll go off somewhere tomorrow, just to cheer Sybs up a bit.'

Which was sensible and what they decided to do. That evening they talked and laughed, made plans and unmade them again, played cards and drank cocoa made with dried milk and saccharin.

It was not until quite late that night, when Sybil was tucked up in the spare bed in Chris's room, that she actually allowed herself to think about the meeting with Lizzie. It had been very strange. For a start, Ralph hadn't seen Lizzie for years, yet he had recognized her unerringly when Sybil herself, who had seen her not three months ago, had almost walked straight past her.

Then there was Lizzie's attitude. She's my older sister and she bosses me a bit, but she's never in her entire life been truly horrible to me until today, ran Sybil's thoughts. Can it be that Lizzie and Ralph are enemies, so she was nasty to me because I was with him?

It made a sort of sense, but the truth was Sybil was tired and confused and mainly wanted to sleep, so she didn't give it any more thought that night. And next day everything seemed different. It was sunny again, and Ralph talked at breakfast of taking them on Filby Broad in a boat belonging to a friend of his, and Mrs Winterton packed a very good sort of picnic, considering, and Lizzie and her behaviour – and her Pole – were relegated to the back of Sybil's mind.

Ralph, on the other hand, found that Lizzie and her behaviour kept him awake for a good two hours that night. The little . . . the little *tart*!

All those loving letters she had written had meant nothing, because it was as clear as the nose on her face that the moment he was out of England she had started an affair with this Pole, and possibly with others, too.

Well, he could take a hint, especially when it was accompanied by the cold shoulder, for she had scarcely acknowledged him at all. And the truth was that pretty though Lizzie might be her sister Sybil was worth ten of her. And she was lovely, with a sweetness which Ralph found both refreshing and stimulating after Lizzie's almost cloying affection.

Not that he had thought it cloying before, but now that he knew he was just one of many . . . and to think I wanted to marry her, he thought, appalled at the trap into which he had so nearly fallen. What sort of a wife would she make for an up-and-coming young solicitor in a big law firm? Sybil was a lady, you could never doubt it, whereas her sister was just . . . well, just a tart who would go with anyone who would spend a few bob on her.

So I'll give Lizzie a miss and concentrate on Sybil, Ralph told himself at last, settling down to sleep as dawn was greying the windows. Sybil's decent and sweet and a virgin and she'll make me a beautiful, decorative wife. If I marry her, that is. I might just – well, I might just have her, because it is wartime, after all.

But all through his anger and his hurt pride, his rage against the Pole, there was a core of aching, a hunger, which he did his very best to ignore. Because Lizzie, the greedy, unprincipled little cow, would never ache or hunger for any one man.

He might have thought a little better of her had he known, as Emil did, that she had cried herself to sleep, and that even in sleep, she wept.

13

On Saturday everyone slept late and had a lazy day, but early on Sunday Ralph took the girls and Toddy out for a spin. Sybil sat beside him and Toddy and Chris sat in the back and they were all very happy and easy together. The lazy relaxed Saturday had dissipated most of Sybil's worries and she had woken determined to enjoy this unexpected break and to do her best to captivate Ralph.

They went to an old grey farmhouse with a lichen-patched roof where the farmer was famous for his cider. As Chris said, it was fun to watch others work for a change. Mr Bickers had a son in Ralph's squadron and welcomed them warmly, selling them a flagon of cider and giving them the sort of meal which his son had boasted about back in Lincolnshire. The great egg and ham pie was served with piles of vegetables and chipped potatoes cooked in pork fat, for Mr Bickers reared his own pigs and usually managed to do well out of them. There were a couple of landgirls on the place and Sybil and Chris told them about their own work whilst the farmer's teenage daughter gazed admiringly at Ralph and laughed at all his jokes. After that they drove back to Norwich and went to a pub – it was Sybil's first visit and she was astonished to see as many women as men in the bar, some of them very smart indeed – where Ralph and Toddy drank beer and laughed rather a lot and she and Chris sipped their way through a sweet sherry each and secretly thought it rather nasty.

Then, tired but happy, they sat in the car outside Toddy's house and did what Ralph described as 'a bit of canoodling', which meant quite a lot of kissing and some very discreet cuddling. And then Ralph drove home, parked the car in the yard, and they trooped indoors armed with the cider and told the Wintertons all about their day until they were chased off to bed at midnight with the reminder that some people had to get up in time for work next morning.

On Monday they slept late, then wandered downstairs and had

an early lunch. Then Ralph went off somewhere and the girls went shopping. Even wartime shops were fascinating to Sybil, who rarely bought anything new. Thanks to Lizzie's good offices – for she was a valued customer as well as ex-staff – they both got a pair of stockings from Curls, though they were imitation silk and would, Chris said, ladder within seconds of being put on. Still, they would need them for the dance that evening.

'Dancing on a Monday?' Sybil said, used to the village hops which always took place on Saturday so that the dancers could lie in on Sunday morning. 'Whatever next?'

'Oh, some other mad gaiety,' Ralph said, teasing her. 'We still haven't danced together, have we?' They were in the kitchen, watching Chris fry up cold potatoes to accompany the sawdust sausages they would presently eat. Ralph leered at Sybil, eyes twinkling. 'Until you 'ave zwooned in by arbs, by darlink, you 'aven't leeved,' he said in a passable imitation of Charles Boyer's romantic tones.

'If she wanted to swoon in your arms she could do so right here in this room,' Chris remarked, prodding suspiciously at her mashed up vegetables. 'Do I smell burning? I most sincerely hope not, since this is the best I can manage . . . we'll have to go food-shopping tomorrow, Sybs. And for unrationed stuff, what's more, which is very hard to lay hands on.'

'She won't want to swoon until I've danced the tango with her and clasped her passionately to my manly bosom,' Ralph explained. 'Not that I'd do such a thing, of course – nothing's further from my thoughts.'

He lied, Sybil knew. He never lost an opportunity to give her a squeeze and a quick, soft kiss and she was looking forward very much to more of the same. It was lovely to be admired and courted by someone as handsome as Ralph – I expect we'll marry after the war, she told herself as she laid the table. What fun that would be – Chris would be my sister! Independence and a career, which had seemed so delightful only a week ago, had suddenly lost its attraction.

They caught a bus to the Lido, which was quite a way out of the city, on Aylsham Road. Ralph did not use the car unless there was no public transport because of petrol rationing, and they would have to walk home since by the time they left the dance-hall no buses would be running.

'And taxis are few and far between and cost the earth,' Ralph told the girls. 'So wear good, sturdy shoes and take your dancing slippers with you in a bag. That's what everyone else does.'

Toddy called for them at eight and, four abreast with arms linked, they set off. They went down St Giles into the city centre and caught the bus on St Benedict's. There were many passengers similarly bound, all the girls carrying dancing slippers in their bags, Sybil was pleased to notice.

She had made a special effort tonight. She had washed herself all over with a couple of kettles full of hot water, powdered with the only talcum available, Johnson's Baby, and then availed herself of Mrs Winterton's offer of scent, dabbing it behind each ear, on her wrists and on the delicate collar bones which showed at the neck of her dance-dress.

The dress was special. It was smoke coloured, somewhere between blue and grey, in soft silky stuff which fitted neatly to hip level and then went very full and swirly. Sybil loved it though she rarely had a chance to wear it but, putting it on that night and covering it with her sensible Land Army greatcoat, she knew it suited her.

The bus rumbled past City station and over a bridge. Sybil, sitting warmly pressed against Ralph, pointed out of the window at the scene outside, the calm water silvered by a huge moon, the shapes of the warehouses sinister and black against the starlit sky.

'What river is that? Isn't it a marvellous night?' she said.

'It's the Wensum,' Ralph said. 'The moon is bright, isn't it? Almost like day. It'll make the walk home easier, anyway.'

'Leeeeedo!' shouted the conductress. 'Come along, ladies and gentlemen, step lively now, we in't got all night, you know. Some of us is a-goin' off duty!'

Chattering and chaffing, the passengers began to leave the bus. The pavement, white in the moonlight, became crowded with young men in uniform, young women in pretty dresses. The Lido, everyone's destination, bulked black against the stars.

'Come on,' Chris urged, pulling at Sybil's coat. 'I want to get my good shoes on . . . we shan't be long,' she added over her shoulder to the two young men. 'Get us a drink, would you? Lemonade or something. I bet it will get awfully hot inside as the place begins to fill up.'

My first real dance, Sybil thought tremulously, heading for the ladies' room. In a few minutes I shall be dancing with Ralph, actually in his arms! Oh, how shall I ever bear the joy of it?

It was easier to bear, perhaps, because Ralph was not a gifted dancer and Sybil, having painstakingly learned the steps for village hops, was just the tiniest bit disappointed. Ralph mainly wanted to plod round, hum the tunes in her ear, and grasp her hotly. And whilst she and Chris went off and powdered their noses, looking anxiously at their reflections for signs of melting or running or incipient spots, he plodded round the floor grasping other girls, all of whom seemed, to Sybil's jealous eye, very much lovelier and more sophisticated than she.

But he came back to her. Quickly, and with excuses. Reasons? No, definitely excuses, Sybil thought sadly – and forgave him at once. He knew both the girls he had danced with, they were the sisters of friends, good manners dictated that he dance with them at least once whilst giving them news of their brothers' progress up in the north.

'It doesn't matter at all, Ralph,' Sybil said cordially. 'Honestly. I'd do the same myself if I knew people here, but I'm a stranger. Still, there's bound to be a ladies' excuse-me presently.'

There was. Mindful of her own advice about Ralph's tendency not to value what came easy, she danced with a small, foreign-looking man who whirled her round giddyingly and snuggled up rather pleasantly during the slow bits of the dance, and with a tall, gangly man who kept trying to have an interesting conversation, only he was a Scot and she found him difficult to understand.

Ralph, who had sat out and sulked, welcomed her back eagerly and monopolized her for the rest of the evening. In fact, during the last waltz, the proverbial time for cuddling, he whispered in her ear that she was the sweetest thing – he had never felt like this about a girl before, and she must come up to Lincolnshire so that they could be together during his leaves – they needed to get to know one another; she must realize that as he did.

When the last waltz had faded into silence there was a rush for the cloakrooms in which Chris and Sybil joined. Rapidly they bundled themselves into their coats and changed their dancing slippers for walking shoes, then they joined Ralph and Toddy in the foyer. The boys were already greatcoated, for despite the fact that April was almost over it was chilly outside, and the four of them linked arms as they crossed the road.

They did not hurry but stepped out nevertheless, amongst a crowd of others going in the same direction both before and behind. The moon sailed above them, a pure silver sphere, spilling brightness and inky shadows, but lighting the pavement so well that their torches were unnecessary.

'Lucky it's so bright; my battery's low,' Chris said, trying to match her step to Sybil's and tugging Toddy across the pavement like a drunk. 'If the moon goes behind a cloud – oh, there aren't any!'

'Too right; it's a bombers' moon,' Ralph said. He sounded uneasy and Sybil realized that to Ralph a clear night meant a bombing raid into Germany, something which would mean more of his friends dead. 'Wonder if the chaps have been scrambled.'

Toddy was answering when, high and eerie, a sound built up, rising and falling, urgent.

'It's the alert,' Chris said. 'Oh hell – where's the nearest shelter?'

'Heaven knows. Keep on walking,' Ralph said. 'Oh, my God!'

They were just about to descend a sloping road with the river at its foot. As they watched, two aircraft zoomed down, looking as though they intended to plunge into the river. Sybil saw them lift at the last minute and saw, by the light of the flares the planes were dropping to illuminate their targets, the bomb-doors open and their cargo of high explosive come tumbling out. She clutched Ralph as the bombs struck and they saw a fountain of water, smoke and fragments of buildings suddenly blown, in slow-motion, into the air.

'Get down!' Ralph shouted. Sybil found herself lying beside some-one's garden wall, the bricks actually pressing against her nose. She felt Ralph's arms go round her with nothing amorous, now, in their grasp, and felt him roll half on top of her. 'Don't move, don't even breathe,' he said against her hair. 'There's more overhead, those bombs are going to . . .'

Earsplittingly, the aircraft noise and the whine of descending bombs drowned the rest of his sentence. The two of them lay against that garden wall whilst the pavement beneath them reverberated to the concussion of the attack and then for a moment there was quiet, though they could hear, above the small sounds – the crackle of a fire, the scream of a child – the booming throb of engines as yet more aircraft swooped low over the city.

'Come on, no sense in staying here,' Ralph said when the noise was at its height. He dragged Sybil to her feet. 'We'll make a run for it. If you see a shelter, give a shout.'

'Where's Chris?' Sybil cried as they began to run down the road, hand in hand. Her dancing shoes in their little bag seemed to have disappeared but she was past caring. 'Oh, Ralph, where's Chris and Toddy?'

'Don't know. They'll be all right, though – ah . . . look, just rounding that corner ahead – see?'

Unmistakably, Chris's flying form, hand in hand with Toddy, then they were out of sight.

'We'd better follow them,' Sybil panted. 'Chris knows the way . . . we might catch them up in a moment.'

Beside her, Ralph shook his head.

'No. Tell you what, let's see if we can race them. Bet we get back home faster my way!'

It was so typical of the Ralph she remembered that Sybil actually choked on a laugh. Trust him to make even an air raid competitive! But soon she had no time to think and no breath to talk with either. She was fit, but even so she had a stitch from running bent double and bruises from suddenly throwing herself to the ground when Ralph gave the word, and her mouth was dry with fear.

But they made it. Somehow, they found themselves back on St Giles, though Sybil had no idea how they had got there. She simply recognized the church, then the house.

'Come on! They'll be in the cellar; it's better than an air raid shelter,' Ralph said. He opened the front door and ushered her in. 'See? They'll all be down there, though I bet we beat Chris and Toddy.'

The door to the cellar was open; from below, they could see a light. Ralph clattered across the hall and stood at the top of the whitewashed steps. He leaned forward.

'Mummy? Daddy? We're back . . . everyone hunky-dory?'

'Daddy's out,' his mother's voice floated up to them. 'Are you all there? Do come down, Ralph, and shut the door. We only left it open . . .'

A crash and a splintering roar made Ralph and Sybil instinctively duck and clutch one another. Ralph took her hand and together they descended the stairs.

The cellar was full. Women with coats dragged on over night-things, small children either hopping with excitement or pallid with fear and exhaustion sat or stood around. But no Chris and Toddy.

'Well? Where's your sister?' Mrs Winterton's voice was sharp with foreboding. 'You were together!'

'We got separated quite early on. I think we were actually blown in different directions,' Ralph said apologetically. 'We saw the first bomb coming out of the aircraft, we were that close. Chris and Tod may be right behind us, or they may have found a shelter and dived in. We meant to do that but it's so bad out there it seemed better to keep on going. Want me to go and search for them?'

He sounded bright and eager, as though such a search would be great fun. Mrs Winterton closed her eyes for a pregnant moment.

'No, Ralph, certainly not. Toddy will take good care of Chris, I'm sure. I have quite enough anxiety as it is without sending you out into that.' Another thundering crash made the walls of the cellar jump; Sybil was sure she had seen them move and cringed away, but though the oil-lamp flickered as though it would have liked to give up, it remained burning.

'Right. I'll stay here, then. Is there anything you need from the house? I'm sure it will be safe for me to nip into the kitchen and fetch anything you may want – the kettle, or some food.'

'We've tea and cocoa in flasks, and biscuits and homemade cakes for the little ones,' an elderly woman said. 'We've been preparing for this for weeks . . . most of these people were on their way to the shelters in Chapel Field gardens when we brought them in. There's a lot of house up above us to take the impact of the bombs first, and this cellar is deep and dry, so when your mother offered to let us make use of it it seemed sensible to kit them out properly and take every precaution against being here longer . . .' she hesitated, looking around her at the exhausted women and frightened children '. . . longer than we perhaps expected,' she finished tactfully.

As another explosion rent the air a small boy, who had been playing cards with two others and had seemed happy enough, suddenly burst into tears. It had all been too much, Sybil saw. His courage had held up, he had been concentrating on the game and keeping two other children happy, and then that last shattering crash had been the straw that broke the camel's back. She cleared her throat.

'Anyone want to play *I Spy*? Or would you rather have a story?'

She had not really known she had a teaching voice until she heard her own words and then she was just profoundly glad of it. Children who had been grizzling and clutching their toys forlornly came towards her. She formed them into a circle and sat in the middle of it. The small, trustful faces were lifted up to her own and she read pleasant anticipation and the beginnings of confidence there. This was normality, a teacher telling a story, an everyday event. And a story would help them to forget the fearsome crashes and the danger just for a little while; perhaps, once they had been brought to a state of forgetfulness, whisked into a fantasy world for a while, they might even be able to curl up in the blankets which Mrs Winterton had provided and go to sleep.

'Once upon a time there were three billy goats,' Sybil began. 'They were known as the Billy Goats Gruff and they lived in a green green meadow, full of green green grass, beside the most beautiful little river. And spanning the river, from one side to the other, was a bridge.'

The power of narrative has proved strong throughout the ages. Adults in low-voiced conversations stopped talking. Ralph, who had been fidgeting round and eyeing the stairs longingly, settled down beside his mother. Everyone was listening. They might all know the story of the Billy Goats Gruff by heart, but as jesters and ballad singers have known for years there is in everyone a strong compulsion to hush and listen to a story.

'Now under the bridge there lived a troll . . .'

You could have heard a pin drop in the cellar as Sybil unfolded her tale. Her voice rose and fell and the children's eyes never left her face, except when their lids drooped in sleep. Vaguely, through the thick walls which surrounded them, they could hear the sounds of the conflict, but they were no longer important. The story was important. Sybil talked on.

Sybil and Ralph left the cellar as dawn was breaking.

'We'd better go round to Toddy's,' Ralph said as they stood in the doorway, looking cautiously out at St Giles in the grey light of a morning which was only moments away from night. The church was unharmed but when they looked towards the city they could see rubble in the road and smoke hanging like a pall over the roadway. Sybil frowned; she could see further than she had seen the previous night . . . that meant houses were down, and shops and offices.

'Yes, all right . . . and I'll have to get to Lizzie's lodgings,' Sybil said worriedly. 'I must find her. I wonder what was hit?'

'Quite a lot, I'd guess,' Ralph said grimly. 'Mother's coming out soon; she'll want to ring Flicky's school – they were evacuated to Devon, you know – to tell her everything's okay. She came up earlier to take a peek and said the WVS will need all the helpers they can get to sort this lot out, and I'll bet we've not seen the half of it yet. Coming?'

'Of course I am. But Ralph, will you come with me to Lizzie's?'

'Sure.' He held out a hand. 'Do you want to go there first? Only to be honest I know very well that Chris wouldn't have gone to Toddy's, because there would have been no point. It's further away, and . . . we'll try Lizzie's place first. Look, it's going to be all right, I feel it in my bones.'

But they nearly lost hope as they walked through the city.

Fires still raged and firemen stood helplessly by broken mains, unable to use water to quench the flames. Everywhere people were digging; soldiers, rescue squads, policemen. Whole areas had been devastated; Brigg Street was unrecognizable, Curls just a blackened shell, the rubble still smouldering. A fireman was wielding an axe, trying to cut away a smoking wooden window frame from Marks & Spencer in case it burst into flames once more.

They reached Orford Place and stopped short. Scarcely a building stood. Fear, which had hovered all night, struck black at Sybil once more; her legs would not hold her up, she was going to faint . . .

'It's all right, old girl, we're still a way from Lizzie's lodgings. Anyway, it's a solid sort of building. I bet there are cellars just like at St Giles. Mark my words, Lizzie will have been snug as a bug in a rug.'

Sybil nodded numbly and never allowed herself to wonder why Ralph should know anything about the building in which her sister lived. What on earth did it matter? What mattered was finding Lizzie alive and uninjured.

They did that sooner than they expected. They had crossed Orford Place and were heading for Timber Hill when they saw a small, determined figure coming towards them. It was Lizzie, accompanied by the young Pole they had met the previous Saturday.

'Oh, you're all right, Sybs,' Lizzie gasped as soon as they were close enough. She, who was so undemonstrative, ran into her sister's arms and hugged her convulsively. Her beautiful, heart-shaped face was dirt-streaked and her cream dress was crumpled and dirty. Furthermore, it was an evening dress, not a day dress, certainly not the sort of garment Lizzie would ever wear to work. She must have been in it when the raid struck and was wearing it still. 'Was there ever anything like it? We thought we were goners several times. The ceiling came down on us but we managed to crawl out, didn't we, Emil? The room positively rocked.'

'It most certainly did,' the Pole said. 'I thought my last moment had come.'

'Didn't you get to a shelter?' Sybil said incredulously. She stared at Lizzie and her companion, then swung round on Ralph. 'I thought you said there was a cellar – oh, Lizzie, if I'd known you were in such danger I'd have gone half mad with worry!'

Lizzie shrugged.

'Then it's a good thing you didn't know,' she said crossly. 'I hate shelters; they smell and they're damp, and the same goes for cellars.

Anyway, I told Emil that if one of those bombs had my name on it then it might as well land on me in my own room, not in some smelly bolt-hole. And we're both okay. I'll get the landlord to mend the ceiling if I decide to stay.'

'Were you under your dining table, Liz? I like to think of you under the dining table,' Ralph said pensively. 'Just like a fluffy bunny rabbit, with your little tail in the air and . . .'

'Yes, of course we got under the table,' Lizzie said shortly. 'No point in being downright stupid. Emil's got to get back to his airfield so I'm going to walk down to Thorpe station with him, though heaven knows whether there will be any trains running. Still, I'll have to get a good wash and brush-up before I go to . . . hell's bells!'

Lizzie had glanced to her left – and seen what was left of Orford Place. Before their eyes the heart-shaped face paled and she actually swayed where she stood. Ralph put out a hand to steady her but Emil was there first, looping a long arm about her shoulders, turning her towards him, shutting out the sight.

'Reaction, I think,' he said briefly to Sybil, over Lizzie's shaking golden head. 'She worked there once, but she will not work there again – no one will. I think we should return to Timber Hill, so that Lizzie can tidy herself. It is only the bedroom that is in a mess. The other room is fine. Will you come with us?'

'Not right now,' Ralph said before Sybil could answer. 'We've got to find Chris and Toddy.'

'The nightwatchman . . . what about old Lou?' Lizzie said suddenly into Emil's shoulder. She tugged herself free. 'Emil, what about old Lou?'

'He was probably safely tucked away somewhere,' Emil said comfortingly. 'There is a basement . . . was, I should say . . . he will have got himself down there with a flask of tea and some grub. Come home, Lizzie, and clean up a bit.'

But Lizzie was shaking her head, pushing the hair off her face, her hands suddenly firm and her chin jutting with determination.

'It's all right, Emil, I'll be fine now. Hope you find Chris and Toddy fit and well,' she added, smiling a little tightly at Sybil and Ralph. 'I'll come round and see you in St Giles later, when I've found out about old Lou.'

She turned and, towing the Pole behind her, began to pick her way over the still smoking rubble.

By the time they got back to St Giles, Chris and Toddy, dirty and tired, were sitting down to tea and toast. It appeared that they had found a shelter, joined the family in it, and stayed there until dawn. Coming out, they had got completely disorientated by the destruction all around them and had been slow in making their way home, but now that they had arrived they were full of the terrible things they had seen and keen to go out and help.

'Mum left as soon as we came through the front door,' Chris said cheerfully, scraping jam meanly on to her toast and doubling it over to make a sort of sandwich. 'She's a member of MAGNA so she's organizing homes for the homeless and trying to get children out of the city for a few nights, just in case they come back. Will they bother, do you think? I mean, they did so much damage last night . . .'

Her voice petered out and she bit into her toast.

'Doesn't matter; they'll be back,' Ralph said. 'I expect my leave will be cancelled; I'll ring my CO today and find out, but if I can stay I'll have to see the civil defence people about giving a hand. I'm not going to sit back and watch whilst they flatten my home.'

'I don't think they'll cancel our leave, will they, Chris?' Sybil said. 'We'll do whatever we can to help.'

'We'll go and find Mummy,' Chris said, getting to her feet. 'She'll find a use for us, never fear!'

What should have been a week's rest and relaxation after the horrors of the Pakeby bombing, therefore, turned into a nightmare. On Tuesday night no one slept much, waiting for the aircraft hum to start overhead. All day Wednesday was given up to helping those who had lost their homes, taking children to relatives in the country, giving Mr and Mrs Winterton as much support as they could.

On Wednesday night the raiders came again. Wave after wave of aircraft darkened the sky and bombs rained down on the city once more. Ralph was out fire-watching but Sybil clung to Chris in the cellar and Chris cried like a baby, because she said she imagined the city lying there in the dark like some great wounded animal, unable to move, waiting for more pain, more destruction.

The Wintertons had invited Lizzie to stay with them for a few days at least, but Lizzie declined. The flat was uninhabitable and since her factory had been bombed she had no work, but she still seemed cheerful.

She came chirpily up to the house on the Wednesday afternoon and told Sybil that she was going home for a couple of weeks.

'I might join one of the women's forces,' she announced. 'After all,

I've been told the WRNS and the WAAFs have a marvellous time – all those lovely sailors and airmen, Sybs! But there's a munitions place at Beccles and quite decent accommodation, so I may end up there – it'll be easier to get home at weekends.'

Ralph had not been there, but when she told him he did not seem much interested.

'She's a pretty little thing, your sister, but I'm afraid she just isn't my type,' he said. He put an arm round Sybil's shoulders. 'I prefer my girls with streaky fair hair and serious little faces and I like them to have brains as well as beauty . . . darling Sybs, it sounds so daft to say I want to take you away from all this, but it's what I mean! I'd like to take you somewhere quiet and peaceful, where we could learn all about each other, where we'd have time for each other, with nothing to come between us. If only we could go away, just the two of us . . .'

It sounded like a proposal, but Sybil was still being careful. She smiled and leaned her head on his shoulder and said it all sounded lovely and perhaps one day . . .

They were walking round the garden because it was so difficult to be alone in the house now, and neither of them could bear to walk through the shattered city, but Sybil knew that before she went home Ralph would suggest a trip out in the car, or a visit to the cinema – somewhere where it was possible for them to be by themselves.

The raid on the Wednesday night was dreadful and yet more of the city was devastated. Toddy's roof was burned off by an incendiary which took hold at the height of the raid, and when Chris and Sybil went to visit a friend in the Rupert Street area they were appalled by the damage on all sides. The friend was safe, even joked about how she had been stuck down a shelter simply longing to spend a penny, and how her cousin, not realizing, had kept making her laugh . . .

On Friday morning Sybil packed her bag. Chris was to stay on to help clear up but Ralph said he would run Sybil home to Pakeby.

'I'm off myself tomorrow,' he said. 'Don't try to dissuade me, Sybs, let me stay with you as long as I can.'

Who could resist a plea like that? Certainly not Sybil. 'I hate leaving you with all this muddle, though,' she told Mrs Winterton. 'I wish I could have done more . . . all that mess!'

There wasn't a shard of glass left in any of the windows at the back of the house, because it faced Chapel Field, which had been badly bombed. Mr Winterton and Ralph, neither of them particularly handy at doing odd jobs, had managed to put a pane into the kitchen window and another into the scullery, and they had to be content with that until they could get an expert to finish the job off properly.

'I can't tell you what a help it has been, having you here,' Mrs Winterton assured her. 'I'm just so desperately sorry that your week's holiday should have turned into the hardest work of your life. And thank Dora for that wonderful food, Sybs, and take good care of yourself. When the war's over you must come back again and we'll make sure you have a marvellous time. They'll have rebuilt the Hippodrome and repaired the theatre ... it's amazing how people will put their backs into a job when there's a war on. Norwich will be a grand city again quick as quick!'

But Sybil, climbing into the front passenger seat of Ralph's noisy little car, thought that she knew better than ever now what a grand city Norwich was, and what grand people lived there. She had seen shopkeepers serving customers from barrows outside their ruined premises, bus conductresses climbing down from their vehicles to shift timber or bricks from the road, little boys making their way to school across the rubble, dragging the family pet, 'because there's nowhere to leave him now the house has gone'. People would tackle anything, do anything now, to see the Nazis beaten. Mrs Winterton told her that born grumblers who never had a cheerful word to say had suddenly turned optimist, as though the enormous destruction and the many deaths had made them see how lucky they were to be alive, made them determined to go on being lucky.

And now, in the little car speeding through the bright spring sunshine, Sybil knew that she, too, was one of the lucky ones. She had found Ralph and he had found her and they would be happy. He had been brave, risking his life in ruined buildings to dig out those buried by falling masonry. He had proved he could turn his hand to anything, he had comforted children, chaffed old people, been bracing or sympathetic with those whose losses oppressed them. War was a terrible thing and Ralph would undoubtedly risk his life for his country many times in the months or years to come, but just at this moment she was sure they would both win through. We'll have a nice little cottage somewhere and I'll teach and grow vegetables and keep the place nice until the babies come along, she dreamed. And Ralph will go off each day into the city and do whatever it is solicitors do and come home every night to me. And we'll live happily ever after.

But when Ralph asked her why she was so quiet she just smiled at him and said she was wondering when it would be warm enough for sea-bathing. Would he come over for a dip once summer came?

'I might, at that,' Ralph said longingly. He wound his window down and the smell of the sea came through, for they were close enough to Pakeby now to hear the murmur of the waves and the cry of the gulls. 'But don't forget, Sybs, you're coming up to Lincolnshire to be with me! You promised.'

She never had, of course. But she knew she would move heaven and earth to be with him. And when they drew up outside the cottage and Lizzie and Mum rushed out she hardly minded at all when Ralph kissed Lizzie, though she could not help noticing that her sister drew back quickly, looking annoyed.

'It's very kind of you to bring Sybil home, Ralph,' her mother said. She did not sound as pleased as Sybil would have liked, however. 'You'll stay to tea? Lizzie and I went shrimping earlier, and I baked this morning.'

Ralph agreed to stay and Sybil waited for him to suggest that the two of them went walking on the beach or into the country . . . anything to be alone. It might be their last opportunity for simply ages! But Ralph was very correct. He and Sybil walked down the lane to the field where the Wintertons' ponies still grazed in spring and summer, and then they went back to the cottage for tea, and whilst they were eating Dora wanted to tell Sybil all about Dad coming home next week, which would be wonderful. She asked about the raids but you could tell that even Lizzie's descriptions hadn't made them real for her. Or perhaps Lizzie hadn't really bothered to describe the raids – she was an odd girl in some ways, quite unable to see things from any point of view other than her own.

'So you'll be back to work tomorrow,' Dora said at last, dishing out delicious slices of bakewell tart. 'Well, dear, summer is coming, your busiest time, so Mr Franklyn will be pleased to have you back. And we'll be able to get into our routine again – I've missed you very much indeed.'

She sounded so surprised that they all laughed.

'Mum, honestly! Anyone would think I hadn't missed you! Yes, it'll be good to be on the farm again in lots of ways.'

And, in saying it, Sybil suddenly realized that she had spoken no more than the truth. She had moaned with the best over the hard work, the cold, the obstinacy of the animals and the way tractors kept breaking down, but she would really be glad to get back to the work she knew and loved.

'Wish I was happy to be going back to the squadron tomorrow,' Ralph said gloomily, when she admitted how she felt to him later, standing beside his car and waiting to wave him off. 'I'll be all right when I get there, of course, but I shall miss you like hell, Sybs my darling.'

'I'll write two or three times a week,' Sybil said eagerly. 'And if I possibly can, I'll come and stay . . . but not till summer, of course.'

'No, not till summer. Take care, my darling.'

'You take care too, Ralph.'

He took hold of her hand through his open window, turned it over and kissed her palm gently. Sybil felt a glow spread through her; he was so romantic, so truly loving!

'Oh, Ralph, I'll miss you so much! Write often!'

'Of course I will, whenever I can, only it isn't always easy . . . goodbye, sweetheart!'

The engine roared whilst she was still trying to answer, still trying not to cry, and then he was gone, the little car belching blue exhaust fumes as he skidded round the corner of Beach Road and out of sight. Sybil sighed and went slowly back indoors.

It was strange to be lying in her own bed again, with Lizzie's warmth beside her. Lizzie hadn't slept at home for ages and Sybil felt as though very much longer than a week had elapsed since she herself had lain here last – she had, she felt, experienced enough for at least ten years. The raids, the terror, the excitement, roared through her head, preventing sleep, but over it all her feeling for Ralph – and his for her – comforted her marvellously. City life was lived at a much faster pace than country life, she decided, but loving someone was the same city or country, it had its own pace and she liked it, wanted more of it.

She regretted that she and Ralph had not consummated their love; she guessed that, had it not been for the sudden and shocking blitz, they would have found an opportunity. She was not at all sure whether it would be an enjoyable business, however. Kissing and cuddling was fine, but she still felt that it might be sensible to wait until they were married for – well, for the rest. She knew the wartime argument used by every soldier, sailor and airman that no one knew whether he would be alive the next day, so it was only right that a decent girl should give the man of her choice her body as well as her heart; but even so she felt instinctively that to give Ralph what he wanted might not be a very good idea in the long run.

Beside her, Lizzie murmured something in her sleep and turned to face Sybil. She cuddled up unselfconsciously and Sybil found herself wondering whether Lizzie had cuddled up equally unselfconsciously to that handsome young Pole – Emil. If Lizzie does it, why do I feel so ambivalent about it? she wondered restlessly. She's older than me, of course, so perhaps she's braver and more experienced, but I do think that love should be enough. If I'm really in love then I should want to give Ralph everything, and perhaps I do. It's just the thought of . . . oh, hang it, how silly I am! Lizzie isn't looking for a permanent relationship with Emil, and anyway Emil probably isn't like Ralph, with his fondness for competition. Sybil was a bit afraid of being bad at it and not enjoying it, and even more afraid that Ralph, once he had got her, would no longer want her. Not that any of this conjecture really mattered; she had not yet been asked to succumb to Ralph's desires, and in the meantime she had better get some sleep or she would look a hag in the morning.

Then her thoughts turned to Dora. Why had her mother been so cool with Ralph earlier in the day? It was not her imagination; she knew Dora too well to have mistaken her mother's reaction. Dora did not really like Ralph, did not approve of his courting her daughter. Why not? He was what was commonly known as a good catch, he was the son of a rich and cultured family, and if they married she would be bettering herself in the very way her mother most desired.

She racked her brains for a bit, then gave up as she felt sleep coming to her at last. What did it matter? After all, it would be she who married Ralph, not her mother, and anyway Dora would love him when she got to know him. It was just that Ralph had never been much in her company. He hadn't been one for females, as a boy.

He danced with another girl when you went to powder your nose, a small voice in the back of her head reminded her just when she was deliciously relaxing. He kissed Lizzie, and he needn't have; Lizzie was quite cross. But none of it made any difference. Ralph was her first boyfriend, her one true love, and she would follow him, if needs be, to the ends of the earth.

And with that highflown and poetical sentiment ringing in her ears, Sybil fell asleep at last.

Lizzie felt her sister relax as she fell asleep and knew that her chance had gone, for the time being at least. She should have spoken – or was it best not? She had not wanted to tell Dora, because Dora knew quite enough about Ralph already – she knew about Tess, whereas Lizzie herself had only known about Phyllis.

Tess had been the other maid at the vicarage the year of the midsummer bonfire, and though she and Lizzie had known one another they had not been close. Half the village suspected that Ralph had fathered Tess's baby, the other half murmured darkly about Mr Winterton himself, but no one, to Lizzie's knowledge, had actually stated Ralph's involvement as a fact until her mother had said it. Lizzie had often wondered about Tess's baby, but she had not really believed Ralph could have fathered little Mikey as well as Phyllis's boy. Yet when she told Dora about Ralph and Sybil, her mother had replied promptly and definitely.

'I don't want him sniffing round Sybs. Look at Tess, twenty-one years old and landed with a son of five,' Dora said sourly. 'All that talk . . . I knew it was young Ralph. Of course Mr Winterton paid up like he should, saw Tess through until she could work again, but it was Ralph who interfered with Tess, like he interfered with Phyllis. He's not the sort of person I want for my daughter.'

Lizzie had been annoyed, indeed very annoyed, but not particularly shocked. Why should she be? She had been there. Running away from Pakeby, pretending she wanted to work in a shop, and all the time she had a bun in the oven and what she wanted was to get rid of it. Ralph's bun, of course, planted one dark night in her father's beatster hut with Lizzie beside herself with delight and Ralph making all sorts of promises . . . and then simply disappearing out of her life, leaving her to manage as best she could.

So now, lying in the dark with the window a paler patch to the right of the bed and her sister's breathing in her ear, she tried to sort out just how she felt about everything and what she should do. She had no wish to harm Ralph in any way, but whether or not he had fathered Tess's child she knew very well that he had fathered hers.

He had not liked it when he had found out about Emil, but it was her belief that he would still visit her when he could, even though he knew about Emil. She had been forced to befriend Emil; Ralph had been abroad and Lizzie could scarcely live on air! Well, perhaps she could have managed, but she needed a man and with Ralph not available . . . and anyway she did not love Emil even a little bit. He was a handsome escort and a generous provider, but although he huffed and puffed and climbed all over her, his lovemaking left Lizzie cold, and perhaps because English was not his first language or perhaps because his heel-clicking and politeness really was a part of him, Lizzie found him extremely boring company and was always glad when he took himself off.

So Lizzie decided she had been faithful to Ralph in her fashion. It had been he who had cheated by going off abroad and then returning and dating her sister. It should not have been necessary for Lizzie to lie here, sleepless, wondering what she should say to her sister – Sybil was a big girl now, able to take care of herself. She would have more sense than to fall in love with Ralph, surely? The fact that Lizzie's heart had ached a little when she had seen Ralph with his arm about her sister was what you might call an occupational hazard – she went out with other men, so in theory she could scarcely object if Ralph dated someone else. But she also knew that he wasn't to be trusted with women, especially not with Sybil. Big girl or not, Sybil was still innocent.

And Ralph? If he had not been sent abroad they would probably still have been going together, because she had liked him very much and had been happy enough to manage on her salary so long as Ralph came when he could and stayed in her room and took her about. He was fun, intelligent, generous . . . she had felt a stab of something very akin to jealousy as well as that unaccountable heartache when she had seen her younger sister hanging on his arm. Emil had many good points, but Ralph understood her and she him. We're two of a kind, she thought sadly. And our kind isn't Sybil's kind, and she's going to be hurt, but if I warn her, won't that hurt more, in the end? Anyway, for all I know Ralph might have come to his senses, decided he really does want to settle down. He's quite old. He must be twenty-four, and that's settling-down age by any standards.

Leave well alone, she advised herself now, turning over as carefully and quietly as she could in the big, saggy bed. Sybil can take care of herself. And Ralph's been taking care of himself, helping himself, for years. Get on with your life, Lizzie Cream, and let them get on with theirs!

Only . . . why Sybil? By Lizzie's admittedly exacting standards, Sybil was really rather plain. She seldom used make-up, wore uniform or dowdy clothes, favoured flat-heeled, sensible shoes. And my standards are – or were – Ralph's standards, she reminded herself. Ralph liked girls to look good . . . and act bad. Sybil wasn't like that. She was all wrong for him, so why had he singled her out?

Lizzie lay awake a long time, wondering. Were men so different from women that a shared sweetness meant nothing to them? Could a man really forget the pleasure he had taken from a woman and simply move on to the next, as though, like cats, all girls were grey at night? Did Ralph not understand that had he been available, there would have been no question of her moving on, taking up with other men? Or was it that Ralph liked good-time girls to mess about with, but wanted the other sort when settling-down time came? When they were kids, Ralph hadn't paid much attention to anyone except Georgie. He had appeared to despise all girls, though he was nice with his sister, showing her how to ride her pony, doing more than his fair share of the grooming if she was busy with other ploys. Perhaps he despised all girls still, but because he enjoyed sex he had to pretend a little. Could it be that Ralph imagined Sybil, the cool and untouched Cream sister, would be a better bet in every way than Lizzie? But Lizzie could still remember all too clearly the way Ralph had behaved, in bed and out of it. She really could not credit any theory which denied Ralph's all-encompassing pleasure in her body and their shared loving.

There was one other reason why Ralph should have chosen to take Sybil out, of course, but surely not even Ralph would stoop that low? If he wanted to keep his jealous eye on Lizzie and make sure that she did nothing without him knowing, what better girlfriend could he pick than Lizzie's one and only sister?

He was jealous, all right. They had almost come to blows when he had visited the room in Timber Hill after Emil had left. He had been on the verge of tears . . . it had taken a lot of cuddles and kisses and other things, too, to calm him. Yet he had gone straight from her to Sybil – she knew it. And the way he hung over Sybil, whispering, kissing – it wasn't Ralph's style, Lizzie told herself obstinately for the twentieth time. He was doing it in front of Lizzie because what better way was there of saying, 'Look at me, cuddling up to your sister, leaving you out in the cold'?

There was, of course, no better way. Except I might tell . . . but he knows me, just as I know him, Lizzie decided. He knows I won't tell, no matter what. I like men all right and I don't kid myself – men's minds are quite different from women's. They don't really see the harm in a bit of malarky, a roll in the hay. If the girl gets herself in the club most men are sorry but not guilt-ridden; they think, in their hearts, that a girl should feel quite proud to have a fellow's baby. If only girls realized that they'd take a lot more care and wouldn't have babies they didn't want, Lizzie thought righteously. Look at me! One mistake, yes, but no more, never again. She had gone to a clinic and got herself fixed up with a thing called a diaphragm. It might be a bit of a nuisance but it did the trick – no more babies – and it meant she could be generous back, when a fellow was generous to her.

So, she would not tell. She would regard Sybil's affair with Ralph as just a part of her sister's growing up. She'll probably keep herself pure for her wedding, Lizzie thought without either censure or admiration, and then she'll meet someone who really cares and see Ralph's affection for what it is. And until then, I'll let sleeping dogs lie. And try not to remember how sweet were Ralph's kisses, how warm his arms, how vigorous his loving. Because despite how I feel about him, despite how I feel about Sybil, I couldn't take him back, not after this.

She sighed and tried to settle and presently she moved surreptitiously away from her sister – to mop the tears which were rolling down her face.

14

The kitchen was full of scented steam and the windows ran so that the autumn sunshine seemed to waver as it came through the glass. Sybil and her mother were making bramble jelly whilst Chris prepared the jars, dipping them in boiling water and then standing them on the top of the range to dry out. Now, she put down the final jar and looked approvingly round the kitchen.

It was the culmination of a week of hard work. Dora had been picking almost every day and the girls had helped whenever they were not working, for blackberry wine and bramble jelly were two of Dora's staples and since Georgie was home on leave in a few days and Henry would follow in a few weeks it behoved the Creams to gather the berries whilst they were at their best, fat and full of juice and sweetness, and Chris, in her capacity as lodger, had been glad to help.

'Dad will want to take some wine back with him,' Dora had said contentedly to Sybil the previous day, as they strained the cooked berries and gathered the juice. 'It's ever so popular on the ship, he's said so several times. And that reminds me, I must make some parkin. Did you say your mother could spare me some medium oatmeal, Chris dear?'

'She said she would,' Chris said. 'I reminded Toddy to go in and ask for it, but you know what blokes are like – he may forget and if so I'll go home at the weekend and get it myself.'

'I'll go with you,' Sybil put in. She was leaning over the range stirring the big saucepan, her face pink and damp from the steam, her hair curling in little wet tendrils about her face. 'But we'll have to give your Mum some of the parkin, that's only fair.'

'She can have some and welcome. But I do want to make it, because it's Georgie's favourite.' Dora poured the boiling jelly in a thin and steady stream from pan to jar. 'Here's another one, Chris – can you put it on the windowsill, love, out of harm's way?'

'Sure.' Chris glanced at the grandmother clock in the corner. Toddy had said he would come over on the five-thirty bus, which meant he could be here in about an hour. 'How much longer is all this going to take? It's like a Turkish bath in here!'

'If you want to go and change, for goodness sake go,' Dora said at once. 'Just so long as you don't mind a cold tea – I thought bread and jam.'

'I don't really need tea, thanks,' Chris said. 'Toddy said we'd get fish and chips after the flicks.'

'Lucky thing,' Sybil said enviously. 'Wish Ralph was on leave too. He doesn't get long enough as a rule to come all the way here, but it's nice when he does.'

'Umm hmm,' Chris said guardedly. She had her suspicions about her brother but she could not possibly tell Sybil how she felt. Several times Ralph had been home on leave, had actually been seen in the city – but had not visited Pakeby. Sometimes of course he had come over, all charm and friendliness, eager to take Sybs out and court her . . . but what about those other times?

There had been something between him and Lizzie, Chris was sure of it. He had affected to despise the elder girl, but Chris thought it was just an act, a smokescreen so that she and Sybil did not suspect. Yet why, if he was crazy about Lizzie, did he bother with Sybil? Except that Sybil was beautiful in a way Lizzie, for all her glamour, would never be, and perhaps Ralph really appreciated both that and Sybil's honest, down-to-earth niceness.

Perhaps it's that thing they say about men – 'Bad girls to play with, good girls to marry' – Chris decided at last. After all, Mummy would welcome Sybil as a daughter-in-law, or I think she would, but she'd be a bit dismayed to find Ralph walking up the aisle with Lizzie!

'You don't want to set too much store by a wartime friendship, Sybs,' Dora said now. Chris, whilst secretly applauding the sentiment so far as Sybil and Ralph were concerned, felt obliged to defend wartime friendships. Some, after all, were made in heaven – look at her and Toddy, for instance!

She said so, mumbling rather.

'Some are okay, Auntie Dora – Toddy and me are pretty serious, I can tell you.'

'So are Ralph and I,' Sybil put in. 'Honestly, Mum, just because Ralph's nice-looking that doesn't make him a – a *spiv*.'

Dora joined in the laughter which followed.

'I know he isn't a spiv, sweetheart, nor anything but a nice young man. But you don't see each other all that often and it might happen that he meets someone else, falls in love . . . I just don't want to see you get hurt.'

'Mothers have been saying that since the dawn of time,' Sybil grumbled. 'And it doesn't make any more sense now than it did then. You say Ralph might meet someone else – well, so might I!'

'No, because you won't go out, except with the girls or with Ralph,' Dora pointed out and Chris, halfway across to the box-stairs, nodded an agreement to this.

'Auntie Dora's right, Sybs. Why won't you make up a foursome now and then, with me and Toddy? I don't suppose Ralph would mind and it would do you good to get out sometimes.'

'Yes, I dare say. But for one thing I don't want to, and for another Ralph would mind; he'd be hurt,' Sybil said, lifting the heavy pan off the stove and beginning to stagger with it to the table where it would cool a little before Dora started the straining. 'Just you live your lives, you two, and let me live mine.'

'Well, don't say I didn't warn you,' Dora said rather obscurely as Chris began to mount the stairs. 'Oh, Sybs, don't slop blackberries all over the table! That stuff stains, you know.'

Chris, almost up to the landing, was struck by the last remark. Blackberries stain – of course they do! And she had an old grey dress which she was heartily sick of – would it go blackberry coloured if she picked enough and boiled them up together? It was a cotton dress and cotton, she had heard people say, dyed well.

It took her mind right off Sybil and Ralph, which was as well, for by the time Toddy arrived to pick her up she was determined to dye her grey dress and equally determined to have a good time. Discovering that Toddy had remembered the medium oatmeal only set the seal on her pleasure, and though she felt rather mean when she saw the moony, wistful look on Sybil's face as the two of them left the cottage, she knew there was nothing she could do about it.

Except to have a word with Ralph the next time he came home on leave. And to keep her eye on him.

In the end, Sybil employed her evening by writing letters. One to Ralph, a fairly short one since she wrote two or three times a week, one to Dad, a rather longer one, and one to Georgie, shortish again, because she would be seeing him so soon and anyway the chances were that he would get the letter when he docked in Liverpool, and would read it on the train home.

Chris and Toddy came in late and bright-eyed; someone's been kissed in the cinema and cuddled all the way home, Sybil thought enviously. Toddy had missed the last bus, but he would spend the night on the sofa where Georgie slept when he was at home and go off on the workers' early bus first thing in the morning.

Ralph never missed the last bus because he usually came by car – another reason, Sybil told herself defensively, why he came so rarely. Petrol was allowed to essential users only and then in very small quantities. Ralph and his friends managed, but it was getting more and more difficult, and Pakeby was out of the way – and he hated buses, poor Ralph!

She and Chris went off to bed as usual and Sybil wondered whether Chris longed to go downstairs during the night and climb on to the couch with Toddy; but she laughed at herself for even having such a thought, for Chris was a sensible girl and would never have abused Dora's hospitality in such a fashion. Besides, she had announced her intention, only a short while ago, of going over to Toddy's part of the country when she next had leave and spending a few days with him there.

'He can get me into some decent lodgings,' Chris said airily. 'It'll be nice, as a change.' But though she made it all sound perfectly respectable she avoided Sybil's eye and Sybil felt ashamed of her own lack of enthusiasm for such a course.

Ralph had suggested that she visit him in Lincolnshire several times, but so far she had always made some excuse. Besides, they rarely got more than a forty-eight, which meant long trips were out of the question. But next summer . . . oh well, I'll let next summer take care of itself, Sybil decided, cuddling down in their shared bed where Chris was already breathing steadily and deeply. The trouble is I don't see enough of Ralph to feel entirely easy at the thought of – of being with him, just the two of us. He'd probably find me boring, and then what would I do?

Next morning, over breakfast, Dora asked the two girls whether they felt like a short expedition that evening. Lizzie was working and lodging in Beccles now, and unless someone told her she would not know that Georgie was coming home on leave in less than three days.

'I could drop her a note, but you know Lizzie,' Dora said. 'I'd like her to come over for tea – it would be nice to have all my children under the same roof for once. And then Dad will be back too, in a fortnight. I could write, but I do feel, Sybs, that if you went over and told her Georgie would love to see her . . . well, she might come home, just for a few hours.'

'Of course I'll go. I'll cycle over directly I finish work and have a cup of tea with her,' Sybil agreed. 'But don't get too excited, Mum, because I don't have much influence with Lizzie now; not any more.'

'None of us do,' Dora said rather sadly. Unspoken, between them, was their dismay at the way Lizzie had grown away, not only from her parents and her old home, but from her sister too.

'Doesn't Lizzie write to Georgie?' Chris said curiously as the two of them cycled to work in a brisk autumn breeze which was already whirling the leaves from the trees. 'I'd have thought she'd have written – you do, after all, and there's a bigger age gap between you and Georgie than between Lizzie and him.'

'I know, but they never liked each other much,' Sybil admitted ruefully. 'When we were kids it was always me and Georgie; Lizzie was a bit detached, even then. And since she moved out – well, I don't really understand it, but you know I miss Georgie horribly, yet I hardly miss Lizzie at all. I think it's because she's shut me out, widened the gap between us, whereas Georgie . . . well, he's a man and not a boy any more, but even so he's the same old Georgie.'

Chris made some noncommittal comment and they cycled on, but Sybil's thoughts continued to nag at the relationship between Lizzie and the rest of the family. Where had it gone wrong? Why did Lizzie continually ward them off, as though she was afraid of a close relationship? It was a mystery.

Sometimes, though, she felt that the old Lizzie was still there, inside the beautiful, grown-up body of the young woman Lizzie had become, and that the old Lizzie looked out wistfully at her sister and longed for the friendship they had once shared.

Only I did nothing to spoil it, Sybil reminded herself. It's Lizzie who's so prickly and strange and difficult. If she could only tell me *why*, what I'm supposed to have done . . .

But it seemed that Lizzie could not tell, so the two sisters shared an uneasy truce, whilst perhaps they both hoped that one day their old understanding would resurface once more.

'Well, Sybs, haven't you got growed up whilst I bin away!'

Georgie grabbed Sybil and swung her up in his arms, pretending to toss her up to the ceiling, looking huge and golden in the small, smoky kitchen. He was so like Henry now that Sybil could have mistaken one for the other, for all Georgie was twenty years younger. Sybil, squeaking and hugging him back, suddenly thought how poverty-ridden the cottage must seem when one had been out into the world a bit. Georgie had been doing convoy patrol in his frigate, but when he was in port he would be in quarters a good deal more luxurious than his cottage home, she guessed.

'Georgie, how you ever fit into a frigate I don't know! Oh, it's lovely to see you again – have you seen Dad lately? Is he all right? You know the worst thing about war is that you don't see the people you love nearly often enough.'

'I've sin Dad,' Georgie acknowledged. He looked round the room and Sybil could see that, like her, he was suddenly aware of its smallness, the low ceiling, the packed earth on the floor. But there was contentment in his glance, even a sort of pride – could it be that war on a frigate could actually make you fonder of your home, no matter how humble? Georgie, settling down on the old sofa, certainly made it appear so.

'Where did you see Dad? How recently?'

'Couple of weeks back. See, the thing is, Dad's on a minesweeper so he's often in the port, but sometimes he come up to Liverpool which is where we dock, and the turn-round's too quick to get home to Pakeby but time enough for Dad and me to hev a pint or two and a mardle. That's grand, seeing Dad.'

'It must be,' Sybil said. She turned to her mother, who was cooking over the stove and watching them indulgently. 'I left a message for Lizzie, Mum, because she was out, but her landlady said she'd probably come over at the weekend unless she's doing overtime. She does overtime quite often; Sundays too, sometimes.'

The last remark was a lie, but at least it would prevent hurt feelings should Lizzie decide not to bother to come home. And Sybil saw by the warm glance Dora shot her that her mother was grateful. She knew that Georgie, so simple and good, would not understand Lizzie's attitude.

'Ah, well. It'll be good to see Lizzie, but I'm not bankin' on it,' Georgie said, walking over to the stove and looking hopefully at the pan Dora was stirring. 'We're had a few hot do's, I can tell you; I could sleep for a week.'

'Nothing to stop you, except that you'll want feeding, I dare say,' Dora said. She was glowing with happiness because she had her boy back again. Casualties at sea were always heavy and Dora must worry terribly with both her men aboard ship, but she seldom let it show. She soldiered on, joked, worked, wrote long letters . . . bet she prays, too, Sybil thought with a sudden flash of insight. Bet she goes down on her knees every night of her life and begs God to take care of her Henry, her Georgie.

Sybil had been brought up to pray and until the night of the Pakeby raid she had gone to church twice every Sunday and watched her mother kneel and cover her face with her hands. Now that the church had been destroyed they went to the Cunningham Hall, which was almost as close as the church itself, being on the corner of the Street and the Causeway. She and Chris and Dora knelt decorously and closed their eyes, but somehow Sybil thought that sort of praying was mere politeness, a way of deferring both to the rector and to the Lord. But down-on-your-knees praying in the privacy of your own room was different and Sybil herself now indulged in a good deal of it. She prayed for the safety and happiness of everyone she loved, for the Allies to be victorious, for the war to be over soon. Yet having thought about it, she realized that her prayers must be mere mouthings compared to her mother's desperate pleadings. Everything Dora valued was at risk, because she had given her whole life to Henry and her children. If they were killed . . . well, Dora's life would be worth nothing.

Shivering, Sybil dragged her mind back to practicalities.

'Well, if you're at a loose end, old Georgie, you might consider taking me and Chris out to a hop or a flick. Chris has got a feller who comes over quite often, but Ralph doesn't get away nearly so much. I'm not proud – I wouldn't mind a bit of an outing with a big, beautiful sailor!'

'I'll bear that in mind, old lady,' Georgie said contentedly. 'Come on, Ma, tell us what's for supper, then!'

The weekend passed in a flash. Georgie took the boat out and brought back a netful of codling, and Dora sold some to people in the village and salted down what they didn't eat. When the girls weren't working the four of them went out after blackberries, trudging the country lanes, talking and laughing. Georgie was so happy, so genial! Most people hated their war work, Sybil found herself thinking, but Georgie simply wasn't like that. Whatever he did, he did to the best of his ability and enjoyed too. How fortunate they were, he and she, to be doing work they loved, with people they liked, for Georgie talked a lot about his shipmates and seemed to know everything about each one of them, even the officers.

'People appreciate a bit of interest,' he said when she commented on this fact. 'Don't you find that, old Sybs?'

Sybil laughed, remembering the present bane of the Franklyn landgirls' existence: Bert Haysell, who had been brought in to supervise the girls when Mr Franklyn had been rushed into hospital for an emergency appendectomy. The girls, kidding one another, had hoped for a tanned, muscular son of the soil who would sweep them off their feet – well, sweep one of them off her feet – flirt with them, help them to cope. Bert was small and wizened, and he hated women. He made sure all the really dirty jobs went to either Chris or Sybil since he felt, obscurely, that they needed taking down a peg, and although he was clearly talented in one direction – that of passing work on and getting out of it himself – the girls rightly considered him a lazy old sod who seldom lifted a pitchfork, talked smutty and swore fruitily, seldom smiled and never washed.

'Did you hear Bernard Whatsisname on the wireless the other night? He said his mother never washed him all winter, she just picked him up and knocked him against the wall to get the dirt off in the spring, as if he was an old tater,' one of the landgirls said. 'That's what old Bert's missus must do. Can't wait for old Franklyn to come back!'

'A bit of interest!' Sybil said now, walking along the cliff path into the port with Georgie beside her. 'If I showed any interest in old Bert, he'd have me shot at dawn. We aren't supposed to speak to him unless we curtsey first. He's a rotten old swine – aren't there any like that aboard your frigate, Georgie?'

'No,' Georgie said thoughtfully, after a moment. 'Well, yes, but not to me, if you see what I mean. And not in front of me, if they know what's good for them.'

And Sybil, looking at the breadth of her brother's shoulders and the size of his fists, thought she saw exactly what he meant.

When the weekend was over, she and Chris returned to the farm and to the rule of Bert, as they called it. But somehow, it was easier to get along with Bert when you thought of Georgie, crammed into a small ship with aircraft and submarines and other warships all gunning – literally – for him, yet managing to get along so well with his shipmates. It made Bert's whiny voice and sharp tongue seem more amusing than dangerous, and it infuriated him when Chris and Sybil were indulgent over his demands, and seemed to find his nastiest cracks amusing. It also made him uneasy, causing him to walk out of sheds when they walked in, to break off in the middle of sentences and find himself suddenly needed elsewhere.

What was more, Georgie had a practical sort of way of looking at problems which helped Sybil quite a lot. Lizzie, for instance. When, by Wednesday, she had not turned up, Georgie said that if Chris would be good enough to lend Sybil her bike, the two of them would go and visit Lizzie.

'I suppose she's been too busy,' Sybil said. 'But I'd like to cycle over with you, Georgie.'

Chris, for her part, announced herself very willing to lend her bike, particularly as it would mean she did not feel honour-bound to accompany them, for a ten mile cycle ride was no sinecure after a hard day on the land.

'Most of the harvesting's over, so now we'll start ploughing in the stubble,' Sybil remarked as the two of them set off. 'Aren't the colours marvellous at this time of year, Georgie?'

Georgie grunted, and presently stopped and dismounted.

'What've you done to my saddle, gal-Sybil?' he enquired plaintively. 'This one, that catch me just where I don't much like being cotched!'

Sybil, clapping a hand to her mouth, dismounted too.

'Oh, Georgie, I'm so very sorry! Mum said it would be all right and it was done so long ago I just completely forgot! I swapped the saddles – yours is in the shed at home, don't worry. This is a girl's one I bought.'

'Oh, ah. Well, that'll be all right when I've shoved it about a foot higher,' Georgie said philosophically, getting the spanner out of the toolbag which hung on the back of the saddle. 'Hold hard a minute, gal, and I'll be with you.'

They rode along through the dreamy golden sunshine, heading for Beccles. Lizzie had found a job in the munitions factory there and lodged with a Mrs Potter in Blyburgate. The house was an old one, full, right now, of bright young girls, most of whom worked, with Lizzie, at Elliott's. Mrs Potter answered the door and told them that the girls would be home in about ten minutes, and would they care to have a spot of supper – nothing elaborate, just what she did for her lodgers. A few sandwiches, homemade crisps in a big dish, sausage rolls with homemade chutney and maybe a bit of apple pie for afters.

Georgie agreed with alacrity; you could see he was used to being indulged by middle-aged women, Sybil thought as her brother sat down in the chair Mrs Potter offered and took the big mug of tea she held out. He also looked with admiration at the table, set with all the things Mrs Potter had described and more.

'How is it you can get hold of sausage meat and pork pies?' he enquired amiably. 'As for those scones . . . I envy your lodgers, Mrs Potter!'

'My son-in-law's the butcher,' Mrs Potter said, smiling fatly. 'We've a good foo ration books, with all the girls, and my sister Rosemary, she work in Barrett's shop, so one way and another . . .'

'Lucky Lizzie,' Sybil said as her own cup of tea was handed to her. 'I hope she isn't planning to go out, though. It's a good cycle ride from Pakeby to Beccles.'

'Ten mile,' nodded Mrs Potter knowingly, though it was easy to see from her round and robinlike figure that it had been a good few years since she had cycled it herself. 'She in't going out tonight, my woman. Not mid-week. That's rare hard work them girls do, up to Elliott's.'

And presently the girls came in, Lizzie amongst them, looking very spruce, though tired. And now that she was home, Lizzie behaved nicely enough. She hugged Georgie and squeezed Sybil's hand, and then they all sat down to tea and whilst they ate Georgie asked Lizzie about her job and her life and Lizzie answered, still in the guarded way which had, Sybil supposed, become second nature to her since leaving home. After tea Lizzie took Georgie off to see her factory whilst Sybil helped Mrs Potter to wash up. It was a small way to repay that lovely tea and it gave Georgie the chance of a few words with his sister.

They could not stay long. Both bicycles had lamps but they would only use them if they heard traffic approaching along the windy lanes which led home. And they were blue-painted lamps, which didn't give very much illumination. Besides, it would take them an hour at least.

Lizzie walked them down to the end of the road and saw them on their way. She gave Georgie another hug and said to Sybil that she would really try to get home the following weekend.

'Only there's shift-work, and overtime,' she said in her cool, detached voice. 'And I do have to enjoy myself sometimes, when I'm not working.'

'And coming home to see Mum and Sybs isn't your idea of enjoyment, Lizzie?' Georgie asked in his mild voice. 'What an odd gal you are!'

Lizzie blushed but stared up at him with no other sign of discomposure.

'No; it's my duty, and I feel I do my duty all week, without having to do it weekends as well,' she said. 'Goodbye, both. Take care of yourself, Georgie.'

Cycling home through the dusk, Sybil said as lightly as she could,

'Well, I suppose we asked for that. I'm sorry she considers Mum and me a duty, though.'

Georgie snorted.

'She don't! That was just the hurt speaking; didn't you twig, gal-Sybil?'

'The hurt? Georgie, what've I ever done to Lizzie? Or Mum for that matter? Just answer me that!'

'I often thought that Mum wasn't there for her when she needed her most, and I'd guess she reckon you've taken her feller,' Georgie observed after a moment. 'I'm not sayin' you did, mind, just that it was what Lizzie would think.'

'You mean Ralph, don't you? Oh, but Lizzie hardly knew Ralph! She was always off with her village friends, she hardly ever played with Chris or Ralph.'

Georgie sighed.

'I maybe don't say much, Sybs, but I do notice a fair old bit! I well remember digging Gran's garden that autumn, after the midsummer party, just afore tha gal Lizzie left. It's my belief that Gran told her to go rather than bring disgrace . . . that sorta thing, anyway.'

'Go? Lizzie? But why, Georgie?'

'Reckon she was in the family way,' Georgie said quietly. 'I in't never said anything to anyone, because that's not my way, but I always did fancy Lizzie left home because she didn't hev much choice. It was sudden-like, wasn't it?'

'Yes, it was, but . . .'

'Told everyone she had a marvellous job but you didn't hear much about that job for a while. And Gran gave her money; I saw her take it out of the sock, count it into Lizzie's hand.'

'Gosh. Yes, that would add up, I suppose,' Sybil said thoughtfully. 'Fancy you knowing all these years, Georgie, and never letting on. Didn't you feel you ought to tell?'

'Nope. Wouldn't have said a word now, only I could see you were hurt by Lizzie's attitude, believing it had no cause. But it had, see?'

'Ye-es. But . . . she should have *told* me,' Sybil said vehemently. 'How could I possibly help her if I didn't know?'

'Ah, but there was the other half. The father.'

'The *father*? Of course, there had to be a feller . . . was it Ralph, is that what you're trying to say, Georgie?'

'Well now, I don't know, and I'm not sure that it matter, much,' Georgie said consideringly. 'No, I'm inclined to think it was someone else, someone Lizzie din't care two hoots about, because Ralph and me was pals and he'd 'a said suffin'. But she liked Ralph, see? Really liked him, I think, and probably she let him see she was keen – and then he turned up wi' her little sister in tow. See?'

'But how was that my fault?' Sybil cried, quite vexed to be blamed for something about which she had known nothing. 'If Ralph likes me, what am I supposed to do about it? Give him the cold shoulder? Tell him I'd rather he took my sister Lizzie out? I think I'm most awfully lucky that Ralph likes me, and I *do* like him, I like him a lot. Oh, Georgie, I don't think I can just give him up!'

'It's all right, old lady, there in't no need for desperate measures,' Georgie said. It was too dark to see his face, though there was a moon, but Sybil did not need to see him to know that he was smiling. 'I'm just saying that Lizzie feel a little stiff towards you because you've got what she want. She's been the same all her life, gal-Sybil, so there's no need to get in a spin over it! Lizzie was spoiled rotten by Mum because she was so pretty, and so like Mum, too. There in't no cure for Lizzie being off-hand with you and Mum, but maybe that's easier to bear if you know the reasoning behind it.'

'Maybe,' Sybil said, 'so long as no one expects me to give Ralph up.'

' 'Course not! Besides, I'm not saying Lizzie would want him, even. So go on being nice to her, Sybs, and understanding. Don't expect her to like Chris, or be polite to Ralph, because Lizzie's a bit like one of them old waspses what hang round the plum tree. A bee will wait till it's hurt before that sting, but the gal Lizzie sting first, in case.'

Sybil laughed, unwillingly almost, at this neat description of her sister.

'All right, Georgie. What happened to the baby, though, if Lizzie did have one?'

'Reckon it was got rid of before it ever was a baby,' Georgie said gruffly. 'Or adopted, maybe. Anyroad, that in't no concern of ours, Sybil. It's just another reason why Lizzie's a bit touchy, like, over family life.'

'And do I tell her I know?' Sybil queried next, cycling along in the deepening dark with stars appearing overhead and a great golden harvest moon swinging in the sky above them. 'It might help her to know I know.'

'No! If she'd wanted any of us to know she'd have told us. And how often do she visit Gran, by the way?'

'Well, never, so far as I know,' Sybil said. 'She's hardly ever in

Pakeby, and when she does come she's always in a hurry to get away again. Why?'

'Because Gran know what happened to Lizzie all them years ago, and Lizzie don't visit her. Read between the lines, Sybs, for goodness sake!'

'Georgie, I never knew you were so wise,' Sybil said in an awed voice as they turned into the village and saw the dark shapes of the houses beginning to loom up on either side of the road. 'I won't say a word. But I'll be ever so nice to Lizzie!'

Sybil was ploughing the ten acre when the storm started. The weather had been threatening all day, the clouds scudding across the sky at a great rate, grey and ominous. Around lunch-time, indeed, she had joined the other girls in the barn, where they were diligently topping and tailing sugar beet, told them it was time for food, and led the rush to the kitchen, feeling certain that by the time they had eaten rain would be pelting down and she, too, would go to the barn.

But she was wrong; as they left the farmhouse a watery sun came out from behind the cloud. It looked as though she might just finish the ten acre before the rain started.

She was on the tractor, carefully taking the deep dip in one corner, when the sun disappeared once more and a little wind blew up. It bent the brown and gold hedges for a second or so, then it went, leaving a flat calm behind. A flat calm and an eerie light, a yellowish, livid light with nothing in it of sunshine or blue skies.

'Hey, Sybs, why's the light all funny? I don't like it,' Selly Cotter said, her round brown face appearing through a gap in the hedge. 'Why's the wind dropped? What's that noise? Is it 'planes?'

Selly had not been a landgirl very long; she was only sixteen and lived in Norwich, where her mother worked as a cleaner at the City Hall and her father, until he was whisked into the army, had been a postman. She was a city child through and through, yet she had taken like a duck to water to the hardest agricultural work. Old Bert, still ruling, could almost be said to like her.

'No, it isn't a bombing raid,' Sybil said cheerfully. Odd how a natural fear could temporarily take away the less natural fear caused by the stillness and the strange light. 'But we're probably going to get some rain.' She spoke quietly but knew that in the almost uncanny stillness her voice could be heard right across the field next door, where Selly and another girl were barrowing away horse dung, which, if left, would sour the ground and give the horses worms.

Slightly reassured, Selly was turning away from the hedge when, out of nowhere it seemed, the wind hit them. It was no ordinary wind either, but more like a hurricane. It bent the tall trees which surrounded the fields, it shrieked and howled around the tractor and sent the birds which had been following the plough up in a wild, involuntary dance. Huddling low over the tractor's steering wheel, Sybil saw broken branches, a couple of last spring's nests and a huge clod of earth sail past her before she managed to get the tractor into the lee of the hedge. Climbing down, she staggered into the ditch and saw, through the quickthorn, Mandy Phillips, who was small and slight, knocked off her feet and bowled over and over like a hoop as she rolled, shrieking, across the grass, whilst Selly, clinging to the wheelbarrow, looked likely to follow her at any moment. Dung, windborne, was already leaving the barrow.

'Come into the ditch,' Sybil shrieked as soon as the wind allowed her to open her mouth again. 'Selly, Mandy, come over here!' They probably did not hear her, could not for the sound and fury of the storm, but she stood up and pushed herself half through the hedge and Selly caught sight of her. Mandy was picking herself up, red-faced, more embarrassed than hurt, Sybil guessed, and both girls ran towards the ditch and bundled into it, Selly grabbing Sybil's hands fiercely in her own large, probably dirty ones.

'Have you ever seen anything like it?' she demanded breathlessly. 'Cor, that's a storm and a half in't it, Sybil? But it's quieter; do you think . . .'

The wind silenced her; this time what looked suspiciously like the remains of a gate came crumping and crashing over the meadow. A huge tree lost a huge branch; it came thundering down on to the hedge and a gap magically appeared.

'Stay where you are,' Sybil said crisply, when Mandy and Selly showed a tendency to make a run for it. 'Here, I'll come through to you; it's more sheltered your side.'

It was probably not true, but Sybil did not want those two foolish young girls to be alone in that wind, so she crawled along the ditch to the gap in the hedge and went through, then crawled back. And all the time the wind shrieked like a maniac and seized branches from trees, roofs from sheds, great cushions of hay from haystacks and endless twigs and loose bits of fencing from everywhere and hurled them up into the air.

'That's a cyclone,' Selly mumbled, staring, round-eyed, from the shelter of the ditch. 'Oh, no, look at that!'

'That' was rain; they could see it coming a field away, heavy silver-grey rain like a curtain of parachute silk, bearing down on them. It hit and it was less rain than cloudburst, as though someone had torn the rain clouds, releasing not merely droplets but bucketsful of water. It was so violent that the girls shrank back into the slight shelter of the hedge, but even so it made them gasp and stung their faces.

The wind had dropped whilst the worst of the rain fell, but as it slackened from a river of water to a mere tropical downpour the wind began to pick up again. They could hear it coming like an express train, roaring through the trees, screaming across open ground, hitting them at last like an explosion, a battering ram of air.

Selly began to sob and Mandy, only a year older and without Selly's physical strength or weight, looked likely to follow suit. Sybil made up her mind.

'We'd better get back to the farm in the next lull,' she shouted. 'Wait till I give the word.'

They waited until the wind seemed to be gathering its breath for another attack, then sprinted in a tight little group across the meadow, through the gateway – the gate had long gone – along the deep lane and across the yard.

There was damage here; a roof off a building, a scatter of broken tiles near the back door, a chimney on the farmhouse itself leaning perilously. The big barn door was swinging on its hinges; Sybil pushed the other two towards the back door and ran to the barn, but there was no means, now, of fastening the door so she ran back, getting into the kitchen just as the rain began again.

The landgirls were all there, sitting cross-legged on the floor, watching the storm through the back window. Chris's face lit up when she saw Sybil.

'What happened?' she asked. 'Where were you? I'd gone into Lowestoft to buy seed; I got back seconds before it started.'

'Ploughing the ten acre,' Sybil said briefly. 'The wind rolled poor old Mandy around in the horse dung like a hoop!'

The girls laughed, even Mandy. It was rather high laughter, but it helped to relieve the almost unbearable tension.

Someone else volunteered that she'd been in the petty and had almost fallen through the hole with shock, except that the wind had come from beneath her, nearly popping her straight up off the seat and through the roof. Someone else observed sagely that there was no longer a roof on the petty, and how did she explain that? Laughter, another voice chiming in, the beginning of conversation.

'Where did it come from?' Chris asked Sybil quietly. 'This is tropical stuff. We don't have storms like this in England!'

'I pity any pilot up in that,' Pat Frewin remarked as great, ragged black clouds began to race across the sky. 'They wouldn't last long up there today.'

'I don't envy sailors, either,' Chris said. 'What'll the sea be like, Sybs?'

'Awful; there'll be immense waves running,' Sybil said. 'Thank God Georgie's home this week, but I hope Dad's all right.'

The kitchen grew dark but Mrs Franklyn declined to light the lamp.

'We don't want no fires should the wind blow a frame in,' she announced, and this was clearly possible. Besides, the lightning began to flash at that point, arcing brilliantly across the sky, and though they all hated this sudden storm no one wanted to look away from the windows.

A crack of thunder directly overhead, so loud that it sounded like a bursting bomb, put an end to their conversation for a bit. Someone started to tell a story but her voice tailed out; the competition from the elements was too great. Then Chris started singing and slowly, falteringly, other voices joined in. Mrs Franklyn tried to start them off with what she would have called 'a good old rousing tune', and Bert, huddled in the corner smoking his noxious pipe, glared balefully at them, but somehow the ones they chose seemed, in the circumstances, more appropriate.

'Run rabbit run rabbit, run run run,' some girls bawled cheerfully, whilst others sang that there were rats, rats, big as bloomin' cats, in the quartermaster's stores, and a third group adjured everyone to bless 'em all, bless 'em all, the long and the short and the tall.

'How about "Bless this house"?' Mrs Franklyn kept suggesting in her soft voice. 'Or we could try a nice ballad. "Greensleeves" is a great favourite of mine.'

Undeterred, the shrill, determined voices rose even above the roar and crash of the elements in the tunes which took their minds off their troubles. 'She'll be wearin' pink pyjamas when she comes,' roared the sugar-beet choppers. 'Oh, *don't* go under the apple tree with anyone else but me,' shouted the dung shovellers. '*Who* do you think you are kidding, Mr Hitler,' bawled Chris and Sybil, whilst the sober indoor people, Ethel who did the dairywork and the charlady and the charlady's dim daughter Mabel, put their hearts and souls into outsinging everyone with the words: 'When the m-moon shines, over the cow shed, I'll be waiting at the k-k-k-kitchen door!'

And all by herself, in lonely defiance, Mrs Franklyn sang, 'We'll gather lilacs in the spriiing again, We'll walk together down an Eeenglish lane . . .'

During this cacophony Chris moved over to sit by Sybil.

'This came out of nowhere,' she said quietly. 'What'll happen in Pakeby, Sybs?'

'The sea will probably come over the bank,' Sybil whispered back. 'But Georgie's home – he'll take Mum into the village if it looks like reaching the cottage. It wouldn't be the first time Creams have run up Beach Road and asked the nearest neighbour for shelter until the tide ebbs.'

'That's all right, then,' Chris said. 'I imagine this is quite local, anyway. I doubt if your father is getting such freak weather conditions at sea.' She turned to Mrs Franklyn. 'Let's beat them all at their own game,' she shouted. 'Let's sing the WLA song! Come on, really loud, drown them out!'

> 'Back to the land, we must all lend a hand,
> To the farms and the fields we must go.
> There's a job to be done, though we can't fire a gun
> We can still do our bit with the hoe.'

The other girls, hearing their official song, began to join in. Mrs Franklyn sang with gusto and Sybil heard one of the girls remark to another, 'So *those* are the words – bit different from what we usually sing!'

Oh well, she thought, that's war for you.

'Well, Georgie, did you enjoy that?'

Dora and her son had eaten well; roast pork, apple sauce, roast potatoes, runner beans and cabbage, followed, joy of joys, by a treacle pudding, sticky and heavy as lead, but oh so delicious! And Dora had not only enjoyed her own food, she had thoroughly enjoyed spoiling her son. He was such a good boy, such a pleasure to be with and so sensible – so very like his father.

'Mum, it was grand, absolutely grand!' Georgie leaned back in his chair and patted his stomach. 'I've not ate so well since I joined the navy . . . where did you get that pork?'

'We killed one of our fatteners a few months back and shared it out; this week Edith Sumner killed hers and did likewise. That joint was part of our share. Done like that, it means we get fresh meat off the ration now and then, but it was just luck that Edith's coincided with your first proper leave.' Dora got up and spooned tea into the pot, poured on boiling water and pottered over to the pantry to bring back a jug of milk. 'You'll have a cuppa now, will you? I'll wash up later. Right now we'll let our dinner settle.'

'Good. And we'll have a bit of a natter,' Georgie said contentedly. 'How are you managing without me and Dad, then?'

'Not too bad. Sybil's a good girl, she helps with the allotment and so on. She's done her teacher training and though she can't use it whilst the war lasts, it'll stand her in good stead in peacetime. As for the Land Army, she loves it, she really does, and I do enjoy having Chris and her about the place. I wouldn't say this to everyone, love, but Lizzie's been a bit of a disappointment to me and Sybil's been marvellous. As you know, Lizzie walked out of this house a few years back and she's never walked in again – that is, she's come in, but only in the body, never in the spirit. She was the apple of my eye, you know that, yet she's cast me off completely. Which hurts, of course, though not so bad now I've got Sybs to comfort me. And you, lad, when you're able.'

'I wish I could be home more,' Georgie said. 'Next time I get a forty-eight I'll do my best to get back. And Mum – don't be hard on Lizzie. It's my belief there's more to her leaving home than meets the eye. And I haven't come back to see you as often as I could have, which isn't to my credit at all, even though I've a good reason.'

'Oh? What's that, then?'

'It's five foot four, with dark curls and big blue eyes . . . it's got the prettiest little face and the sort of figure a fellow wants to cuddle. In short, Mum, it's a girl.'

'A girl? Well, I never did! You've kept her pretty quiet, young Georgie!'

'Mm hmm. Wanted to be sure she felt the same's me, and now I know she does. I bought her a little ring . . . Mum, we're engaged! Me and Emily Lewis are going to get married one of these fine days!'

'Well, Georgie, that's grand!' Dora exclaimed, though there was a tight sort of feeling in her chest and a dryness in her mouth. Her firstborn, about to fly the nest, so keen on some little bit of a girl that he'd spent leaves away from his home and his mother! But it would never do to show her dismay, and besides, she realized that it was not really dismay but a sort of stupid jealousy. The girl must be a darling or Georgie would not love her. Dora turned bravely back to her son. 'Going to bring Emily home with you some time, so we can all meet her?'

'I thought I would,' Georgie said shyly. 'She's one of the best, Mum – you'll love her. Comes from a little village in North Wales she does, so she talks real pretty, though she's worked in Liverpool in the shipping offices for a year or more. She's a Wren . . . did I say? Good at her work and all, types like lightning. I reckon I'm a lucky bloke.'

'You'd best write to your father and tell him,' Dora said, sipping her tea. 'Lord, I've eaten too much – shall we take a walk on the beach, see if some exercise will make room for supper, later?'

'Dad knows; leastways he's seen me with her,' Georgie confessed, drinking his own tea down in one long gulp. He stood up, then bent to peer through the low kitchen window. 'If we're having a walk we'd better get going – that sky looks odd. Reckon there's a storm coming.'

'I'll put my coat on,' Dora decided, finishing her own tea and walking over to open the back door. The freshening wind made her shiver as she turned away. 'You'd better take your coat, too.'

'Right,' Georgie said. He unhooked his duffel coat from the door and put it on, but left the toggles unfastened. 'Which way d'you want to walk? Towards the port or towards the abandoned cottages?'

The abandoned cottages were no more than a smudge on the horizon but it had been a good while since Dora had gone that way and she felt in need of exercise. She had to get used to the idea of losing a son, because she did not fool herself that Georgie would hang around working a Pakeby fishing boat when he could be earning decent money in a big city with his little Welsh sweetheart by his side.

'Let's see if we can get to the cottages before the weather breaks,' she said, raising her voice as they left the shelter of the kitchen and began to cross the yard. The wind was rising, and out to sea you could see those strange flat patches on the waves which mean a squall. 'Good thing my coat's got a hood.'

'Aye, and mine,' Georgie agreed. 'Shake a leg, then, or we'll get drownded by the look of those clouds.'

They walked the short distance down to the cliff-path which ran along the top of the beach. The beach itself was usually deserted at this time but today there was a young couple strolling des-ultorily across the sand, making for the waves. They were hand in hand, a dark young man and a slim girl, the girl's fair head resting on the man's shoulder. Young lovers, taking a walk on the deserted beach.

'They look pretty moony; I wonder if we ought to warn them that there's a storm brewing?' Dora said nervously. It was safe to walk right along the cliff-path but there was only a very restricted area of beach which had been left unmined so that the fishing boats could go out to sea. 'They might walk along the tideline and forget . . . oh, no, not today.'

The barbed wire entanglement and the warning notices stretched down to low water mark but theoretically at least it was possible for someone walking actually beside the water at low tide to go past the entanglement without realizing. However, today the tide was already more than halfway in, and still coming. The young couple would have to go in over their heads before they reached the end of the wire.

'No, they'll be all right,' Georgie said placidly. 'I expect they're looking for somewhere quiet and private where they can do a spot of lovemaking.' He laughed. 'First upturned boat they see they'll be in under it, snogging away.'

There speaks the voice of experience, Dora thought sadly. It was clear that innocent Georgie, who flirted with girls for fun but thought more highly of fishing, football and a night out with the boys, was long gone. Life would never be quite the same again – the Cream family really was breaking up, with Lizzie in Beccles and likely to stay there until she could move back to Norwich and Georgie contemplating marriage and, probably, a family of his own.

I won't mind so much once Henry gets home, Dora comforted herself. This girl, this Emily, sounds a nice little thing – there'll be children for me to fuss over and a nice little home somewhere for Henry and me to visit . . . it won't be so bad. And I'll still have the girls – how does that saying go? *A son is a son till he takes him a wife, but a daughter's a daughter the rest of your life.* Whoever made that up never said a truer word!

They were halfway to the cottages when the wind became almost too strong for them, hurling itself at their backs, forcing Dora to break into a trot. Up at this end of the beach the sea was already only feet from the path so it was impossible to tell when the spray that was suddenly lashing into their faces was joined by rain. Georgie took his mother's arm.

'This is no joke,' he yelled, his head close to hers. 'We'd better shelter in the cottages – we shan't make much headway against this wind and I don't like the look of the sea – it'll be over the bank at this end if the wind doesn't drop soon.'

'All right,' Dora gasped. 'So long as we don't get hit by the roof caving in.'

But this fear proved groundless, for the abandoned cottages, when they reached them, were roofless, sand piled up inside, the windows letting in both wind and spray. But in the second cottage along there was a small room facing inland with all its sturdy walls intact. In here, Dora and Georgie found a temporary refuge and sat down on the piled sand with their backs against a wall.

'Dad says in a few years these cottages will be under the sea,' Georgie observed presently. 'It makes you think, Mum.'

'Yes, it does. Your grandmother remembers when these cottages weren't on the beach at all, and there was a wide barley field between them and the coast. I think of that sometimes, when the wind's blowing a gale and I'm lying alone in bed, listening to it trying to grab the rooftiles and hurl them into the Malverns orchard.'

'Good thing you've got Sybil and Chris with you,' Georgie observed. 'If Sybil was still in teaching she wouldn't be able to stay on in Pakeby, so being a landgirl is good all round. And when the war's over Dad will be back to take care of you.'

He did not mention himself because, Dora knew, he was too honest to pretend. But he was right; she was lucky to have the girls. Many a woman with sons and daughters of an age to fight was left alone to do the best she could until her loved ones came home – or didn't come home.

'Yes, I wouldn't be without the girls for all the tea in China, though I miss you and Dad more than I can ever say.'

'That's nice to hear, but . . . oh, to hell!'

There was no doubt that it was raining now. The rain came down on them in sheets, soaking them in seconds. Georgie turned to her, peering out of his hood, eyes twinkling.

'We'd better get out of here, take our chance on being blown all anyhow,' he roared. 'What price under a boat now, eh?'

Dora laughed.

'A boat, when they could have a beatster hut? That's where they'll be if they've got half a brain between them.'

Mother and son grinned at each other, this time with the camaraderie of knowledge shared. No young lover in Pakeby could possibly be unaware of the various uses to which beatster huts were put during the season; clearly Georgie's interest in football and fishing had never entirely submerged his interest in girls!

'Aye, you're right. C'mon then, let's start battling.'

Georgie seized Dora firmly round the waist and the two of them bent their heads and began to charge into the gale.

But it was hard work, and tiring, and the sea shocked them by suddenly mounting the bank and pouring over the path to a depth of a foot at least. Mother and son were forced to push their way through the thick hedge, tearing clothes and skin, in order to walk in comparative safety in the meadow on the further side.

'We could go further inland, walk through the wood,' Dora shrieked, but after a frowning moment Georgie shook his head.

'Not safe; trees won't all be able to withstand this,' he bellowed. 'You don't want to be brained by a falling branch. We'll stick to the fields.'

It was a long way back; presently, in order to breathe, for the wind was trying to push its way down into her lungs when she was trying to exhale, Dora had to turn her face into Georgie's shoulder and he, too, turned his head so that his breath was on her cheek. Despite the terrifying power of the wind and the slashing discomfort of the rain, both of them were giggling at their antics as they strove to continue on their way. Dora had lived by the sea now for twenty-five years and she had never seen such a storm and hoped she never would again, but she was still conscious of pleasure in the sudden warmth of Georgie's company and the closeness, both physical and mental, which their ordeal was engendering.

'This is dreadful,' she muttered against Georgie's shoulder. 'Does it get like this at sea, Georgie?'

'Never known it this bad,' Georgie assured her. 'I reckon it was a storm like this which drownded the village. Glad we're off the cliff-path – I reckon we'd have been knocked off our feet by now.'

In the field where the Winterton ponies were kept a mini-tornado caught them. It whirled them round, still clinging together, bashed them against a stunted hawthorn tree, then dropped them as though it disdained their earthbound weight and whirled on, taking with it anything loose it could find – branches still heavy with leaves, hay, sand and a sizeable piece of timber.

'Christ almighty!' Georgie gasped, and Dora knew that it was not blasphemy but a devout prayer. 'Christ almighty, pity poor sailors!'

Henry! Henry might be at sea in this! Henry . . .

'Dad'll be snugged down safe in harbour somewhere,' Georgie roared as though he had read his mother's thoughts. 'We're almost home – can you see the church?'

Through eyes filled with water and sand particles, with the wind actually daring to dictate whether or not she could peer between her lids, Dora managed to make out the remains of the church and, against that crouching animal-shape on its mound, the comforting bulk of the three cottages. Thank God! Another few yards, and . . .

'We'll be indoors in a moment,' Georgie shouted. 'Oh, heck! Remember those kids on the beach? You go indoors, Mum, and I'll just . . .'

He tried to release her but Dora clung on, so together they rounded the side of the cottage and made for the shore. To Dora's horror waves were breaking here right into the churchyard, the cliff-path was completely hidden, the bank somewhere beneath the white, flurried water. The boats were riding all anyhow, some inverted, some filled with water, others only had a nose above the waves. But they'll be all right if only it eases soon, Dora told herself. They're well anchored, so they should be all right, and if they go it's not as if they had people aboard . . .

The water was halfway up the beatster huts. One door had been broken in by the elements and you could see the loose nets drifting in the doorway. Dora was about to say that those kids couldn't possibly be in the huts, so they might as well go home and get the kettle on, when Georgie gave a shout and let go of her so abruptly that she nearly fell.

'My God! Look out there, Mum! See?'

Dora's glance followed his pointing finger and she saw, with cold horror, just what had happened to the young lovers.

They were adrift on that boiling and treacherous sea in a small boat which must have dragged its anchor at the start of the storm. And Georgie was stripping off his duffel coat, his thick jersey, even his boots.

'I'll get 'em, tow 'em ashore,' he said breathlessly. 'Go and put the kettle on, Mum. I'll need a hot drink and a hot bath by the time I'm through.'

'Georgie, don't . . . you can't . . . no one could swim in that,' Dora began, but her son shook his head at her, grinning.

'I'm taking the boat out, Mum, I'm not a fool! I may have to swim to bring them back, but I'll go out in style.'

And with that he turned away from her and waded into the surf.

Dora watched with clasped hands and bumping heart. She dared not turn her eyes from the scene before her, she literally dared not. She watched as Georgie got into a boat which was still riding relatively high, and waved to the two children – they were scarcely more – in their cockleshell craft. She watched as her son manoeuvred his craft neatly with one oar, through trough and crest, until he was almost alongside.

She watched as he threw a rope, hauled it in, threw again . . . jumped into the sea and took the rope to the youngsters, supervised the fastening of it, began to swim back.

He must have thrown out the anchor but it hadn't held, and, empty and alone, his craft was now making its way determinedly along the coast. With the sea running the way it was they would probably find it tomorrow cast ashore by the abandoned cottages, so Dora took her mind off it and watched Georgie.

He was a strong swimmer. Even in the impossible conditions prevailing he managed to fight his way nearer to the shore with the rope wound round one arm so that he was pulling the small boat with him.

He shouted something to Dora when his feet touched bottom, and turned to wave at her and grin; and an incoming comber of huge dimensions picked up the little boat and its two occupants and crashed them with its many tons of green and white water down on Georgie. He went under like a felled ox, then rose. Blood was running, pale and watery, from a great cut across his brow, and for a moment he staggered before coming on whilst the little boat which had downed him was carried ashore by the force of the waves.

Dora shouted and ran towards him; the surf was only knee-high on him now and the youngsters were climbing out of the boat, but it was easy to see that Georgie had been stunned by the impact of the wave for he was wandering, heading off to the right.

One moment he was there, head bent, blood running across his face, and the next there was a tremendous explosion. Water jetted, church-high, into the grey and lowering sky, and sand, and . . .

Dora shrieked and ran into the surf, convinced that Georgie was there somewhere, that he had fallen when the explosion happened and was even now just below the swirling white water. The girl had fallen over and the boy pulled her to her feet, spitting shingle, weeping. He called to Dora, who shook her head and continued blindly feeling for her boy, for a shirt, a hand.

She found nothing. It was moments later before she realized that the surf around her feet was stained with red.

Georgie's death changed all of them in different ways. Henry came home looking twenty years older, ashen-faced, haggard. He and

Georgie had always been close, working together, thinking in a similar manner. And it would be down to Henry to tell Georgie's fiancée, a job which he was dreading.

As for Dora, all she wanted, at first, was to deny his death, to find someone who would agree with her that the whole thing was a mistake, that somewhere Georgie still sang his silly songs and rode his wretched bicycle and talked broad Norfolk outside the cottage and standard English within its walls. She put her blue Christmas dress away in mothballs, then got it out and wore it constantly because she loved it so and because it reminded her of that long-ago time when Georgie had saved all his money to buy his mum her dream-dress. Conveniently forgotten, now, were the evenings which Dora had spent secretly taking in the waist and letting down the hem. All that mattered was that the dress was a sign of Georgie's love for her.

Had she been able to erect a memorial, tend a grave, that might have eased her grief. But though the main part of the Cunningham Hall was now used as a parish church there was no place for a memorial, no body to bury in the neglected churchyard. And the weekly dances for those members of the forces who needed entertainment, the whist drives, the small social events of a village driven into itself by war were all held at the hall. Dora could pray there, but she could not go there to be quiet and alone, to talk to Georgie, as she would have done in the church.

Lizzie grieved. She had never been as close to Georgie as the rest of the family, but it was Georgie who had dispelled for ever Lizzie's deep inner conviction that she was damned.

She had destroyed life. At the time, when she had had to decide for herself what best to do, destroying life had been the last thing on her mind, and when her ordeal was over, when the child that had never been a child was gone, there had been precious little guilt. The guilt had come later, to haunt and terrify her, with dreams of hell and terrible punishments and worse dreams – nightmares, really – of her father's reproaches, her mother casting her out.

Defiance had come next. Sod the lot of them – if she was damned, then she would make the first move. She would cast *them* out, treat *them* like the pariahs she felt herself to be.

Georgie alone had examined her attitude and understood. In Beccles, whilst Sybil washed up and talked to Mrs Potter, Georgie had gone with Lizzie to see her factory, had told her that he'd guessed about the baby.

'You've paid the price ten times over, Lizzie Cream,' he had said robustly. 'Stop paying it, and stop hitting the rest of us. You had a choice: to hurt the family and have an unwanted baby or to save the family and not have the baby. I think you done right . . . good Lord, Liz, you were only a baby yourself!'

It was the weirdest thing – as if a heavy burden she had carried for years and years, until she no longer remembered life without it, had suddenly rolled off her back. She had stared at him, feeling light and free and . . . well, and *good*. For the first time since she had left home goodness was hers again. No one assumed her a sinner, so she need not be one!

So Georgie's death had been a terrible blow to Lizzie. It was as if she had lost the only person in the world who really knew her . . . and it had been such a brief relationship, for his death had occurred only two days after their talk. She had had the much longed for 'forty-eight' in which to appreciate Georgie and then he had been torn from them all.

But because he had released her from what he had made her see was an unnecessary torment, she was able to go home at last. Naturally, as any loving daughter would. Able to comfort Dora, to give Sybil a hug, to tell Dad, before he left, looking big and bewildered and suddenly old, that she would keep an eye on them all.

'I've changed my job, so I'll be working at the port from now on,' she told him, still speaking noncommittally, as was her way. 'It's better, because I'll be able to visit regularly and see that Mum doesn't pine.'

Chris thought Lizzie was still a bit cold, but Dora was pathetically glad to get her elder daughter back again. It was almost as if Lizzie had felt her need and had answered it in the only way she knew. She had simply done her best to take Georgie's place, or perhaps she was giving Dora back the gift of herself, so unobtrusively but definitely removed when she had first taken a job in Norwich.

And whilst Sybil and Chris did their best to see that Dora did not dwell on her loss, Lizzie took practical steps. Dora had always visited her mother-in-law two or three times a week, baked for her, cleaned her house for her, seen that someone – once Georgie, now mostly Sybil or herself – dug the small garden, weeded and planted. Dora belonged to the WI and once a week she went to the rectory and knitted balaclava helmets and khaki gloves for the forces with the rest of the Ladies' Sewing Circle. But Lizzie, though she said nothing, must have guessed where Dora's thoughts went winging as soon as the girls were out of the house and she had time to think.

Watching her face, the hands that had once lain still in her lap after a long day but now clenched and unclenched, Lizzie thought her mother was probably remembering what they had said to her at the inquest when she had protested that the beach was safe just there, that it could not possibly have been a mine, since Georgie was still on the stretch of sand between the rolls of barbed wire.

'Mines creep around under the sand,' the expert who came to talk to her told her. 'There was rough weather when your son was killed, too – it could have been a sea-mine carried ashore. It's a terrible thing, Mrs Cream, but at least you know your son didn't suffer; his death was mercifully quick.'

That was all very well, but Lizzie, from her own experience, knew that her mother would blame herself for other things. If she had thought faster, could she have saved him? If she had seen the wave, warned him . . . if he had not stopped to smile at her, anxious to reassure her that he was safe, that his feet were on firm ground . . .

So Lizzie thought about it, and then took herself off to St Luke's Hospital, which was only just up the road. When she was small she and Sybil had often walked past and waved to the TB patients who slept out on the wide balconies, part of their treatment being plenty of fresh air. Henry said it was a kill or cure policy, but Lizzie was sure it had worked. Now, however, the hospital was taken over by the forces, so she went and talked to the matron.

'They've got a thousand sick sailors in there, Mum,' she said when she got back. 'I know how busy you are, but they need someone so badly. To talk to the lads, be with them when they come round after an operation, write the odd letter for them, explain what the doctor means if it's a bit obscure . . . you could do it standing on your head. And they'd pay you, though not much.'

Sybil said it sounded like a good idea so long as Dora didn't over-reach herself, and gave Lizzie a tiny thumbs-up sign when Dora turned away from them for a moment. Chris wondered aloud whether Dora would be able to cope – and Dora, who had been saying she did not think she possibly could, promptly turned round and said that she would do anything she could to help sailors because was not Henry in the navy? Had not Georgie been at sea?

After her first day at St Luke's she came home and ferreted around amongst Georgie's old books. There was a boy called Paul in there, blinded by fire, with very little use in his hands – but so brave, with such a lovely grin! He had been a Barnardo boy so he had no relatives that he knew of, no friends save for his shipmates, but he did love

books, so Dora intended to read all the old favourites to him ...
she would go in the evenings, in her own time, if matron thought she
should be doing other work during the day.

Her cure, Lizzie saw, was beginning.

Lizzie now worked at a factory in the port, a light engineering works
making parts for aero-engines. She enjoyed her work, though the pay
did not compare with that of a munitions worker, and she was able
to get home at least once a week.

She had meant to tell Ralph she would not see him any more unless
he stopped seeing Sybil. But the trouble was, whatever Ralph might
think of her – and she suspected he looked on her as a 'naughty girl'
who was fun to be with but not to be taken seriously – Lizzie was in
no doubt what she thought of Ralph. She loved him, wanted him,
could not imagine life without him. So she went on seeing him and
despising herself for it.

But as she told herself one evening, when she and Sybil had been out
to a dance together and had enjoyed one another's company as well as
that of several anxious young men, a sister is still competition so far as
marrying is concerned. Sybil and I may have fallen for the same man,
but only one of us can actually get him. So all's fair, presumably, in
love and war, and Sybil must look out for herself.

It enabled her to justify her continued meetings with Ralph, which
all ended in bed. Sybil, it seemed, was saving herself for marriage. And
if the worst comes to the worst and he marries Sybil, at least I'll have
something good to look back on, Lizzie comforted herself, when Ralph
fell asleep in her arms. At least I'll have known good times.

15

It was a lovely day, too lovely to hang about the base talking to his friends, far too lovely to catch the liberty truck into the City of Norwich. Fenn found himself, for the first time since he had arrived in England, with time on his hands and no one telling him what to do or where to go. Not that he had any doubts; he had waited eagerly for this moment ever since he and his crew had touched down on English soil.

He wanted to see the country. Oh, not the country as in England, but the countryside, the scenery he had viewed only from the great height his B-24 attained as it swept across the channel, heading for Germany on a daylight bombing raid.

Of course there were landings, when the ship was skimming the trees, losing height, as eager for the ground as a tired horse for its stable. But you simply didn't notice the scenery then; you were going so fast and concentrating so fiercely – the sheer strength needed to depress the rudder pedal had made your legs trembly from fatigue long before you'd completed the mission – that it just wasn't practicable to look about you.

But now it was different. A whole day, Fenn thought greedily. A whole day in which to find out what it was really like out there, in rural Norfolk. He had borrowed a bike, and if he liked riding it he would acquire one of his own. Thus armed, with English shillings and pence in his trouser pocket, he intended to enjoy his day. He was strong and used to physical work; the coast was not too far away. He would reach it and spend an hour or two on one of the long white beaches he had only seen from the air.

He cycled off the base, getting used to the feel of the machine. It was a good deal older and heavier than the bike he had ridden in the States, but it would do, and once he was on the country road which wound down to the coast, his eventual destination, he decided that there was a lot to be said for a bike which scarcely needed any skill to ride. It gave him time to stare.

And there was plenty to stare at. A city childhood had not prepared him for the sight of meadows of standing hay nor the luxuriance of the foliage on the trees overhead. Birds whistled and piped all about him, some soft, some shrill, some hauntingly sweet, and there were flowers everywhere and wild roses in the hedge. He knew about wild roses because the huts were built into the shadow of a wood and someone had told him what the pink and white flowers were called, but there his knowledge ended. Tiny flowers no bigger than a fingernail, others gaudily yellow, tall and purple, small and brilliant blue, he could no more have named them than flown his B-24 to the moon.

He got off the bike because he wanted to examine a stream, chattering alongside the road. He crouched, absorbed, seeing an occasional flash of silver, suspecting fish, yet . . . in a stream this small? Surely not! Presently he got back on his bike and found that he could see over some of the hedges into the meadows and fields beyond. He could feel a sense of wellbeing pouring into his very soul, which had been taut with fear, bravado, exhaustion . . . heavens, it seemed like years since he had last truly relaxed.

He turned randomly off the road on to a smaller, narrower one; this one was more like a lane, the tarmac wearing thinner as he continued until it petered out altogether. His sense of direction, which was good, told him he was still heading for the shore, but now he had all but forgotten his objective. The place was so beautiful! The lane wandered along between tall banks and trees, squat and slanting, grew on the bank, brambles tumbled down it, moss and more tiny flowers studded it.

The further he went, the narrower and bumpier grew the track. Finally he dismounted and wheeled the bike, the better to admire his surroundings. Soon the ground beneath his feet grew softer and sandier, and he knew he must be nearing the coast. It became more difficult to push the bike, but he persevered; he had every intention of continuing right down to the shore and did not fancy leaving the bike here, out of his sight.

Presently the banks grew shallower and he could see over them into the fields on either side. Barley, still green, flourished its beards on his right, pasture lay to the left. Presently he came to a five-barred gate and, leaning against it for a moment to allow his breathing to steady after the slog of forcing the bike through the sand, he saw three ponies grazing there – a fat little cob, a sturdy grey, and a chestnut with a white star on its forehead and a darkly wicked eye.

Fenn dug into his pockets; shillings and pence were not much good to a pony, but . . . ah, some Lifesavers! Would they be acceptable? He called softly and held out a hand, the peppermint flat on his palm. He had fed horses in New York and had always loved the sensation of velvety lips nuzzling his skin. The ponies came quickly towards him, plainly neither shy nor nervous. They jostled each other, the chestnut snatching the mint and crunching at once, without the nervous lipping of a horse offered unknown substances. These ponies were near enough to the lane, Fenn imagined, to be titbited by any child lucky enough to have a lump of sugar – or a Lifesaver – in its possession.

The ponies ate the mints, then wandered off, blowing gently down their soft noses. Fenn was enchanted by them, by the smell of them, their gleaming hides, the barrel sides tapering to those ridiculously slender chorus-girl legs. Pretty things, with their big, dark eyes and their skittish movements!

He began to push the bicycle again, plodding along, head down. It was no real hardship, though, for now he could smell and hear the sea, the murmur of a retreating wave, the thunder as one advanced. And that fresh, salty smell, which was at once fishy and not fishy at all, could come from nothing but the ocean.

The lane ended in a sandy road. Looking to his left, he saw the ruins of a small church crouched on a grassy mound. Opposite the church, a short row of flint and tiled cottages . . . and beyond them, the sea! Blue today, crisply capped with white, the waves broke on the hard white-gold sand. Fenn saw a gull floating above the water and other birds, long-legged, long-beaked, strange, poking about on the wet, sky-reflecting strand. Then he was laughing, leaning his bicycle carelessly against the flint wall which surrounded the church and heading for the shore. He would paddle . . . no, dammit, he would swim, it was warm enough! His friend and co-pilot, Will, had taught him to swim while he was at the Advanced Flying School, and though he had no trunks with him he was wearing underpants. Besides, the place was deserted. Not a soul walked along that tideline or wandered through the lazily splashing surf. He knew that many of the beaches were mined against invasion, but it was clear he would be safe enough here, because of the fishing boats pulled high up the dunes. The rolls of barbed wire which prevented one from straying too far along the shore looked new, though there was an older, saggier barricade half-buried in the sand and more than half eaten away by rust. He supposed that the new barbed wire had been laid down because in the summer children would begin to frequent the sands once more.

Fenn sat down at the top of the beach, where it was pebbly and tufted with spiky, light-coloured grass, and took off his shoes and socks. Then he rolled up his trouser-legs, abandoned his shoes and the light jacket which was no longer necessary with the sun climbing towards its zenith, and set off for the sea. He waded in and the cold gripped him; perhaps a swim was a bad idea after all, but his feet would soon get used to the chill.

Paddling through the shallows, however, was so absorbing that he soon forgot the temperature of the water. As the tide retreated it left long, shallow pools which were full of marine-life. Fenn, whose childhood had never included so much as a day-trip to the seaside, pursued tiny flounders the size of penny pieces, delicate, transparent shrimplings, silver-sided fishes which could whip across the pool in a flash with one flick of their tails. He hooked up marvellously colourful seaweed, pea-green and transparent, dark red and fernlike, flat and shiny like strips of chestnut leather. When he had finished with the pools at last he went back to the sea, to the little wavelets and the chill and thrill of it. He found cuttlefish eggs, the strange creatures known as dead men's fingers, tiny green crabs and starfish by the dozen. He pursued and lost a sizeable jellyfish, bobbing just beyond the surf. It was the jellyfish which was responsible for his trousers getting very wet indeed . . . but they would dry off on the ride home, Fenn told himself cheerfully. This was marvellous – the long stretch of deserted beach, the splashing of the waves, the shells with which one pocket was already laden. He could not imagine why the guys had not come over in a body with him, why a trip into Norwich was deemed preferable to this.

He must have been paddling for over an hour when he first noticed the girl. The sun had gone in long since and a chilly breeze had sprung up, but Fenn had no intention of leaving the beach just yet and when he saw the girl he was pleased that she might share his own pleasure in this marvellous place. She was up at the top of the beach, on the grassy little path, walking with easy, loping strides, but as she neared the roadway she slowed down and Fenn was able to walk up towards her without having to hurry. Nearer, he saw that she was barefoot, as he was, and wore a faded cotton skirt which she held bunched up with one hand so that her long legs were free of it. Her streaky, windswept hair fell across one side of her face and was hooked back on the other side behind one small ear. She was not looking at him.

She had a basket over her free arm and was gazing dreamily ahead of her, and when she got near enough Fenn could hear that she was singing.

> 'Loud roared the waves, wild raged the sea,
> Yet boldly to our boats went we,
> To cast our nets into the deep,
> To feed our childer, ere they sleep.'

The tune was haunting; a lament and a lullaby in one. Fascinated, Fenn stood still, listening, whilst the young singer drew nearer, still unaware of his presence as she looked down at her feet and at the path's uneven surface.

> 'Our fragile craft, blown far from shore,
> Will ne'er touch land nor harbour more,
> The childer we have toiled to save,
> Will mourn each . . .'

She had looked up and seen herself observed. The hand which had held her skirt bunched at her side released it to fly to her mouth, and the skirt clung to her wet, bare legs. Fenn wondered if she had been in the sea further up, and also whether it was safe to do so, for beyond the strip where he himself had been paddling was the area of sand which must, surely, be mined. He smiled at her and saw an answering smile warm her amber eyes, though her hand was still clamped over her mouth.

'Did I startle you? I'm sorry . . . can I carry your basket? It looks heavy.'

She shook her head but took her hand from her mouth. Her eyes met his frankly, though there was shyness in her glance.

'No, it's all right. I'm used to the weight.'

'Sure, but it'll do you good to have a break. Where are you going?'

She jerked her head towards the town in the distance.

'I've been up the coast, netting herring. Now I'm going home to cook it for my tea – and my mother's.'

There was a breeze here on the beach and her long streaky hair, which now that he was closer he could see was every shade from palest gold to glowing chestnut, was teased into elflocks. Her skin was pale and clear, the sort he most admired. Her lashes were thick and a couple of shades darker than her hair, and she was very slim, almost thin, though her body had a grace which not even the clumsy clothes she wore could hide.

'Where do you live? Is it far? May I walk you home?'

She looked at him and raised her brows, which were pale brown and no more than delicate brush-strokes above the large, clear eyes. She smiled a little and inclined her head slightly.

'Of course; the road is as much yours as mine, so I can scarcely forbid you! Do you like the smell of fish?'

She was teasing him, her head tilted, and Fenn grinned.

'Hey, ma'am, your fish don't smell, not out in the open like this. I guess they're fresh, anyway, aren't they? And fresh fish smell of the sea.'

She laughed and looked up at him with a mixture of coquetry and shyness which he found irresistible.

'Do they? But my basket smells of yesterday's fish and last week's fish – and last month's fish for that matter!'

He laughed too. There was something very attractive about this girl even though her hair needed brushing and her skirt and blouse looked as though she had borrowed them from someone very old and poor. She walked beautifully, he decided, straight-backed, moving from the hips, with such grace that he could have watched her for hours. Her bare feet were pretty too, the toes as straight as though she had never worn shoes in her life, and the hand holding the basket, work-roughened, chapped and red, was nevertheless finely made, the delicate bones of wrist and knuckle tender beneath the skin.

'I don't mind the smell of fish – in fact, I like it. C'mon, let me carry your basket!'

'There's no need. I do a lot of heavy work in my job, so I'm used to it. You don't live locally, though; I can tell from your voice. Have you come far?'

Fenn grinned.

'Well, I've been living in the States, but I come from Manchester, England. You're from the village here, I suppose?'

'That's right.' She turned away from him to climb up the short bank on to the rough shingle road which ran between the church and the cottages. Fenn went to follow her, then remembered his shoes and socks. He could scarcely light out after the girl and walk down the village street in bare feet, even if she could!

'Hold on, ma'am . . . I shan't be a tick.'

He grabbed his footwear and sat down on the bank, pulling on his socks, pushing his feet impatiently into his shoes. His toes were gritty with sand but he sensed that she would not hang around waiting for him; she was not that sort of girl. He stood up before his laces were properly tied, therefore, and turned to speak to her, then stopped short. She was no longer standing on the bank behind him. He looked wildly about, on both sides of the road, then towards the port, then in the other direction. She had disappeared as completely as though she had never been.

Fenn sat down again; suddenly. It was the weirdest thing, wasn't it? Here one minute and gone the next . . . but where? And how?

She must have gone into the ruined church, he decided. Softly, so as to surprise her, he walked along the road to the churchyard gate. He crossed the grass, avoiding the tombstones, to the arches which were just about the only part of the building still standing. He peered in, but there was so little left that it was easy to see the place was empty. Slowly, he retraced his steps. The church had been bombed and set alight, so much was obvious from the smell and the blackened timbers within. The girl was not here then – so where?

Frowning, Fenn turned away. Where the hell had she disappeared to? She had simply not had time to get far along the road, for he had not been more than a couple of minutes putting on his shoes and socks. Still, he would walk into the village, see if she was waiting somewhere in the street. He could ask at the nearest shop, describe her, try to track her down.

There were a few people about but not many; it was getting near tea-time, Fenn supposed, when most people would be indoors either preparing or eating their meal. He asked a little boy who stared at him, open-mouthed, whether he had seen a girl with golden-brown hair and a dark blouse, walking along with a basket of fish on her arm. The child frowned and then, face clearing, said, 'Got any gum, chum?'

'Can't say I have,' Fenn admitted. 'Then you've not seen a girl . . . a young lady, I should say . . . in a cotton skirt, with no shoes on her feet?'

'I in't seen nobody, 'cep' for you,' the infant said impatiently. 'If you in't got no gum, how about nylon stockings?'

'I came here to see the sea,' Fenn said with what patience he could muster. 'Not to chew gum or wear nylon stockings! Oh, hell, where can she have gone?'

But since it seemed there was to be no finding her, he walked down Beach Road again, picked his bicycle up from where he had slung it against the church wall, and began to retrace his steps along the grassy lane, wondering all the while just why the girl had fled. He was halfway home and getting increasingly eager for his supper, when a thought struck him. The girl could have gone into one of the cottages facing the ruined church. Or suppose she hadn't been a girl at all, but a ghost? After all, how else could she have pulled off that extraordinary disappearing trick? And why should she want to disappear, unless she had a good reason for doing so? Fenn had no illusions about himself, but he did not think he was so repulsive that a pretty girl would run off just at the sight of him!

By the time he cycled on to the base once more he was almost certain that he had either imagined the whole incident or seen a most delightful ghost. And, being Fenn, he had told the whole of his squadron by bed-time that the coast was haunted and that he had actually stood and chatted to a girl whose luminous beauty had made an unforgettable impression on him, until she had slowly disappeared, Cheshire-catlike, before his eyes!

And once he had made it into a good story, it occurred to him that if she was not a ghost, it would not be all that long before they met. The airfield was not far from that village, Pakeby, and he was bound to visit there from time to time.

Sybil could not have said just why she had decided to run off when the young American serviceman had been chatting so pleasantly to her. Partly, of course, it was the fish. She had staked out a longshore net the previous day when the tide was well out, waited for a tide to come and go, and then gone out and gathered up a whole basketful of fish from tiny ones to a few reasonable two or three-pounders.

She should not have gone down the far end of the shore, really, but if you went right along to where the great shingle ridge started the beach was not mined. It would have been too dangerous to try to bring a landing craft in there, she supposed. And because the shingle went right down to low water mark, the fish came in closer to the land, which meant a better chance of a reasonable catch.

Still, that did not explain her flight. And why should I have to explain it? she asked herself crossly, standing at the sink with a bucket of fresh water, furiously gutting her catch. If I don't want to stay and talk to a young man, why should I?

But part of the trouble was that she *had* wanted to stay and talk to him, that was the rub. Because for one thing she was Ralph's girl, and for another she hated to think that he would assume she was a fish-seller. He would smell the fish on her hands and on the big wicker basket and associate her with the smell of fish for the rest of their acquaintance, no matter how short – or long.

So she had run away, really, because she liked the young man. They had only talked for a few minutes, but she had felt definitely attracted to him. He was not handsome, like her own dear Ralph, but his ugly face was strong and interesting. He had a lovely grin, curly hair . . . but she hadn't taken that much notice, after all, and would soon forget him.

Dora and Chris, who had been shopping in the port, came in when the fish were just beginning to spit in the pan and congratulated her on her catch.

'You've got so many that I'm sure we can spare some,' Dora decided. 'You can take some to Mrs Franklyn, dear, if you think she'd like them.'

'Mrs Franklyn would be delighted to have anything that isn't rationed,' Chris put in. 'I wish we could get some to Mummy and Daddy, but it would have to wait till we get a spot more leave, and the fish wouldn't be very fresh by then!'

Thinking of leaves and the Wintertons made Sybil think of Ralph. He wrote to her, though not often; Sybil wrote three or four times a week. Lately, though, Ralph's letters had been a trifle peevish – he could not understand, he said, why she would not come up to see him in Lincolnshire for a few days. Other people got leave, so the Women's Land Army must have time off too. I need you, he wrote piteously. We'll never get to know one another if we never meet, and if I were to come down to Pakeby your family – and my sister – aren't likely to leave us alone for long!

So why did she hesitate? Next week they were going to start haymaking at two of the farms in Irewood and the schoolchildren were going to be given a few days' holiday. No one would go to school when they might legitimately be out in the hayfield, making sheaves or leading the horses to and from the stacks, so Mr Franklyn could easily spare me for a few days, Sybil told herself. I could go up to Lincolnshire and welcome, so why on earth don't I? If I love Ralph – and I do – why won't I go to him? I am true to him, I never flirt with other men, I seldom even smile or chat to those brash young airmen with their funny haircuts and tight trousers who are beginning to turn up to every social event for miles around. I didn't even encourage the young man on the beach and . . . well, I liked him at once, as soon as our eyes met. But when you love someone you want to give them everything, and I love Ralph. So why can't I go to Lincolnshire and let him make love to me properly, all the way, as other girls do?

And then there was the incident of the Liberator bombers.

It was a misty early morning with a promise of fine weather to come, ideal for haymaking. There had been an epidemic of tummy upsets amongst the landgirls on a nearby farm so Sybil and Chris were sent off to help the farmer get his hay in before the spell of fine weather broke in torrents of rain. Since the girls would make a full day of it they set off at sun-up, with a couple of flasks of weak tea and some sandwiches to eat in their first break.

They went first to the farm, where they met four other landgirls who took them along straggling country lanes to the meadow they were to help cut. Sybil stripped off her jersey and folded it, laying it with her food under the hedge. She had not realized the airfield was quite so close until, through the mist overhead, they heard the roar of many engines. The other girls, used to the sounds, called out that it was the Liberator bombers going out on a daylight raid over Germany.

Sybil and Chris, fascinated by the closeness of the aircraft, moved over to the hedge and peered through it. They could see the runway, and the planes, although the early mist hid them completely, could be heard revving up their engines for take-off.

As they watched the noise grew deafening and suddenly, in the sky above them, they saw the aircraft, huge under any circumstances but made to look twice their real size by the looming mist and the frightening suddenness with which they had appeared.

'I say! Aren't they immense? And so many of them – it must be a special raid, I should think.'

Sybil spoke to Chris even though she realized that her friend would be unable to hear a sound above the roar, but Chris nodded nevertheless and mouthed back what looked like agreement.

And then, as they watched, above them another plane loomed out of the mist, directly below one already in sight. Sybil heard herself shout a warning as though the pilots could actually hear her – 'Look out, boys, there's another plane too close for comfort!' – but it was too late even had they been able to hear. She clutched Chris, shouting soundlessly above the roar.

'Oh, God, don't let them, don't let them . . .'

There was a grinding roar, and then a terrible shrill whine, as of souls in torment. The two great aircraft seemed to Sybil to go into slow motion. They hit, wavered, seemed to bounce laboriously apart . . . and then they were diving to earth, the whine growing louder and louder, a great plume of black smoke following them.

They struck. Sybil felt the earth shake, saw a tree no more than fifty feet away dragged up by the roots as though it were no more than a sapling, and then, suddenly, there was nothing, no sound, no movement, nothing. Overhead, faintly, they could hear the engine noise receding but the mist still hid the sky. On the other side of the hedge . . .

For a moment no one spoke or moved, then as they heard the muffled thump of the impact the girls turned with one accord and ran beside the hedge, searching for a thin spot, finding one, bursting through on to the misty runway, seeing the great, broken, reeking shapes, smelling the pungent scent of fuel and hearing the first sharp scream . . . a figure rolling free from the wreckage, coming towards them, gesturing them back . . . and then the explosion, the flames shooting higher than a house, the great, stinking cloud of oily smoke.

The heat was like a furnace; there was no getting near it. From far away they could hear the bells of vehicles charging to the rescue. The man who had waved them back . . . Sybil had seen him engulfed, shrivelling, dropping. There was no hope for him, no hope for anyone in that burning mass. The best thing they could do now was to get themselves out of the way so as not to impede the rescuers who were fast approaching, crashing out their disaster notes as they came.

Like whipped puppies the girls retreated through the hedge. The sun was coming up, flooding their field with gold, and the mist was thinning so that they could see blue sky now. It was a lovely early summer's morning, except for the scene beyond the hedge, where the smoke would hide the sky.

'Best get on with the harvesting,' someone said. 'Not a thing we could do . . . Oh, but those poor young buggers. I can't bear to think of it!'

It was, Sybil supposed, an epitaph of sorts.

Lying in bed that night, trying to banish the scene on the runway from her mind, Sybil knew that she had shilly-shallied long enough. What she had seen could easily happen to Ralph. He risked his life every time he took off in his Spitfire, every time he landed. She would go to him this very weekend. Mr Franklyn was quite willing to let her have a couple of days off, so tomorrow she would catch the bus into Norwich and then the train to the station nearest Ralph's lodgings. She would explain to Dora and Chris that she would only be gone a couple of days, just long enough to see Ralph and perhaps go to a dance or a flick with him. They would guess what she was intending to do, or they might, but she knew that Chris, at least, would understand. She could telephone Ralph's aerodrome from the village, leave a message telling him when she would be arriving, how long she would be staying.

Comforted by the decision, she slept at last.

On Friday Sybil woke to find sunshine spilling through a gap in her bedroom curtains and Chris, who had applauded her decision to go and see Ralph, already washing and abominably cheerful. Sybil herself felt odd; surely she was not going to come down with the wretched tummy bug which both she and Chris had managed to escape so far? She decided she did feel a bit squeamish, but not truly ill, and began to get, rather reluctantly, out of bed.

And then she remembered that it was Friday, that she was going to see Ralph, and the day seemed as bright as it really was, Chris's cheerfulness a natural thing. She felt okay, she decided, though her face was warm and she ached a little. Tension from the previous day, she supposed, taking her place at the washstand; it will ease as the day goes on.

She didn't fancy breakfast but had several cups of tea, and at her mother's insistence ate a piece of toast. Dora knew where she was going but although she frowned and sighed and told her, rather jerkily, not to do anything foolish she seemed to accept Sybil's decision. But she did keep starting sentences and not finishing them, glancing meaningfully at Chris, and when Chris left, sending Ralph her love and telling Sybil to be a good girl, Sybil flew upstairs to pack, thus neatly avoiding the moral lecture which she felt sure was in store.

When she set off, her suitcase banging against her leg and unaccustomed shoes on her feet, she became aware that she had a thumping headache and was already beginning to wonder whether her decision to go to Ralph had been the right one. When she had phoned to hesitantly suggest she should stay with him he had been delighted, but . . . She could have changed her mind, of course, but thinking it over she decided that a decision taken at a moment of crisis should not be altered in cold blood.

She was sorry that Dora was not altogether pleased that she was becoming friendly with Ralph, but also rather puzzled by Dora's obvious lack of enthusiasm. There seemed to be no earthly reason why her mother should not have been delighted that one of her old dreams had come true, even though it had happened to the wrong daughter. She did not think Dora disliked him. It was merely that, on the two or three occasions he had visited the cottage, Dora had seemed rather cool, rather unimpressed.

Making her way to the bus stop, it occurred to Sybil that the bag containing the hard-boiled eggs and a cake was heavier than she had at first thought, and the suitcase, with only a change of undies, a nightdress, her toothbrush and flannel, and her purse and ration book, weighed far more than it ought. Probably it was just the fact that a mixture of anticipation and a sort of dread was making her slow and hot, she thought. She was glad, though, to set both case and bag down when she reached the bus terminus on London Road.

She had wanted to take Ralph some strawberries – there were a few early ones about – but it had not seemed a good idea to lug fresh fruit halfway across the country by train and bus. As it was, because of a daylight raid, a faulty engine and various other vicissitudes of wartime travel, she didn't reach her first change until after seven o'clock, and it was nearly midnight when the train finally chugged into the station where Ralph was to meet her.

Sybil had slept for the last hour of the journey, waking each time the train jerked to a stop. Now, she got out, bleary-eyed, hot, and thoroughly uncomfortable. She was tempted to abandon the bag with its cake and hard-boiled eggs because they were so terribly heavy, but finally lugged the whole lot along, searching the faces of the few people still hanging about. She was about to give up and ask directions when she was seized and hugged.

'Sybil, darling, you came! Oh, you wonderful girl, I was so afraid you'd get cold feet and change your mind. I don't know how I'd have borne the disappointment. Come on, let me carry that great suitcase . . . bet it's full of food!'

It was Ralph, looking marvellously debonair in his uniform, his cap rakishly tilted, his eyes sparkling.

'Oh, Ralph, I'm most awfully tired . . . yes, I brought a cake and some hard-boiled eggs . . . where am I to stay? Will your landlady have a room for me?'

'Borrowed a flat,' Ralph said, squeezing her so hard that it hurt. 'My landlady's a sour old bugger. Come along – it's not far.'

It may not have been far, but the walk seemed interminable to Sybil. She was hot from the train but shivery in the night breeze and she could not always hear what Ralph was saying through the drumming inside her head. The headache with which she had started the morning had got worse and worse as the day progressed, and what a moment it had chosen! She desperately wanted to be at her best . . . it must be miles to this wretched flat . . . her shoulders ached so badly. It must have been that hard seat on the train. And the sharp pain jabbing at her lower back would surely ease once they could stop walking.

They reached the flat. Ralph unlocked and hustled her up a flight of dark, urine-smelling stairs into a small room. He had fixed the blackout earlier, and now he lit a lamp. As it flared up, Sybil looked timidly about her. It was a funny sort of flat, just a room with a bed in one half and a cooking stove and two chairs in the other. Still. Sybil shrugged off her coat and collapsed into one of the chairs.

'Oh, Ralph, I'm sorry, but I'm so terribly tired . . . can I go to bed straight away? I'm asleep on my feet!'

He chuckled. He was taking off his own clothing – good God, he was going to strip! Sybil hastily averted her eyes from him, staring down at her blue cotton dress. This was not at all how she had imagined it would be. She knew he wanted to make love to her and that meant sharing a bed, she realized, but . . . now? After that terrible journey, when she felt so . . . so very *odd*?

She spoke the thought aloud, her voice small and hoarse. Ralph laughed indulgently.

'Sweetheart, we've all the time in the world – the whole weekend! And then I'm on for forty-eight hours and off for twenty-four. If you're exhausted we don't have to rush anything! Shall I help you to undress?'

'I can manage.'

But she couldn't. Her fingers were all thumbs and in the end she was quite pleased when he came over and unbuttoned her, though she gave a squeaky sob when he unfastened her brassiere and slid her knickers down. She tried to hide herself with her hands but really did not have enough hands to do a good job, and instead of putting on her nightgown she just slid straight into bed, shuddering at the coldness of the sheets.

'Well, aren't we eager?' Ralph said, but he spoke kindly. 'Want a drink or anything, sweetheart?'

'Oh . . . yes *please*,' Sybil said fervently. 'Anything, water or anything.'

'How about some lovely gin and orange? It will help you to sleep.'

'Water.'

'Oh. Right you are, you're the boss.'

The water was warm and brownish, but Sybil drank it straight down, then collapsed on to the pillows. She wanted her nightdress, though; she was cold.

'Ralph . . . could I have my nightie, please?'

'Of course, honey. Of course. You're sure you wouldn't . . . no, all right. Here it comes, down over your head.'

He was tender, pulling the nightie into respectability, then getting into bed beside her. She was shivering and he put his arms round her, one hand, to her dismay, immediately shrugging the nightgown aside to clasp her breast, to fondle, for a second, her hardening nipple. Then he pushed her away. He sat up; she felt the cold air funnel between their bodies.

'Sybil? You're on fire!'

She thought he was being sarcastic and felt bitterly ashamed of herself. To come so far and then to be so tired that all she wanted to do was sleep!

'I'm sorry,' she said humbly, teeth chattering. 'I do love you, Ralph, it's just that I'm so very, very tired. I'll be all right tomorrow.'

'All right nothing – you're running a fever, girl! You're like a perishing furnace!'

'I'm cold,' Sybil said drearily. 'My bones ache. I'm so cold.'

He sighed.

'Summer 'flu – just my luck,' he said crossly. 'Well, let's hope it's one of those twelve hour bugs. Goodnight.'

He rolled away from her and Sybil got as far down the bed as she could and presently fell into a nightmare-haunted sleep.

She woke with the dawn. She ached so badly that she could not stop herself from groaning. Ralph woke presently and got her a cup of tea; she had never been more thankful for anything in her whole life, but as soon as she drank it she vomited it back again.

'You can't be ill here, poor little Sybs,' Ralph said, when she tried to get up and couldn't even keep her balance. 'Look, I'll take you home . . . where does your mother think you are this weekend?'

'With you,' Sybil said hoarsely. 'It's all right, she knows.'

'She *knows*? My dear girl, have you gone mad? No mother would be too pleased to think her child was . . . Oh well, since you've burned your boats, get yourself dressed whilst I go and arrange things.'

Her arms wouldn't work properly but she managed somehow to get the dress on over the nightie and the coat on over that. She drank some water and vomited that back, too. The ache in her back and legs was beyond belief, and she could not imagine how she was going to reach the car. Whilst she waited for Ralph she leaned back on the pillows and felt darkness descend, tried to fight it, gave in. She would rest for a little, make herself stronger for when she had to reach that car.

Ralph carried her to the car. Being moved hurt awfully, but she bit her lip and would not cry out though tears rained helplessly down her hot cheeks.

He put her in the back because she could not manage to sit up properly, and drove with all the windows tightly closed because the cold air hurt so much. He is a nice person, Sybil thought. When we get home I'll tell Mum and Lizzie how kind he's been – I might give him to Lizzie, she'd like that. When we get home I'll have a cup of Mum's tea, I won't be sick after Mum's tea, I'm never sick . . . I wonder why I was sick just now, after drinking water? Perhaps the water here is bad, perhaps it's poisoned me, that's what it is. Only then she remembered that she had not felt at all well on the train, even before drinking the water.

It was a puzzle, the whole thing. I've never had a day's illness in my whole life, it was always Lizzie who was ill, she thought next. When I get home I'll ask Mum . . . oh, when I get home, how I want to get home!

She did not reach home. Ralph talked to her, tried to explain something, but she could not understand. It was as though one of them were under water and trying to speak to the one on the surface. She could see his face wavering around, see his mouth opening and closing, but what came out might just as well have been gibberish for all the sense she could make of it.

When the car stopped she thought she was home, and she was so confused that even when they brought a stretcher out and loaded her on to it with infinite gentleness she somehow managed to believe that it was Mum and Lizzie taking her in.

She came to herself for a moment on the ward, with little white beds all around and uniformed nurses hovering. She said, quite brightly, 'Where's Ralph gone?' and saw a fat and kindly face loom over her.

Then, with one terrifying swoop, she was in another place, another time, fighting constant pain, unbearable heat, unquenchable thirst. She knew she was in the plane that had crashed and cried out to them to save her, to get her out before it blew up, to bring water from the pond to douse the inferno.

The pain, which could not get worse, got worse. Faces came and went. She saw a woman with a face just like Dora's and the woman wept and tried to touch her, only it hurt to be touched, even the sheet hurt. She saw Lizzie, pale and wide-eyed, scared at what was happening to her beloved little sister. There had been times when Sybil had doubted Lizzie's love for her but not any more; love and fear for her shone out of Lizzie's big, shadowed blue eyes.

'You can have Ralph if you'll stop the pain,' Sybil meant to say to her, only nothing came out but groans. Somewhere inside her frantically thudding head she realized that she should never have tried to have Ralph for her own, that what she was suffering, this hell of heat and pain, was her punishment. It seemed a very cruel and terrible punishment considering that all she had wanted was to be loved, but she would just have to bear it. She wished she could tell Lizzie that she was sorry, but when she opened her eyes Lizzie had gone, and Mum had gone as well, and someone gave her a drink of something soothing which stayed inside her and gave her, for the first time, a thread of hope. Might it end? Might she emerge from this one day?

Night came, and lasted ten years; the next day dragged on. Someone came and pulled her around, the pain was unbearable but she was too weak to protest, all she could do was be brave. The voice boomed out, saying that this might hurt a little, that it was for her own good.

But she clung on. Different things helped her; memories mostly. The beach, her friendship with Chris, the feel of a pony's lips nuzzling for a titbit. Then there was the cold wind tugging her hair, the sun dazzling on the waves, a face, dark and ugly but interesting too, which looked down and pitied her; all these things were inside her head. Often she did not think of them because the pain would not allow it, but then the pain would ebb a little and the memories would come back. She had had good times and bad, but mostly good. This was a bad time – it would pass. Inside her, she knew it would pass, and that made clinging on just about possible.

Sometimes it would have been much easier to let go, to slide down into the darkness which she sensed was very near. But she could not. Life was too good, and besides, there was something . . . something better to come, if only she clung on!

16

Chris missed Sybil more than she had expected. In fact, when she got back to the cottage that Friday evening and found Dora and Lizzie sitting on opposite sides of the stove, companionably discussing what they would do to celebrate Henry Cream's next leave, Chris decided to go home just for a day or so. She got on fairly well with Lizzie, but had never felt the older girl really liked her much, and it was only fair to let Dora have her daughter to herself for once.

Accordingly she set out early on the Saturday morning, taking an overnight bag with her, and was in St Giles before nine. Her mother greeted her ecstatically and they had a good day out together, visiting relatives, but in the evening Mrs Winterton had to go to a first-aid lecture so Chris went home alone. When she unlocked the front door – there was nobody else in the house as her father was in London and Norah had long since moved out into her little retirement cottage – the telephone was ringing. She hurried across to it, because it might have been Toddy, or Ralph, or even her father, but when she picked it up – no maids to do so now, no one to answer the door or cook her a meal – she could tell at once it was none of them. There was the long pause she had come to associate with a public call-box and then the rattle of the button being pressed.

'Hello? Who's that?'

'Chris Winterton speaking; how can I help you?' Chris said cheerfully. The caller, a woman, breathed heavily for a couple of moments, as though making up her mind what to say. Then she spoke.

'Oh, Chris dear, it's Dora. Chris, I'm at the Ryder Hospital just outside the city. Have you spoken to . . . to your brother?'

Immediately all sorts of terrible suspicions began to jostle in Chris's mind. Ralph was ill, perhaps dying, and Dora was trying to find a nice way of breaking it to her. Or Sybil had failed to arrive – no, it couldn't be that, they would have known sooner. Or Toddy had been shot down and Ralph had got in touch with Dora because he couldn't find anyone in at the St Giles house. A second's thought would have shown her how unlikely these things were, but she was too worried to think.

'Dora! What's wrong? No, I've not seen Ralph for weeks, but Sybil's with him for the weekend, isn't she? Has she phoned to say he's ill?'

'It's not Ralph, it's Sybil.' Dora gave what sounded like a sort of sobbing gulp, then continued. 'She's in hospital, and I just wondered . . .'

'Sybil!' Chris's immediate concern was real. Sybil was her dearest friend, closer to her than anyone apart from her immediate family. Dear God, what had Sybil done to herself . . . an accident? 'What's happened, Auntie Dora? How can I help?'

There was no mistaking the sob this time, but Dora rallied quickly. 'Oh, Chris, you're such a *good* girl. How like you to ask at once! My dear, could you come? We're at our wits' end, Lizzie and me . . . Lizzie's paying what she can but the cost . . . it isn't just the cost . . . Chris, she's terribly ill. The doctor said . . . he said . . .'

'Of course I'll come. I'll catch a bus and be with you in thirty minutes, perhaps less. Whereabouts in the hospital are you? How can I find you? Which ward is Sybil on?'

'I'll be in the foyer, waiting for you,' Dora said unsteadily. 'Lizzie's sitting with her for a bit, not that it'll make much difference. She doesn't know us, you see.'

'Right. I'll leave a note for Mummy; is there anything I can bring, anything you might need?'

'We'll manage. Just come, dear. Oh, I wonder if you might . . .'

There was a clatter as the money ran out and the dialling tone sounded in Chris's ear.

Chris hung the receiver up slowly, then turned and made for the stairs. She found a clean flannel and a new tablet of soap, some lavender water and a box of scented talc which she had been hoarding for a special occasion. She put the articles in a shopping basket and folded a small towel over the top, then ran down the stairs and went into the kitchen.

There was not much food about, but Mrs Winterton made oatcakes which were nice with jam spread on them . . . nice with cheese, too. Chris jammed half-a-dozen into a brown paper bag, put the paper bag into her shopping basket and headed for the dresser. There was a chalk board with a wooden frame round it which she and her mother had rescued from the nursery. Now she picked up the chalk, thought for a moment, and then wrote in her firm, teacher's hand, which not all the farmwork in the world could destroy:

Mummy, Sybil in Ryder Hospital. Mrs C desperate. Have gone to see what I can do. Love Chris. P.S. Have taken soap and a flannel and some oatcakes in case they need things.

She stood a moment longer, wondering whether to add anything more, but decided against it. Her mother was unlikely to read the message much before Chris herself got back with more accurate information as to Sybil's illness. As she ran down St Giles and across the market, heading for the bus station in Surrey Street, it occurred to Chris to wonder why Ralph had not got in touch with them himself, seeing that Sybil had been taken ill in his presence, if not in his room. But she still did not know what had happened. They might have had a car accident, and if so Ralph would still, presumably, be with poor Sybs, though not hurt himself. Dora's voice on the phone had been clear enough on that score – *It's not Ralph*, she had said.

Chris was in luck with the bus; the one she wanted stood in its place, the driver about to climb aboard, the conductor putting a new roll of tickets into his machine.

'Do you go to the Ryder Hospital?' Chris asked breathlessly, clambering aboard, for she had run most of the way across the city. 'And when's the next bus back?'

'There's one when visiting ends, at eight,' the conductor decided. 'You're early, miss . . . hope everything's all right?'

'Oh . . . I don't know myself,' Chris said, grateful for the concern on his elderly face, for he was far past retirement and must have been brought back now that the younger men had mainly been called up. 'My friend's mother just rang and said Sybs had been admitted. She said to come right away.'

The conductor adjusted his machine and rolled out a thin paper ticket with pink printing on it. He tore it off and handed it to her.

'There you are. Fivepence, please. Hmm, doesn't sound too good. Well, you'll soon know; we're off!'

The journey was uneventful, but Chris was in such a state of nervous tension that she would probably not have noticed had the bus filled up with Martians complete with green skin. She knew where the Ryder Hospital was and as soon as they neared the stop she was on her feet and hurrying down the aisle.

'Thanks very much,' she called to the conductor, swinging off the platform and down on to the pavement.

'That's all right; hope your friend in't too poorly,' he shouted back. 'Don't forgit, last bus is eight o'clock, midweek.'

Chris nodded, waved, and set off up the long drive. The last time she had seen the hospital grounds had been in peacetime; now the lawns had disappeared and potatoes, leeks and other vegetables flourished. Much more sensible and useful for the patients, Chris told herself, than lawns would have been – but she was glad to see that the big old laburnum trees still dripped their gold along a side path, and the fruit trees which had always grown in the side garden were there still even though vegetables now surrounded them, making it difficult to reach the trees, Chris imagined, when the fruit was ripe.

The hospital, which had once been a stately home, faced her across a gravel sweep; she crunched over to the front doors, pushed them open and went in. She found herself in a small foyer with benches round the walls and low tables with elderly magazines scattered over them. The walls were painted a rather depressing shade of green and the benches had been upholstered in black, but someone had filled a big bowl with late tulips and branches of white lilac and the scent and colour made the foyer seem almost pleasant.

There was no one about, however. Chris looked round and saw a hatch with a bell-push beside it. She walked over to it and was about to ring the bell when the double doors across one end of the foyer were pushed open by an impatient hand and Lizzie strode into the room. She smiled at Chris and passed a hand across her brow. Lizzie could never look anything other than beautiful, Chris reflected, but now she also looked exhausted and pale with worry.

'Lizzie! What's happened? How is she?'

'She's very ill,' Lizzie said. Her crystal clear voice was fogged with tiredness, subdued by it. 'I don't suppose Mum had a chance to say, but she's got something called infantile paralysis. I thought it was a disease only kids caught, but the doctor says a lot of young women have been getting it – he reckons it's in the water or something, he said.'

'My God! Oh, Lizzie, I'm so sorry. Can I see her?'

Lizzie nodded.

'Yes. She woke so I fetched Mum and Mum said to come down here and bring you up as soon as you arrived. She . . . she looks different, mind. You can see how ill she is. Mum's booked in at a guesthouse place down the road, but we'll have to go home tomorrow, I think – I've got to go to work – and try to come in whenever we can. So with you being on the spot for a day or so we thought, Mum and I . . .'

'I'll do anything I can, but I've only got two days' leave. I'll be back in Pakeby myself tomorrow evening,' Chris said at once. 'Mummy will hold the fort, though, when she knows. Dad's in London, but he'll help when he gets back. Lizzie?'

They were walking together down a long corridor but something in Chris's voice drew Lizzie to a halt. She looked down at her feet as though she did not want to meet Chris's eye.

'Yes?'

'How come Ralph didn't let me know? He could have telephoned.'

'He didn't have time, Chris. He drove straight to Pakeby from the hospital and brought Mum and me back, and then he had to get back to his airfield. He was ever so upset, and he did telephone you, only no one answered so he had to leave. They say at the hospital that there's another landgirl from our area been diagnosed as having the same thing, so they did know it might well be that. Don't blame Ralph, Chris. He did everything he could.'

'Yes, he would. He was awfully fond of Sybs – like the rest of the family.'

'Was?' Lizzie said sharply. 'She's not dead yet, you know!'

'Did I say was? That just shows how shocked I am,' Chris said at once. 'She's lovely, is Sybs.'

'I know. We haven't always . . . Oh, by the way, I had a word with Ralph and he told me she was ill when she arrived, so no matter what people may think it all came to nothing, her visit to Lincolnshire.'

Was that satisfaction in Lizzie's voice? But she continued to walk fast so Chris hurried along beside her, wanting to hear as much as possible before they reached the ward.

'So there you have it; no naughty weekend for poor little Sybs. Here we are – Mum's by the bed.'

She held a swing door wide and Chris went into the room. It was a long, narrow room with long, narrow windows. Sybil was in a partitioned-off section of the ward. The door stood open and Chris could see straight inside. There was a window, sealed shut, blackout curtains ready to pull across, and a locker on which stood a jug of water and a glass. Apart from the bed and two hard-looking wooden chairs the room was empty. Chris moved forward into the doorway and gazed pityingly down at Sybil. She lay very still, looking small and defenceless, and Dora, beside her, glanced up as the two girls entered. She smiled and half got to her feet, and Chris could sense the older woman's relief at their presence. Though what I can do, God knows, Chris thought rather despairingly, tiptoeing towards the bed.

I know nothing about sickness – apart from measles and chickenpox I've never had a day in bed in my life. What good can I do?

But she knew as soon as she reached the bedside that just by being there she could relieve Dora of some of her anxiety. Lizzie, good though she was undoubtedly trying to be, was not the sort of person to fill a mother with confidence. Selfish, perhaps, but she was certainly putting herself out for Sybil.

'Hello, Auntie Dora,' Chris said softly. There was a second chair by the bed and without waiting to be invited she sat down in it. 'Do you want Lizzie, or can she go and get something to eat?'

'I wouldn't mind a cup of tea and a bun,' Lizzie admitted. 'There's a staff canteen which they say we can use. The prices are reasonable, too.'

'You go,' Dora said. She had looked up and smiled at Chris again but then her eyes returned to the figure in the bed. A long tube led from a bottle on a stand into Sybil's thin arm and Chris saw that her friend's thick, shoulder-length hair had been cut amateurishly short at ear-level. Sybil's face was deathly pale save for a bright spot of scarlet on each cheekbone which only served to emphasize her pallor, and she had dark circles around her eyes. She was taking rapid, shallow breaths but every now and then her breathing would be suspended altogether before starting off again a few seconds later. She sounded like a tiny, quiet steam train which is finding a hill too much for it.

Lizzie left the ward and Chris pulled her chair closer to the older woman's.

'I've brought a flannel and a bar of soap and some lavender water,' she said, keeping her voice low. 'I thought you might like to bathe Sybil's forehead, it might cool her a little. And I've got some cheese and oatcakes if you'd like a mouthful without leaving the bed.'

'You're very good. Chris, I haven't said so to Lizzie, but this must be costing the earth! I'm not at all sure whether Sybs kept up her sickness payments . . . and even if she did and the club will cover the cost of the hospital, how am I to manage without Sybs's money coming in each week? I can't even get in touch with Henry to let him know our poor little one is ill.'

'Don't worry. Sybs is working for the government, so they'll continue to pay her wages whilst she's sick, I'm sure. As for paying into the club, I know very well she did, because we often discussed it.' Chris tried to speak with complete confidence, though she longed to cross her fingers against all the lies she might well be telling, for she had no idea whether the Women's Land Army would continue to pay Sybs now that she was ill and unable to work. 'Anyway, Auntie Dora, money is the last thing you have to worry about! If you need a loan you know very well that Daddy and Mummy would be happy . . .'

'Oh, Chris, I hoped you'd say that,' Dora said. She heaved a deep sigh and leaned back in her chair. 'The anxiety! You've no idea! Every time they come to give poor Sybs an injection or to fill up that bottle thing I start worrying about the expense . . . and you feel so guilty, you know, when money's on your mind instead of your child's welfare.'

'Don't worry any more,' Chris advised. 'Can she hear us, do you think? What have the doctors said?'

'They say she's bad, but not the worst they've seen,' Dora said. 'I don't know whether she can hear us or not, but she doesn't seem to recognize me or Lizzie. Her breathing worries me, though – and it worries them, too. They're afraid that the paralysis may affect her chest muscles, which could . . . could interfere with her breathing. That's why they keep that' – she pointed to a large cylinder standing behind the bed – 'handy, in case she needs oxygen.'

'I see.' Chris drew the lavender water and flannel out of her basket and tipped a little of the scent on to a corner of the cloth. 'Shall I bathe her forehead? It can't hurt, surely?'

'You go ahead,' Dora said. 'Chris, do you mind if I close my eyes for a minute? Lizzie and I have been here now for the whole day, in a state of dreadful anxiety, and I don't mind admitting that if I don't have a rest I think I'll collapse. Wake me if . . . if things change, though, won't you?'

'Of course I will,' Chris said. She leaned over the bed and applied the flannel delicately to Sybil's shiny forehead. 'You have a bit of a rest.'

And presently, she had the satisfaction of seeing Dora's head fall sideways and hearing small, exhausted snores.

As good as alone with her friend, she picked up one thin hand in hers and began to rub the skin on the back of it, very gently, with her thumb. And she talked, so low that it could not possibly have disturbed Dora, but she hoped she might get through to Sybil.

'Sybs, my love, you must hang on and get better . . . keep on fighting, don't give up. Think of Ralph . . . he's waiting to hear that you're up and about again, so he can come and visit you. And Lizzie's going to come over each evening after work so that when you do wake up, she'll be here. And there's me, too. I won't go back to the farm until I know you're all right . . . think of the Franklyns and the other girls, having to cope without both of us!'

As she said the last words she thought she saw Sybil's eyelids flicker.

Frowning, she repeated the sentence: 'I won't go back to the farm until I know you're all right . . . think of the Franklyns and the other girls, having to cope without you!'

She was right; the amber lashes moved, ever so slightly. Still holding Sybil's hand, Chris leaned nearer the bed, so near that her breath moved the wisps of hair on her friend's cheek.

'Sybs? It's me, Chris – what shall I tell the Franklyns?'

'Te-ell . . . them . . .'

In the chair by Chris's, Dora leaned forward. She must have been woken all in a moment, Chris thought, by some sixth sense which had brought Sybil's voice to her even in the depths of her exhausted sleep.

'Yes, my dear child? Tell them what?'

'Te-ell . . . them . . . I'll come . . . back.'

'Of course we will. Chris will tell them, because I want to stay with you until you feel a great deal better. How do you feel now, sweetheart?'

The heavy lids lifted and just for a second Chris felt the weight of them, the effort which had gone into opening those eyes for the briefest of moments.

'All right,' the thin, exhausted little voice murmured. 'Oh, Mum, I ache, I do ache!'

'Get the nurse,' Dora hissed at Chris. To her daughter she said, in wonderfully calm and loving tones, 'It'll pass, darling. Now that you've begun to get better you'll be a bit stronger every day, you see!'

Chris almost ran from the ward. It was dusk but since the staff had still not drawn the blinds there were no lights showing. The patients in the other beds must have been almost asleep for no one so much as stirred as she shot through the swing doors and into the corridor. Where would she find a nurse? There must be an office or a sluice or something . . . she would try the next door she reached.

She had her hand on the door knob when it opened. A short, plump woman stood there, looking as startled as Chris felt.

'Sorry, my dear, I didn't realize there was anyone outside. Can I help you?'

'Yes! My friend, Sybil Cream . . . she's got infantile paralysis . . . she has just spoken to us, to me and her mother! Mrs Cream says would you come, please?'

'Well, that's good news,' the woman said placidly. She fell into step beside Chris and they returned the way Chris had just come. 'No hurry now. It's been a bit of a worry, her falling into what amounted to a coma, but it may have been due to the high temperature – diseases of the central nervous system are always nerveracking to nurse because we don't know too much about how things work – or there may have been some other cause. Still, if she's awake and talking, perhaps we could persuade her to take some water by mouth. Saline drips and so on are all very well, but . . .'

She chattered on and Chris longed to beg her to hurry, but in fact they were back in the partitioned room in no time, the nurse taking Sybil's pulse, checking the drip, moving her patient's limbs with such care and gentleness that Chris marvelled at it – yet still Sybil cried out, on a high, agonized note.

'It's all right, girlie, it's all right, just lie still and you'll be asleep in no time,' the nurse comforted her. She had been leaning over the bed and now she straightened, a hand going to the small of her back. 'There; let her sleep now. Talking will exhaust her more than you would ever guess.' She turned to Dora. 'Have you had a meal this evening yet? I understand you'll be lodging with Mrs Burbridge, so there's no need for you to stay here. She's only fifty yards away and I can send the porter to fetch you if we want you, though I don't think we will. Go and get some rest, my dear, or you'll be ready to collapse just when we want you to take girlie home.'

'Take her home? Oh, sister, is she going to get well?'

The nurse murmured reassuringly and led them both out of the tiny room and into the corridor. There she stopped and faced them.

'Mrs Cream, I hope and believe Sybil will get better, but I don't want to discuss her case in front of her because she may well hear us. The trouble with the disease she's suffering from is that we don't know too much about it, only that it can kill and it can also cripple. Sybil will need a great deal of care and love over the next few months, and you must be well enough to give it, so it won't do her or your family any good if you wear yourself out in what, I have to tell you, are the early days. I'm afraid, my dear, that you've a long row to hoe before Sybil is her old self again. Now go and find your other daughter and take yourselves off to Mrs Burbridge's place. I don't want to see either of you until about ten o'clock tomorrow morning.'

'Can I sit with Sybs for a bit?' Chris asked. The nurse started to shake her head, then thought better of it.

'Very well, just for a short while. I or one of my nurses will be within call, and we'll pop in every few minutes to make sure she's all right. Then you must go and catch your bus home . . . wherever home is.'

Chris glanced at her watch. It was almost nine o'clock; the last bus had gone nearly an hour before. But she could always walk, or thumb a lift, or ring for a taxi. So she assured Dora that she would be all right, saw her go off in search of Lizzie and the canteen, and turned back into the ward. The nurse drew her away from Sybil's little room, however, a finger to her lips.

'Hush; you may sit with her presently, but first we must talk. The mother's been distraught, the sister's not easy to talk to, but you seem like a sensible young woman. Just how bad is the situation at home? They're obviously desperately short of money, yet Mrs Cream seems . . . she talks like a lady, has no local accent, thanks me politely for everything I do. I can't make it out.'

'Sybil's father is a fisherman, only he's on a minesweeper at present,' Chris said. 'They don't have much money but Lizzie contributes what she can and Sybil's a landgirl, like me, though we are both trained teachers. I lodge with the Creams so I pay Mrs Cream for my keep and Sybil hands over almost all her money apart from what she needs for herself. But my parents will help. My brother is Sybil's young man, and we're all very fond of her, so you needn't worry that bills will be unpaid or anything like that.'

Chris must have spoken in a slightly censorious tone, for the sister jerked her head reprovingly in Sybil's direction and lowered her voice still further.

'No need to be snooty with me, young woman. Your friend's getting the best medical care regardless of the cost. Besides, she's in government service, so she'll be in some sort of sick club, no doubt. No, what worries me is sending the girl home when she's well enough. We need all our beds, we're understaffed, and once we've done all we can . . .'

'When she's fit again, you mean,' Chris said. 'The Creams live in a cottage down by the sea at Pakeby. Sybil will be all right there.'

But the nurse was shaking her head.

'No, not when she's fit again. When we've done all we can for her, I said, and that's precisely what I meant. There will come a point when she'll have to go home and her mother must manage as best she may. That's why I wondered about their circumstances.'

'Circumstances? I'm afraid I don't understand.'

'No, I see that. You haven't spoken to the doctors, of course, and Mrs Cream has been far too worried to take in what has been said to her. I very much fear, my dear, that your friend may never again be the young woman you once knew. It could have been worse, of course. Young people have died from the results of infantile paralysis, especially those whose breathing has been seriously affected, and Sybil's breathing is not too good. I hope we'll pull her through. Only I fear she's almost certain to be severely crippled; she may never walk unaided again.'

Sybil lay very still in the bed. She ached all over but her hips, knees and ankles were white-hot agony when she moved and pretty painful when she did not, so for the most part she lay still as stone. Chris had been here just now and had talked about the Franklyns . . . what would happen if she was going to be ill for a longish time? Would she lose her job? Oh, she didn't want to, she had worked so hard to learn how to do the work required of her, and though she had loved her brief teaching career, looked forward to resuming it when hostilities ceased, she knew that no other war work could suit her the way farming had. But Mr Franklyn needed every pair of hands he could get at this time of year, with summer coming on and the crops needing more and more attention. What on earth would they do if she was away for ages?

They would have to apply for someone else. They would take her job and she would have no money . . . this hospital must be costing an awful lot of money . . . Lizzie would do what she could and Chris would help . . .

Her thoughts rushed off at a tangent. Ralph. He had been with her when the illness had first struck; he had been kind and gentle, had brought her here, and then of course she had no idea what had become of him, she only knew he had gone. He had to go, she knew that. He was flying Spitfires; you couldn't just send a message saying my girlfriend's ill, you'll have to find another pilot. There was a war on, and Ralph was needed in Lincolnshire.

If only it didn't hurt so much to move! If only she could envisage the day when she would be really better, could get out of this bed and walk down the ward, chat to the people whose voices she sometimes heard, raised in argument or laughter. What was the matter with her, anyway? No one had said . . . there was something holding her arm down, it hurt, she wanted her arms free, she must, she must . . .

'Sybs?' That was Chris, her voice gentle, scarcely above a whisper. 'You go to sleep now, Sybs. I'm here. I'll stay until they say I must go.'

Chris stroked her forehead gently with something damp which smelled lovely, then touched her cheek. Sybil opened her eyes.

'What . . . will . . . Mr Franklyn . . . ?'

'I don't know, but I'll find out,' Chris said honestly. 'I'll do my best to make sure they keep the job open for you, but you aren't to worry, the sister says so. You want to get well, love, don't you? Well then, just lie there patiently and do as they tell you and I'm sure you'll be feeling better in no time. I'll sit with you until you go to sleep, shall I?'

'You will? Oh, Chris!'

Lizzie went off with Dora to the lodging down the road after they had had a meal at the hospital canteen. Both tired, both very unhappy, they climbed into the double bed and settled down to sleep. Dora was soon breathing deeply, almost snoring, but Lizzie lay there for a while, her mind chasing itself round and round.

She felt guilty, that was the trouble. Guilty for grudging Ralph to Sybil, even though she knew, or was pretty sure, that Ralph would never have looked at her sister had he been able to have Lizzie herself. And now look what would happen! If Ralph followed his heart and left Sybil, everyone would say he was heartless and self-seeking. If he stayed with her and she really did spend the rest of her life in a wheelchair, he would be miserable. Ralph would not want a wife who was just a burden to him, especially whilst Lizzie was free.

It makes it so awkward for me, Lizzie thought resentfully, lying there in the dark. She had always intended to take Ralph back when his unfortunate affair with Sybil was over – and Lizzie did not doubt that the liaison, as she called it, would not last more than a few months. Ralph, bless him, was too like Lizzie. He was an eager lover and he liked beautiful people. Sybil was all right, Lizzie supposed, but she was no beauty. Oh yes, Ralph would tire of her sister and turn to Lizzie once again. If he had not been so annoyed with her about Emil – and that was Sybil's fault, come to think – then they would never have broken up in the first place.

It was awful, though, to see poor little Sybs so ill. Although the last thing Lizzie wanted was to work on the land, she had rather admired Sybil for the way she had thrown herself into the work. She was a teacher, after all, had worked very hard to get her qualifications, and yet she buckled down and slogged, rain or shine, planting, sowing, reaping, mucking out stables, milking cows, handling that heavy tractor as well as any man.

It was a pity, really, that Lizzie intended to reclaim Ralph, because there was no doubt that in many ways Sybil deserved him. But she, Lizzie, could not help herself. She had had other men, she would not deny it (or rather she would have denied it had Ralph not caught her out), but that did not mean she was not in love with Ralph. Because she was. Body and soul. She loved him in a way she had never loved any man, before him or since. And only he could satisfy and quieten the restless yearning that was in her.

Besides, Ralph wasn't really right for Sybil. He was right for Lizzie, though; we're meant for each other, Lizzie thought contentedly. Sybil would find the right man – someone not quite as selfish as Ralph, someone not quite so obsessed with a pretty face and figure. It would all work out for the best, Lizzie told herself, snuggling down. She had no doubt of it; no doubt at all.

'But I never even knew there was anything between them! Oh yes, he took her out a few times when you were all here on leave together, but that didn't mean . . . oh, Chris, love, I'm not saying she isn't a lovely girl because she is, but . . .'

'But you don't want Ralph held back by a cripple,' Chris said unkindly. 'Don't pinch your mouth up, Mummy, because that's exactly what you mean and you're probably right. I never did think they were right for each other, but don't you see? This is just going to make it difficult for Ralph to break the relationship without feeling really bad about it. Without looking bad, what's more. He won't just be fluttering on to the next flower, which he's done often enough in the past not to have a conscience about it, but he's leaving a girl who may be crippled for life. Oh, Mummy, don't cry. It'll all come out in the end, it has to!'

Mrs Winterton and Chris had been sitting one on each side of the big kitchen table. But seeing her mother's eyes filling once more Chris jumped up and put both arms round her slim shoulders.

'I'm sorry,' Mrs Winterton sobbed, rubbing her eyes fiercely with her handkerchief and then turning to hug Chris. 'I didn't mean to be horrid about Sybs or anything like that, and it isn't true – well, not very true – that I don't want Ralph tied to a – a cripple. But what you said about Ralph being tied to Sybs for all the wrong reasons, that does upset me. You see, love, I can't bear him to be unhappy or badly thought of and it seems to me he's going to be one or the other no matter what he does.'

'Leave it to Sybs,' Chris advised gently. 'She'll see that Ralph escapes if he wants to, without embarrassment on either side. Tomorrow I'm going to talk to the Powers that Be about Sybs's job, which she won't be able to keep, I'm afraid, so I lied my head off when I told her she could. They told me at the hospital that one reason why Sybs may have a fight to get well is that she was doing a very energetic job, and the disease thrives best on muscles which are being constantly used. But we'll all help her and visit her and Mummy . . .'

'Yes, dear?'

'Don't *worry*. We'll work something out.'

17

When *Stompin' Suzie* was crossing the English coast Fenn saw the first long lines of pale but brilliant gold light up the white beaches and knew they were even later than he had expected to be, for usually they returned in the grey light of dawn, seeing little of the country below them save for shapes which gradually grew clearer as the sun's strength increased.

They had been over the Ruhr last night, factory-land. And there had been some pretty stiff opposition, both from the ground and in the air. Fenn and the crew had put *Suzie* through every sort of hoop but they had still not managed to escape entirely unscathed. Nipper, the tail gunner, had reported damage and because it had been such a helluva long ride home Will and Fenn had taken it in turns to handle the stick. Even so, when Fenn took over as they neared the coast he began to worry at the feel of her. A B-24 was always a heavy, some might say sluggish, airplane, but this was ridiculous. It took all Fenn's considerable strength to keep the rudder pedal down – as he shouted to Will at one point, he was beginning to feel that he was supporting all thirty tons of airplane instead of *Suzie* supporting them.

Then Krantz, the engineer up in the top turret, reported that there was damage to a wing. He could see a line of smoulder which now and then seemed to flame for a minute. Fenn felt cold, then hot. Damn, damn, damn! No one ever got off entirely untouched, but this was his last mission before a long leave period and he had been looking forward to it ever since he had made up his mind to go home. Back to Manchester.

He had written to Rachael more than two years ago and made up as best he could for his long silence. She had written back, a letter full of love and understanding, telling him she had a nice man friend and a good job, that she was a nurse now, not just a cleaner at the Jewish hospital. But then he had moved on from Basic Training

273

School and somehow he had not managed to write again. He had not intended to lose touch, but somehow, with the exigencies of war, it had happened.

Guys often said it didn't do to anticipate; living for the day seemed to be best. And Fenn had done just that, lived each day as it came, gone with pretty girls, never arranged to see them again, played cards with guys in the Mess and tried not to notice when, in a week's time, everyone round the poker table was different.

Until now, when, because he had five whole days off, he felt he must take the big decision. To go back to Manchester and find his family, or to stay shtum, to enjoy his time in England as a sort of bonus of war and then return to New York and pick up his life there as though it had never been interrupted.

Rachel wouldn't need to know he'd ever been back; he could send letters to Sammy's girlfriend, Ada, and she would post them as though they had come straight from the States. His curious reluctance to see his mother was not easy to explain, but he acknowledged that it existed. Was it because, once he had seen her again, he would worry about her? It was bad enough worrying about his crew, himself, Sammy up in Scotland, without worrying about Rachael too. Yet he knew he wanted to go back. He wanted to see Manchester again, see whether it was anything like his mental picture of it.

And he wanted to see Cecil, and the other Finaglers. Even Saul, if his cousin was still in the city and not abroad somewhere. It was not that he hadn't fitted into New York because he had; he felt like a New Yorker from the top of his head to the soles of his feet, but that didn't stop him from knowing that his roots were buried deep in the little streets and parks and places where he had been brought up. Gamps slept beneath a big, carved gravestone out at the cemetery in Crumpsall. Who visited him now that Fenn was no longer there; who put little bunches of stolen flowers on his grave? Rachael worked at the Jewish hospital where Gamps had breathed his last but she was a busy woman, probably had a whole life of her own by now which Fenn knew nothing about. She would never neglect Gamps . . . but it would be Fenn's presence which the old man wanted, Fenn's tatty bunches of flowers.

It's my childhood, Fenn told himself defensively. So he had never been any of the various things he had pretended – not rich, not famous, not wonderfully popular and beloved – but that did not mean to say his childhood had not been a happy one. He had been very happy until Gamps's death, but even after that there had been long periods when he had been as happy as any boy could be. Mainly when Great-Grandpa and Uncle Joseph were nowhere in his vicinity, but even so! As the time for his leave drew nearer he found himself remembering with increasing clarity every little street and alley, every room in the house, every face in the classroom. Becky whatsername! Pretty little kid – wonder what she made of it when I vamoosed? And Cecil, my best friend. They had not exchanged letters because Fenn had not dared to send an address until he was in the Army Air Force, but he had written cards to Cecil two or three times a year, telling him . . .

Oh, well. What he'd told Cecil might not have been true . . . well, it wasn't true . . . but that didn't matter. Cecil knew Fenn, he would read between the lines. And Rachael? She loved him, he knew; she would forgive the years between. He could just see her, the big, dark eyes tear-filled, her arms held out to him . . .

No use dreaming, though. They were starting their approach, and it would take all Fenn's concentration to get her down, judging by the way the rudder was responding. The tower had already been informed of their plight and position, and now they went into their landing procedure. Their bombs had all gone down over the Ruhr, so that was all right. Fenn began to talk to the tower, then to bring the big airplane into the right position for landing.

'Krantz, check the auxiliary hydraulic pump's off and open the flight-deck escape hatch,' Fenn said automatically. There was damage, so they might yet have to crash land, though the main wheels had come down with their usual spine-jarring crunch and the nose-wheel seemed to be in position. Because of the smouldering wing-edge the fuel sight-gauge valves had been turned off and drained in the forward bomb-bay. The crew had been together now for long enough to have the drill off by heart but Fenn always went through it, anyway. It was a brave – for brave read foolish – pilot who did not go through the check-list.

The tower had given them the go-ahead to land so Fenn lined up with the end of the runway and slowed his speed to around 155 mph. He turned shallow into his approach, dropping the speed still further. He was down to 135 mph when the wheels touched and he immediately brought the throttles full back, raised the nose a fraction and began to use the brakes.

'We're down, Kitzie, we're on terra firma,' Will said exuberantly into his interphone. You could feel the relief from tension as an almost physical thing as the big airplane trundled to a halt. 'C'mon, boys, the blood wagon ain't needed jest yet!'

'Trust *Suzie* to bring us home safe,' someone else remarked as they made their way to the truck which would run them back to the mess. 'We're last ones back, though.'

'No, not quite; there's one more to come, I hear it,' Benny said. He was the nose gunner, a skinny, active guy with big ears. It was said he could hear a mouse fart a mile away and now he was proving it, since Fenn could hear nothing. He listened, then caught the faint, far-off purr of an aero-engine.

'Yeah, there's somethin' . . .' he began, to be interrupted by Bob Ennis, the bombardier.

'That ain't no bomber, Benny; that's a fighter. Escort, or . . .'

He came out of the clouds, a narrow, wicked shape, guns blazing. Fenn, flinging himself flat, fancied he could even make out the pilot, the helmeted head, goggled eyes, the hands gripping the stick. And then they heard the rip and roar of the guns and covered their heads, all cursing together as they heard the splintering crash and the roar. Fenn glanced over his shoulder and jumped to his feet with a yell. *Stompin' Suzie* was on fire from nose to tail.

'Git outa here!' he heard himself bawling at his companions, only just beginning to uncurl from their pre-natal positions on the grass. 'She's afire, there's nothin' we can do, so *run*.'

They obeyed. The fire engines came sirening across the airfield and the truck, waiting for them a short way off, gunned its engine and tore over to them. They leapt aboard, the heat on the backs of their necks telling them what was happening to their B-24.

'She's a goner,' Benny said miserably as the truck drew up outside the offices where they would go to debrief. 'I should've know that warn't no Lib engine – too light, too high, like a wasp.'

'Nothin' we could've done,' Evan, one of the waist gunners said philosophically. 'Our big bird's a roast turkey.'

She was. In an hour – less – there would be nothing left of *Suzie*, not so much as a whisker.

'But we're all okay,' Fenn pointed out. 'Say, our five days will likely be a week now, maybe more! We're runnin' kinda short of B-24s. We're gonna be grounded for a while, guys!'

So his visit home, which had seemed to recede when the B-24 been hit, had suddenly become not a possibility but a fact. Just goes to show, Fenn thought; poor old *Suzie* – but I'm going home after all!

*   *   *

He went into Norwich on the liberty truck, seeing the city through new eyes now that he was going home. It was a small city, and old. The castle high on its grassy mound looked down on fifty churches and a hundred pubs, or so the locals said. Fenn reckoned he'd been in most of the pubs – he hoped to visit them all before he left the area – and a good few of the churches, though only as a sightseer. Fenn's religion sat so lightly on him that he had never even looked for a synagogue in Norwich, far less in New York, where Sammy and Yacob Kopinski had talked about the synagogue but never, to Fenn's knowledge, actually visited it. They were always going to do so, but that was as far as it went.

The liberty truck was obliging and dropped the men as near their destinations as possible, so Fenn, with his possessions in a knapsack on one shoulder, was put down right outside Thorpe station. He strolled across the concourse and into the echoing central hall, bought a ticket to Manchester Victoria, listened to the clerk's instructions for changing at Ely, and then went into the rather dingy refreshment room to get a cup of coffee and a sandwich to pass the time until his train arrived.

He was sipping a cup of awful coffee with distaste when the girl walked in. She was small, slender, blonde, with the sort of wide-open blue eyes and curvy mouth which usually meant 'available' in Fenn's experience. She looked all round, as though searching for someone, and then went up to the counter. She bought a cup of tea and an iced bun – she had a very clear voice, every vowel-sound as perfect as cut glass – and then went to sit at a table by herself.

There were very few people about; Fenn cleared his throat and stood up, a hand going to tug his cap from his head. He smiled at the girl.

'Excuse me, ma'am . . . haven't we met? Weren't you at the Samson & Hercules ballroom a week or so ago, with a friend of mine – Alby Bichstein?'

It was a good guess; she looked the sort of girl who might well mix with a number of men and not be able to name them all. She smiled up at him, but did not suggest that he sit down.

'Alby? That's an unusual name. I don't think . . .'

'Gee, what am I thinkin' of?' Fenn thrust out a hand. 'Fennimore Kitson, ma'am, at your service. And you're . . .'

She nearly let the little hesitation drag on so that he would have been forced to say something, admit defeat, but instead she laughed suddenly and held out her own hand.

'I'm Lizzie Cream, and you're picking me up,' she said gaily. 'Do sit down. When my friend arrives I'll be able to introduce you as respectably as though we'd known one another for years.'

Fenn had always thought on his feet; now he wondered whether to look hurt and exclaim that he really did think he knew her, or whether to meet her with equal honesty. Between one blink and the next, he had decided, for once, on the truth.

He laughed across at her, showing all his strong white teeth.

'Well, ma'am, scrapin' acquaintance is how I'd have phrased it, myself, but I guess that's just a nicer way of sayin' pickin' up! You catchin' a train?'

'No, I'm meeting one. I've a friend coming on leave for a forty-eight – as it's such a short time I thought I'd meet him off the train. That'll give us an hour or so longer together. What about you? Taking yourself off to London for a bit of fun? They tell me the London clubs for you boys are the last word in luxury.'

Fenn smiled politely. He did not like to say that so far as he could see luxury, to the British, meant cakes without butter, bread without jam and coffee without coffee! The food here was simply unbelievable. They'd never even heard of waffles or grits or chilli. Yet he remembered his mother's cooking with watering mouth, so perhaps he ought not to blame them for the food; there was a war on, as people were so fond of remarking. Though why that should make them give corn-cobs to the hens and eat Brussels sprouts which looked mighty like warts was more than he had yet fathomed.

'No, I ain't London bound, not this time. I'm headin' for the city of Manchester.'

'Really? It's not everyone's favourite place – I take it you have friends or relatives there?'

'Uhuh. Relatives. I'm from English stock, you see. My great-grandpappy owned the railroad from London to Manchester and my grandpappy's big in property development. Got a great old town-house in Altrincham; that's where I'm bound, though I've never seen the place.'

That, at least, was true. Fenn's knowledge of Altrincham came solely from the fact that his mother had once said, with rare viciousness, that when Joseph died she would see he was buried in Altrincham, because that was the only way he'd ever get there. Uncle Joseph, Fenn remembered with satisfaction, had been furious.

'Well, I hope you find them all well,' Lizzie Cream said politely. 'And your pa . . . I mean your father? What does he do?'

Fenn shot her a quick glance; had there been just a trace of sarcasm in her voice? Was it possible she thought him a liar, a romancer? But her blue eyes were guileless enough.

'My pa? Aw, he went to the States when he was no more'n a kid, married Mom ... she came from the South, her family owned plantations in Jamaica, big estates in Louisiana, rich ain't the word ... then Mom and Pa moved up north, took on a ranch, and now the whole family's in cattle ... my brother Sammy, he's the baby of the family, me an' ole Sam, we'll share the ranch between us one of these days. But I like city life, which is why I went into the theatre.'

She smiled at him. Her eyes were dancing as though she were enjoying every word he spoke. Fenn was gratified, and yet ...

'The theatre? Are you an actor, then?'

'Gee, no ma'am! I back shows, finance 'em, you might say. It's a way to lose a lot of money unless you've got the knack.' He smiled modestly. 'I ain't never lost money at it yet,' he finished truthfully.

'Well, that's very impressive!' Lizzie Cream looked over his shoulder, half-smiled and got to her feet. Her tea was almost finished, the iced bun no more than a few crumbs. How she had managed to get them both down whilst listening to him was a mystery to Fenn, who had not noticed her so much as sip at her cup. 'I must go, there's a train drawing in!'

He tried to stand up but she pushed him down again, smiling, excitement lighting her up.

'No, it'll be a while before your train arrives and there'll be a flood of people in here soon, off the London train. It's been nice meeting you. Er ... perhaps we'll bump into one another again some time.'

She fluttered a white, beautifully manicured hand at him and was gone, hurrying out on to the platform.

Thoughtfully, Fenn got up from his seat, but left the chair tipped up so that no one would think it untaken. He moved over to the half-glassed door and looked out.

The train had arrived and people were running up the platform, casting themselves on the bosoms of those who waited. Lizzie's friend proved to be an officer in the Royal Air Force, a handsome, fair-haired young man, tall and athletically built, who picked her up and hugged her, then stood her down and kissed her with an intensity and fervour which made Fenn feel quite envious. When had he last felt like that about a woman? When had he ever felt like that about a woman, come to that?

The officer's cap was tilted to the back of his head and he wore a white silk scarf which he now removed and hung rakishly around

Lizzie's neck. He pulled on it, and began to hug her again. What a spectacle to make of themselves, Fenn thought sourly, carrying on like that when the platform's nearly empty.

He stood watching until they had sauntered, still entwined, out of the station, and then he returned to his table. He sat down and shrugged philosophically, picking up the curly, dry-looking sandwich he had purchased earlier. He took a bite – strong cheese and a tiny smear of some sweetish pickle. At least the cheese tasted of something – a boxer's training shoes – which was better than the insipid seed cake he had seen displayed under the glass counter, or that dreadful concoction known as 'spam'.

And Lizzie Cream, who had preferred her Royal Air Force guy to a red-blooded Yank (who was born and bred in Manchester, Fenn reminded himself, in parentheses)? Oh well, you win some, you lose some. And the conversation had done two things. It had revived all Fenn's story-telling instincts and it had made him realize that he must decide what he would tell Rachael, Joseph, Saul, and anyone else who asked about his life in the States. He had better get his story sorted out on the train journey otherwise he might make some fatal error, like claiming one thing to one person, something different to someone else, and not realizing they would compare notes when he had gone back to Flacton once more.

Not that he intended to lie, of course. Would he lie, and to relatives he hadn't seen for years? Fenn never lied, though he did embroider a bit when such embroidery made everyone happier, including Fenn himself. His mother would like to hear he was successful; Saul would perhaps not really like to hear he was rich, owned a car so long that one half of it was in Manhattan whilst the other half was in Brooklyn, and had gotten himself engaged to be married to an up and coming film star, but he would be interested and envious. Fenn told himself virtuously that it was better for a guy to be interested and envious than bored . . . and besides, he had his reputation to think of. It would never do if he did not dazzle half the congregation with his exploits – they would think he had changed indeed!

It did not occur to Fenn that as first pilot of a B-24 he might well expect a certain amount of genuine adulation – the great bombers droned overhead in Manchester no doubt, defending Mancunians from the Luftwaffe – without having to tell a single lie. What was the point? Besides, that was what he *did*; he had no desire to talk about that!

*   *   *

The station was the first surprise. It looked different, though Fenn would have said that stations never change and that he had not noticed it, particularly, when he had fled all those years ago.

Within seconds of descending from his train he realized what had changed; it was lighter because most of the glass roof, supported by iron girders, had been blown off. He frowned, left the station and began to walk towards the city centre, hoping to pick up a bus.

The destruction was a horrible surprise, a kick in the pit of the stomach. He was used to seeing the debris and rubble of earlier air raids, the bomb craters and ruined buildings in Norwich. The bomb-sites already overgrown with rosebay willow herb were as much a part of that city, to Fenn, as the sight of the castle towering over Castle Meadow, or the Elizabethan houses with their beams and jutting upper storeys which lined so many of the small streets.

But he had never known Norwich before the Luftwaffe came; his own city, Manchester, he had known only whole and complete. The sight of Deansgate and what had been Market Street, the Shambles a shambles indeed, made him feel ashamed of his absence, his involvement with another country, another culture. He walked the battered streets and ached for the people who had been killed whilst he had been safe on the other side of the Atlantic.

But he had been learning his craft, learning how to hand it out instead of just taking it, as the citizens of Manchester had been forced to do. He had felt neither guilt nor pleasure in the past as he gave the order to Bob to open the doors of the bomb-bay, but in future he would do it with satisfaction. A church for a church, a street for a street, a life for a life, in fact. Let the Germans feel what it was like to see the senseless destruction of buildings which had been beautiful, areas which had been much loved.

He saw a bus approaching but ignored it, walking now towards the Cheetham Hill area. He might as well see what was what before going to the hospital to find Rachael. Once he'd seen how things stood he could either decide to get himself a hotel room or move on. It all depended on his mother, really. He could go up to the cemetery and pay his respects to Gamps in a day easily, so he had no need to stay if she didn't want him to.

But he hoped she would want him, would make him welcome. He had done wrong to run away all those years ago, he acknowledged, but he had come back, hadn't he? It would be all right, it was bound to be.

Rachael was a generous, loving person – she would not turn her back on him now.

Cheetham Hill Road was in darkness by the time he reached it, though it was the darkness of summer, with lots of stars. He knew his way blindfold, he discovered, but his way would have led to the house in Belstrode Street and his mother wouldn't be there. Instead, he turned left into Elizabeth Street. The hospital was blacked out, of course, but he would have known it anywhere. He walked up to it, glancing to where the nurses' home stood – and stopped short. His mouth dried, and his heart began to beat out a frantic tattoo with the sheer, awful shock.

The nurses' home, which had stood up against the hospital for as long as he could remember, was a shell. Gape-eyed, the windows showed only sky and the roof had gone altogether.

He was running; stupidly, blindly, running up the road, away from the carnage which might have happened yesterday for all he knew. He was sobbing beneath his breath, going over all the old charms . . . let her be all right, let it be a bad dream, let it not be true that I killed her by pretending she was dead, let her be all right, all right, all right!

Someone was coming down the pavement towards him; a policeman, the familiar domed helmet on his head. Fenn slowed and stopped.

'Excuse me, officer . . . the nurses' home attached to the Jewish hospital; what happened? Was anyone killed?'

The constable glanced back at the hospital as though he had forgotten its existence, forgotten the nurses' home altogether.

'The nurses' home? Eh, that were blitz, sir. Bin done a while, that. I don't know about casualties, I weren't here at the time . . . you'd best ask at 'ospital itself, sir. They'll know for sure.'

'Yes, of course.' Fenn turned and walked back with the constable, trying to pull himself together. No point in panicking when he had ignored his mother for years. What was I thinking of? he asked himself now. I knew she loved me . . . how could I have done what I did?

'You over here in the forces, sir?'

The constable was making conversation, Fenn realized.

'Oh . . . yes, that's right. American Army Air Force. I fly B-24s.'

'Aye, I know 'em. Liberators. Well, sir, here's 'ospital. Go in careful, like, because they've got double doors so's there's no light can get out to show Nazis what's what.'

'Right. And thanks, officer,' Fenn said.

He walked briskly up to the entrance doors. He pushed them open

282

and all at once a wave of nostalgia hit him. It was exactly the same! Amongst so much change, this familiarity caught at his throat, filling him with a bitter-sweet sense of belonging. The times he had crossed this foyer to go into the long corridor which led to Gamps's ward! The times he had sat here waiting for Rachael when he was small and she was working a late shift! Even the smell . . . The kosher kitchens must be hard put to it to provide their patients with the right food because of all the shortages, but if smells were anything to go by Meaty and Milky were going strong, just as they always had!

There was a hatch across the hallway with a bell beside it. He walked over and pressed the bell-push and after a pause the hatch shot up and a woman's head appeared in the aperture. She wore rimless glasses and her short gingery hair was untidy, her face pale with tiredness, but even so she smiled brightly at him.

'Good evening. Have you come to visit someone? The hours are really seven till eight, but I can see you've come a long way, so if you could just give me the name . . . or do you know the ward?'

'Umm . . . Rachael Kitzmann,' Fenn mumbled. 'She isn't on a ward. She works here . . . well, she used to work here. I'm – I'm – '

'Rachael Kitzmann . . . Kitzmann . . . Wait a moment, I'll have a word with matron. She knows everyone. You said Kitzmann worked here? And she's a patient now? Matron's bound to know.'

Before he could explain further she had got off her chair and clicked out of sight.

Sighing, Fenn leaned against the wall and found his mind returning again and again to the gaunt ruin next door. The nurses' home. She had been so proud of her lovely room in the nurses' home. But that had been longer ago than he thought, probably. His mind began its ritual again; let her be all right, let her not have been killed by that bomb, if she's all right I'll be good, I'll never lie again, not even a little bit . . .

A woman rustled round the corner. She wore a blue dress and an imposing air. She smiled, her kind, intelligent face creasing with friendliness.

'You're wanting Rachael Kitzmann that was, am I right?'

Fenn's heart dived into his boots. That *was*?

'She's . . . that's to say is she . . . she was . . .'

'She's on Sereno ward. She shouldn't be there, of course, but when the pains started . . . come along then. You're a relative, are you?' She indicated Fenn's kitbag. 'She'll be glad to see you, a fine surprise, and she has one for you, too!' She turned to the ginger-haired woman and once more the bright, lively smile transformed her round, plain, over-powdered face. 'Thank you, Miss Spycer. Well done to fetch me!'

She bustled through the swing doors and into a corridor, waiting for Fenn to catch her up. She smiled encouragingly up at him.

'Where've you come from? You're one of those American boys, eh? A Yankee, that's what the girls call you.' She laughed breathily, hurrying along. 'Well, well. You've not come from America today, I don't suppose; where are you stationed?'

'On the Norfolk-Suffolk border. At an airfield called Flacton.'

'And you've come specially to see Rachael, when you don't even know her married name! Mind, it's a mouthful – she's Mrs Balonokov now. Amos, that's Mr Balonokov, wanted to change the name to Baker, thought it was nicer, more English, but Rachael she liked the name as it was, said he should be proud of his heritage. So she's Mrs Balonokov now, and very happy they are . . . you'll see.' She turned left so abruptly that Fenn was nearly caught out, only swerving to follow at the last possible moment. They were in a very short corridor this time, with windows at intervals and a pair of double swing doors through which matron advanced, holding one door open courteously for Fenn to follow.

'Here we are, second bed from the door.' She raised her voice, addressing the woman in the bed. 'Well, Mrs Balonokov, what a surprise! A visitor, come a long way to see you, so sit up and tell him thank you!'

Fenn stared and then a big grin spread right across his face. She was all right! Rachael was sitting up in bed, propped up by a good many pillows, knitting. She looked up and smiled, then blushed. She looked pretty and confused and extremely pleased with herself. The long, dark hair he remembered so well hung in loose curls down to her shoulders, her nightgown was pink and white with a frilly little collar. She was staring, still smiling, but there was a frozen quality about her smile which told him that she had not recognized him.

'Rachael? Don't say you've forgotten your own son!'

'Fenn!' She actually shrieked his name, and came half out of bed before he could stop her. She threw herself into his arms, crying, laughing, hugging. He hugged her back, tenderly, felt his own eyes wet. That he could have thought for one moment she would hold his running away against him . . . that he could have done her such an injustice!

'Mum – Rachael – oh, it's good to see you again. You look grand, absolutely fine! When I saw the nurses' home I thought . . . I thought . . .'

'My boy! Oh, my dear boy, you've come back. I always hoped you would, I prayed you would, and here you are. You've grown, and your hair's even curlier than it was when you were a lad . . . eh, Fenn, aren't I proud!'

'Not as proud as I am,' Fenn said, still holding her, though now he was sitting on the bed and Rachael was back between the covers. 'But why are you here? Are you waiting for an operation? Have you been ill?'

'Ill? No, I'm fine, absolutely fine! Didn't matron tell you? Have you had my letters?'

He shook his head. 'Only one, years ago.'

She was trembling with excitement. 'Matron told you I'd married Amos? We're happy as happy, Fenn, and just three days ago, whilst I was helping matron with the paperwork in her office, I started having pains. Fenn, you've got a little brother, Mark Balonokov. He looks ever so like you when you were three days old.'

Fenn stared, shaking his head, grinning like a lunatic.

'A *brother*? Gee, a ready-made family! I can't believe it!'

'Well you better had, for it's true as I'm lying here. Fenn, you must stay with Amos, you mustn't go to any old lodging house! I'll give you the address and you must go right round. He'd be very hurt if he thought my son Fenn hadn't stayed under his roof . . . oh, you've done so well for yourself, I'm so proud of you!'

She wrote the address down on an old envelope, insisting all the while that Amos would quite understand, he knew all about Fenn, he would be delighted, would tell Fenn the story of how he and she had met . . . oh how he would laugh when he heard what a *shlemiel* his mother was!

Fenn left the hospital walking on air. He had seen his brother, had been taken to a tiny ward containing five cots with high metal bars. There were two pink-faced and slumbering children who had had their tonsils removed, two empty beds and, securely tucked down in the last cot, his brother.

Fenn hung over the cot for a long time. He felt so warm towards the baby, so entranced by him. He watched the small, puzzled face, the eyes so tightly closed that not a lash showed, the delicate wisp that was an eyebrow, the pouting, full-lipped little mouth, moving hopefully even in sleep. My brother, Mark Balonokov! Fenn Kitzmann looks as though he's got himself a whole family to love – a mother, a step-father, a brother. Gee!

When he left the hospital he had the envelope crushed in his hand and he did not consider going off and finding himself lodgings even for a moment. He trusted Rachael – had he not always trusted her really, in his heart? She would not let him down; this Amos would be a good man and would welcome Rachael's son into his home. Besides, he was very tired and very excited and badly needed somewhere to lay his head. The flat was above a baker's shop on Cheetham Hill Road called The Jolly Baker and it was Amos's own shop. He made the best cakes in Manchester, Rachael had said, and the finest, crispest matzoh.

Fenn walked up Elizabeth Street and down Waterloo Road, passing his old school and feeling, even in the dark, a friendly kinship with its familiar shape. Rachael had told him about Uncle Joseph and Great-Grandpa being killed in the blitz and that Aunt Anna and cousin Saul were living in Denbighshire because Saul was digging coal. She had laughed and so had he – Saul was so work-shy, how would he like digging coal, eh? Serve him right, Fenn thought, but idly, without malice. The night was fine, clear and warm, and he hummed a tune as he strode along. The only thing which worried him was that Amos might be in bed and asleep when he reached the flat, but he need not have worried.

The blackout was excellent. You could not see so much as a thread of light, but Fenn went up the iron staircase round the side and found the bell-push by the door at the top. He rang and quite quickly he heard footsteps in the flat.

'Yes? Who is it?'

'I'm Fennimore Kitzmann. Rachael told me to come.'

He felt a fool saying it, but not for long. The door shot open and a shortish, squarish man came out. He had thick white hair, dark eyes, and an intelligent, humorous face. He put his arms round Fenn and gave him a quick, unembarrassing hug, then held him back and stared intently at him.

'My boy . . . Rachael's son! Yes? You are Rachael's Fenn?'

'That's right,' Fenn admitted. 'It must seem kinda strange, me just comin' in out of the night without a word, but . . .'

Amos Balonokov shook his head and put a finger to his lips, then closed the door, locked it, and beckoned.

'Not strange, wonderful,' he declared. 'A miracle for which she has prayed. Two sons in three nights . . . eh, wouldn't you call that a miracle, Fenn, after years of longing?'

'Yeah, I guess.'

'Then come into the kitchen, Miracle, and let me give you something to eat and drink. Anything particular you fancy?'

'Bread and water 'ud be fine,' Fenn confessed. 'I haven't eaten since this morning.'

'Well then, we can run to toasted cheese, a nice mug of cocoa and a piece of my famous fruit loaf. How does that sound?'

'Wonderful,' Fenn said. He looked round the kitchen. He grinned to himself, with pride and loving memories. Two sets of pans, both gleaming with cleanliness. A neat gas stove, not a range, but much cleaner and more convenient. Walls of gleaming tiles with pictures and copper utensils breaking up the almost sterile whiteness. A tall blue jug with a burst of bright flowers, marigolds, ornamental thistles, tiger lilies, exploding from its neck. Printed tea-towels hanging on hooks on the door and soft, colourful rugs scattered over the scarlet linoleum. A room to enjoy, not just a room to work in. A long shelf over the stove held cookery books and a few paperback novels. Rachael had always loved to read. There was a fireplace but at this time of year no fire burned in it, so someone had filled a big copper jug with ornamental grasses, chinese lanterns, blue and purple statis.

'Sit down, my boy, sit down. Take the weight off your feet and put it on your *tochis*.' Fenn sat in a saggy, comfortable armchair and leaned back luxuriously, stretching his legs to their fullest extent. A steaming cup was placed on the arm of the chair and soon after that the toasted cheese arrived complete with homemade chutney, or mustard if he preferred it.

Whilst he ate, Amos made sure the spare bed was aired, took Fenn's kitbag through, supplied him with a clean towel, told him where the bathroom was and said that though he himself would be in the shop by eight, Fenn had no need to get up early, could lie in as long as he liked.

'You soldiers work to defend us and when you're on leave you should get a good rest,' he observed, and was not at all abashed when Fenn said that in fact he was a Liberator pilot.

'There you are, then. All the more reason to rest whilst you can,' Amos said, chuckling. 'And I should rest too, since I'm so tired I can't tell a birdman from a landsman. Go to bed, Fenn. I'll be along with a cup of tea for you about ten, when I have my mid-morning break, and then we'll talk about you getting up.'

Fenn's room was small and clean and bright. It had a single bed, a dressing table, a tallboy and a couple of rugs. The window, which was open to let in the fresh night air, overlooked the garden where Amos grew as wide a variety of vegetables as he could manage and, he told Fenn proudly as he drew the blackout blind down, an apple tree which bore huge fruit on the right of the clothes line and a plum which did pretty well too on the left.

'When you're ready for bed, let the blind up, then you can enjoy the air,' he advised. 'It's a small room and it gets hot, nights. Sleep well, my boy.'

And Fenn, so tired that even getting between the sheets was an effort, thanked his host, let the blind up and stood for a moment looking out over the dark garden before climbing thankfully into the small bed.

Just before he slept he reviewed his day. A baby brother, a mother who loved him despite what he had done, and a step-father who was easily the nicest guy Fennimore Kitzmann had ever come across. And so far he had not felt bound to tell one single, solitary, over-embroidered lie!

18

Sybil was in hospital for three months before the sister on her ward told Dora she was going to send her home.

'There's really nothing more we can do for her, except to ease her pain, which can be done just as well at home,' she explained to Dora. 'There's no cure as such for infantile paralysis, we simply make her as comfortable as we can and keep her limbs as still as we can and wait for the virus to work itself out. And it seems to have done so.'

'So she won't walk? Not ever?'

'Now, Mrs Cream, you should know better than to make such a wild assumption. As I must have told you at least twenty times, Sybil's trouble was her job. Anyone doing hard physical work suffers the worst with infantile paralysis; it's almost as though the virus can get a better grip in actively moving bodies. She was very lucky, in fact, that at the onset of the disease she was on leave and taking a train journey. But even so she's been very ill, and now that the disease has run its course it's largely a matter of waiting to see how much movement can be brought back to her limbs. There's very little muscle-wasting, as yet, which is a good thing, and if she can be helped by a physiotherapist, who will teach her the sort of gentle exercise which can be most beneficial to her condition, then we may well see her walking after a few months. And another good point is that we've found she still has quite a lot of feeling in the affected limbs.'

Dora knew all about that. She had been present when some of the tests had been done and had suffered for her daughter as Sybil's limbs were probed for a reaction, but Sybil knew that such apparent cruelty had a purpose and never complained. The doctors had to know how far the paralysis had spread in order to help her.

And now she was coming home! Despite Chris's loving and helpful presence and Lizzie spending almost all her spare time at the cottage, Dora had missed her younger daughter sorely. First Georgie and then

Sybil, she had thought. Only I can't lose my baby girl, she must get well!

She told Paul all about Sybil and knew that Paul was rooting for her, adding her to the list of people he cared about though the two had never met. Paul, despite his blindness, was one of the best people Dora knew and she was touched by the fact that he always asked after her daughter – he, who had so much to bear.

'But I can walk,' he said soberly when she reminded him that he, too, had a disability to fight. 'I can get about – I will, too, once they'll let me.'

'When they let you out you're going to come and stay with me for a while, don't forget,' Dora said firmly. 'There's always Georgie's bed . . . well, it's the sofa really, but you'll find it comfortable, same as my boy did.'

'I know, Dora. And I will come, if I possibly can. Now tell Sybil from me that once she's home things will seem much easier to bear. Why, she'll have my favourite lady with her, for a start!'

Dora laughed.

'Soft soap butters no parsnips,' she said obscurely. 'As for having me there, I hope you don't think I shall neglect my work here, for that's the last thing Sybil will expect me to do. Besides, she'll have plenty to occupy her; these exercises, the physiotherapist's visits, all her friends popping round . . . oh, yes, she'll keep busy, will Sybs.'

She never admitted even to Paul that her secret belief was that Sybil, under her own guidance, would make a complete recovery. It sounded silly put like that, but Dora was a great believer in the efficacy of being at home. And it would be good to have Sybil back on other counts, too. The worries which had weighed her down would not seem half as heavy when her daughter was there to share them. The bills for Sybil's treatment, for instance, would be paid for by the insurance, with any extra being handled by the Wintertons. Mr Winterton had said, gruffly, that he understood that Dora's girl was . . . hrrumph . . . tied up in some way to his boy Ralph, so naturally anything the Wintertons could do . . .

They would have helped anyway, but it was nice to hear Mr Winterton talk as though he was thrilled to consider Ralph and Sybil a couple. Which he cannot be, with the poor little soul likely to be crippled, Dora thought understandingly. The money they had already laid out was only a loan – Henry had written to say this must be made clear – but if Mr Winterton really felt that because of their children's friendship there would be no hurry to pay it back, it would take a deal of worry off Dora's shoulders.

'I can go back to teaching now, can't I, Mum?' Sybil had said the other day. 'I know I can't work on the land, but I could teach! And why not be useful? I'm sure, once I start to walk . . .'

'You'll have to give yourself a few months,' her mother said. 'You mustn't try to run before you can walk, love.'

'Funny joke,' Sybil said, smiling. 'But it's a good sign that I've got feeling in my legs, isn't it? It means I will walk one day, doesn't it?'

'Of course it does. It'll just take time,' Dora said comfortingly, and hoped that she spoke the truth.

And Sybil returned by ambulance on a fine September day when the nearest farm was harvesting. Everyone was helping bar Dora, who was walking up and down Beach Road in mixed anticipation and nervous dread that something would happen to delay her daughter. A few hundred yards away the shouts and laughter of the harvesters came gently on the breeze and the glorious scent of ripe, sun-kissed wheat was even stronger than the smell of the sea.

The ambulance drew up outside the gate and the attendants brought Sybil in on a stretcher. It was the first time Dora had seen her daughter out of a hospital bed and she was shocked by how pale and thin Sybil looked. The ambulance men were tanned and fit, Dora herself was golden-skinned, but poor little Sybil looked like skimmed milk and not even the excitement of being home could bring more than the faintest flush to her cheeks.

Chris, hearing the ambulance, came hurrying over from the harvest field and blew Sybil a kiss over the gate. She had arranged a 'swop' so that she might be near at hand today and now she beamed at her friend.

'Sybs, you're back! I can't stop, we're just starting to stand the stooks, but when we have our break I'll nip home for two minutes and see how you're settling.'

Dora, seeing the ambulance men looking round the kitchen, had a pang of severe doubt. She wondered suddenly whether Sybil would have been better off downstairs, small and dark though it was, but on the other hand upstairs she would be away from the heat and cooking smells and in her own attic room the two windows could be left wide and the door, too, could be opened, creating a through-draught. And what was more, Sybil had a marvellous view from that window. She could see the meadows, the line of beechwood up by the farm, the raggedy hedges, the yellowing corn. And the sea. The white-gold of the beach, the sea in all its moods, could be hers whilst she lay in bed, whereas the front room, with its tiny little window facing north, only offered a view of Beach Road and the ruined church opposite. Before the war, when the church was in use, it would have been quite interesting to see the people coming in their best to morning and evening service, but now it was a pretty dull scene. No, the bedroom would be best.

She said as much to the ambulance men who looked doubtfully at the narrow, boxlike stairway and in fact were quite unable to manoeuvre the stretcher up the treads. Then the younger, fitter man said he would carry Sybil, no difficulty, and took her up the flight as though she weighed no more than a child – which was probably the truth, Dora thought ruefully, eyeing her daughter's sticklike arms.

Dora saw the ambulance men off and went back indoors to put the kettle on. She had put clean sheets on the bed and had used the hand-embroidered pillowcases she had been given as a wedding present, but even so the elder ambulance man had told her she would simply have to get hold of a decent single bed.

'She need a firm base do her back won't get strong, and that there's a feather bed,' he pointed out severely. 'What's more, feathers are hot; she'll swelter on a warm day. And when you get the new bed, get someone to make you boxes, one for each leg, so's you can raise it like a hospital one, do you'll get awful backache, bending to the gal.'

'I'll get a single bed,' Dora said, but with sinking heart. Dear God, would the expense never end? And it was so difficult to buy any furniture at all, let alone something large like a bed! People just weren't making furniture whilst all materials were being eaten up by the war effort, and although utility stuff was being produced it was bound to cost more than she could possibly afford.

The boiling kettle took her mind off beds for a moment and whilst she made up a tray and cut two slices of cake she was simply happy that Sybil was safe home. But mounting the stairs with care and pushing open the door of the bedroom, she was horrified to find Sybil with her face buried in the pillow and her thin shoulders shaking, obviously in floods of tears.

'Sybs! Oh, love, does it hurt so badly?'

'Hurt? No, it doesn't hurt . . . well, not more than usual, though I've got awful backache . . . but somehow, I thought when I got home . . . oh, I'm being stupid! And to tell you the truth the view from the window is so beautiful and I've missed it so much that I started to cry over that more than anything.'

Dora put the tray down on the table she had carried up earlier and sat carefully down on the bed. It creaked over to one side and she saw Sybil slide helplessly towards her. The ambulance man was right; she would have to get a new bed somehow. She took Sybil's hands in hers.

'You thought you'd be all right once you got home, like in one of those miracle plays! And so you will be, love, but like they said at the hospital, give it time. You were always a patient kid, and now you'll have to have endless patience to do your exercises and put up with my clumsiness, because I'm no nurse, and somehow the two of us will struggle through.'

'I should never have let them send me home,' Sybil muttered. She knuckled her eyes with her fists, a child again for a moment. 'How on earth will you manage? All the work of the house and looking after me, too! And the money . . . how long will the government go on paying me? What will happen to us when they stop if I'm not back at work? Oh, Mum, why didn't I think about you before jumping at the chance of leaving hospital? I was so damned selfish!'

'Rubbish. All right, in some ways it will be hard, but it'll be a great deal better with you here than without you. You can have a go at your books again, because I'm sure you're right and they'll want you to teach, and once you get a bit stronger you can shell peas and slice beans and so on, which will be a great help. And Sybs, I can *talk* to you! You've no idea how hard's been without someone to talk to, because though Chris is wonderful, she isn't family!'

Sybil shifted a little; beads of sweat stood out on her forehead and Dora saw, with love and despair, that the ambulance man was indeed right; the feather bed was too soft and yielding, Sybil's weakened limbs would never cope with it, and it was terribly hot, too.

'Look, love, drink your tea and eat a piece of cake whilst I go down to the vicarage,' Dora said. 'In all the excitement of getting you home I'd forgotten I was supposed to be finding a single bed for you, but I really ought to get that sorted out. You'll be all right? Chris will be coming over in a minute, when they stop for their break, but if you like I'll get her back right now.'

'No, leave her. It will be so nice just to drink my tea and then lie back and look out of the window and not have people clicking about and chattering,' Sybil said. 'But I'm all right in this bed, honestly.'

'Don't start. You're having a modern bed; it'll be better for your back,' Dora told her. 'I shan't be long . . . are you sure you'll be all right?'

Sybil said she was sure so Dora poured the tea, moved cup and plate so that it was easy for Sybil to pick them up, and left the bedroom. She hurried downstairs and went to the jar on the mantelpiece. Not enough money for a new blanket, let alone a new bed.

Right. Charity it is, then, Dora Cream, Dora told herself, fetching out her grey cardigan and pushing her feet into her one and only pair of respectable shoes. You will go to the vicarage and throw yourself on the mercy of the Rev. Fulthorpe and his wife. You won't ask them to give you a bed but to lend one until Sybil's better. Goodness, in a great old house like the rectory surely they'll have a bed they can spare?

Under other circumstances Dora would have enjoyed the walk through the village. Dappled golden sunshine and blue shadows danced as she walked under the tall beech and elm trees which lined the road, and she did not even have to knock on the rectory door since the Fulthorpes were sitting on deckchairs on the little round front lawn beneath the monkey-puzzle tree, he in his shirt-sleeves reading a book, she in a cotton skirt and blouse, shelling peas. They were clearly intent on making the most of this Indian summer, for who knew what winter might bring, but they both looked up and smiled as she entered the garden, the Reverend actually waving his book at her and beginning to scramble to his feet.

'Don't get up,' Dora said with automatic politeness. 'I'm afraid I've come to ask a favour.'

Mrs Fulthorpe was wearing a wide-brimmed straw hat which had seen better days and her spectacles were pushed right down her nose so that she could look over the top of them. She had once been a pretty woman but hard work and marriage to a devout but unpractical man had given her face a resolute serenity which was, Dora thought, better than mere prettiness. Now, she waved her colander full of peas at the empty deckchair.

'Do sit down, Mrs Cream. If there's anything Mr Fulthorpe or I can do to help you we will, you know that. Is Sybil home?'

'Yes, thank goodness. But the ambulance man told me that she needs a modern bed, a single one, with a firm mattress and things on each foot to lift it up for easy nursing. Ours is feathers, and he says that's too hot for her, beside perhaps hurting her back.' Dora sank into the deckchair and found herself at an immediate disadvantage, being virtually on her back with her feet almost off the ground. From a reclining position she twisted round to look earnestly at Mrs Fulthorpe. 'I can't afford a new bed even if I could get one, which I doubt. I was wondering if you could lend us one, just until Sybs is better.'

'Oh, my dear! We did have plenty of beds, but what with the shortages and the difficulties of buying such things most have already been given away . . . Dr Rudkin's family is so large and his widow, poor dear, so desperate. Do we have any spare beds, Humphrey?'

The Rev. Fulthorpe laid his book down across his bony, flannel-clad knees and considered. He had a long, narrow face speckled with the huge freckles known locally as grave-spots, and the eyes that had once been forget-me-not blue had faded to an indeterminate, milky grey. His panama hat with its black ribbon hid a hairless, freckled scalp, Dora knew, just as she knew that his rather stern aspect hid a sweet nature and a notoriously soft heart.

'Beds,' he said musingly. 'No, my dear, we have only the one which we share, beside the bunks the boys use when they're on leave. But just lately, someone mentioned beds to me . . . let me see, let me see, now where was I? I seem to recall I was standing in someone's kitchen . . . dear me, what it is to be old . . . and someone was telling me they'd thrown out a bed because what did they want with an old . . . that's it! Though whether you could possibly make use of it, Dora my dear, I can't tell.'

Mrs Fulthorpe sighed and smiled, then leaned across to give her husband's hand an affectionate squeeze.

'Humph, old chap, who's thrown out a bed? And where is it now?'

'Oh, didn't I say? It was young Mr Hutchins, I think he said his name was Sid, who took over Elm Tree Farm when old Hutch died. I went over to see him because the milkman offered me a lift, and there was young Mr Hutchins lugging out a couple of single beds. Said the old people must have been mad to sleep on them . . .' he peered shortsightedly across at Dora '. . . but of course they did no such thing. The Hutchins liked a bit of comfort. I imagine they were for the maids – they had two or three girls working there before the war – because they were simple things, built of boards with a mattress atop. I doubt they'd be suitable for poor little Sybil, but they were definitely beds and he was definitely throwing them out.'

'And they're still at the farm? Or did he send them off on the dustcart or take them to the tip?' Dora enquired without much hope. She would not have been at all surprised had Mr Fulthorpe announced airily that young Mr Hutchins had trundled the beds down to the beach and cast them into the sea, but the old man frowned and put a finger to his brow in thought.

'Now where did he say they were going? Ah, I know! He was going to put them in the big shippon, because he said they could go to the auction next week. In wartime the most unlikely things fetch a few bob, he said.' He beamed triumphantly from Dora's face to his wife's and back again. 'Does that help you at all, my dear?'

'In the big shippon,' Mrs Fulthorpe said thoughtfully, before Dora could answer. 'It's good and dry in there – not that we've had any rain for the past week, as my tawny chrysanthemums keep reminding me. Another two days and I'll have to start watering. Now young Hutchins is harvesting today, so I gather from the noise. If you were to run down now, dear, and ask him about the beds, offer him a couple of bob, he might put them on to the cart and bring them round this very evening!'

'He might think I'd got a nerve, asking,' Dora protested. 'But there's no harm in approaching him, I suppose.'

She made to get out of the chair – no easy task – but Mr Fulthorpe waved her down again, standing up himself with the agility born of long practice.

'Sit down, Dora, sit down! No need for you to run over when I'm going that way myself. Keep Mrs Fulthorpe company for half an hour and you shall have those beds, though whether they'll fit the bill it isn't for me to say. I've been meaning all afternoon to go along to the harvest field about tea-time . . .' he beamed at them with innocent naughtiness '. . . because I have a real weakness for those big jugs of cold tea and the meat pies which farmers always seem to produce from somewhere.'

'No, really, Mr Fulthorpe . . .' began Dora, but was shushed by the vicar's wife.

'Let him go, Dora, it'll do him good to get some exercise. And whilst we wait, we'll go into the kitchen and make a pot of tea and you can give me your opinion of my latest fatless sponge.'

'Well, Mrs Cream, that's my final word; tek it or leave it as the saying goes.'

Young Mr Hutchins had brought the beds right to the door. Now he stood there looking mulish.

'But five shillings for the two . . . it seems very little,' Dora said feebly. 'Surely five shillings each would be fairer?'

He shrugged. He was sandy-haired, serious, with a receding hairline – he was in his mid-forties – and the sort of bulldog jaw which made people call him obstinate, but Dora was sure he was just determined. Which he would need to be to pull his old uncle's farm back into profitability, she concluded.

'Look, all right, seven shillings for the two, but that's my final offer.'

Dora laughed; haggling this way must be unusual, to say the least.

'Very well then, you've persuaded me. Seven shillings, and any time you need someone to cook or clean just let me know. Seriously, Mr Hutchins, I'm very grateful. A decent bed will make all the difference to Sybil.'

Mr Hutchins snorted, then turned to his wagon and began to manoeuvre the first bed on to the ground. They were sturdily built of pine planks, unpolished and plain, but the mattresses were modern and looked clean and firm.

'She might as well sleep on t' floor,' he said roundly. 'But Vicar said as how it's what her back needs.' He began to heave the first bed up the garden path to the front door. 'They take to bits; want me to do that for you and get them upstairs? We can leave 'em outside girl's room until you're ready to swop her over.'

Dora thanked him but decided she would rather the beds remained all in one piece.

'Sybil's friend Chris lodges with us, so we'll do it when she gets home tonight,' she decided. 'Thanks very much for all your help, and here's your seven shillings.'

He grunted and the back of his neck, which was all Dora could see, turned brick red.

'Any time. If you need owt else let me know. I go to auction most weeks.'

After thanking him and seeing him off, Dora returned to the house. She looked again at the beds, propped untidily at the foot of the stairs, and thought how war and adversity brought out the best in people. Mr Hutchins was a foreigner to the village and therefore suspect; he had come down from Yorkshire and folk said he was tight, wanted slave labour, never thought of anything but money. Since Dora thought this applied to most of the farming community she had not been much worried by his reputation, but it had proved thoroughly undeserved. He had wanted to give her the beds, had sold them for less than half the price he would have got at auction, had delivered them in his own time and would have dismantled them downstairs and put them together again upstairs had she not refused his offer.

Partly it was because Sybil was sick, of course, and partly because, as everyone was so fond of saying, there was a war on. But most of all it was because he was a pleasant young man trying to fit into a tight little community which was suspicious to the point of paranoia about anyone not born and bred within a five mile radius of the village.

Still, she had best go up and tell Sybs that the beds had arrived. She went swiftly up the flight and popped her head round the door. Sybil was lying facing the window. She looked young and vulnerable, no more than a child, her mouth drooping, her lids half-shut. But she turned as the door opened and tried to smile cheerfully at her mother.

'Oh, it's you, Mum! What was that row about?'

'Sorry, did I disturb you? I bought two beds from the new chap at Elm Tree Farm, and he delivered them just now. Don't listen to a word they say about him in the village, though – he's really very nice.'

'I'm not likely to hear what anyone says about anyone else, in the village,' Sybil said lightly, but with a trace of bitterness in her voice. 'Where's the new bed now, then?'

'Downstairs. Lizzie's coming over to see you this evening so I thought when Chris gets home the three of us would be able to take the old bed down and the new beds up, if you don't mind being lugged about a bit, you poor little soul.'

'Lizzie? And Chris? Oh, that'll be nice,' Sybil said, with more animation than she had yet shown. 'Gosh, and I've only been back a couple of days!'

'And there's that lady from the hospital coming to give you exercises, and Dr Lewis popping in – you'll find yourself worn out by the social round before you're much older,' Dora said cheerfully. Poor Sybs, she was putting such a brave face on it all! 'What would you like for your tea?'

'Oh, just a drink. I'm not hungry.'

She never was, now. It seemed an effort even to finish a cup of tea and food was merely pushed around the plate. In hospital, Dora supposed, they must have insisted that she eat, but although she did her best Sybil never made inroads into any meal she provided. Of course, it wasn't easy to think of new ways of using their rations, but Sybil had always eaten well before. Perhaps after the woman from the hospital had been . . .

'If you're not going to eat then you'd better have a milky drink,' Dora said tactfully. 'Tell you what, suppose I make you some semolina? I've got some, and some milk. Would you eat semolina pudding if I made it?'

'Oh no, don't go to any trouble, it only makes me feel guilty when

I can't get it down,' Sybil said. 'I'll have cocoa instead of tea if I must, but tea's more refreshing.'

'I'll get you a cup of tea, then,' Dora said resignedly. 'I'm going to make some sandwiches for Chris and Lizzie; perhaps you'll feel a bit more like eating when they arrive.'

'Perhaps,' Sybil said. But she did not sound convinced.

Lizzie had spent the weekend at home and had gone back to Lowestoft on Sunday evening really worried about her sister. Sybil had been home for a month now, yet there seemed no change at all in her condition. What was worse, her sister, who had always been so hopeful and bright, was depressed, uncertain, prone to tears.

Lizzie was walking round the deserted shopping centre wondering what was best to do for Sybil and absently window-shopping when a hand was placed across her eyes and an arm encircled her waist. A voice she knew well said: 'Guess who?'

She would have known it was Ralph without a word said. She tightened her mouth and tried to draw away, but the arm only gripped her more firmly whilst the hand slid from across her eyes and began to stroke lovingly along the line of her jaw.

'Don't maul me,' Lizzie said. She tried to sound brisk but only succeeded in conveying a sort of breathlessness. 'What are you doing here? You know what we agreed when we knew poor Sybs was so ill – no messing around until you'd made up your mind for sure. And anyway, aren't you supposed to be flying 'planes?'

She turned as she spoke and looked up into his face and the expression she saw there made her sigh and take his hand from her chin quite gently.

'Oh, Ralph, what *is* it?'

'I've got a forty-eight. Can I stay with you?'

'You'll be going over to see Sybil. Dear Ralph, I was with her earlier today. She talked about you so lovingly – you haven't told her you want to break up, have you!'

He shook his head, still looking down at her. The close-cropped fair curls made him look what he was – boyish, young. But the haunted expression on his lean face, the dark hollows around his eyes and the lines which ran across his brow made him look as old and as knowing as Methuselah. Lizzie, who was not imaginative, suddenly thought of all old-young men she now knew; men who had to live for each day as it came because there might never be another, men who had learned to acknowledge that the sunrise they had seen as they ran across the short, dew-wet grass towards their aircraft might be, for them, the last sunrise.

'Lizzie? I'm a coward, I suppose, but we see so much pain, so much suffering . . . it's as though I can't bear to inflict that sort of pain on poor old Sybs. But I will tell her – when she can cope better, I'll tell her. And now, can I come home with you?'

He was still Sybil's young man, then; all Sybil had if the truth were known. She lay in her hard bed and her only lover was pain, but Ralph was her hope that one day things might be better. Lizzie loved her little sister very much in her own way. When they were kids she had been glad that Sybil was clever because she wanted good things for the younger girl and did not think that Sybil's looks would ever amount to much. Looks, to Lizzie, were all-important. And she had been right. Even before her illness Sybs had been, in Lizzie's eyes, pale and plain. How she had ever attracted Ralph in the first place Lizzie could not imagine, but she had accepted it, shrugged and moved on, telling herself that there were better fish in the sea than had ever come out of it, reminding herself that she, Lizzie, was destined for better things than the junior solicitor in a family firm.

But in her heart she did not believe that there was anyone better, for her, than Ralph. He had been her first lover; she supposed that must be why she wanted him so desperately. She had been unfaithful to him because she wanted fun whilst she was young, but she would never have looked at another man had she not found herself so lost without him. She might tell herself until she was blue in the face that she could do better than Ralph, but she knew it was an empty threat. If Ralph still wanted her she was his.

Now, Ralph looped his arm round her waist and began to lead her firmly along the pavement. People idly strolling in the evening chill scarcely looked at them, but feeling Ralph's hip moving gently against hers as he hurried her along was like a draught of strong and heady wine to Lizzie. She could still remember that very first time, his hands on her, smoothing across the young, untried mound of her stomach, setting her on fire with his touch! She shivered, trying half-heartedly to pull away. This was madness – impossible! They still wrote often but she had promised herself time and again that she would stop seeing Ralph and Ralph had agreed. And now, with Sybil crippled, unable to leave her bed . . .

'This your flat still? Come on, then, get your key out!'

Frowning, she shook her head. She began to expostulate, to tell him that he might have no conscience but Sybil was her sister . . . the key turned sweetly in the lock and they clattered up the stairs, Lizzie impelled by Ralph's hand in the small of her back.

She tried to turn into the tiny shared kitchenette but Ralph dexterously swung her past it and into the bedroom. He had been here before, of course, but not since Sybil's illness. This was so unfair; why did God do it to her? Why did he let her hunger for Ralph so much that it was like a wild beast clawing at her, making her body ache to melt into his, throwing caution, conscience, everything, to the four winds?

'Lizzie? Do you love me, Lizzie Cream?'

She was lying on the bed cradled in his arms and all she could think of was how desperately she wanted him, how there had never been anyone else who could stir her like this. She wound her arms round him, hooked a leg over his hip, pressed herself close, the clamour of desire so loud that she could scarcely hear the words he whispered, nor her own panting, yearning replies.

'Lizzie . . . oh, dear God, how could I ever look at another woman? Oh Lizzie, you're the best, the most . . . oh, Lizzie . . .'

There was no restraint, no more muttering Sybil's name, no denials. They shed their clothes without thinking, stripping each other, mouthing, nuzzling, clutching, kissing.

To be sure as they joined and began the frenzied dance of love she saw, for one moment, Sybil's face in her mind's eye, the eyes shadowed with sadness, the mouth drooping, but then they began the long, sweet journey to fulfilment and all Lizzie knew was that she was where she wanted to be, where she was born to be.

We're nothing apart but together we're wonderful, she thought exultantly as they collapsed against each other at last, slippery with sweat and love. Just two ordinary mortals who, together, can experience ecstasy.

Ralph tugged at her until her head rested in the hollow of his shoulder and his hand caressed the roundness of her breast, peaking her small pink nipple into a tiny wild strawberry. She was purring with relief and satisfaction, rubbing her cheek languorously against his lean chest, deeply and ecstatically satisfied, like a hungry man who has eaten his fill and yet cannot prevent himself from contemplating his next meal. Nothing mattered now, not Sybil, not Chris, not her job . . .

With startling suddenness she fell asleep, only to wake in the dark of the night with Ralph nuzzling her, caressing.

'Darling Lizzie, I'm awake!'

'I'm asleep,' Lizzie groaned, trying to curl down the bed again. 'I've got to go to work in the morning, you know.'

'Never mind tomorrow; love me again, little one!'

She woke to find it was broad daylight. She sat up and gasped and in a moment he was awake too, screwing up his eyes against the light, for they had not pulled the curtains the previous night.

'Oh, God, Ralph, I was on earlies this morning – what time is it?'

He had taken his wristwatch off because once when they had been making love it had got entangled in her hair; a salutary experience which had, on that occasion, almost put them off their stroke. Now he picked it up off the bedside table, tilted it to read the face, put it down again.

'Almost ten. You can say you felt ill, forgot the time, were called home to see a sick relative. Say anything you like but you aren't leaving this bed for the next hour or so. And when you do leave, it won't be to scuttle to work. You're mine, Lizzie Cream, until I have to go back to Lincolnshire.'

She lay down again. She could no more have denied him now than flown to the moon. But mention of a sick relative stirred her sleeping conscience into momentary wakefulness.

'Oh, Ralph, what about Sybil? She is my sister.'

'Yes. But I don't love her, little Liz. I never did. I just wanted a girl, you'd made it obvious you weren't available, and she'd made it equally obvious that she was.'

'You're a real swine, Ralph. She's a . . . she's ill. Does that make no difference?'

Ralph sighed and his breath stirred her hair as he gave a long, low whistle.

'How can it make a difference? I don't believe I've ever loved anyone in my whole life the way I love you. I tried to change and I couldn't and Sybs being ill has made it more difficult for me to love her, not easier. But I won't pretend, Lizzie. I'll drop her a note.'

'It'll hurt her.'

'So? It would hurt her more if I went on pretending to love her whilst shagging you whenever our paths crossed. Wouldn't it?'

302

'If you pretended to love her I wouldn't let you *shag me* as you so vulgarly put it. I can say no, you know!'

He leaned over her and pulled, rolling her on top of him. She lay across his stomach, half laughing, half annoyed. She wriggled, got half off, turned to try to slap his face and found herself dragged until she was astride his waist. He could not have done it without her co-operation and he knew it, grinning up at her, his eyes bright blue, his mouth wickedly curved, but as his hands held her she saw the expression in his eyes subtly change from amusement to the beginnings of revived lust.

'Well, well, well!' he said softly. Strong hands cupped her smooth shoulders and began to pull her inexorably forward. 'So you can say no, can you?' He stopped talking for a moment as she began to collapse on top of him. He ran his tongue across her small collar bones and down between her apple-shaped breasts, then he turned his head sideways and gripped her hips hard, bearing down so that she groaned softly, letting her lips stray across his bristly chin. 'Well, go ahead, you iron woman; say no!'

'No-oo,' Lizzie crooned hypnotically. 'No-oo, no-oo, no-oo.'

He muffled a laugh against her smooth skin.

'Oh, Lizzie, Lizzie, what a pretty little liar you are; and how much I love you, lies and all!'

'If I had the wheelchair at least I could get over to the village school, talk to Miss Payne, perhaps give a hand with the kids. As it is I'm stuck here, a bloody useless good for nothing!'

It was not like Sybil to swear; Chris leaned over the bed and patted the thin white hand as it lay on the coverlet.

'Ask Miss Cole – no, *tell* her you're not getting better stuck up here all day,' Chris advised. It was a cold day in mid-December and she knew very well that Sybil was fretting for some kind of chance to have a normal Christmas. 'Tell Miss Cole . . .'

'Miss Cole hates me; she thinks I'm not trying, when she must know . . .' Sybil turned her head away but Chris could see the tears welling up in the big amber eyes. 'It's no good, Chris. I'm never going to be able to walk, so I might as well . . . I might as well . . .'

'Tell Miss Cole that, walk or not, you need that chair,' Chris commanded forcibly. The room was dark despite the candle, for it was Chris's turn to do the early milking so the blind was still drawn. She and Sybil preferred to keep the lights out and sleep with the blind up and the windows open even when it was cold, but when she was doing the early milking this was impossible. 'Don't forget, Sybs. Speak firmly to that wretched woman.'

'I'll do my best,' Sybil said weakly. 'Take the candle with you; I shan't need it.'

Chris was about to say she'd leave it anyway when she heard Dora moving around downstairs. That meant the kettle would be on and the stove poked into life. Good! And it would enable her to spend a few more minutes with Sybil, who looked dreadfully down today.

'Lie down again for a bit and I'll bring up some tea and sit with you whilst I drink mine,' Chris coaxed. 'Auntie Dora's down already so the kettle will be on.'

'I'd love some tea.' Sybil leaned back on her pillows, sighed at the state of them after a night's tossing and turning, and tried to put them right, which brought on the pain. The useless legs which could not walk and would not respond could suddenly curl and jerk with agonizing spasms of involuntary muscle contractions. When this happened there was little anyone could do to help, but watching without attempting to bring aid was something Chris knew she would never master.

'I'll rub your legs,' she said. 'Oh, Sybs, you poor darling, hang on, it won't last.'

It didn't, but it left Sybil weak and trembling, exhausted by the fight which could never be won because the enemy would only retreat in order to return again and again. Chris could tell when the pain began to ebb because Sybil's sweat-beaded brow and upper lip smoothed out, the deliberate stillness of her body eased into a more natural pose. Then Sybil's shadowed eyes opened and her lips tilted into her own sweet smile.

'Sorry, my own fault, I shouldn't have twisted round like that. Could you do my pillows for me, Chris? And then we can have our tea.'

'Of course. Here, don't move, I can manage.'

Chris plumped up the pillows and made Sybil as comfortable as circumstances allowed, then made her way down the stairs. In the kitchen she smiled at Dora and said that she was taking Sybil's tea up. Outside in the yard she could hear the chickens purring and scratching, the fattener grunting as he poked a pink, ringed snout into his empty trough, the birds beginning to shout as they saw the approaching dawn. Further off, the sea sang its quiet continual song and gulls squawked and squabbled on the tideline.

Another day, with fun and hard work for her. Just another day for Sybil.

Sybil leaned back against her pillows after Chris had gone and told herself that she was a lucky girl. There had been other people struck down at the same time as herself. Two of them had died, which meant that she was lucky just to be here, lying in this narrow, firm bed, seeing the glint of the sea on the horizon, the wings of a passing gull as it swooped and dipped above the cattle in the meadow next door.

If you never walked again you would still be lucky, Sybil Cream, she told herself vigorously. If you spent the rest of your life in this room . . . Tears, uninvited, began to fill her eyes, to spill over, to chase each other down her cheeks. Oh, God, how could she bear it? The pain, the long, dull ache in her back which she could never lose no matter how constantly she shifted her body from one position to another. And the boredom, the loneliness, the sense of total isolation, of being no longer even a member of the human race but a thing apart, an Invalid, a Poor Soul.

There was another name, but that one was so bad she tried never to think of it. The Cripple. Suppose they called her that? People who hadn't seen her for years, who knew she was imprisoned in the little bedroom in the end cottage on Beach Road, might shake their heads sadly over her in years to come. Oh yes, you mean the Cripple; Poor Thing, shut away up there. They say she's lost the use of her legs; just a Cripple and quite young!

She was crying in earnest now, knowing that Dora was busy tidying up after breakfast, getting ready to go down to St Luke's for her morning stint, and not caring if her whole face puffed up like a balloon from the tears, the scrubbing of her reddened eyelids with her fists. What did she care what people thought? No one could possibly know how unhappy she was, how determined that, sooner than spend the rest of her life as an invalid, she would walk into the sea and end it all. Only she couldn't walk, so she would have to devise some other method of putting an end to her life.

Could she jump out of the window? Ha, and probably bruise her knees or break other bones so that she was more helpless than ever? What a bright idea, Sybil, she said sarcastically to herself.

Poison was out of the question since she was stuck up here in bed, unless she persuaded Dora to go out and pick a big bunch of deadly nightshade to brighten the room, which she could then munch down after dark. Or there were asps, of course, a well known if not popular method of ending it all. *Finish good lady; the bright day is done, and we are for the dark.* Cleopatra to Charmian, or Charmian to Cleopatra? Not that it mattered. What mattered was the non-availability of your average asp, even if you settled for an adder, a good deal commoner in East Anglia. But she could just see herself asking her mother to bring her an adder. *They make lovely pets, I believe, Mum. It'll keep me company when you're busy downstairs. A basketful would be nice.*

Fortunately the absurdity of her thoughts made her smile and then give a little giggle, and since it is impossible to pursue thoughts of suicide once you've giggled Sybil hitched her useless body a bit higher in the bed, wiped her nose on one of the large white hankies her mother had tactfully provided, smoothed her hair with both hands and tried to recapture a sense of purpose.

What about Susan Coolidge's Katy, then? Katy was crippled and rose above it; she became an example to everyone, an adored elder sister, a saint, no less! It was unfortunate that Sybil had found Katy a prig once she had fallen off the swing in the barn, because no one wants to model themselves on a prig. Besides, Katy was a book for children. I want to marry Ralph and have kids of my own, Sybil thought desperately. And Ralph . . . he's most awfully nice, the best bloke you could imagine, but I know very well he won't want to marry a crip . . . I mean someone who can't walk!

But you're going to walk, a little voice reminded her bracingly. You're Sybil Cream, you've got your whole life ahead of you, and you are most certainly going to walk, you aren't going to be beaten by any stupid damn disease. Go *on*, legs, twitch when I tell you to! Twitch, will you! For God's sake just give a teeny twitch, just to let me know you heard!

Her skinny, hateful legs! Not a twitch would they give, not even the tiniest shudder. She reached down the bed and pinched herself spitefully on the inside of her knee. She could feel *something*, couldn't she? Just the faintest something, a sort of buzz, a frisson of sensation? Or was it that the wish was father to the thought? Did she feel something because she so desperately wanted to, so wildly longed for a sign that she would get well!

You had to have feeling; if there was feeling then the limb could recover. Not would, but even could was better than couldn't. So just as soon as she could she would get well. But it would be so much easier to work at it if she had a wheelchair, some hope, somewhere other than the bedroom. She had always loved the room, but to be told, as she had been told by the hated Miss Cole, that she would be marooned up here until she could walk – when she was doing her damnedest, trying her hardest, and getting nowhere – that was unfair and gave you this feeling of helplessness which was almost worse than being crippled.

There was so little that she could do, up here. She wrote to Ralph and he wrote back, of course. He had been to see her a couple of times in hospital, awkward for once, not joking or twinkling, not hugging, even. Just a chaste kiss on the brow, half an hour of awkward conversation whilst he sat on the chair beside her bed and told her in a rather desperate monotone all about life in Lincolnshire, and then the relieved leavetaking, the jaunty air he could not quite hide as he strode back down the ward again.

She believed he loved her, but some people could not cope with illness in those they loved and Ralph was one of them. When she was well again, when she was walking . . . ah, then it would all be the same as before, perhaps even better. They would laugh and joke again, and Sybil would tell him about the silly things that had happened in hospital, the times she and one of the nurses had laughed themselves into a state of semi-collapse over some ridiculous little incident. Somehow, when she tried to tell him things like that in the ward, they had fallen flat. He had stared solemnly, seeming not to understand that she was joking so that her voice had faltered to a stop, as embarrassed, in the end, as he.

Once, long ago, a blind piano tuner had come to see to the piano at St Leonard's. And there had been a teacher who had lost both legs in the First World War. She had never been taught by him but had seen pictures of him with his class, his wheelchair brought level with the boys, a rug over the useless legs, a bright smile on an intelligent, even handsome, face.

Those people had overcome their disabilities to continue with their normal life. Then why could she, Sybil, not follow suit? Of course she could, once she was stronger, once the pain attacks were not so close or so mind-burningly bad. She would walk again, but

until that time she must make Miss Cole see that the wheelchair
was essential to her. After all, there was no sin in begging for a
little help instead of the constant nagging criticism and accusa-
tions of laziness which had been her lot from the physiotherapist so far!

19

Fenn decided, ten days before Christmas, that he did not like winter. He had two days free and absolutely no idea what he wanted to do with them. It was too cold to ride the bike, he had done his shopping so didn't fancy taking the liberty truck to the city, yet he was sick and tired of the base, the boring food and conversation, the tensions which seem unavoidable amongst men who are constantly battle-ready.

He was not even looking forward to Christmas, when in common with everyone else he would have two days off and then continue to wait for the right weather conditions for flying. You couldn't go far at such times, because no one, especially not the met. boys, knew just when the clouds would roll away and the sun would come out. So if he went home to Manchester – and he was tempted to do so – he might find himself in the most awful trouble if the weather suddenly brightened.

More and more, he longed for a family Christmas. He wanted to be with Rachael and Amos and his new little brother, sitting round a nice coal fire and not around the stove which burned fitfully in their mess room. And at home in Cheetham Hill he could take a hot bath! The bath-hut at Flacton was another Nissen hut with cold water only and no glass in the windows. Ice formed on the surface of the water if you left it too long before leaping into the tub – showers were best, since at least you could get out quicker.

But it was not worth the risk, to go home and then find the bloody trains were not running, or the city was snowed up.

So what to do? Having decided to put up with a Christmas on the base, with a quick rush to Norwich, to the excellent Officers' Club in Bethel Street where everyone made a real effort to see that the guys felt at home, Fenn still had to decide what to do with his day off today.

Other guys had made contacts in the village; they would go and visit their friends, farmers and their wives, girls and their parents, even the rector of the local church or the landlord of the local inn. Fenn had plenty of friends on the base but he knew very few locals. It was not that he was unfriendly, far from it, but he was absorbed in the life he was leading. He had survived so far, he gave no hostages to fortune, he wanted to end the war alive and fit, not a nervous or physical wreck.

There was a dance at the Samson & Hercules ballroom in the city. It would be a festive pre-Christmas occasion, but he didn't feel like dancing. He mooched around for an hour or so and then, since it did not actually rain though it looked as though it would like to do so, he got out his bicycle, put on his waterproof, and cycled off the base.

It was odd how he turned at once towards the coast. The last time he had gone this way it had been spring, he remembered. He'd had a lovely day, the sort of unforgettable day which came one's way perhaps once or twice in a lifetime, so he did not expect to repeat it. But there was quite a big town there, as well as that village with the ruined church . . . what was it called . . . Pakeby? And he'd met a girl . . . or had she been a ghost? He grinned to himself and bent all his energy to the pedals, suddenly full of enthusiasm for the thought of a trip to the coast, a mooch round another town. Lowestoft? Yes, that was it, Lowestoft. There would be some life there; sailors, shipping, girls!

Fenn's enthusiasm lasted until he reached Pakeby – and discovered that it was early closing. He cycled along London Road until he came to the turning into Pakefield Street and slowed; then he saw the shops were all firmly closed, with that smug, secretive look they wear when you want them open and they can thumb their noses at you. He sighed. For the last mile he had been thinking wistfully of a large teacake and a bottle of Corona, but he cheered up when he remembered the Tramway Hotel. He had never been in it, but he might be able to get a beer there. He crossed the road and approached the hotel.

It was closed too, or as good as. They had a sign on the door saying that residents could get in round the back but that the hotel would not be open for business until seven o'clock.

Disconsolate, he turned away. One-horse joint, he was thinking resentfully when he saw a bus draw up. It had come from Lowestoft and shoppers were descending from it. One of them was a landgirl, with dark hair which fell in bangs across her forehead. She looked happy and pleased with herself and she carried a shopping basket on one arm. She saw Fenn watching her and smiled.

'Hello . . . are you lost?'

'Yes, ma'am . . . the hotel's closed,' Fenn said. 'Ain't got nowhere to get me a bite of food nor a drink. You know anyplace else around these parts where they'd maybe sell me some chow?'

'Well, there's Mr Battell's tea-garden . . . only not in December, perhaps,' the girl said thoughtfully. 'He sells Wallers' cakes, though, and they're delicious. Only he's closed, of course. Or there's Foreman's shop. You could get tea and a bun there, except that it'll be closed too.' She looked at him thoughtfully. 'Look, would you like to come to my place? It's only a cottage but it's nice and cosy on a winter afternoon and Auntie Dora will make us a pot of tea and probably produce a cake from somewhere. And you can tell us how the war in the air is going. At least it'll be preferable to a picnic of seashells on the beach.'

Fenn grinned. Here was a girl after his own heart, who could give him a big smile and invite him home with no thought of danger. She was a lady, too; she had a pleasant, low-toned voice and although her hands showed that her work was hard and physical she had beautifully clean nails and her hair shone with washing. In Fenn's opinion, ladies always took good care of themselves.

'Gee, ma'am, that's mortal good of you! Do you live far?'

She did not look the type to merely want a lift, though – especially on an ancient push-bike. But he drew his machine alongside her and began to push it in the direction she indicated, then slowed and stopped, tugging at his cap.

'Durned if I've not thought to introduce myself! Fennimore Kitson, ma'am, at your service.'

The girl held out a hand.

'Chris Winterton. Hello, Fennimore.'

'Hello, Chris; only I'd sooner you didn't use the whole durned mouthful. All my buddies call me Fenn.'

The girl laughed.

'Right, Fenn. I understand how you feel since my full name's Christina, but only school-teachers call me that! No, I don't live far – how well do you know Pakeby?'

'Well, I guess I know the beach, the ruined church . . .'

'There you are, then. We live opposite the church, in the end cottage.'

A faint memory stirred in Fenn; he looked thoughtfully at Chris.

'Have you got a sister?'

'Yes, but she's away at school. But I've got . . . oh, here's a coincidence.' She began to wave to someone ahead of them. 'Lizzie! Hey, Liz!'

A figure was walking down the road towards them; a small, slim girl with golden curls bouncing on her shoulders. She wore a biscuit-coloured macintosh and high-heeled brown shoes and she had a brown velvet alice-band holding her hair back from her face. She glanced cursorily at Fenn before turning her full attention to his companion and Fenn, taking in the big blue eyes, the rosebud mouth, the creamy complexion, thought he had never seen a prettier girl – and thought, too, that he knew her from somewhere.

'Hello, Chris! Been shopping in the port? What a way to spend your day off!'

Immediately he heard that cool, crystal clear voice, Fenn knew who she was: the girl in the refreshment room at Thorpe station – the girl who had almost let him pick her up, but had left him for a tall young Air Force officer.

'I wanted some stockings,' Chris said. 'And Auntie Dora needed some bits and pieces, so it seemed the sensible thing to do. Sybs was very depressed today, so we didn't both want to leave her.'

'No. I thought I'd pop over and have tea with you because I'm on the night-shift. Who's your friend?'

Chris coloured; Fenn liked the way the rich pink swept in a tide across her tanned face.

'Oh, how rude I am! Lizzie, this is Fenn Kitson; Fenn, Lizzie Cream. I lodge with her mother.'

The two murmured greetings; Fenn wondered whether to remind Lizzie Cream that they had already met, but decided against it. The other girl – Chris – might think it was a ploy to get to know Lizzie better, and indeed it might have been just that, for Fenn still thought her the prettiest girl he'd met. But right now he wasn't into picking up girls, or not unless they had the sort of mothers who might invite him over for Christmas, anyway.

They reached the cottage, went round the back, and Chris took Fenn's bicycle from him.

'You go in and meet Auntie Dora whilst I put your bike away,' she said briskly. 'Lizzie, you introduce him.'

'Right.' And then Lizzie, turning to usher Fenn inside, recognized him.

It was an extraordinary moment. Lizzie glanced, and then in the middle of glancing away did a double take. She stared, and Fenn could see the slow comprehension dawning – and with it, a sort of horror. For some reason, he could not imagine what, she remembered their brief meeting with very mixed feelings – embarrassment certainly, and something more, something deeper.

'Hi,' Fenn said softly. 'Hi again, Lizzie Cream.'

And Lizzie turned in the doorway and pushed past him – almost rudely, he thought, astonished.

'Oh, Chris, I quite forgot,' she called across the yard. 'I've got to go up to Gran's; I did some shopping for her. See you later – tea-time.'

'What've I said?' Fenn asked her, keeping his voice low but not as low as all that, for Lizzie hesitated, then turned and came back.

'I can't tell you now,' she whispered. 'But I'll hang about at the top of the street . . . no, that's no good . . . can you not say anything about me? Can you . . .'

Chris reappeared at the door of the shed, now minus the bicycle.

'What was that, Lizzie? I heard you say something, but not what it was.'

'I've got to go up to Gran's to hand over some shopping I did for her,' Lizzie explained again.

'Shopping? For Gran? Oh, but I did her shopping earlier, though I'm not taking it over until tomorrow. She said . . .'

'It's Christmas, Chris, so don't ask questions,' Lizzie said briskly. 'See you at tea-time!'

'Look, if you're going to Gran's you might as well take . . .'

Chris stopped short as Lizzie continued round the corner of the cottage, stared after the other girl's disappearing back for a moment, then shrugged and turned back to Fenn.

'That's our Lizzie for you,' she said resignedly. 'She's always up to something. Well, just let me introduce you to Auntie Dora and then perhaps I had better pop round to Gran's with the stuff.'

'And find out why Lizzie fled,' Fenn said, grinning.

Chris looked over her shoulder at him as she opened the door which Lizzie had firmly shut.

'Are you calling me nosy? Well, I might ask a question or two. In the meantime . . . oh, Auntie Dora's upstairs. I'll give her a yell.'

Chris disappeared into what looked like a cupboard, but since he could hear her footsteps ascending he assumed it was a staircase. Left to himself, Fenn stood in the warm, dusky little room that was the family's kitchen and looked around him.

He liked it. A cooking range with the front open roared away, a kettle hissed contentedly to one side of the hot rings, and all around the room were signs of family life and of baking. A big cake cooled on a wire rack on the dresser, four large cottage loaves stood out on the scrubbed wooden table, the spicy tang of gingernuts came from a tray of crumbly homemade biscuits which were still steaming slightly on top of the stove.

'Hang your coat on the back of the door,' Chris said, suddenly reappearing in the room and making Fenn jump. 'Auntie Dora won't be a tick; she says sorry about the mess, she's in the middle of baking. Would you like a teacake?'

'Well, gee,' Fenn said uncertainly. He knew all about rationing; they were often reminded that it was unfair to eat at the Britishers' expense, but those teacakes smelt so good . . .

''Course you would,' Chris said comfortably. Another set of footsteps began to descend the stairs and she turned to smile at the pretty, middle-aged woman who appeared. 'Here's Auntie Dora. Auntie, this is Fenn Kitson, the bloke I told you I'd invited to tea.'

Fenn smiled politely, and said how good it was of Mrs Cream to invite him into her home and then, realizing that it had been Chris who had asked him in and her not even a daughter of the house, he was overcome with embarrassment and felt his face go hot.

Dora saw that he was flushing and shook her head chidingly.

'When I hear your planes roar overhead in full daylight, going to teach the Nazis a long overdue lesson, I want to hug the lot of you,' she declared roundly. 'It's a privilege to have you under my roof, young man. You're much appreciated by us British, I can tell you. And now you can just sit down and appreciate my teacakes. If you pour the tea, Chris, I'll do a tray for Sybil.'

'Right away, Auntie,' Chris said cheerfully. She had shed her overcoat and boots and must have changed out of her trousers whilst she was upstairs, for now she wore a pale grey skirt and a pearl-grey jumper. 'When I've done that, though, I'm just going to trot down to Gran's with her shopping. I won't be two ticks – I'll probably walk back with Lizzie.'

'Good,' Dora Cream said absently. 'Fenn – that's an unusual name. But one thing I have noticed about you boys is your unusual names. Kitson's ordinary enough, of course – do you come from English stock?'

Fenn, in his most deprecating manner, was in full flood on the history of the Kitsons and his mother's family when Chris left, but since Dora was clearly fascinated and listened avidly as she pottered around preparing a tray Fenn continued anyway. His stories, he thought with rare detachment, really were improving; Dora was as caught up in this one as he was himself. He must remember to tell her about his rich cousin, Albion Fennimore, who had invented a new type of automobile with an automatic pilot setting on the gear-stick.

Dora was toasting teacakes now, holding them out to the fire impaled on a fork. She toasted half-a-dozen and then spread jam thinly on each one. Butter, Fenn remembered, was scarcely ever available in Britain.

'Here, eat this one whilst it's hot,' Dora said. She put a teacake and a cup of tea on a small tin tray. Then she headed for the narrow doorway in the corner of the room through which she had so recently entered. 'Just going to take Sybs up a tray – you know about Sybs, of course? She's Lizzie's little sister.'

'No, I can't say . . . is she ill?'

Dora had a foot on the bottom stair but she hesitated as they both heard the sound of someone thumping on the front door.

'Ill? Well, yes, she's . . . oh, goodness, can you take these whilst I go to the door? I can't imagine who it might be!'

Fenn took the tray and, as Dora rapidly left the room, began to mount the stairs. The poor kid, ill up there – he might as well take the stuff up to her. It wouldn't hurt her to see a stranger, and uniforms, to most kids, were an added attraction. Besides, Dora had been good to him, and it was a small enough repayment to save her legs on the steep little stairs.

He reached a tiny landing, hesitated between two doors, chose the nearest. He balanced the tray on one hand, not without difficulty, and pushed the door open.

Sybil had been promised a visit from the area physiotherapist that morning, after complaining to the doctor that she seemed to be getting nowhere with Miss Cole.

It was eleven o'clock before she heard voices down below followed by footsteps ascending the stairs. She had combed her hair, rubbed her cheeks to make herself look healthier and done her best to tidy the bed, though she no longer tried to move her own pillows. It led to bouts of severe pain and that, of course, deepened her depression.

Outside on the tiny landing she could hear a low-voiced conversation; Dora's voice and that of another woman. Then Dora creaked down the stairs again and the door opened wide, and that was because the woman entering the room was wide, too. She was not very old, probably no more than thirty-five or six, but her weight made her look older. She was fat but also thickset, the arms protruding from the short sleeves of her green overall muscular and covered with down, her dark hair cut almost as short as a man's, and her brown eyes flickered across Sybil and the room with an air of weary disdain, as though she saw too much suffering, too many small attic rooms.

'Good afternoon,' she said curtly, plodding across the sloping floorboards and lowering herself heavily into the cushioned cane chair by the bed. Sybil's heart bled for the chair but it stood up to the punishment admirably, only creaking protestingly whenever the woman shifted her weight. 'I'm your area physio, Miss Lang. You are Sybil Cream?'

'That's right,' Sybil said, wondering who else she could possibly be, up here in Sybil Cream's bed and paralysed to boot. 'How do you do?'

She held out a thin hand which was ignored. Miss Lang had produced a notebook from somewhere and was apparently checking through it, her lips moving soundlessly as she did so.

'You're suffering from . . .' A mumble of technical jargon which Sybil had heard and hated before. Instead of answering she nodded, some of her hope draining away. She had given up on Miss Cole who simply didn't seem interested in Sybil's condition, but had had great hopes of the area physio. One glance at Miss Lang's face was enough to convince her that the other woman had probably listened to most of Miss Cole's stories about Sybil, and believed them. She wondered for the first time whether there was anything anyone could do for her or whether the visit would simply prove that she was beyond help.

'Do you have movement in your left leg?'

'Well, not really, although sometimes my legs jerk when –'

'Involuntary muscular spasm is not movement,' Miss Lang interrupted with a curl of her thick upper lip. 'No movement in the left leg, then. And the right leg?'

'No movement,' Sybil said miserably.

'Trunk?'

'Well, I can hitch myself up from lying to sitting, but –'

'Yes, yes. Motions normal? Bladder control normal? No catheterization?'

'It's just my legs,' Sybil said. 'The rest of me's all right. It's only my legs that won't work.'

'You should be in a wheelchair,' Miss Lang snapped. 'Prefer your bed, I suppose, to getting downstairs and making yourself useful.'

It was a statement, not a question, but Sybil answered it anyway. She felt sore with disappointment – why had this woman taken such a dislike to her? She could scarcely be blamed for the absence of a wheelchair, when she had been begging Miss Cole to provide one for her for months.

'No I don't prefer my bed! Life would be much easier for me with a wheelchair, but Miss Cole wouldn't do anything about it until you'd come and seen me yourself.'

'Hmm. Well, I've been extremely busy, and I'm sure if Miss Cole hasn't seen fit to provide you with a chair there's a very good reason for it. There are a great many cripples needing wheelchairs, some probably far less fortunately placed than yourself . . . members of the forces maimed in action, for instance. I'm afraid you'll just have to wait until we have a chair free. But I'd better take a look at you, I suppose.'

She got laboriously to her feet and tugged the covers down. Sybil looked at her skinny white legs with a feeling akin to despair. They looked so damned feeble, lying there, as though they never intended to be useful members of society again.

'Hmm. Try to lift your right leg. Now your left. Hmm.'

She had left soon after, leaving the room in the middle of Sybil's apologetic explanation as to why she could not do the exercises, why she so desperately needed the chair. There are few things more irritating than having someone put the 'phone down on you when you are in mid-sentence, and when you can't walk and someone simply leaves you, you get the same feeling of frustrated fury. Sybil had wept bitterly at the time and now, waiting for her tea and knowing that someone had come to the door, which would delay Dora's bringing it up, she could not forbear shedding a few more tears. It was awful to be denied the one thing that would, perhaps, give you a little bit of independence, allow you to practise what tiny movement there was in your lower limbs!

So when she saw the door begin to open again, she had been crying, believing herself safe for a while at least. Dora was busy with a caller, and rain had just begun to slant across the windowpanes. Dora had been washing, so Sybil guessed that her mother's first action, when she noticed the raindrops on the glass, would be to rush out to the line. Getting the washing in, hanging it round the range on the clothes horse and across the backs of the chairs, would take a while. Sybil had at least twenty minutes before Dora came up with her cup of tea and the newly baked teacakes.

Fortunately, the door opened slowly, so she had scrubbed her eyes fiercely with the backs of her hands and was pretending to read her book when a voice said, 'Excuse me.'

She looked up. A young man in American Army Air Force uniform stood there, with a tray in one hand. He was smiling at her. And just for a moment it was as though time had stood still, as though this stranger was vitally important to her, as though his entering her room at this particular moment would have a deep and dramatic effect on her life.

She knew him at once, of course; he had spoken to her months ago on the beach and she had liked him then, felt an immediate affinity allied to a strong physical attraction. But she had not expected to see him again and having him actually in her room was a weird experience, as though a film star had stepped off the screen or a character off the page of a book. And then he moved and the spell was broken and she looked at him again, having a good stare whilst he was concentrating on getting through the door with the tray, then carrying it carefully over to the bed, eyes down, concentration total. She stared because although at their first meeting she had liked the look of him, she had never in her life felt like this, never known such strength of feeling. And he had called it up, apparently, merely by appearing in her room with a tea-tray and smiling at her.

He wasn't particularly tall, though he was broad-shouldered and thickset, but somehow he seemed to fill the room. He was bareheaded so she could see his black, close-cropped hair and he was tanned and healthy looking, with very white teeth. His chin was long, with a cleft, and although it was only mid-afternoon his jaw was already blue as the strong stubble began to show. Used to her blond brother and red-headed father, and to Ralph's fair complexion, Sybil had not previously encountered the phenomenon of five o'clock shadow, and she could not decide whether she liked it or not.

'I've brought your tea, ma'am; can I come in?'

That made her laugh because he was in already, wasn't he? But she nodded shyly and he placed the tray very carefully and gently across her knees and then decided to move the teacake which had slid across the tray when he had put it down. As he did so their fingers touched and an extraordinary feeling chased up Sybil's spine. It was not the normal frisson of excitement which a young man's touch might engender in a girl, more a tremendously heightened sense of *awareness*, as though all her sensitive nerve-endings were affected by this man's mere presence, and even being in the same room with him was somehow right, as though fate had foreseen it, matched them.

But you could see he had no idea how she felt. He was smiling down at her, the very dark eyes sparkling with amusement because he had

surprised her. He had smiled at her on the beach, too, but that had
been long ago and obviously it had not stayed in his mind as it had
in hers. She must be calm and natural, must not embarrass him. The
last thing she wanted was for him to guess the effect he had on her.

'Thank you very much. Where's Mum?'

'Someone came to the front door and she went to answer it, so I
thought I might as well bring your tea up. How are those pillows?
Need a bit of life shaken into them?'

'They're fine,' Sybil said quickly. 'Who are you? And why are
you here?'

'Well now, my name's Fenn Kitzmann, but suppose you guess how I
come to be here, honey? Or do you have scores of strange visitors?'

That made her laugh again, because now she came to think of it he
was just about her first real visitor. He was settling himself in the cane
chair now and glancing out of the window, giving her the opportunity
to study him again. She saw that his eyes were not dark brown as she
had at first assumed but a very deep blue, and she also saw that though
his chest was broad, it tapered to a small waist and narrow hips. How
strangely different are men from women, she thought to herself. He
isn't really handsome or even good-looking. I'm sure he isn't a patch
on Ralph, yet . . . he's special to me, even if others don't agree.

'Well, honey? You've had your thinkin' time, now start guessin'!'

'Must I? I really can't imagine who you are, or why you're here,'
Sybil said. She felt like adding that it did not matter who he was, it
was enough that he was here, in her room, that they had found each
other. But she must not forget the finding was all on one side. To him
she was just a bedridden girl, a cripple. It was a bitter thought, but
even the bitterness could not take away her incredulous pleasure in
his presence.

'Right, I'll give you a clue. I biked here, thinkin' to get me a cup
of tea and a bun, but . . .'

'But it's early closing, of course!' Sybil crowed. 'You poor thing! So
then what happened?'

'Well, I was wonderin' what in Hades to do next when the bus
stopped beside me and a purty girl stepped down. Any ideas?'

'Chris! But do you know Chris? She's my best friend but she's never
mentioned – oh. I know – you're Lizzie's Yank!'

It should have distressed her, the sudden suspicion that he was the
American airman Lizzie had talked about, but she knew Lizzie too
well. Lizzie was bound to have better game in view; she would not
waste herself upon someone of only moderate importance.

The suddenness and frankness of her reply amused him. He squeezed his eyes into gleaming slits and threw his head back and roared. He finished laughing, shook his head at her, and was about to disabuse her when something stopped him. So Lizzie had a Yank now, did she? Well, he would keep shtum about it for the moment.

'That's one way of puttin' it, I guess. I'm Fenn Kitzmann and I do know Lizzie.' He pointed accusingly at her teacake. 'I brung that up on my own initiative, so why don't you take a bite?' he said coaxingly. 'I'll be in trouble with your mom if you won't eat.'

'No you won't, she's used to it,' Sybil observed, but she took a bite out of the teacake nevertheless. With her mouth full, she said, 'Didn't Mum give you one? I'm sure she means to invite you to tea, so why don't you go down and bring your own tea up here – if you don't mind, that is? It's awfully nice to talk to someone who isn't family.'

'Sure.' But he was frowning. 'You been ill long?'

'Quite a while.'

'How long before you're up and about?'

It was a fair enough question but suddenly there was a lump in her throat and tears brimmed her eyes. No one had told him she was a cripple! Lizzie wouldn't, of course, because to Lizzie Fenn would be just another ship that passed in the night, and Mum had scarcely had time, whilst dear Chris had only just met him and would scarcely jump in with a remark about Sybil's unfortunate state until she knew him better. Sybil turned her head to look out of the window and could see only grey, with the blurring of tears and the falling rain combining to wipe out the view altogether. She swallowed. So he didn't know a thing, which meant that any explanation must come from her – and come right now. She had no wish to let him believe she would be 'up and about', competing on even terms with Lizzie, in a day or so.

'Sybil? Oh, honey, what's the matter? What did I say?'

He had forsaken his chair and crouched by the bed, taking her hand in both of his. His hands were warm and strong but his touch was compassionate rather than exciting. You're a fool, Sybil Cream, Sybil told herself, pulling free and wiping away her tears.

'Sorry,' she muttered. 'I'm fed up because that hospital woman . . . Miss Lang . . . came this morning and she isn't going to do anything about getting me a wheelchair and I do so desperately want one. I can't do the exercises without a chair. It does get me down.'

'A *wheelchair*? Gee, I thought you'd had flu or measles or something! What's the matter with you, hon?'

'I had infantile paralysis, and now my legs are paralysed,' Sybil said. 'The first physio, Miss Cole, gave me exercises but I can't do them. I have to swing my legs out of bed, which I can't do, and even if I could I wouldn't be able to swing them back. I've done my very best to explain that my legs won't move enough – well, they won't move at all – but she's always in a hurry, she just won't listen, and it's been m-m-months since I left hospital and they said there that I should have a wheelchair and it isn't as if . . .'

The bed creaked as Fenn sat on it in order to gather Sybil into his arms. She rested her hot wet cheek against his blue jacket and sighed deeply. If this was pity, and if pity was the only reason for his putting his arms round her, then she would have to settle for it. Oh, lucky, lucky Lizzie to get someone so special. If only . . .

'You shall have that wheelchair, honey, if I have to go to the hospital and shake it out of them! Now, what's this about exercises?'

'I haven't told anyone. I don't really know why I've told you, because it's no use crying over spilt milk. If I can't do the exercises, and I can't, then it must mean I'm incurable. But because I can't even get my legs out of bed no one really knows whether I can do them or not! I can't put any more on Mum and Chris, nor on Lizzie, because it's Miss Cole's job to watch me doing the exercises and then tell me what I'm doing wrong. But whenever I ask her to watch or try to tell her what a fix I'm in she walks out of the room, knowing very well I can't follow,' Sybil said. 'You see, the exercises are meant to strengthen muscles but you can only do them if you can move your legs a bit and I can't and she knows it, so why on earth won't she give me something I *can* do? If I'm so bad that exercises can't help me then you'd think she could at least get that wheelchair! So you see I'm not crying for nothing, not really.'

Fenn squeezed her shoulders. Then he rubbed his sandpapery chin against her hair. Sybil longed to touch him back, to run her fingers along his chin and feel for herself the dark roughness of it, but she knew better. This was Lizzie's Yank and he was used to the breathless, amazing beauty of her elder sister; all he could possibly feel for her was pity. Lizzie would undoubtedly dump him when something better came along, but it would not do to pretend, even to herself, that she could attract a man. Men, most of them, were embarrassed by cripples, so she might as well get used to the idea.

'You're certainly not crying over nothing, and I'm sure you'll get better given the right treatment,' Fenn said firmly. 'You're a brave kid. You'll work hard once you know what to work at, and that ain't gonna be long, I'm tellin' you. Say, my mom's a nurse. She might be able to help.'

'But she's in America,' Sybil said weakly. 'Even if you wrote today . . .'

'No, she isn't in the States. I was born and brought up in Manchester and my mom's still there,' Fenn said. 'Don't say though, will you, baby? I never tell anyone that.'

'No, I won't tell,' Sybil said. She moved in his arm to look up at him. Close to like this she could see that he had a big nose, that he had a bit of a shaving rash, that his tan was fading. But she could no longer even begin to compare him with Ralph. Ralph was handsome, kind in many ways, a decent enough bloke. He wrote to her, he had visited her in hospital, but she was sure that when she was strong enough he would tell her that he was not cut out for marriage, that they were wrong for each other. It was one of the many things she had cried secretly over, but not any more, she told herself firmly. Not any more. Because Ralph was right, she could never have loved him or she would not now feel so entirely comfortable, so completely at home, in the arms of this young man she had barely met.

'Good. Knew I could trust you. Now tell me the name of the hospital and I'll . . .'

The door opened and Dora's face appeared round the edge of it.

'That was the vicar, asking if we'd any spare fish since the – oh!'

'Sorry, ma'am,' Fenn said. 'Ain't misbehavin', jest tellin' your pretty daughter there'll be somethin' done for her before too long.'

'The physiotherapist comes,' Dora said. Her voice sounded defensive. 'I keep hoping . . . I asked about the wheelchair today but I think she feels it's too soon. She says wounded soldiers and airmen need the chairs so there aren't many left over for civilians. I suppose we must be patient.'

'Not unless you want to be at the back of the queue all your life,' Fenn said decisively. 'There'll always be an excuse for some people not doing their jobs, and that's what it amounts to – that Miss Cole, she's a lazy woman, that's what. Time she was sorted, and I'm the guy to do it. As I was telling your daughter, I've relatives in nursing so I know how the system works.'

'The trouble is, I complained about Miss Cole and now Miss Lang resents me just like Miss Cole does,' Sybil said. 'It's no use looking uncomfortable, Mum, because it's the truth. Miss Cole hates me and despises the pair of us . . . you're afraid to stand up to her in case she makes my life even harder and I'm the same. If you ask me, she was telling lies when she said soldiers and airmen need all the wheelchairs, because the hospital isn't a military one. Fenn's quite right, we really should do something.'

Dora looked curiously from face to face, then nodded.

'Fenn, you've given me hope, and I believe you're right. If we're not prepared to fight for Sybil, who will be? I'll catch a bus into Norwich . . . oh, but how will you manage, love? If I leave . . .'

'No need for you to lift a finger,' Fenn said grandly. He swung his legs off the bed and stood up. Sybil felt as deprived as a new-born kitten moved from its mother's warmth but she smiled up at him. Never let your feelings show, she reminded herself. He's a friend, just a friend. You're lucky to have such a friend! 'I'll go into the city with the liberty truck tonight and get it sorted. Take my word for it, honey, you'll have that wheelchair by this time tomorrow. I'll deliver it myself!'

Fenn had his tea upstairs with the child Sybil and then went downstairs with her mother and the other girl, Chris.

'Lizzie's getting Gran's tea for her,' Chris explained. 'And then she'll have to go straight to work. She said to say cheerio to you, Fenn, and she'll see you some other time.'

But he was sure she would be lurking outside somewhere, when he left the Creams' cottage just as the rain began to ease. He shouted up the stairs to the kid, thanked Dora for her hospitality, and having spent the best part of his visit mentioning how he hated Christmas away from his family back Stateside, got himself invited for Christmas Day.

'It'll be just family,' Dora warned him in the cool, cut glass voice which was so like that of her daughter Lizzie and seemed so at odds with her surroundings.

'That'll be great,' Fenn said, meaning it, as he shrugged himself back into his uniform macintosh and wrapped his scarf round his neck. 'I'll be there, ma'am – wild horses wouldn't keep me away.'

And that would have applied equally well to Lizzie, he thought, when he saw her under a big black umbrella, waiting at the bus stop on London Road. She saw him at the same moment and waved, then crossed the road and came towards him.

'Hello again. Look, I hate too many explanations but I suppose I do owe you one. That fellow you saw me with – the family don't approve. They don't like us meeting.'

'That's bad. But why?'

'He's more or less engaged to – to someone else. He's going to tell the – the person that they don't suit but he's waiting until the right moment. It would ruin everything if my parents found out and I was really scared you'd let the cat out of the bag without realizing it. So . . . Fenn, would you be a sport and pretend you've never met me before?'

'No can do,' Fenn said cheerfully, and saw the blue eyes narrow. So the beautiful Lizzie had a temper – well, she had better not vent it on him. He explained.

'Sybil jumped to the conclusion that I was your Yank, whoever he may be, and because I didn't know what was goin' on, I just let the remark stand. So I guess your family think we're old friends.'

'Oh! Well, that could be useful. Yes, really useful,' Lizzie said thoughtfully. 'There are times when I need to be with my – my friend, but I can't let the family suspect. So I could say I was with you, perhaps.'

'Be my guest,' Fenn said courteously. 'Except that you'll have to give me due warning; I've been invited to spend Christmas with your family.'

'Oh, lor', you really are getting your legs under the table,' Lizzie said, but she did not seem displeased. 'Sybil's a lovely girl, isn't she?'

'She sure is; she'll be lovelier once she's got her wheelchair,' Fenn said, and saw by Lizzie's expression that he had in some way disappointed her. Still, she smiled and agreed, promised to let him know in good time if she needed him as an alibi and stood in a puddle to watch him cycle off down the road, turning once or twice to wave.

Odd, Fenn mused, hunching his shoulders against the light drizzle which had replaced the downpour. She's the sort of girl who could have any feller, but she sure is dead-set on that young officer. Well, it's no skin off my nose, he decided, pushing hard on the pedals, and driving the bike forward with all his energy. Tomorrow I'll get that kid her wheelchair . . . and I'm all fixed up for Christmas Day!

His pals were delighted to welcome Fenn aboard the liberty truck; they shoved up so he had room and began to tell him all about the delights he would presently encounter. The small, country city with its friendly people – particularly its friendly girls – the dance halls, the clubs, the cinemas, all pleasant places on a cold December evening where a man might warm himself and forget the war for a while.

They were surprised when he said he had to go to the hospital first, but resigned to his ways. Fenn was an odd guy. He'd talk your head off but you never somehow felt you knew him. His crew acknowledged that he was a first-rate pilot with a flair for knowing where the shrapnel would hit, behind which particular cloud formations the enemy lurked. They got along with him fine aboard *Stompin' Suzie Too*, but he had never confided in any one of them. They had seen him with various pretty girls and envied him his ability to wangle himself into most women's good graces, but he rarely talked about the girls, never brought them along to dances at the base. Perhaps he was not as confident as he appeared, but on the whole his pals thought not. It was just Fenn's way, they concluded, and were glad to welcome him aboard the liberty truck.

Fenn, for his part, endured the bumpy ride, chatted, and wondered just how he was going to deal with the hospital authorities. In many ways he was an easy-going guy but seeing that little girl so unhappy had been like a punch in the gut. Poor kid; she was no more than thirteen or fourteen, he supposed, yet no one had been concerned enough about her to make trouble at the hospital.

To be sure, once her mother got him downstairs again, she had done her best to explain.

'Miss Cole didn't just make excuses about the forces needing the chairs, she said the chair was no use unless Sybil begins to co-operate and tries to do the exercises,' she explained, shamefaced. 'I didn't like to interfere. That Miss Cole's a funny woman and Miss Lang was worse, but I know Sybs can be difficult sometimes. She hardly eats anything, and she won't do the exercises in front of either me or Chris.'

'She can't do them; they're for someone with more muscle control than she's got,' Fenn had said in a tight voice. That a mother should not have realized her daughter was a real little fighter, that she should have simply accepted an unpleasant woman's bitter words against her own child, shocked him. His own mother had been weak, he had thought – but that weak? That careless of her child? Never!

325

'She can't do them? Oh, but are you sure – did she say so? Miss Cole says she's perfectly capable, just unwilling to put herself to so much effort.'

'Tell me, Mrs Cream, who do you know best, your little girl or that thar Miss Cole?'

'Oh, Sybs, of course. But . . .'

'And who is the more truthful?'

'Why, Sybs, definitely. Miss Cole often tells untruths to save herself from trouble. But . . .'

'No buts, ma'am. Why, Miss Cole won't even stay to watch Sybil try to move her legs, she just shoots off out of the room. So I'm gonna find out what gives, because you can't leave the kid, she needs you. But I can be in Norwich and out again before you know it.'

'It's very good of you, Fenn, but do you think the hospital authorities will accept your word on how things are?'

'They sure will,' Fenn said grimly. 'Don't worry, Mrs Cream, I'll be back here with that wheelchair tomorrow.'

He would do it, too. He liked Sybil, thought her hard done by. She was gentle and soft-spoken and she had a pretty laugh; she'll grow up real nice, he told himself as he left the liberty truck behind and began to make his way to the hospital. Or she will if she's given the chance. What has that pretty mother got against her, though? It was clear she took loving care of her, so why not go the whole hog, see the kid got her wheelchair and the sort of exercises she could do? She seemed a sensible and courageous woman, so why had she simply let that Miss Cole push her – and her daughter – around? But he was already beginning to realize that Dora Cream had too much respect for authority so far as Sybil was concerned. He knew nothing about her background, but he did know that if you love someone you want the best for them. If Miss Cole had already proved herself a vengeful sort of woman then Dora would not want her on the opposite side in the fight for Sybil. The fact that Miss Cole was already ranging herself with the enemy had not, until today, occurred to Mrs Cream. I shouldn't criticize her, Fenn told himself, mounting his bicycle. But I'm going to do my damnedest for that poor kid!

Then there was Lizzie – but it didn't do to think too much about Lizzie. She had never mentioned a paralysed sister, never spoken of the kid. It seemed odd, but perhaps the entire family were a bit odd, Lizzie with her singleminded selfishness, the mother ignoring the child's obvious needs, the kid herself, never telling anyone she couldn't do the exercises.

But Fenn had reached the hospital; he turned into the driveway and began to rehearse his story.

20

The wheelchair was a cause of some merriment amongst Fenn's pals
when he got it out of the taxi. The driver, an elderly man with the
red and bulbous nose which spoke of much dedicated drinking, had
grumbled about such unusual luggage but helped Fenn load it up and
didn't go too fast round corners so Fenn, though squashed, wasn't
entirely flattened by his capricious companion.

The liberty truck was always crowded, so the guys put the chair
in the well of the vehicle and everyone put a steadying hand on it.
After all, by the time the truck was loaded and ready to leave the
city, most of the airmen were high on excitement and whatever alcohol
they had managed to consume. Their contrary travelling companion,
quick to seize the chance to career from one side of the truck to the
other, crushing toes and mangling kneecaps as it went, caused a lot
of hilarity and some bad language, but no one questioned its right to
be there.

Which was as well, a sober Fenn thought ominously, for he had
been forced to stretch the truth until it squeaked to acquire the
damned thing. First he had insinuated himself into the Cream family
by marriage (his mother was now Henry Cream's sister, living in
Boston and married to his father, a surgeon at the foremost hospital
for spinal diseases in the whole of the United States). Then he had
told the matron that her Mrs Lang had not visited his little cousin
for over three months, and since that time had refused to acquire the
wheelchair which was the only possible means by which Sybil might
move around once more.

Matron began defensive and ended charmed. She promised to
speak severely to Miss Cole and Miss Lang and said she would
see that a wheelchair was despatched to Miss Cream the very next
time an ambulance was in the vicinity of Pakeby. Not good enough,
said Fenn, and told her about the useless exercises and the rapidity

of Miss Cole's exit when she should have been working with his cousin.

Matron was shocked; genuinely, Fenn could tell. She was also a nice woman, he decided, when she shelled out a well-maintained wheelchair and waved him off the premises. He signed forms quite merrily, did Fenn, and asked what Miss Cole would be like on her next visit.

'I'll send someone else,' matron said. 'That poor girl, to receive such treatment! We have another physio working the district, a girl in her twenties, and I'll see she calls. Indeed, if she hasn't arrived by next Wednesday, please get in touch with me again.'

Fenn promised to do so and travelled back to Flacton in a happy daze, scarcely noticing when it was his turn to be crushed or mangled. He had succeeded; so far as he was concerned the wheelchair might ram him in the shins and welcome.

And next day, early, he began to plot. He needed transport, and several of the men drove jeeps or army vehicles. He decided to go to his colonel. After all, a wheelchair for a youngster was just the sort of scheme likely to appeal to a man who was always reminding them of the importance of 'gettin' along good with the Brits'.

Fenn was right. He was lent an army vehicle and a driver, though as he pointed out he could perfectly well have driven himself.

'Not on these roads you don't,' Abe Harness, the colonel, grunted. 'Jest be sensible, boy, and let Josh, who knows the roads, tek the pair of you.'

Josh was black, cheerful and a brilliant driver. The two young men enjoyed the short run though it was typical December weather. Yesterday's rain, it seemed, had scarcely abated all night and on a couple of occasions they drove through what appeared to be sizeable streams.

'They're fords, man,' Josh said when questioned. 'Ain't you never sin a ford afore?'

Fenn, thinking back, supposed that he had seen tiny streams trickling across the road, but that had been in summer, when you went through them without a thought. Now they swirled round your hub-caps and you slowed and tested your brakes as you emerged on the further side.

When they reached Beach Road Josh helped Fenn to manoeuvre the wheelchair on to the path but declined to go inside.

'I'll come back for you,' he said. 'Got a friend lives in the port; she'll be mortal glad to see me. I'll pick you up again in . . . say an hour?'

'No, man,' Fenn said uneasily. 'They won't want me for an hour.'

'Aw, g'won,' Josh wheedled. 'You stay a while – how's the kid goin' to git down them stairs without you?'

It had not occurred to Fenn before, but now he saw that Josh had a point.

'Right; an hour, and I'll walk towards the port along that lane,' he said, pointing. 'Otherwise toot the horn.'

'Okay,' Josh said. He jumped back into the jeep and revved the engine, then disappeared round the corner of Beach Road. Fenn stood and listened to Josh's strong voice telling anyone who cared to listen that there would be bluebirds over the white cliffs of Dover until it faded into the distance, then he turned and began to push the wheelchair round the side of the house.

The yard was puddled and forlorn, the sheds apparently empty. Rain still fell greyly on everything in sight. Fenn pushed the chair doggedly over to the back door and knocked. There was a short pause, then he heard footsteps. Dora smiled as she opened the door, then she saw the wheelchair and her eyes widened.

'Goodness! I never thought you'd do it – not right away, like this. Come in, come in, you must be soaked to the skin.'

'The chair's a bit damp, but it'll dry, same's me,' Fenn said cheerfully. He and the wheelchair clattered into the kitchen, both shedding water on to the hardpacked earth floor. 'Gee, I'm sorry 'bout the mess.'

'Mess? Nonsense, a splash of water isn't a mess,' Dora said bracingly. She took a roller-towel off the back of the door and began lovingly drying the wheelchair, stroking the worn leather seat as though it were fragile as porcelain. 'Well, just wait until Sybil sees –' She stopped short and stared up at Fenn, then turned to glance at the steep, narrow cupboard-staircase. 'Oh Lord, it never occurred to me – it won't go up the stairs!'

'What does that matter? Sybil's gonna come down,' Fenn said. 'It'll do her a power of good, ma'am. Turble bad for a youngster, being cut off from the family like that. I'll fetch her now for you.'

'It's so good of you . . . do you want a hand? I could go up the road and fetch . . .'

'She'll be safe as houses with me,' Fenn said, beginning to mount the stairs. 'We'll have her sittin' here like a queen, watchin' every move you make, before she's much older. Shan't be more'n a minute.'

He took the stairs two at a time, bumping his elbows and once his knee, so anxious was he to reach Sybil's room. He knocked perfunctorily, then threw the door open and strode towards the bed.

'Ma'am, your carriage awaits,' he announced. 'Got a warm jacket to wrap round you? You're goin' places, babe!'

Sybil had known he would come, was absolutely sure of it, but as the day wore on she began to see the impossibility of the task he had set himself. She remembered matron vaguely from her time in hospital and doubted that anyone could pull the wool over eyes so shrewd. Yet when she heard the knock on the back door and then the step on the stair she never doubted for one moment that it was Fenn, come to announce mission accomplished. When he opened the door and crossed the room, saying that her carriage awaited and she was going places, she glowed with excitement and a vicarious sense of achievement.

'Oh, golly,' she said inadequately. 'However can I get downstairs, though? My legs won't hold me, but if I swing . . .'

She took hold of her white legs and began to heave on them. Fenn chuckled, bent over the bed and lifted her bodily into his arms. He smiled down at her, then a tiny frown stole across his face. The arms cradling her tightened a trifle.

'Sybil, honey, I've just made a discovery. You're no little girl, you're a very lovely young woman!'

'I'm twenty-three,' Sybil said. 'How old did you think I was?'

Her voice seemed to be coming out in jerks; that was his closeness, of course. Her body lay in his arms just as though . . . just as if . . . but it was no such thing. She might have been a pound of sausages – or more likely a telegraph pole – for all the feeling she would be engendering in him. But she did wish she'd had the forethought to grab that jacket he'd mentioned. One of her small breasts was pressed against him and, shamingly, she could feel the nipple hardening. She prayed fervently that he would not look down, would not see and realize how he affected her.

'I thought you were about ten years younger than that, I guess. How about a blanket? We don't want you to git cold.'

He struggled a blanket off her bed, holding her safe against his chest. She murmured incoherently; he really should not bother, she was far too heavy for him, just let him put her back in bed . . .

'Too heavy? You're like a feather, sure you are. You ought to see my old airplane, *Stompin' Suzie Too*. Now she is heavy, that I'll grant you, heavy's lead when we're draggin' home, tired out. But if you wuz

331

to put your arms round my neck you'd take what little weight there is on yourself.'

She could feel the heat fly to her cheeks and heaven knew they were hot enough already, but there was sense in what he said. She put her arms round his neck, then rested her cheek against his collar bone. He somehow managed to collect the length of her useless legs into neatness and they got down the stairs without Fenn falling or Sybil being dropped. And at the foot of the flight the room she had not seen for months was waiting for her. Smiling at her. The fire was roaring, the table was set for tea, even the rain driving against the windowpanes helped to make the place seem, in contrast, warmer, more homely.

And she could not be that heavy, because Fenn just stopped at the bottom of the stairs, still holding her, letting her look around. Dora, fussing over the table, beaming, turned and pointed.

'Well? What do you think? I don't know how this young man did it, but there's your chair!'

It was beautiful! It had shiny wooden arms, a slippery leather seat, big wheels and smaller ones, a footrest which could be folded up if you didn't need it – it was the wheelchair of her dreams, or would have been had she been in the habit of fantasizing about wheelchairs.

'Oh, Mum!'

'Nothing to do with me,' Dora said gruffly. 'It was all Fenn, his idea, he got it, everything. It's him you should thank.'

'I do thank you, Fenn, more than I can possibly say,' Sybil said. 'I say, it's a new one . . . oh, can I sit in it?'

'Sure; but I was gettin' to like carryin' you,' Fenn told her, settling her with great gentleness on the slippery leather seat. 'Now just let your legs go limp and I'll wrap the blanket round them, then put your hands on the wheels . . . let the brake off first – can you see the brake? . . . and you can start by wheeling yourself up to the table.'

'It's wizard,' Sybil said breathlessly five minutes later. She had wheeled herself to the table, then to the back door, she had done a three-point turn to go and peer out of the front window. Now she felt capable of going all over the ground floor of the cottage. Perhaps tomorrow she could somehow get over the doorsill and into the back yard! She said as much, but Fenn, smiling at her, shook his head.

'No you don't. Take it slow, hon. One of the things matron told me at the hospital yesterday was that too much exercise can harm. Increase it little by little, a bit more each day, she said. And you're getting a new physiotherapist, a gal not much older than you. She's to come by Wednesday or you must let matron know.'

'Not Miss Cole? Oh, that's best of all,' Sybil gasped. 'Why don't you just lift my front wheels over the doorsill, Fenn, then I can scoot over and say hello to Beattie. I've missed her horribly, you know.'

Dora laughed at her but shook a reproving head.

'Sybs, you heard what Fenn said, too much too soon isn't good for you at all. And besides, it's raining cats and dogs still, and pretty chilly. Show us how nicely you can eat your tea, instead.'

It was a good high tea, with shrimps, Dora's own brown bread and margarine, homemade strawberry jam and a mock-chocolate cake which, Henry always declared, was impossible to tell from the real thing. Fenn obeyed Dora's injunction to 'eat up', and because she was watching him and talking, an amazing amount of food somehow found its way on to Sybil's plate and thence into Sybil. Indeed, instructing Fenn how to shell shrimps – the little brown ones which are hardest to shell but all the sweeter for the work – telling him how they caught them in the low-waters left when the tide swept out, inviting him to try his luck at it one day when the weather was finer, boasting that once she got the knack of the wheelchair she would very soon be bowling along the beach, was just what Sybil needed. She could feel her confidence returning, making it almost impossible to remember how very unsure and unhappy she had been up in her room only an hour or so earlier.

Tea over, Fenn offered to wipe whilst Dora washed, but Sybil vetoed this very firmly.

'No, indeed! It's months and *months* since I was last useful. Mum will wash up, of course, and I shall wipe. Fenn, you may put away since that's probably beyond me for a bit. I'll tell you where things go.'

'What a bossy gal she is,' Fenn said to Dora. 'Was she always like this, Mrs Cream? You'll be calling curses down on my head for bringing her downstairs, soon.'

The three of them quickly had the meal cleared away and the room tidy again and Fenn glanced towards the window and shivered.

'Gee, I'm glad I'm not cycling today. I wonder where my driver's got to? He was seeing a girl in the port, but he should've come back by now.'

Sybil immediately shot across the room and manoeuvred herself neatly through the kitchen door and into the front room; she managed to reach the window without knocking anything over, then came back, smiling.

'He's outside in the car, snoozing,' she announced. 'Oh, Fenn, I do hope you'll come and see us again – and Chris too, of course. I dare say you see Lizzie in the port,' she added.

'Before I go anywhere, I'd better carry you back to bed,' Fenn said gently. 'You must be tired, honey.'

Sybil, about to stoutly deny it, realized that he spoke no more than the truth. She smiled ruefully.

'Yes, I am rather. But what'll I do tomorrow, when you aren't here to carry me downstairs? Oh, I can't be stuck in the bedroom and unable to get at my wonderful chair until someone strong happens by!'

'How about if I bring your bed down for you, before I go?' Fenn said at once. 'If you'll excuse me for a moment I'll go out and ask Josh to give me a hand. It won't take no time at all . . . that is, if Mrs Cream doesn't mind having you in the kitchen all night?'

'It'll be grand,' Dora said at once. 'If you and your driver don't mind I'd sooner the pair of you brought the bed down because I doubt I could manage it alone! If you bring the bed and the mattress I'll follow with the bedding. I'll be quiet as a mouse and let Sybil rest most of the evening, and tomorrow we'll start the day off with the new exercises. We'll see you on Christmas Day, Fenn, and by then there'll be a great change in Sybil, I'm sure of it.'

Dora had watched, enchanted and delighted, as Sybil not only came out of her shell in the young American's presence but began to sparkle; she could pass for a pretty girl she thought at one stage, and promptly felt ashamed of herself. For goodness sake, Sybs *was* a pretty girl. Just because Dora's yardstick of prettiness began and ended with Lizzie – *had* begun and ended with Lizzie, she reminded herself – that should not mean she did not appreciate the subtler beauty of her younger daughter.

Because she was ready, at last, to see that Sybil most certainly had a kind of beauty. Her very fine, streaky fair hair did not curl, was not thick and bouncy like Lizzie's, but it had a shine on it like a horse-chestnut fresh out of the husk and to stroke it was like stroking the finest silk.

Her eyes were not sparkling sapphire-blue, like Lizzie's, but amber gold with a darker line round the iris. Her lashes were not an inch long, neither did they curl, but they framed eyes which had a straight and sincere glance. Her face was not an adorable heart-shape, it was a small, thin little face, but her mouth had a sweetness about it which was lacking in Lizzie's shapely, pouting lips and Sybil's pointy chin was determined enough for strength but not for obstinacy or selfishness.

Of course she's too thin, but her figure was good once and will be again, Dora told herself. Those poor skinny legs may fill out as she finds how to do the exercises and it will be good to hear her laugh, sing, make jokes. Dora was not deceived by Ralph or his letters. The lad would never stand by Sybil and she must know it. Ralph was a lightweight. He wanted a pretty girl who could keep up with him, enhance his life. He would not be held back by a cripple, no matter how bright and sensible she might be.

How thrilled Chris would be, though, when she returned from her day out in Norwich, to find Sybil, if not on her feet at least in her wheelchair – and downstairs, furthermore, where Chris was so anxious to see her. And she was right, of course. Now that it had been pointed out to her so forcibly, Dora knew that she had been wrong to keep Sybil marooned upstairs, even if she told herself that the child would have less aggravation from the everyday tasks being done in the kitchen. And the story of the exercises had shocked her; that poor little Sybil had not liked to give her more worry by telling her how Miss Cole was behaving! Still, thanks to Fenn the whole miserable situation was being rectified.

Dora had no doubt that what with his getting her the wheelchair and generally treating her with such kindness, her younger daughter had got a sizeable crush on Fenn Kitson, but there was no harm in that. When Ralph decided to dump her it would be grand if Sybil was already keen on Fenn. Sybil had said that Fenn was Lizzie's Yank but then Lizzie had been around with a dozen lads since the start of the war and would surely raise little objection if she could see that Sybil was in love with Fenn? Though of course there was more to being in love than gratitude and a few long, soft-eyed glances. Sybil doesn't know many men, Dora reminded herself. The fact that she can't hide her feeling for him may mean nothing – she's probably a little upset because Ralph hasn't visited her since she got home. And his letters are so stilted and short! Besides, if Fenn is Lizzie's Yank and Lizzie wants to keep him, he's not likely to look twice at Sybs. Not that you could ever tell with Lizzie; she was a mystery to her mother.

The two young men took the bed to bits and brought down the pieces, the mattress last. After some thought, Josh – whose black but cheerful visage had almost frightened Dora into a fit at first glance, since she thought that a large white grin had walked into the kitchen unaccompanied by a body – had suggested that it might be an idea to put the bed up in the front room which seemed to be little used.

'Then Sybil can be in the kitchen with you all day, but go to another room at night so's you don't disturb each other,' he said with rare tact, and Dora had agreed that this seemed a sensible solution. The bed fitted neatly into the front room after the two young men had lugged out a velvet footstool and an occasional table with inlaid mother of pearl across the top. These treasured objects were reverently carried up to Sybil's bedroom and put in the walk-in cupboard. They would be restored to the front room again when Sybil was able to walk up and downstairs, it was agreed.

So Dora waved the boys off and then followed Sybil into the front room. It scarcely took a moment to unwrap Sybil from the blanket which Fenn had tenderly put around her, pop her into bed and cover her snugly. And though Sybil protested that she would like to stay up for a little longer, once she was settled she leaned back on her pillows and smiled gratefully up at her mother.

'Who would think that an hour in a chair could be so tiring?' she marvelled. 'Isn't he nice, Mum – Fenn, I mean?'

'Very nice,' Dora said, feeling both truthful and diplomatic for once. 'I'd say Lizzie was a lucky girl, except that, knowing her, I doubt that her fondness for him will last long.'

'I dare say you're right,' Sybil murmured. Dora noticed the little smile which lingered on her lips after this remark. 'I wonder if Chris . . . ?'

'I think Chris has become rather attached to someone else,' Dora observed. Sybil, who had noticed Chris's attentiveness to Paul Holness from St Luke's Hospital, nodded understandingly. Toddy had been fun, but his visits to Chris had tailed off with Ralph's to Sybil, and Chris certainly gave no sign of missing him overmuch. 'Now rest for a bit, dear,' Dora went on. 'I'll get us a bite of supper presently and come and sit on the end of your bed to eat mine. Then we can plan what to do tomorrow.'

'Yes. Isn't it wonderful to be able to say that I have a choice?' Sybil said. 'Before, all I could do was read a book or lie and look out of the window, but soon I'll be really useful again. And in a couple of days the new hospital lady will be round and I'll begin to move my legs – I'm sure of it!'

Sybil had got all her presents packed away now, in pretty paper with clean string round them. She had knitted Fenn a pair of gloves, a real labour of love, for she was an incredibly bad knitter. In fact Chris, examining the gloves just before they were packed away, had demanded to know why she'd done such a lacy, openwork pattern considering the cold to come?

'It's not a lacy pattern, it's just plain and purl,' Sybil said indignantly. 'Unless you mean the holes I've left for his fingers.'

'How many fingers does he have to a hand? A dozen?' Chris said, and giggled at her own wit. 'Honestly, Sybs, you couldn't give these to an octopus . . . well, you could to an octopus, but not to a feller!'

'Don't be so critical,' Sybil snarled, snatching her knitting back and curling her hands defensively round it. 'I've dropped one or two stitches but Mum will put them right she said.'

The gloves, then, were a labour of love because the Yanks seemed to have so much that it was difficult to find a suitable present, but the rest of Sybil's gifts were shop-bought. Chris had taken Sybil's hoarded coupons and bought Dora a beautiful headscarf in dark blue woollen material patterned with pansies. Large khaki handkerchiefs had been bought and despatched to Dad. Ralph would receive a packet of Players and some of Dora's special fudge, and the present for Chris was wrapped and hidden. Even Lizzie's gift was now ready, though Sybil had had qualms over Chris's choice of make-up. But Lizzie would be pleased with anything, she thought hopefully. And she did love powder and paint!

Everything's ready, Sybil thought contentedly as she lay in bed on Christmas Eve; and Fenn's coming here, which will mean it'll be perfect.

Fenn had a marvellous Christmas. He threw himself into all the celebrations and enjoyed everything from the best dinner he'd eaten for months to teaching Sybil, Dora and Granny Cream to play poker. Lizzie wouldn't play but sat and watched them, laughing and decorative. Fenn liked all three girls, but Sybil was his favourite. She was pretty, of course, but it wasn't just her looks because Lizzie knocked them all into a cocked hat in that department. It was, he supposed doubtfully, her personality. She made him laugh a lot, listened to his stories round-eyed, admiring, collapsed into gurgles of mirth when he said something deliberately ridiculous . . . he liked her a lot.

It was a pity she was a cripple, he found himself thinking as evening drew on and they played silly games in the firelight and Mrs Cream – only she was Dora to him now – invited him to spend the night on the sofa, since Sybil was in the front room and Lizzie would be sleeping in the attic. If she hadn't been a cripple ... but she was. He had asked her how the exercises were going and that was the first time that the bright animation had left her face all day.

Still. It didn't really matter about her being a cripple, he decided, because the last thing on his mind was any sort of permanent relationship with a woman, no matter how sweet. Anyway, he had quite decided he must marry a very rich girl, not just a pretty one. Seeing the way the guys could just disappear into whatever oblivion waited for bomber crews, he had made up his mind that, should he live through it, after the war he would go all out for the good life, and that meant, for a guy like him, a rich wife.

What a shame that the Cream girls weren't rich, though Lizzie was out of the running, being very much in love with that RAF guy. Chris was quite well-heeled, but that wouldn't be rich enough to keep Fenn in the style to which he intended becoming accustomed. Anyway, she was fond of Paul Holness, who was a great guy, one of the best.

He accepted Dora's invitation to sleep on the sofa, therefore, on the grounds that he might as well enjoy two days before going back into hell. And Boxing Day was even better than Christmas Day, because he wheeled Sybil out in her chair, just the two of them. They went right along to the ruined cottages, with Fenn having to physically lift the chair over some awkward obstacles, and Sybil was in ecstasy over everything, from the ice on the puddles to the ridiculous gannet which lumbered clumsily along the beach to get into the air, looking for all the world like a Liberator bomber on take-off. Even shells which Fenn collected and dropped into her lap seemed to give her pleasure.

She was a good kid. Oddly, he found himself telling her the truth, though he stuck to his old style of narrative with the rest of the family. But he told Sybil all about running away from Manchester, and about Sammy and his dad, about the hard times and the good.

Yes, she was a good kid, he mused that evening as they played marbles like four kids on the hard dirt floor, Sybil leaning down from her chair and bowling a pretty accurate alley. Pretty, too, in her way. She was a girl who could grow on a guy. She had a boyfriend, Sybil said so herself, but he hadn't been to see her for a while, so ...

Pity she was a cripple.

Lizzie loved Lincolnshire, or perhaps it was more that she loved being with Ralph. If Sybil could have seen her she would scarcely have recognized her sister, for Lizzie donned wellington boots, mac and headscarf and she, who hated walking, tramped for miles beside Ralph over the Lincolnshire wolds. Ralph wanted a few days in the country, he explained, seeing different parts, so they packed nightclothes, a change of underwear, a change of socks and set off.

There had been no question of letting any member of the Cream or Winterton family know the true state of affairs, of course. So far as they were concerned, Ralph was flying and Lizzie had gone to visit a friend so that the two of them might take a holiday together. Lizzie talked as if the friend were a woman, but thought that Dora was not fooled, and probably not Chris nor Sybil, either.

But Lizzie was too busy to worry about what people might think. What with arranging time off from work, getting someone to keep an eye on the flat and packing sufficient clothing, she had her work cut out just to be ready on time. And she needed clothing quite different from the sort of thing she usually wore, and sturdy boots, for though the winter had not been too bad, February was not the best month for hiking.

So she and Ralph set off on a wild wet morning on their first holiday together. Naturally they called themselves Mr and Mrs Winterton and Lizzie wore a gold band on the third finger of her left hand. They spent the nights in small village inns, sometimes being fed royally by the landlady, at other times resorting to picnics in their room with Lizzie squatting cross-legged on the latest bed making sandwiches from anything they had managed to acquire and Ralph lounging beside her, watching her animated little face as though it held, for him, some deep and fascinating secret. Which, perhaps, it did.

On the third day, coming into the inn soaked to the skin, they ran themselves a bath and climbed into it, one at each end. Feet and legs tangled, bodies gradually warming in the soft water, Lizzie smiled lazily across their pinkening flesh and Ralph smiled lazily back. They had ordered dinner and the smell of it cooking had hastened their descent into hot water but now, hungry though they were, the comfort of their positions made them linger.

'Good, Liz?'

'Oh, marvellous! Just to relax . . . just to be warm again! Why you wanted a walking holiday I can't think.'

'Oh, c'mon, peachy Liz, of course you can think – you're enjoying it as much as I am, which is saying something.'

'Ye-es, but it isn't really *me*, is it, Ralph? I mean, striding across hills and down into valleys, wading through streams, being soaked and muddy and cold . . . that's for others, I've always thought.'

'And now?'

Lizzie thought of walking through a glade of tall dead bracken, every curled frond bedewed with raindrops, in her nostrils the smell of wet peat and grass and gorse. They had emerged from the bracken into a stretch of marsh, where pools of amber water glinted up at the cloudy sky and they had to jump from tuft to tuft of grass just to keep dry-shod. Further on they had crossed a meadow, the turf spongy and good to walk on, poached into creamy-brown mud by cows beneath the shelter of a leafless chestnut and near the sagging five-barred gate. Hedges still thick with curled brown leaves had hemmed them in, water tinkled along a ditch, a group of toadstools growing on a mossy tree-trunk added a splash of brilliant colour to the scene.

'And now, Lizzie? Don't moon whilst the water goes cold!'

'Now I wonder why I've not walked more at home. Only I expect it's just being with you, Ralph. You make walking in the rain seem fun when the sensible side of me knows it's sheer, unadulterated madness!'

Ralph chuckled and sat up with a great crashing of water. He held out his hands.

'Right, now I've got an admission out of you, dinner! Let's get out of here and eat before we fall asleep and miss our grub.'

The best part, Lizzie thought contentedly, climbing out of the tub and wrapping herself in a towel, was never *having* to do anything. For the first time in their relationship they had time. Time for loving, time for just warmly cuddling, time to learn each other's ways. Now they could afford to have a splashy hot bath, get dressed, enjoy a meal, without that terrible hungry urgency which usually beset their brief meetings. No need, now, to grab and cling just because they were alone together; that could come later. In a proper bed, with gentleness and pleasure shared, both of them thinking not just of themselves but of their partner, too.

'What'll you wear? It's a posh dining room and the landlady says there's several people staying.'

Lizzie giggled. With only one knapsack to contain a change of clothes there was not much choice, but she had a thin wool dress in a glorious shade of blue which she wore in the evenings when they wanted to appear respectable. She knew, gladly, that they were thoroughly unrespectable; a man and his mistress, a lover and his lass. Did the landlady wonder as they trekked tiredly up the stairs? Would she eye them covertly next morning at breakfast, noticing how fond they were, how constantly they touched, how sweet their smiles, their voices?

But it did not matter. Nothing mattered but Ralph and their love. It was love, for both of them – she knew it anyway, but had it confirmed as they prepared for bed later that evening.

'Only two more days, Liz. We're on the down-path now, heading back to the airfield, back to reality. Tell you what, why don't we make it official?'

'Make what official?'

'You know very well what I mean – Mr and Mrs Ralph Winterton, that's what I mean. Why don't we get married?'

Lizzie heaved the blue dress over her head, tossed it on to a chair and began to wriggle out of her vest. Naked but for a pair of knickers and her precious nylon stockings – her Christmas present from Fenn – she smiled across at him, hooking her thumbs into the knicker elastic at the waist prior to pulling them neatly off.

'Get married? Why ever?'

She did not know why she had not at once jumped at the idea, for she had never been so happy, had never felt so right, so completely at home. It was as though she and Ralph had been made for each other, two halves which, together, formed the perfect whole.

'Well, for one thing, suppose something awful happened and you . . . suppose you had a baby?'

Lizzie completed the removal of her knickers and then took off her stockings by the simple expedient of standing on first one leg and then the other. She unrolled the nylons and threw them on to the chair, then picked up the little white shirt which she wore in bed and slipped it over her head. Pulling it down, she pushed back the covers, sat on the edge of the mattress and then swung her legs on to the bed. She lay back on the pillows, dreamily contemplating her lover.

'A baby? But I use my Dutch cap; I told you ages ago.'

Ralph snorted.

'Yes, but suppose . . . well, suppose you had a puncture? If it can happen to a bike it can happen to a diaphragm. What'ud you do then?'

'If I was pregnant, you mean? Well, I'd have the baby.'

'Yes, and the poor little bugger would be a bastard. You wouldn't want that for him, would you?'

'Language, dear,' Lizzie said absently. 'I see what you mean, though. It would be easier to tell people I was going to have a baby if I was a married woman.'

'Right. Oh, Lizzie, I never thought I'd feel like this about anyone!'

Ralph had stripped and now he came and sat on the edge of the bed by Lizzie. He turned and put his right hand on one side of her, his left on the other. Then he bent and began kissing the tops of her breasts. Lizzie shivered; God, she loved him! Being married to him, having a right to say she loved him, would be about as near perfection as she was ever likely to get. So why hold back, why not just agree and then go through with it?

'All right, I will. We will. Marry. But not till you've told Sybil.'

The words came out jerkily; it was all very well to tell herself that they had all the time in the world, that there were two whole days left before they would have to say their goodbyes, but right now the desire which he was churning up with his mouth on her skin wanted to have its moment.

'Truly? You'll marry me? I'll tell Sybs, all right! Oh, Lizzie, Lizzie, Lizzie!'

The candle on the bedside table was a good one and would have burned for many an hour, save that Ralph's jerking elbow caught it and it went out as it fell. It lay there, as candles will, rolling first to the right and then to the left until momentum ceased to drive it, and all the while it smelt of hot wax and smouldering wick. It was lucky it went out, in fact, and did not drop to the carpet or set fire to the sheets.

Neither Ralph nor Lizzie would have noticed. They were far too busy with their own affairs.

2.

Fenn was up early with the rest of his crew, because you were always called at around 0300 hours when you were flying a mission. This one was supposed to be special, though, so he shrugged himself into his clothes and went at a run through the pre-dawn dark, the March wind blowing a snow storm into his face. There were real eggs on the long tables at breakfast instead of dried ones, and the coffee was hot and stronger than usual. Last night they had been given whisky so that they might relax a little, get some sleep, so now the crew of *Stompin' Suzie Too* were apprehensive but excited, as well. They were going to hit Berlin, right in the centre of Germany, instead of the Ruhr where all the factories were, or cities nearer at hand.

It was Fenn's twenty-fifth mission, and he, like everyone else, had been briefed for Berlin before, but adverse weather conditions had always made the planners draw back at the last minute. This time, however, it was for real. In the time they had been stationed in East Anglia they had faced so much, counted their blessings, limped home on a wing and a prayer, seen others die, some horribly. Fenn, and most of his crew, were battle-weary, prone to the shakes after ten hours in the air, but on the other hand they were hard-bitten and experienced, and they knew that they reacted not as eight separate people but as one when the chips were down.

Not that team spirit could save them if the tracer – or the flak, or the ground-fire – had their number on it, but being an experienced fighting force helped. When things went wrong it had become almost force of habit to put them right. You knew how to deal with a kinked pipeline to your oxygen supply because you'd dealt with it before, you were careful with your electric suit so that you didn't get it wet. A wise man carried a bottle for emergencies, not that it was easy, peeing in a bottle when you were four miles above the earth, with the countryside like a miniature relief map below you and the enemy attacking from every angle, but it could be done. They had had several crew members injured, too. An engineer in the top turret had been shot through the palm of the hand, a tail gunner had lost fingers from frost-bite, Fenn's first co-pilot had been killed by a bullet ricocheting around the cockpit and going in through his temple. He had taken off his steel helmet because it got in the way of his oxygen mask; now Fenn and Will, his present co-pilot, wore their steel helmets at all times regardless of any minor inconveniences.

Stompin' Suzie Too soldiered on, too, as her crew did. Best ship in the fleet, the men enthused, lovingly patting the picture, on the nose, of a curvaceous brunette in cowboy boots and little else. *Suzie Too* had been holed just about everywhere but somehow her ground-crew always found the parts she needed and managed to patch her up. And right now, because of the importance of the mission, everything had to be just right. *Suzie* stood on the hardstanding, bombed up, fully fuelled, as ready as she ever would be for what lay ahead, whilst occasional snow-showers tore across the runways and the crews hunched down into their layers of cold-weather clothing.

'Checks first,' Fenn said to Will as soon as they reached the hardstanding. Will nodded grimly. They trusted their ground-crew but even so the most rigorous checks were carried out before every mission. Pilots who let mistakes go didn't last long.

Having satisfied themselves that all was as it should be outside, the pilots climbed through the nose hatch to do the cockpit checklist whilst Bob Ennis checked the bomb-load, the gunners mounted their machine guns and checked the ammunition and Krantz, the navigator, tried to get his mass of maps and charts under control.

Fenn sighed and stretched, peering through the glass; it was still dark though it was almost seven o'clock and the weather showed no signs of improving; even as he watched another gust of snow tapped against the windscreen.

'Do you reckon this is one more false start, Will?' he said amiably, his eyes checking, always checking. 'Weather looks bleedin' awful, as them Londoners say.'

'The meteorology guy said the weather 'ud improve,' Will said doubtfully. 'Aw, let's act as if we believed him. All checks completed? Warm her up, then.'

Take-off was signalled by a green flare from the control tower. All too soon, Fenn thought, *Suzie* had lumbered into the air, fooling them, as she always did, by her reluctance to rise much above the treetops until suddenly, as though she had seized the bit between her teeth and decided the mission was worthwhile after all, she began her determined climb towards the clouds.

Over the North Sea they test-fired the guns; each gunner was checked out over the interphone to make sure that his gun was not jamming. The mighty airplanes continued on their way, the biggest fleet ever, Fenn was sure. He thought wistfully of Lizzie and Sybil, waking perhaps to hear the booming thrum overhead, knowing that the great raid had started, the one they were all hoping would end the bloody slaughter of daylight bombing.

'Well, who's for a little poker?' one of the waist-gunners said into his interphone. 'Gee, what with the sheer excitement of it, how'll we ever manage without a mission a day?'

Laughter, but subdued, greeted this. Everyone hated the boredom – until it vanished in the battle, then they longed for it to come back. Fenn thought about it; boredom, cold, your frightened thoughts chasing around in your head, then the flak, the tracer, the heat of battle, the cry 'Bombs away!' and the euphoria, which never lasted, as you turned to head for Britain and your airfield. After that, the Nazi fighter planes, diving, chasing, trying to knock you out of formation so that they could come down and finish you off. Friends who'd jeered and horsed around with you at dawn were dead before noon, others injured, some taken by the enemy. Oh, God, let the boredom last, he prayed as the foul weather showed no signs of breaking. Let's turn back, why not? God knows we'll not see the target on a day like this!

There were recall signals, but they lacked a vital ingredient; Krantz waited for the lead ship to confirm them and waited in vain.

'Enemy intelligence is sure good when they've got our call-sign, though not our greeting,' he remarked into the interphone. 'We're gonna keep on goin', then?'

'Yup. Unless someone tells us different,' Fenn said. His legs were shaking from the effort of flying the heavy plane; he gestured to Will to take over whilst he had a rest and closed his eyes for a few seconds. He heard radio silence being broken by various comments on the recall signals but his group kept on so *Suzie* would follow suit.

'Hey-hey! Me-109s attacking . . . Ginger's gone! My God, there are hundreds of them. Pity the cloud's still too thick, though it's thinning . . .'

They were approaching their target, the force having thinned considerably after the mysterious recall signals. The kraut fighter planes seemed to appear from nowhere, as they always did, and whilst the gunners trained their guns on the new targets flak began to burst below them. Immediately the interphone became noisy as information about the enemy fighters was passed from 'plane to 'plane.

'Fighters at twelve o'clock high – watch your tail, Wally, there's a fighter . . . my God, that was *flak*, he's been blown sky-high by his own flak . . . fighters at three o'clock low, they're comin' right on through, tryin' to break our formation . . . hey-hey, hold your fire, them's our "little friends" comin' right on the 109s' tails . . . hold your fire, fellers!'

'It's sticky,' Fenn bawled, as the small formation drew closer to fill in the gap left by another airplane plunging down into the cloud below. 'Did anyone see the guys leave *Fightin' Filly*?'

'Yeah,' drawled Nipper, the tail-gunner. 'Some of 'em got out. Thank God for our little friends, eh, fellers?'

'They're great,' Fenn said fervently, squinting out at the blissful sight of P-51 Mustang fighters diving fearlessly through the tight formation the Liberators were forced to keep. 'That'll take the heat off us for a bit – Jesus, those guys can fly!'

'Sure can. You ready, Ennis? Soon's you can see something, drop 'em!'

A flak shell burst too near the ship and she rocked with the force of it, one wing dropping. Cannon fire ripped through the fuselage but missed the crew, though only by inches. Me-109s plunged past, guns spitting viciously. Fenn kept her steady, kept her in formation, tried not to watch as another B-24 began to slip downwards, smoke and flames streaming from her port wing and fuselage.

But below them, the cloud was thinning, disappearing; and in the clear March sunshine they could see, as though it was a relief map of the city especially supplied for their benefit, Berlin. Hitler's capital city, the spot he believed inviolable, too well defended to be hit by enemy bombers, too far away for them to reach it.

Fenn had never been to Europe, only knew Berlin from books and briefings, but he could clearly see the great road Hitler had built so that his armies could march in triumph through the city – the East-West Axis – and he could pick out the Brandenburg Gate and the Unter den Linden. But clearer than that were the flak bursts, the enemy fighters swooping again and again as the great 'planes droned over the target.

'Bombs away!'

A joyful cry, a marvellous moment, and then the shout they had heard a score of times but never failed to enjoy as the whole of the great formation began to turn.

'C'mon, let's get the hell outa here!'

Home! Going home!

Not Norwich this time, not the liberty truck, Fenn vowed to his trembling legs, his tense and terrified body, his mind which, he knew, would try to trick him into remembering the horrors he had seen today as soon as he relaxed. No, he would go not to the city but the countryside. This was his twenty-fifth mission, which meant a much-needed break from the fight. He would go to Pakeby, to the end cottage on Beach Road, where he was sure of a warm welcome, and tell them that he needed a quiet break for a few days and yes, thanks, Dora, the sofa will be just grand. Pretty Lizzie could soothe him with talk of her work, Chris could tell him all about whatever it was landgirls did in snowy March. And with Sybil he would at last begin to relax. He would sit beside her and watch her gentle, animated face with the expression of patience hard-won engraved upon it and talk gently, of happy things and happier times.

After twenty-five missions a guy could go back Stateside and no one would blame him – it was his right. Even if he stayed here, and he knew he would because this was his war on two fronts, the British and the American, he would be entitled to a long leave, to catch up with ordinary life, to get over the battle fatigue which meant that sometimes he laughed too loudly, drank too deeply, and shook like a leaf when he thought about the next mission – and the next, and the next.

They were over the North Sea, almost home, when the JU-88 fighter roared out of the cloud and *Stompin' Suzie Too*'s left outer engine was hit. Fenn watched the prop slow and then begin to idle as the engine lost all power. But you could get home with an engine out, provided you took the proper precautions. Then as they crossed the English coast a solitary fighter sprayed them with cannon fire and the tail-gunner's shouted commentary ended in a gurgle and repeated calls through the interphone failed to raise him. Fenn felt sick; Nipper was closer to him than any other member of the crew, for he reminded Fenn of Sammy, who had been like a brother to him. But there was nothing he could do save fly the 'plane. And presently he saw smoke pouring from the left inner engine and knew they would have to get down fast.

Fenn and Will fought to keep her going, fought to remain in the air; and succeeded, more or less. They were way off course when they saw from the fuel gauge that time was running out for them – but they could scarcely miss the airfields, spread out over the flat fields below them. It would mean an emergency landing, though. Fenn drew near the likeliest strip – it belonged to the Royal Air Force and was built for fighters – and began to try to contact the tower. If they didn't get down here it would mean ditching, not a procedure he wished to contemplate.

He gave their call-sign and heard, crackling through his earphones, the tower below respond.

Sybil was woken by the thrum of the big bombers going off on yet another daylight raid. She wondered if it was Fenn up there and felt she could almost see his Liberator, so many times had he described it to her. She had yet to meet his crew, but this would be – if it *was* Fenn up there – his twenty-fifth mission. Most of the crew had flown twenty-four, like Fenn, so after the next raid there would be a long leave for them, and she was sure that Fenn would bring the guys over to meet the Cream family then.

She had never asked Fenn about other girls, but that did not mean she did not occasionally wonder. After all, when she had asked him if he was Lizzie's Yank he had not exactly denied it, though whatever might have existed between them was clearly well and truly over. He and Lizzie were simply not on close terms, though they chatted politely enough when they were in the cottage at the same time. Indeed, Sybil had heard all about Fenn's mythical family from Lizzie and Chris, but she had never told either of them that it was all Fenn's imagination. If it gave him some sort of security to tell all these tall stories then who was she to dissuade him or, worse, to give him the lie? Besides, the stories hurt no one except, in an odd sort of way, Fenn himself. Because he was denying his own background, his own parents, every time he launched into yet another epic about the Kitson family.

He told Sybil the stories too, but always as stories, never as fact, and Sybil had to endure being told by Chris what a coincidence it was that Daddy Kitson was an attorney like Mr Winterton, and had a country house like Malverns, though the Kitsons' country home was a cattle ranch where Fenn played tennis beneath the palm trees and swam in the big, blue-tiled pool. That was what Fenn wanted when the war was over – his cattle ranch where he could sell his wheat and cattle by flying from the remote hills in the blue grass country where the place was situated straight down to the big centres, Chicago, New York, Washington. His father had insisted that he learn to fly long before the war, because it was so useful to a businessman such as himself. And when Chris wasn't talking about the ranch Lizzie was enthusing about the car Fenn's father had bought him, longer than the Creams' whole house and *coloured*, either bright blue with silver trimmings or bright orange with grey trimmings, she could not quite remember which owing to Fenn's having described the cars of the whole family to her at one time or another.

And Sybil had to admit that Fenn's imaginary life was fascinating. His grandparents on his mother's side lived in the deep South, and had a plantation and grew cotton just as they did in the films. His grandmother was a wonderful old lady, imperious, cultured. She wore her hair the old-fashioned way, piled up on her head. Granddaddy had sideburns, white ones, and a thick white moustache. He drawled and pronounced the word 'yes' as though it had three syllables – Fenn demonstrated, *yeh-ah-ess* – and gave Fenn a silver dollar to hang around his neck on a thin chain and told him marvellous stories. Then there were the blacks – slaves no longer yet still so deeply attached to the Masa that they might just as well have been. And the aunts and uncles, some married but most single, all working on the plantation, all of them adoring Fenn, the only grandson, though he had pretty cousins in plenty, all with names like Aimee and Desiree.

That was the Curzons, his mother's family. His father's parents were different. More modern, more in tune with the sort of life Fenn lived. This grandmother was smart and handsome, a famous hostess who had brought up her son to believe that justice must not only be done but must be seen to be done. Grandma Kitson had been delighted when Fenn senior – for Fenn was named for his father and grandfather too – had taken to the law; it had made up for her husband's early demise. Killed when Fenn was only four in an accident whilst viewing Niagara Falls, Grandpa Kitson had been a judge and, as such, a highly honoured member of Boston society. And now Grandma Kitson ran her lovely old Boston mansion effortlessly, with the help of devoted servants including an English butler, and gave soirees for which invitations were zealously sought.

But that was Fenn for you; he was a natural storyteller, someone who could no more be tied by the truth than he could have said 'no' to a request for favour. And because she loved him, Sybil took the stories in her stride, though she did wonder, sometimes, what Fenn would do when he went home to the States – invent an English family every bit as rich, titled and delightful as the American one, she supposed.

She was lying on her back in the pre-dawn greyness listening to the aircraft taking their flight path to Europe but she could see nothing from her present lowly position – the window in the front room was only small – so she began to hitch herself further up the bed, feeling the little thrill of purpose which always came to her as her legs responded, however feebly, to her command. *Move me*, she told them, and they just had! But even hitched up she could not see the planes thundering overhead and she knew better than to try to get out of bed, let alone reach the window. A painful and ignominious tumble could put her back weeks, if not months.

Chris, in her small room under the eaves, could now be heard getting out of bed. Even without seeing her, Sybil knew how easily she did it, with what aplomb! She could see, in her mind's eye, Chris's long, sturdy legs sticking out of bed, her feet thumping to the floor, and then her friend would go over to the window to take a look at the morning. Sybil tried not to feel envy and succeeded more or less because at last she was beginning to get some response from her efforts, and presently she heard Chris padding downstairs, coming to fetch water for washing. She came straight into the front room, as she always did.

'Morning, Sybs! Horrible weather . . . there's snow and a beastly cold wind. What about the aircraft, though; that's a big raid.' Chris walked over to the window and peered upwards. 'Wonder if Fenn . . . ?'

'They've been going over for ages; I should think it must be just about every aircraft in East Anglia,' Sybil told her, pitching her voice to be heard above the noise of the engines. 'It's exciting, isn't it? Fenn says the crackling we sometimes hear is the gunners testing their cannon over the channel. I wonder if this is the big one, the one they've been waiting for?'

'If so, they'll probably have to turn back, like they did last time,' Chris observed, turning away from the window. 'Well, this snow is not the answer to a maiden's prayer. Here was I hoping that 'forty-four was going to be a better year, weatherwise, than 'forty-three. Not good for your first day either, old Sybil.'

Sybil gasped. She had actually forgotten that today she was to trundle down the road to the local school to help with slow readers. As Sybil knew, individual attention could work wonders, and Miss Payne, who took the fives to sevens, was very keen that she go in and give a hand.

'We need another teacher,' she had said earnestly. 'And you were always such a sensible girl, Sybil. Of course the headmaster can't offer you a paid position until the County Council have approved another appointment, but in the meantime, if you could just do a couple of hours a day . . .'

It may not have been a paid position but it was a chance to prove herself and Sybil intended to seize it with both hands. What was more, if she could stay the course – and she intended to do just that – it would prove to all and sundry that she was independent – and employable.

But fancy forgetting, she scolded herself as Chris nipped back to the kitchen. Good thing the 'planes woke me up, or I'd be late on my very first day and that would never do. It was a pity, though, that it was the day of the big raid, because she would have Fenn on her mind all morning. It was strange; she had accepted completely that she would never be the girl of Fenn's dreams, yet he still mattered to her more than anyone else on earth.

Chris filled her enamel jug at the sink and could soon be heard stumping up the stairs. Presently Dora popped her head round the door to ask if Sybil needed a hand and Sybil said ruefully that she would be very grateful, but she knew Dora would want to get Chris off before she began the considerable task of readying Sybil herself for the day ahead.

Dora said, 'See you in an hour, then,' and disappeared again and in due course Chris pushed the door open with a cup of tea in one hand. Sybil drank the cooling liquid and then faced up to her first task of the day – getting out of bed.

But not yet, it appeared. She knew better than to try without someone standing by because if she fell it made more work, so she was doubly glad when Chris popped in again with her own cup of tea and a bowl of steaming oatmeal.

'I'll have my grub with you,' she said cheerfully. 'Shove up!' She sat down on the bed, then looked guilt-stricken. 'Sorry, Sybs, am I on your legs?'

'God knows,' Sybil said, trying to sound airy and not bitter. 'A herd of elephants could be on my legs and I'd just go on drinking my tea and waiting for my breakfast. Those were Liberators going over when you got up, weren't they?'

'As if you didn't know! You've got so good on engine sounds that they ought to employ you to identify them,' Chris said cheerfully. 'Yes, of course they were Liberators. You worrying about Fenn?'

'No, why should I be? Well, yes, of course I am,' Sybil said all at once. 'He's a friend, isn't he? I mean, maybe he was Lizzie's friend more than ours at first, but he comes here a lot, and I don't see when he gets the time to see her, quite honestly. And I – I've grown fond of him. I hate the thought of any sort of harm coming to him.'

'Me, too. Oh, I'm not fond of him the way you are, but I like him enormously. He's a nice bloke. Oh, and that reminds me, Auntie Dora is bringing Paul back for tea. I'll come straight home tonight, because there isn't much point in hanging about at the farm in weather like this.'

'You like Paul,' Sybil stated. 'He likes you as well.'

'Oh, sure. He likes all of us. But that doesn't mean . . . it's so difficult for him, having so little independence.' Chris's cheeks were tinged with pink. She sighed. 'Oh Sybs, I *do* like him, but it's difficult. I'm sure you can see that.'

'Yes, I can. We're in the same boat, as I'm sure you know. I – I like Fenn.'

'And he likes you,' Chris said robustly. 'If you're worried about Ralph just remember he's probably meeting girls all the time and . . . well, he's my brother and I love him, but if you meet someone else I'm sure he'll understand. Gosh, look at the time and I'm still eating breakfast!'

'I'm beginning to realize that if I can feel the way I do about Fenn then Ralph may not mean as much to me as I thought,' Sybil admitted whilst Chris bolted her porridge with one eye fixed on her wristwatch. 'Ralph's most awfully nice, but – well, I don't think we'll end up engaged or anything like that.'

'Good,' Chris said. She scraped her spoon wincingly round her plate. 'Better to know where you stand. Oh, God, I'm always hungry. My hips are going to be like a carthorse's if I don't quit this job soon. We're drilling oats and barley today, if the weather will let us – aren't you the lucky one to be snug in a classroom?'

'Ye-es,' Sybil said. All of a sudden the great adventure was beginning to seem not quite such fun after all. Doubts which had plagued her the previous day raised their ugly heads. 'Oh, but Chris, what if they make fun of me – run off? What if they call names? Or chuck things, or fight each other, or . . .'

'You're no different from any other teacher; no teacher can hit back, they all have to rely on their personalities to keep the kids in order,' Chris said briskly. 'Go on, Sybs, you'll do fine. And anyway, I doubt Miss Payne will leave you alone on your first day.'

'No, perhaps not. What'll you do if it's too nasty to drill?'

'Clean out the shippon and mend fencing, probably,' Chris said.

'And eat spuds and meat pie for dinner and put more weight on my btm. Oh hell, I wish I had self-control over food.'

'You are not fat!' Sybil said, sitting up higher in the bed. 'For goodness sake, Chris, you really aren't fat at all! Give over and go and remind Mum that I'm starving to death in here!'

At ten o'clock Sybil was wheeled briskly out of the cottage and down the road. It was a familiar route and one which made Sybil feel young again – down Beach Road to Saxon Road, past the Carters' cottage, past Miss Denvers' place with its high flowering hedge, past the neat little house where the Bowers family lived, past what she and Lizzie had called the witch's house where the hedge grew so far across the pavement that one had to step into the street to avoid it. On to London Road, linger on the pavement's edge, cross when it was clear to do so, and there was the school – just the same, just the same! Dora, surely as nervous as she, kept talking brightly in a high voice. She was leaving Sybil at school and going straight on to St Luke's.

It was a cold day. Sybil did not go out much and she usually enjoyed the fresh chill of the wind on her face, but by the time she was wheeled into the school she was glad enough to be under a roof again. There were still snow-flurries and she saw, with dismay, that the puddles had cat-ice forming round the edges.

And things were different when you were in a wheelchair. Sybil had attended the school as a pupil and yet she had forgotten that the main school entrance meant climbing steps to reach playground level. Fortunately for her, Fred Carr, the school caretaker, had remembered. He was hovering when Sybil wheeled herself across the pavement and gestured to her to go through the double gates at the south end of the playground and then round the side of the building, where she went straight – and flat – into the main corridor. She wheeled in, and thanked him for his help as he turned into his room, just past the cloakrooms.

'You all right now, miss?' he said, lingering in the doorway.

'I'll be fine,' Sybil said. She had glanced up the stairs as she came in, thinking ruefully that the upper storey was now closed to her, enjoying the evocative smell of damp coats, rubber boots and disinfectant as she passed the cloakrooms, but now she wheeled herself past the assembly hall on the left and along to Room 4. Miss Payne came out to greet her, looking harassed.

'Oh, good, dear, you've arrived. Now we'll have a quiet minute or two whilst the children finish with assembly and then I'll take you along to meet Mr Parkinson, who'll tell you what your work schedule will be. Then I'll introduce you to your class . . . will you be able to manage them on your own for an hour, just until break-time? I'm afraid poor Mrs Eccles is away again – she's bronchitically inclined, you know.'

Sybil followed Miss Payne, a tall, spare woman in her mid-fifties with horn-rimmed spectacles and rather unconvincing grey curls, into the classroom, sniffing the school smell of chalk, dusters, floor polish and cooked cabbage appreciatively as she went. Odd how smells took you back better than any other *aide-mémoire*; just one whiff of the school smell and she was five again, a skinny, ugly little girl coming into the babies' class for the first time, half delighted, half terrified.

Miss Payne took her to see the headmaster after Sybil had taken off her coat and tidied herself.

'I hope you'll enjoy being with the children and we're most grateful for your help,' Mr Parkinson said. He was elderly, with a harassed expression – and no wonder, Sybil thought, considering the strain which was put upon teachers to manage large classes in difficult conditions during wartime. 'I intend to speak to the education authorities with a view to employing you full time, but we're still running on reduced numbers so it may take a little while. Now Miss Payne will explain where you'll be working and with which children and so on. We've kept you to the ground floor, of course, and haven't put you on the rota for cloakroom duties since you'd find it difficult to get your chair between the rows.'

'I just hope I'm useful,' Sybil said. 'It's been a few years since I stood before a class!'

'You'll manage,' Mr Parkinson said. He smiled; he had an engaging grin and very blue eyes and suddenly he looked a bit more like a colleague and a bit less like . . . well, like a headmaster, Sybil supposed. 'They're nice children, Miss Cream – good luck!'

And they were nice children. Sybil liked them from the first moment that Miss Payne led her into the classroom and she saw a dozen pairs of eyes swivel in her direction.

'Now, children . . . less noise, if you please!' Miss Payne said briskly, leading the way across to the teacher's dais. 'This is Miss Cream, come to help us out whilst Mrs Eccles is ill. Be good children and get on with your work. Miss Cream will come to you as soon as she is able to hear your reading.' She turned to Sybil. 'Will you be all right, dear? If you need anything, just rap on the wall or send a child into Miss Isaac's room. She's next door to you that side . . .' she gestured to the left-hand wall '. . . and Mrs Frewin is on that side.' She pointed to the right-hand wall. 'Now, children, what do you say?'

'Good morning, Miss Cream,' chorused a dozen young voices. A dozen assorted faces were turned towards her, a dozen pairs of eyes scanned her curiously. Many mouths hung open in a manner which boded ill for scholastic achievement, but you never knew; the best of us can look idiots at times, Sybil thought charitably, flicking her wheelchair neatly into line with the desk on the dais.

'Good morning, children. Thank you, Miss Payne.'

It was odd how it all came back, the friendly authority, the quick smile of dismissal directed towards a too-protective colleague. Miss Payne left the room and Sybil turned back to her pupils.

'Well now, we must introduce ourselves. I'm Miss Cream, you all know that, but I don't know any of you yet. Let's start with you.' She indicated a small boy with one of those mouse-nibbled haircuts which are usually the result of parental indifference. 'What's your name?'

The little boy stared and a burning scarlet blush rose from his grey neck to his forehead. The small girl sitting next to him turned a glance of kindly contempt on her neighbour, then addressed herself to Sybil.

'He's Graham Wallace, miss; he don't talk much. He think he's a car, doncher, Graham?'

Loud laughter from the rest of the class and a tiny smile from Graham.

'Graham Wallace. Right.' Sybil wrote the name down in her notebook, then turned an enquiring look on the small girl, who did not need prompting.

'I'm Tessa Fricks, miss. My mum know you, she help at St Luke's. And you was in school with my sister Annie. Do you 'member Annie Fricks, miss?'

'Yes, of course I do,' Sybil said, glad to have established a point of contact so early. 'Annie was blackboard monitor when I was milk monitor; she was awfully good at sums.'

The young Fricks nodded importantly.

'That's the one,' she said, as though there were a dozen or so Annie Frickses to choose from. 'She've done ever so well, miss. She've gone into the ATS as a cook. She do love that!'

'I'm very glad to hear it,' Sybil said temperately. From her hasty recollection, Annie Fricks had not only been blackboard monitor and a dab hand at sums, she had also been skilled at jumping rope and the first behind the bicycle shed when boys wanted to play dirty. There had been stories about Annie . . . but Tessa looked a bright kid and Annie had been bright enough, if you discounted . . .

She looked back at Tessa, who was blonde and blue-eyed and had just inserted her finger about an inch up her nose. Oh well, that was kids for you. She turned to the child at the next desk.

'Hello! What's your name?'

By lunch-time Sybil knew all her class by name and by tea-time they were standing out as individuals. Seven little boys with dirty knees and large muddy boots and five little girls with runny noses and spots. As she moved amongst them they became people, each one with their own hopes, dreams, aspirations.

Graham was indeed a car; in the playground he changed gear as he ran, revved his engine going uphill, screamed his brakes when cornering. Otherwise he was a silent child. Then there were Ron and Don, the twins. They had identical faces and enjoyed changing places so their mother, in a fit of pique brought on by bad behaviour, had shaved a highway down the middle of Don's curly crop and a sort of side-road round the back of Ron's head. It worked all right, provided you could remember that Don was highway and Ron was side-road which Sybil, at first, found difficult.

Then there were Freddy and David, inseparable pals, Freddy red-haired and belligerent, David meek and biddable save that he was possessed by a terrible urge to be as bad as Freddy. And there was Philip whose mother dressed him like Little Lord Fauntleroy but never did a thing about his nits, and Bert, who lifted the girls' skirts and pinched their pale bottoms.

The girls, despite the fact that there were fewer of them, would take longer to get to know, but going on what she managed to pick up there was Lottie, who had hair down to her knees, flirted desperately with any man but despised all small boys. Tessa was calm and competent, good with her fellow-girls and bossy with the boys. Sandra's dry brown hair was twisted into unlikely ringlets and she never knew she needed the lavatory until it was too late, which was why the teacher's desk contained two spare pairs of knickers. Elizabeth (Betty) was plump and easy-going and chewed gum whilst Elizabeth (Liza) was skinny and spiteful and fought with nails and teeth when the playground erupted into violence.

At the end of her first day Sybil ached in every limb, had a thumping headache – and knew she was going to be very happy in this school. She wished that the children in the class were hers and grudged them to Mrs Eccles, who seemed to be a lazy woman with none of the instinctive love of children so necessary in an infant teacher, but she would continue to work here until she was thrown out – or made permanent. Even the worry about Fenn and the big raid had been pushed to the back of her mind, especially as the roar of returning planes had been heard, on and off, throughout the late morning and early afternoon.

Raid aborted, Sybil thought with shamefaced satisfaction. Please God let Fenn be down safe!

Dora came to meet her, with Paul, who was coming to tea. Paul was a tall young man who had once been husky but his horrible experience in the engine room of his doomed destroyer had taken the flesh from him and now he was just tall and bony. He had wavy brown hair, a pleasant high cheekboned face which was puckered with scar-tissue, and sightless eyes which were hidden behind black glasses. Sybil, who had been wondering how on earth she would get home without help – for though she could propel herself about very well indoors she thought the unsurfaced shingle of Beach Road would prove an insurmountable obstacle – waved gladly and then felt guilty and went slowly across the playground, calling out as she went.

'Hello, Mum, Paul! How marvellous to see you. I was beginning to think I'd be stranded here for hours. Who's going to give me a push?'

'I would,' Paul said, 'but you'd probably land in a ditch,' but Dora told him firmly that she had no intention of pushing a wheelchair when she had a young man perfectly capable of doing it for her, so Paul pushed, Sybil guided, and they got back to the cottage in good order.

'What sort of a day was it?' Paul asked curiously as Dora helped Sybil off with her outer clothing and pushed the chair over to the stove. 'Did you do much teaching or did you watch?'

'I was rather thrown in at the deep end; I taught because Class Two's teacher is away,' Sybil confessed. 'I only had a dozen kids and they were lovely – I wish I could stay with them for a while. They were good, too. No cheek or silliness, but friendliness and a very real desire to learn.' She waited until Dora was busy with the fire, opening the front of it, poking the ash through vigorously, then propelled herself sneakily across the floor, intending to nip into the front room to have a look through the window.

'Nice that you enjoy it,' Paul said. 'Where are you off to?'

His hearing was acute; Sybil laughed.

'Blow you, Paul! I was trying to sneak a look down the road without drawing Mum's attention. It's getting dark; Chris should be home soon.'

'You're worried about that Yank,' Paul said. 'Don't worry. There were too many aircraft going over for me to count them in and back, but most of them seem to have aborted. Didn't you hear them humming over just before noon?'

'It's the uncertainty,' Sybil said. 'It's not that I worry about him, exactly, but he's a good friend and I can't bear to think . . . well, when Chris gets back I'll see if she's heard anything. The Franklyn place is very near Flacton and there's always someone who knows something hovering around. Mrs Franklyn does the washing for some of the lads, so she's quite clued up.'

Dora had riddled the fire and now the flames were roaring up the chimney. She straightened and put a hand to her back, then smiled across at Sybil.

'Fenn's thoughtful; he'll either bike round when they've debriefed or send a message. Just settle down, love, and you shall have a nice cup of tea and a sandwich. What was your school dinner like?'

'Nice. They don't cook at the school any more, though, the dinners come in big sealed containers from a central kitchen somewhere. Not like your cooking, exactly, but still pretty good. The kids love it even when it's spam, or sawdust sausages, and they get their share of them, Miss Payne says.'

Paul, who had been gazing sightlessly in front of him with his hands lying idle in his lap, suddenly smiled. The smile lit his face, made him look young again, so that you forgot not only the puckered purple tissue which was slowly mending but the strain on the face scarred not only by fire but also by experience. He cocked his head.

'She's just coming down Beach Road,' he said. 'I can hear the crunch of the bike tyres on the shingle.'

'How do you know it isn't someone else?' Dora teased. 'It might be anyone!'

Presently Chris could be heard outside, pushing her bicycle into the shed and whistling tunelessly. She seemed to be taking her time tonight, Sybil thought restlessly, wondering why her friend did not immediately erupt into the kitchen to demand how her first day's work had gone.

Paul got to his feet and seconds later Chris came into the room.

'Hello, Paul, everyone,' she said. She looked tired and uneasy, Sybil thought. 'How nice, tea on the go already.'

'Chris, have you heard what happened to the big raid? You've not seen Fenn, I suppose?'

'No, I've not seen him. I understand the raid was aborted, or at least an awful lot of planes came back early.'

'Yes, we heard them. You can't wash in here tonight, Chris, since Paul's here . . .'

'Yes she can,' Paul said quietly. 'I've heard you can be struck blind for peeping, but you can't peep when you're already blind.'

Dora gave a tiny gasp which was overridden by Chris.

'There you are, Paul, it's impossible to think of you as blind because you don't give that impression. So I shall now clean up.'

Singing under her breath she began to wash and presently Sybil wheeled herself over to the sink and spoke to her above the splash of water and Chris's determined song.

'Chris. Do you think they're all back?'

Chris turned from the sink and put a soapy hand on Sybil's.

'No, love, they aren't. One squadron went on, and Fenn and *Stompin' Suzie Too* were with them. It was a long raid, and those who didn't abort came back awfully late. I asked about *Suzie*, of course, as soon as I saw someone from the airfield, but all he could tell me was that they were straggling home slowly.'

Even as she spoke an aircraft came in from the sea, flying low, the engine note uncertain and faltering. They listened, speechless, until the sound had faded into the distance, then Sybil exhaled softly and spoke.

'I wonder what went wrong? I wish we knew a bit more! I do wish I could get up to the post office to telephone. It – it was his twenty-fifth mission, Chris. They can go home after the twenty-fifth if they like. Oh, Chris, I do wish we knew what was happening.'

'That's war,' Paul said quietly when Chris did not reply immediately. 'That's war, Sybs. It's mostly about waiting and being bored whether you're on a destroyer or in an aircraft or sitting at home worried out of your mind. But if Fenn's been on the big raid everyone's been talking about . . . what was it Churchill said? Something about this not being the end, nor the beginning of the end, but perhaps the end of the beginning? I think, if they've reached Berlin, that it really will be the beginning, at last, of the end.'

22

It took Fenn and his crew a whole day to get back from Debden, where they had landed, to Flacton, and then there was the debriefing, the explanations, the promises that *Stompin' Suzie Too* would be brought down to Flacton, injured though she was, and taken back into active service as well if such a thing were possible. If not, *Stompin' Suzie Three* would be born.

None of the others cared much, but Fenn was still struggling to come to a decision. He could go back to the good old US of A and return to his old life as a garage mechanic, or he could stay on in the USAAF and fly more missions and hope he didn't either get killed or get the shakes for good. What he could not do was remain in Britain as a non-combatant.

You were running an enormous statistical risk the more missions you flew, of course. But Fenn was no great believer in statistics. And it was his war in a way others might find difficult to understand.

He talked to his crew about it.

Will, his co-pilot, had only done eleven missions, so the two of them might stay together if Fenn decided to remain in Britain. Poor Nipper was dead, shot with a dozen bullets as he crouched over his gun in the tail of the airplane. The waist-gunners, Evan and Lou, would be off back to the States with twenty-five missions each to their credit. Bob Ennis, the best bombardier in the squadron it was rumoured, would be staying since he had already passed his twenty-fifth. And Krantz, who found the way to and from their targets, was in two minds. Now that they had reached Berlin and handed out punishment to the city which Hitler valued above all – and believed to be invincible from the air – most of the guys believed the war was nearing the finish. But . . . it was such a mean, cold, cruel, uncomfortable business! And Fenn felt that with *Suzie Too* being shot from under them, so to speak, their luck might have begun to ebb at last.

Nipper's death had shaken Fenn to the core, that was the truth. Right from the moment that the young, ugly, cheerful tail-gunner had walked into Fenn's life, his resemblance, both physical and mental, to Sammy had meant that Fenn had found him easier to get along with than any other member of the crew. Nipper's habit of prefacing every remark with 'Hey-hey!' had made him instantly identifiable over the interphone and his cheerful attitude, his jokes and stream of light-hearted chatter had convinced Fenn that whilst Nipper was catching the enemy in the deadly fire from his cannon they were all of them fine and dandy.

But Nipper was dead, *Suzie* a wreck who might never fly again . . . and Fenn was scared that his luck might suddenly desert him.

That night, tucked up in a strange bed in a strange hut with English airmen all round him and a cold wind howling under the door, Fenn thought about it. He would have a long leave, which meant he could relax, visit Manchester, spend time with the Creams. Then it would be back to the noisy, terrifying business of daylight bombing raids on Germany. Once again he would take his life in his hands – and not only his life, but the lives of seven other guys – and never know, from one hour to the next, when he might breathe his last.

He was struggling with his problem and knowing, in his heart, that it was no contest, that he would stick to Flacton until the war ended and he was at liberty to please himself, knowing that both his countries were safe, when he found he was thinking the stupidest, most inappropriate thought of all. *I must let Sybil know I'm okay first thing*, his thoughts ran. *I wish she wasn't a cripple.*

What the hell? What *difference* did it make, for goshsakes, when you remembered that he wanted a rich wife, a *useful* wife? It wasn't even as if he was in love with the girl, who had a boyfriend anyway, for how could you be in love with a girl who couldn't – well, who couldn't do it? I'm a red-blooded guy and I want a normal girl, Fenn reminded himself. And a rich one, to boot. There's no way I could even think of taking on a cripple.

Odd, though, the way the human mind works. I must be more tired than I thought, I'm actually thinkin' slow and stupid, Fenn told himself. This bed is harder than the Creams' sofa – wish I was on the Creams' sofa right now. Relaxing, he imagined waking up in the morning to find Dora at the stove, getting the kettle on for an early cup of tea, himself one of the family, accepted, made much of, knowing that presently Sybil would wheel herself in and they would begin the casual, easy chat which he found so reassuring.

Gee, but I wish she wasn't a cripple was his last coherent thought before he fell asleep.

Sybil knew she was at least a little in love with Fenn on the day the Liberators launched that first daylight raid on Berlin. By the next morning, she knew she loved him deeply, helplessly, would love him for the rest of her life no matter that he would live out his existence three thousand miles from her, probably with another woman beside him.

She had behaved well enough whilst the family were there. Everyone else was worried about Fenn because they all liked him, but not in the way she did, she realized. Dora had Henry and Paul, Chris had her family – and Paul, because it was plain as the nose on your face that Chris was getting extremely fond of Paul and that her feelings were reciprocated – but though Sybil had her family, she wanted no one else beside Fenn. Just Fenn, alive somewhere, so that she could say to herself as she struggled with her class, or with her walking, 'Fennimore Kitzmann is grinning at someone at this very moment; now he's scratching his nose. Now he's winking at a child; now he's telling incredibly tall stories about how he won the war.'

A world in which Fenn did not exist did not seem to be a world worth tuppence to Sybil. That night she lay on her firm mattress in the dark of the front room and prayed for a long while and then, regrettably, she threatened. If he doesn't come back I shan't try to get better, because what's the point? If he doesn't come back I'll never go to church again, and I'll certainly not sign petitions to get the real church rebuilt. Think about that, You up there, and see whether it isn't worth bending the rules a bit and letting Fenn come through despite the fact that this is his twenty-fifth mission!

By morning she ached all over and felt as bad as she had months ago, when she had first come out of hospital. She greeted Dora listlessly and her mother was horrified at the dark circles round her eyes, the pallor of her cheeks.

'You just stay right there,' Dora said roundly when Sybil tried to struggle into a sitting position. 'You're ill – I'm going to send for Dr Lewis straight away.'

'It's all right,' Sybil had said wearily. 'I've just had a bad night, that's all. I'll be right as rain once I've had some rest. I've got to go in to school, Mum, or I'll lose any chance of getting a permanent post there.'

Dora knew she was right, of course, and wheeled her off at

eight-thirty, though she said she would return at dinner-time just to make sure that Sybil wasn't sickening for something.

Sybil worked hard with the children that morning to get her mind off things, as she phrased it to herself. And to an extent it worked; she only thought about Fenn twice a minute instead of constantly. And she learned to hide her feelings; the children had griefs and worries of their own, as did every soul in school, she supposed. The least she could do was to keep her worries to herself.

Dora and Paul called for her when school finished and Paul pushed her chair home as he had the previous day. It's probably good for us both, Sybil reflected, steering desperately, for Paul, with new self-confidence, began to pick up speed the moment his hands found the grips.

The knock came on the back door when they were all sitting down to tea; Sybil half rose from her chair, her heart beating a wild tattoo against her breastbone. Was it? Oh it must be, it must be!

It was. Fenn stood there, a little uncertain, his grin at half-cock.

'Thought I'd jest drop by . . .'

'Oh, Fenn!' Sybil exclaimed. 'I had a sleepless night worrying over you – how good it is to see your ugly mug again!'

Being rude made it easier to speak to him without giving herself away and he came across the room in a couple of strides to pick her up out of her chair, half hugging, half shaking her.

'Thank you very much, little Miss Gorgeous! How'd you like a good spanking?'

'Where've you *been*?' Sybil demanded. She clutched him hard, trying to shake him back – anything to hide the depth and strength of her feeling for him. 'You usually come over or send a message when you've been debriefed . . . what went wrong?'

'*Suzie Too* did,' Fenn admitted gloomily. 'We was way off course, shot into holes . . . had to land on a Royal Air Force fighter field down in Essex miles from here. It took a while to get back. Gee, Sybs, I'm real sorry if I've give you a bad time, but there warn't no way to get in touch, see? They put us in a jeep and brought us back to Flacton, and then we had to go through the mill again.'

'Anyone hurt?' Sybil asked. But her relief and pleasure at seeing him were such that the question sounded wrong, uncaring. She heard it and hastily added: 'Did you get *Suzie* down without too much damage?'

'She's a wreck, just about,' Fenn said. 'My tail-gunner was killed. Nipper.'

'Oh, Fenn!'

Sybil knew how he valued his crew, understood their closeness, knew that Nipper, especially, was dear to him. He'd called him a Bowery boy, whatever that might mean, said he was a tough little cookie, four foot tall with a heart as big as a barn. Nipper had been the youngest crew member at just twenty, and now he was dead.

'Yeah. Poor old Nipper. Only consolation, he never knew nothin'. Reckon if I had to choose . . .'

'Don't, Fenn!' Sybil's voice was too sharp; she saw her mother's eyes turn consideringly on to her and hastily continued. 'Have you written to his people?'

'I wrote his mom. It's the part I hate most, when –' Abruptly he looked round the table. Paul's head was slightly cocked the way it always was when he was trying to picture the scene, letting the tone of a voice convey not only the words but also the emotions which one strove to hide. And Fenn realized that Dora's face was sympathetic, Chris's too, but Sybil's mirrored his own pain, and there was something else in her expression which he did not want to see – did not want anyone else to see either, he realized. Hastily he turned his most melting smile on his hostess.

'Any chance of some tea, Dora? I could drink a well dry.'

Later, he took Sybil for a walk around the roads of Pakeby because he had to talk to someone and knew she suited him best. Chris and Paul, huddled over the wireless because the batteries were running down, were listening avidly to ITMA, and Dora, also listening, was knitting. It was dark outside and Fenn had come over on his bicycle with its faint front light, which meant that on the way back he would have to dismount and take to the ditch whenever a car came by. Not that many would, not on a cold evening in March with snow-flurries still what you might call an occupational hazard.

Normally Dora would have told them that it was no night for a walk, but not tonight. She was a sensitive woman and though she glanced uneasily up at Fenn and then across at Sybil, she merely told them to wrap up well and keep it short.

'Sybil mustn't catch cold; she's teaching whilst Mrs Eccles is away,' she said rather reproachfully, and Fenn realized he had not asked Sybil how she had got on and felt ashamed.

'We'll go round the block, that's all,' he said reassuringly. 'I'll walk briskly and the motion will keep Sybs warm. Or . . . do you think I'd best go alone?'

But Sybil would not hear of it.

'I need a breath of air myself,' she said firmly. 'Get my coat, Fenn, there's a dear.'

Outside, in the windy dark, Sybil discovered that it was not too bad a night after all. The snow-flurries seemed to have ceased and it was dry and not nearly as cold as it had been earlier. She sat in her wheelchair as Fenn pushed her up Beach Road, left into Florence Road, left again into Nightingale Road and up Cliftonville Road until they reached the main London Road. They could not really talk properly, not with one ahead, so to speak, and the other behind, pushing, but there was an old wooden shed on the other side of the road and Sybil guessed they were heading for it.

They were. Fenn pushed her into its shelter and then squatted down beside the chair. He leaned against it, still saying nothing, his curly head bent so that Sybil could not see his face. She put her arm round his broad shoulders, or as far round them as she could get.

'Fenn? Oh, I'm so sorry about Nipper.'

'He was the best,' Fenn said. His voice sounded rough, almost hoarse. 'He couldn't've known a thing . . . Sybs, he was smiling, I swear he was.'

'I'm sure he didn't know what happened,' Sybil said gently. 'Everyone else was all right, weren't they? Not hurt at all?'

'Oh, bruised and cut, I guess, but not hurt,' Fenn said drearily. 'Say, did I ever tell you . . .'

The story was one she had heard before but she would not have said so for the world. She listened, chuckled, put a hand down and stroked Fenn's cheek – and felt the wet of tears. He caught her hand, pressed it hard against his face for a moment, and then turned and buried his head in her lap. She knew he was crying and she could have wept for him – did weep for him – yet at the same time her heart almost burst with pride. He trusted her with his most secret emotions. A young man could not weep in front of his buddies, but he had to have someone he could trust – and Fenn trusted her, Sybil Cream, cripple. She stroked his curls almost shyly and then bent until her face rested on his head and cuddled him fiercely.

'That's right, Fenn; let your grief out, don't keep it bottled up. He was a good guy, he was your friend. You *should* cry for him.'

There was no sound from Fenn, but Sybil felt the hot tears soak into the thin grey gabardine of her skirt.

And then, abruptly, he was himself again. He sat up.

'Sorry, honey,' he said, and his voice was Fenn's ordinary voice;

quiet, deep, pleasant. 'There was only Nipper . . . he was like me, from the Bronx, a fighter. I never told him about my family.'

Sybil chuckled.

'Which family? Grandpa with the white whiskers, or . . .'

Fenn grinned; even in the dark she could see his white teeth flash. He put his hand over hers and shook it slightly.

'Don't git uppity, gal! Yeah, *that* family. Everyone else knows my family, but Nipper, he knew where I was really from; the only one.'

'What about me? I know where you're from and everything.'

'Oh, yeah, but you're . . .'

She was sure he had bitten back the words 'a cripple', and felt the hurt like a knife in her heart. He had told her once that he had never known a day's illness in his life, had always been strong and healthy, but must this mean he could never look on her as a normal girl, never see her as anything but different? Must she conclude, then, that he had told her about his real family not from love or friendship but simply because, as a cripple, she did not matter, was not important?

He sensed her withdrawal but did not understand it. He stood up, stretched, took hold of the wheelchair once more.

'Sorry about that. You're a pal, Sybil, the best. Like Nipper. I'll take you home now, so you can get warm before bed-time.'

Fenn wheeled her home without saying much more. It was true that Nipper's death had hurt him deeply, affected him more than any of the other deaths had done. But even so, he should not have let go the way he had, sobbing with his head in the kid's lap and all, like . . . well, like a child of five. He knew the strain of war was beginning to tell on him, that he was letting it get to him, but a few weeks' leave would put that right. Give him a chance to get himself together, get a new airplane, and he would face it all without a qualm, the noise, the danger, the terror that any second a spray of machine gun fire would catch you and that would be that. Finish. Kaput. Finito.

He had nearly given himself away, what was more. He had nearly said, 'But you're all right. You've got your feller. With Nipper gone, I've got no one.' But he had thought better of it, because that made it sound as though he grudged her her feller and he had no such unworthy feeling. He was glad she had a guy who valued her, because when a girl was crippled most guys would think her something of a liability. He knew he couldn't have coped with her, even if she had been free . . . but she was a great gal, one of the best. Someone who drew the truth out of him because she was so truthful herself. Like

Nipper, she appreciated the stories, enjoyed the characters he had brought to life, but was never for one moment taken in. She deserved the truth, as Nipper had.

They reached the cottage, went round the side, and Fenn opened the back door and wheeled Sybil in. She looked very white and strained and he felt a pang of pure compunction. It was too bad of him; he had taken her out, piled all his troubles and grief on her head and as a result felt very much better himself. But she looked so worn and vulnerable . . . he was a selfish swine, that's what he was!

But Dora dealt with them all. She took Sybil off to bed whilst Chris made hot drinks, then came back and asked Fenn, nicely but firmly, to walk Paul back to St Luke's whilst she coped with her daughter.

'Did I overtire her?' Fenn said humbly, and Dora said yes, she rather thought he had, but not to worry since Sybil would be fine after a good night's rest, and did Fenn want to come back and sleep on the sofa or was he expected back at the airfield tonight?

Fenn had intended to stay but something in Dora's face decided him to return to the base. He accordingly said his goodnights, thanked Dora for the meal and helped Paul into his coat. Walking back to the hospital, he said rather plaintively to his companion, to whom the dark was no darker than the brightest day, 'I upset Sybs, I guess. Dora was real annoyed with me, I could tell.'

'Yes, she was,' Paul agreed, not mincing matters. He was shrewd, Fenn knew, because he was having to judge emotions from voices alone, so since Fenn had seen annoyance in Dora's face and Paul had heard it in her voice . . .

'But I can't think what I said – it weren't nothin' I did, that's for sure. Unless . . .'

'Unless what?' Paul said quietly. The two young men had got to know each other well just from occasional meetings at the cottage on Beach Road. Fenn sighed.

'Aw, I was upset about my tail-gunner, I guess. I mebbe put it on to Sybs.'

'That won't be it; Sybs would be glad you felt you could tell her. It's how any of 'em would feel. You like Sybs, don't you.'

It was a statement, not a question, but Fenn answered it anyway. 'Sure I do. It's a pity . . .'

He stopped short. Beside him, Paul gave a brief, hard sigh.

'That's right; it's a pity she's a cripple, same as it's a pity I'm blind and just about bloody useless. You want to remember, Fenn, that Sybil's a girl first and crippled – not *a cripple*, crippled – second. I'm

367

learning, as she must, that pity isn't an emotion which does anyone much good. And you shouldn't take it for granted that she'll go on being crippled, incidentally. Chris was reading a medical book about infantile paralysis victims and it seems that if she was fairly inactive when the disease first made itself felt then she has a good chance of learning to walk again. As luck would have it, she was on a train travelling up to Lincolnshire at the time, which is pretty inactive by Women's Land Army standards. So you see, she could be as good as the next person once she gets herself together and begins to work at it. Whereas I . . . well, I'll be blind until the day I die. Here we are, then . . . many thanks for bringing me back.'

Fenn had not noticed the gateway to St Luke's in the darkness; now he laughed and held on to Paul, who would have pulled himself free to go indoors.

'Hang on a minute! For a blind man you find your way pretty good – better than this sighted guy, because I damn near missed the gate. Look, Paul, are you serious? Is it really possible that Sybs might walk again?'

'I'm deadly serious. She's got great courage and with her family and friends behind her, I think she'll walk. But these things take time, and she's impatient, wants to be toddling off down the street tomorrow. Apparently she has to take things slowly or she really might mess up her chances – so Chris says, and she's looked into it.'

'Yeah. Chris is a good friend,' Fenn said absently. 'And of course her brother's Sybil's feller, ain't that so?'

'So I believe. Only . . .'

'Only what?'

'Well, hasn't it occurred to you that he doesn't visit much?'

'No, but he writes, though.'

'Oh, yes, he writes. You didn't mention the chap – Ralph – this evening, did you, Fenn? When you took Sybs walking, I mean?'

'Gee, no,' Fenn said, not needing to stop to think. 'I ain't never met the guy, I ain't liable to talk about him. Do you think he's going to throw Sybs over, then? Give her the go-by?'

'Probably not,' Paul said. 'She doesn't talk about him much, though, Fenn. In fact she talks about you a good deal more.'

'Hmm,' Fenn said. 'Well, thanks, Paul. Do you know, I feel a heap better? You're a great guy.'

They parted at the door of the hospital and Paul stomped off, a hand on the banister, to make his way back to his ward. Fenn watched him out of sight and then turned back into the darkness. Wasn't it the

368

durndest thing that a blind man could see so clearly what he, Fenn, had totally failed to see? That Sybil hated being unable to walk and simply wanted to be treated as normal? Also, that she liked him. Oh, she wasn't *in love* with him or any nonsense of that sort, she had her regular guy, but she liked him a lot.

And I like her, Fenn told himself buoyantly, striding out down the road once more. I like her very much. Tell you what, Fenn, that Paul's a good guy and he thinks the kid could walk. Well, now, just you say to yourself you'll damn well *teach* her to walk and before you know it the war will be over and . . . and you can start looking for that rich and useful wife!

'It's a flying visit,' Ralph said cheerfully, when Dora opened the kitchen door and let him in. 'Just wanted to see Sybs; we're either in the air or on standby almost constantly now, so I hardly seem to get time to answer her letters properly.'

Sybil, sitting in the wheelchair and peeling a big pan of potatoes, smiled across at him, but inside her mind was in a turmoil. She had known, of course, that the crunch would come, that one day she would have to tell Ralph that she'd fallen in love with someone else, but somehow she had always thought of it happening after the war, because Ralph wrote such short letters, and had not been to see her for – oh, ages. But here he was . . . she looked at the bright, handsome face and wondered honestly what she had ever seen in him. Pretty boy, Brylcreem boy, you just don't compare with my tough, square, black-browed lover, who isn't a lover at all but merely my good friend.

'I thought we could go for a spin; I managed to wangle some petrol,' Ralph said to her now. His eyes were darting all over the place. Poor old Ralph, I'm not the only one who's going to make a confession, Sybil thought with a flash of insight. He's dreading this interview; it's much worse for a fellow.

'I'd love a ride, but you'll have to carry me to the car,' Sybil said. Outside, she could see through the window how a sweet April breeze rustled the long grass in the churchyard and the sunshine gilded the stone arches, the great, blackened beams of the church itself. 'Do you mind if we go off, Mum, just for an hour or so? I don't often get the chance.'

Dora did not mind; how could she, when she must guess that Ralph wanted to talk to the girl he was supposed to be in love with, the girl of whom, Dora had made it clear, she thought him unworthy? So Ralph carried Sybil out and sat her gently in the front seat of the rather battered little sports car and the two of them drove sedately past the church and crunched along the Causeway and into Pakefield Street, then out on to London Road.

'We'll go to a quiet part of the Broad and watch the birds feeding their young and building their nests,' Ralph said. 'Because I think we should talk, Sybs, don't you?'

'Yes. We should. But why not as we drive along, Ralph? Why must we wait until we reach the Broad?'

'Oh, because. Shut up, Sybs, and enjoy the sunshine. God knows we haven't had all that much of it lately.'

They reached the Broad, Ralph parked, and then they turned towards each other. Sybil closed her eyes and spoke rapidly.

'Ralph. I've met someone else. I'm most awfully sorry. I don't fool myself that he loves me or anything like that, but I know I care for him. I should have told you before, but ... well, if I had it would have made it look as though I believed you were in love with me, that we were a couple ...'

'Well, we almost were,' Ralph said. He put his arm round her shoulders. 'Sybs, I'm the same, there's someone else. I wanted to tell you, but it seemed such a dirty trick, somehow. With you being ... being ill and that. Only she says I must, and I suppose she's right. Will everyone be awfully annoyed with me, do you suppose? Your family, I mean?'

Sybil giggled. It was so typical of Ralph, to want his freedom yet to want people to love him despite it!

'They won't mind, not once I tell them it was me as much as you who wanted to finish. They may think I'm mad – well, Lizzie may – but they'll understand. Even Chris ... we've talked about it and she knows I'm in love with someone else – she approves, dear Chris. Only ... Ralph, do we have to tell them? You see, my chap, if I can call him that, comes to see me and takes me out because he thinks I'm more or less engaged, and that makes him feel safe. I'd hate him to know you and I had split up, because then I'm sure he'd feel awkward about visiting so often. He'd feel ... he'd feel ...'

'Compromised,' Ralph said quietly. 'The way I did. Because you're not fit yet, Sybs. I do see what you mean, and I won't say a word. Not until you think it's okay. As a matter of fact, I'd prefer not to say anything either. My girl thinks it would be best to keep it under our hats for a while.'

'Then let's,' Sybil said eagerly. 'You see, it makes me feel more normal, to talk about life after the war as though it will contain a man, a marriage, a family. So if you don't mind, Ralph . . .'

Ralph did not mind, said it suited him, too. And presently they went into the village and had a cup of tea and some rather good cakes, and then Ralph drove her home and Dora looked at her doubtfully, then with love, and gave her a big hug.

And Sybil knew she would never regret parting with Ralph, because the relationship could never have succeeded. She had fancied herself in love with him because he had been the first boy to take any notice of her – since then she had met a man with whom she had found instant rapport, a man not a boy, whose ways exactly suited her.

But she would not tell Fenn that she and Ralph had split up. Just the opposite; she knew deeply, instinctively, that Fenn did not even consider her as a partner but only as a friend, and since she preferred his friendship to being without him altogether, she must learn to make do with that.

'Don't look down at your feet, look up at me! Up, up, up, Sybs! Atta girl, atta girl!'

Fenn and Sybil were on the beach, Fenn armed with his friend Nasty's box brownie. Sybil was posed against a beatster hut, wearing her best cotton dress and trying to look nonchalant, but due to the fact that she was determined to be photographed standing and not sitting in her chair she kept checking on her unreliable legs, hence Fenn's urgent shout.

'Hold it . . . ho-oold it!'

The camera clicked and Sybil's smile unfroze and became natural.

'Quick, chair!' she shouted, laughing, sliding. She sat on the sand with a bump and pulled a face as Fenn came unhurriedly from behind the hut wheeling her chair. 'Damn, now I'll have a sandy bottom and it'll be all tickly until bed-time!'

'I'll brush you down,' Fenn offered, but she just laughed and held out her hands to be pulled up.

Abandoning the wheelchair, Fenn went towards her and took the proffered hands. She was looking particularly fetching today, he considered, with her long, streaky hair blown into confusion by the strong easterly wind and her cheeks flushed with excitement and exertion. She was smiling up at him, with a mixture of coquetry and shyness which he found particularly charming, when all of a sudden something clicked in his head. He dropped her hands and fell to his knees in front of her, shaking his head slowly from side to side in self-admonishment.

371

'Well – I'm – darned!' he said slowly. 'If it isn't the girl on the beach . . . the girl I told the guys was sure to be a ghost. And I never thought, never guessed . . . Of course, you went into the end cottage, you didn't just disappear! Why in heaven's name didn't I recognize you earlier?'

Sybil smiled very sweetly at him.

'Because you never saw me as a person, let alone a woman,' she said simply. 'You thought I was a sick child at first and then I was just . . . well, just Sybil Cream, the girl who can't walk.'

'But you knew me! How come you remembered me?'

Sybil shrugged and looked away. Her eyes, cast down, took on a sad slant somehow. Fenn wanted to take her in his arms . . . but that would only give her the wrong impression and besides, she had her guy, that Ralph Winterton, to hug her, or would soon. D-Day had come and gone, the buzz bombs had closed London to weary troops needing a little light relief from the constant bombing raids, but no one doubted, now, that the war was going to end quite soon, and in the Allies' favour. Ralph was still flying Spitfires, and he, like Fenn, would be on round-the-clock flying raids when the weather allowed. So you don't go round hugging other guys' gals, Fenn told himself severely, and then, because she looked so sweet yet somehow vulnerable sitting on the sand, he hugged her anyway, lightly, enjoying for a brief moment the feel of her in his arms, the small, strong bones, the suppleness of her, before he squatted back on his heels once more, her hands in his.

'C'mon, how come you remembered me?'

'You aren't easy to forget,' Sybil said honestly. 'You were the first American airman I'd spoken to and you were rather nice to me. Cheerful. Chatty. *You* know!'

'Oh, sure. Well, since we're playing the truth game, I thought you were the prettiest gal I'd ever come across . . . you walked so well, too, straight-backed but sort of fluid; and your bare feet never faltered, you came on without looking down, carrying that basket of fish as though it weighed no more'n a basket of feathers.'

'Thank you,' Sybil said wryly. 'Wish I walked well now!'

'You can; you durned well will! Sybs, all you need is the confidence to get up an' go, the doctor says so! Look at your purty li'l legs, rounding out right nicely!'

'It isn't just that. I don't seem able to balance,' Sybil said uneasily. 'But you're right, I will one day. Come on, give me a tug and lean me against the hut whilst you bring the wheelchair over.'

'It's too hard to push through the sand,' Fenn objected. 'C'mon, honey, let me help you toddle up the beach.'

'Don't be so silly,' Sybil said crossly from her seat on the sand. 'How can I possibly walk even a tiny bit on soft sand? I'd only fall . . . not that I care about falling, except that I don't want to snap my leg like a dry stick . . . wasn't that what Dr Lewis said?'

'I dunno,' Fenn admitted. 'I waren't there. Right, if you won't walk I'll carry you.'

He loved handling her, feeling her light, warm young body in his arms. Even though they were only friends, though it was clearly impossible for a man to be physically attracted to a cripple, he still enjoyed touching her. But she shook her head, looking obstinate as any mule.

'No. It makes me feel so dependent when you carry me around. Besides, I'm getting too heavy for you now that I'm putting on a bit of weight. You bring the chair over and I'll try to help with the wheels.'

'You're stupid, Sybil Cream,' Fenn said, resorting to childish jibes. 'You're spoilt rotten, you are. Why won't you let me help you? Aren't I your friend?'

It made her laugh as he had known it would, but though she laughed she was serious; she would not feel any more dependent than she need.

'Oh yes, you're my friend . . . that's why you'll struggle with the chair, even though I weigh more than an elephant.'

They both laughed but he fetched the chair from where he had abandoned it earlier. He lifted her into it, though lifting her was not the easy task it had once been; her legs were much stronger, she could stand, it was just that she seemed to lack the confidence to take a step forward, then another, and another.

'Right, ma'am? Off we go, then. Hold tight!'

She clung, white-knuckled, to the chair and Fenn, who had wanted to carry her, tugged the chair along backwards and told himself it served her right when she was jounced and bounced all over the place. But then he was sorry when they reached the path and she grinned elfishly up at him, as though she was well aware that her rough ride had not been entirely because of the soft sand and the large pebbles.

'Thanks, Fenn. Shall we go in now? Mum's getting tea and Lizzie's coming over. She'll be glad you're here, you always manage to make her laugh. She's got a boyfriend in the Royal Air Force, you know . . . she worries about him.'

'Yeah, we'll go in now,' Fenn agreed. 'Bet I got a good picture; you looked like a film star leanin' against that hut. No one'll ever guess you'd not walked there.'

'Thanks for not saying *no one would ever guess you're a cripple*,' Sybil said soberly. 'Oh, Fenn, sometimes I wonder if I ever really will walk. It's all so hard!'

'You'll walk,' Fenn said comfortably. 'Believe me, kid, I know about these things – my mom's a nurse.'

Sybil gave the little purring crow of amusement which Fenn found so attractive.

'Oh, you and your relatives,' she scoffed. 'One of these days –' She stopped short.

'Yeah? Go on, babe, never stop in mid-sentence. One of these days what?'

'Oh, one of these days you'll forget which story you've told who and you'll come a cropper. Something like that.'

But it was not what she had begun to say. He pushed the chair harder and fairly ran up Beach Road just as from the sea behind them the persistent throbbing buzz of an engine came to their ears.

'Daylight raid?' Sybil said, cocking her head. 'If they strafe us make for the church, Fenn. Oh, oh, oh! It's a beastly doodlebug! Run!'

'It's miles off; you can hear 'em comin' across the sea for miles,' Fenn said reassuringly. 'Wish they'd get the coastal defences sorted out, though. It's possible to shoot 'em out of the sky, you know – the artillery are doing it wherever they can.'

'I hate them,' Sybil said uneasily. 'They aren't fair, are they, Fenn? There's no risk for the Nazis, only for us. I mean, with bombing raids the pilots and gunners and the rest of the crew are all risking their lives, but with doodlebugs all they do is set them going, like clocks.'

'Yeah, I see what you mean; that's why they call the VIs flying bombs, because that's all they are, I guess. But they're timed to fly inland, to London, honey. No need to be scared unless the engine stops.'

'I hate them,' Sybil repeated obstinately. 'I'd rather anything but them.'

'Right, let's get moving. Hey, there it is!'

There it was, coming in over the sea. It had a cigar-shaped body with stubby, squared-off wings and as it passed above them Fenn could see the jet of flame which powered it coming from its tail. A long-range, arbitrary instrument of death, it buzzed on over their heads and disappeared into the distance.

They stood and watched it out of sight, and were about to go inside when they heard the rhythmic, pulsing buzz of its engine stop abruptly.

'Good thing it was well out of our vicinity,' Fenn said cheerfully. 'Bet it'll land in fields. They usually coast a way; we probably won't even . . .'

An earsplitting explosion drowned the rest of the sentence. Sybil cowered in her chair as the back door shot open and Dora and Lizzie erupted into the yard.

'What on earth . . . ? Is there a raid? Sybs, thank heaven you're here. I was afraid . . .'

'Didn't you hear it? It went right overhead – a doodlebug!' Sybil said. 'Where do you reckon it landed . . . should we do something?'

'There's nothing we can do,' Dora said before Fenn could answer. 'I've got the kettle on. Come indoors.'

'Whatever will they think of next?' Fenn said as he pushed the wheelchair across the Creams' small yard. 'Since D-Day we must've dropped thousands of bombs on Europe, but the krauts still keep fightin' back. They're born killers, if you ask me.'

He swung the wheelchair sideways to the door, lifted the latch, hauled, then walked in backwards, pulling the chair behind him. Lizzie was already in the kitchen, examining the colander full of strawberries she had been picking over. She looked up as Fenn brought the chair round in a neat circle so that Sybil was sitting alongside her.

'My nerves are shot to pieces,' she said gloomily. 'I've never known worry like it. Never fall in love, Fenn; it gives every explosion the potential of halving your life and making what's left seem pretty hollow.'

'That sounds very profound,' Sybil said lightly, before Fenn could answer. 'Poor Lizzie, you really do love your bloke, don't you?'

'Yes, I do,' Lizzie said briefly. 'We're going to get married when we can.'

Dora, making the tea, raised her head.

'I hope you'll bring him home first, introduce him to your family,' she said rather reproachfully. 'Doesn't he ever get leave? Well, no, I suppose it's difficult at the moment with so many troops in Europe, but next time he's home, Lizzie, we'd love to meet this paragon.'

'He's a Brylcreem boy, isn't he?' Sybil said. 'Like Ralph.'

'That's right,' Lizzie muttered.

'What's his name?' Sybil asked idly. 'I don't think you've ever said.'

'Er . . . Phil. How's the walking going, Sybs?'

'And how come you didn't hear that buzz bomb until it exploded?' Fenn put in hastily. He knew how sensitive Sybil was about her progress, or lack of it, and did not want her to start saying again that she would never learn, or relearn, that particular skill. He came over and sat by Lizzie on the sofa. 'What were you doing, for God's sake? Community singing? It went right overhead, we could see it plain as plain.'

'That's right,' Sybil agreed. 'We saw the fire coming out of its tail and its horrible little squared off wings and everything.'

'Is that the first one you've seen? Nasty, aren't they?' Lizzie said, eating a strawberry and handing one to Sybil. 'Last time I was in London you couldn't move in the underground for people keeping out of their way. They do enormous damage. But we've had Workers' Playtime on the wireless, it drowns out most things.'

'Uh-huh,' Fenn agreed. He turned to Sybil. 'I'm probably busy tomorrow, but the day after I'll cycle over. By then I might have a surprise for you.'

He loved to see her small face light up, her eyes grow round and speculative. She was easy to please, little things delighted her. All through the long, rather cold spring, because it was impossible for her to go through the woods in her wheelchair, he had brought her spring flowers to identify for him.

'That's golden archangel,' she would say instructively. 'No it does *not* look like a nettle, Fenn, or only the leaves. See the big top petal, way above the little, freckly face? That's the angel's halo. Why, if this was ten times the size people would have greenhouses full, but because it's small and sweet and wild no one takes any notice of it. And that tiny blue flower with the round leaves is ground ivy, but the one with blue flowers in a sort of spike is bugle.'

'The woods are full of archangels and bugles,' Fenn said delightedly. 'What a world it is – what a mad world!'

'True. Now are you pressing these flowers, Fenn, to take home for dear Granny Pi-anny?'

She teased him mercilessly about his phantom family and indeed used them ruthlessly at times to get Fenn to do what she wanted. In a moment, Fenn sometimes thought, of total madness he had made the remark that his Boston Granny, Grandmother Kitson, would no more dream of calling her baby grand a pi-anny than fly to the moon, yet his Granny Curzon always referred to a piano thus. From that moment on Sybil had referred to Granny Curzon as Granny Pi-anny and had begun to invent for her habits so strange and tastes so bizarre that even Fenn was sometimes forced into reluctant laughter. But of course he was hoist on his own petard, fallen into a pit of his own making. He could not uninvent Granny Pi-anny nor, without risking belief, could he deny too many of Sybil's dreadful stories, so he was forced to accept that Sybil's tales of his family were here to stay. Granny Pi-anny was now into wild flowers, a keen stamp collector, a champion spaghetti eater and a tap-dancer who, at the age of seventy-eight, had just won a gold medal for being the spryest toe-tapper in the blue grass country.

But now she was thinking about the surprise; he had taken, lately, to setting her small goals in the hope of encouraging her to get on her feet – a box of chocolates when she stood for longer than thirty seconds, a pair of the sheerest nylon stockings when she pushed one foot before the other, though she had not, as yet, changed her weight from one foot to the next. And now he had the best bribe ever – or thought he had. The means to get about.

But he did not intend to tell her about it; not yet.

'That's right, Sybs, a surprise. I'll bring it the day after tomorrow, when I come round.'

Sybil thought about the surprise, off and on, for the rest of the day, but Fenn said nothing and Dora clearly did not know, since she played the guessing game as avidly as Sybil. Lizzie was quiet, though. She kept starting sentences and then not finishing them, frowning over her stitching – she was making herself a new dance-dress out of parachute silk – and occasionally coming out of her abstraction and having a guess at the surprise too.

But in bed that night, Sybil began to think. Not just idly, seriously. Just why was it that she was not keener to start walking? As Fenn had pointed out, her leg muscles were actually building up, getting stronger. There should be nothing to stop her from walking – exactly what was she afraid of?

Deep inside her, there was that little voice which sometimes told her the truth when she would much rather not hear it, and it was muttering away to itself right now. You don't want to be ordinary again too soon, the little voice said contemptuously. You don't want to have to compete with Chris and Lizzie, because they've got boyfriends and proper jobs and their futures all mapped out, and you haven't bothered with things like that because it seemed pointless. Once the full-time job in school had finished and you were only working a couple of hours each day, teaching the slow readers, you decided that you'd never get anywhere so you stopped trying. And you aren't any too keen to start all over again.

Then there was Fenn. He came round a lot because he wanted to see her getting better – but supposing she did? Suppose she got better, and he went off once more on his own business and no longer bothered to come round to the Creams' cottage. What, after all, would be the point if she could take herself off down to the beach, to the woods, over to the school to do a proper job of work?

But that was no reason for not learning to walk – that was being idiotic as well as cowardly. That was actually courting dependence – how could she even think of it, let alone believe that she was doing it?

No, but that isn't why I can't walk, she scolded the nasty whiny little voice in her head. My legs aren't strong enough, not yet. I need an awful lot more physiotherapy and practice and . . .

You need a kick in the seat of the pants, the voice said unkindly. Just you wait till Georgie . . .

But Georgie wouldn't be coming home, telling her off, making her put all her effort into walking. And Ralph belonged to someone else, had no more interest in Sybil Cream, so he was unlikely to care one way or another whether she walked or not.

That wasn't true, either; Ralph was a good friend. He had come to the house last week and now that there really was nothing between them they were able to act naturally, teasing one another, squabbling, until even Dora said what a nice couple they made. Daft, but that was how it went; release Ralph and he immediately became his own nice self. Try to hold him and he was stiff, unnatural, awkward.

And what of Fenn? He was another good friend and he wanted her to walk desperately badly.

I'll really try, Sybil told herself just before she went to sleep. I'll start when he comes round again, the day after tomorrow. And then I'll get the surprise, whatever it is!

23

The surprise was a bicycle made for two, like the one in the song. Fenn had thought long and hard how he could make Sybil more mobile, take her to the places she longed, wistfully, to see once more, and the tandem seemed like the answer. It was narrow enough to wheel along the woodland paths she loved, it could take her as far as Fenn could pedal, and that was quite a way, yet there would be no difficulty with fuel or fare-paying which would have been the case with a car or public transport – and he doubted whether she would have taken public transport anyway, because she would have needed the chair to be available at the end of the journey.

He knocked on the back door and when Dora answered it, gestured proudly to his steed.

'There, Dora! What d'you think of that?'

Dora laughed and then hugged him. Then she laughed again and pulled him – and the bicycle – into the kitchen.

'Fenn, you're a genius! Why ever didn't I think of that?'

'Oh, my God,' Sybil said faintly, from the sofa. 'You don't expect me to ride that, do you? I mean, my legs will just dangle . . . they'll be in the way, we'll fall off.'

'You'll get on that saddle and hang on to the handlebars and I'll do all the work – at first,' Fenn said autocratically. 'Look, there are little straps so's you can fasten your feet to the pedals. They'll go round whether you want them to or not, which will be awful good for those lazy muscles of yours. And every now and then I'll take a rest, and I'll holler, "Push, you at the back there! Pedal, gal!" and before you know it you'll be doing your share.'

They went out on it that very day and Fenn discovered all over again that the best way to forget your troubles is in activity and laughter with a friend.

Because the raid the day before had been bad; real bad. His friend

Nasty, short for Nastiasus, was in *Flirtin' Fanny* and Fenn had seen the tail section shot clean off over enemy territory. The guys had baled out, but out of the eight of them only six 'chutes had opened and Fenn had been sure that Nasty was one of the unlucky ones. That night he'd had nightmares one after the other until he grew scared to even try to sleep and wandered around the airfield, longing for dawn.

Even cycling over on the front half of the long tandem he had been unable to forget the fate of those two men. Good guys, guys who were doing their best, were dying to finish this war. Yet like a hen without a head which persists in racing round and round the farmyard, the damn krauts went on fighting back. They couldn't win, everyone was sure of it now. But when would it end? When there were no more men? No more Nippers, Wills, Bobs, Bennys . . . no more Fritzes, Franzes, Helmuds, Erichs? For him, he supposed, it would end when there was no more Fenn, but it was no use looking at it that way; that way madness lay.

And now, having lifted Sybil on to the second seat and heard her scream with a mixture of delight and fright, having got on in front of her and teased her because she was shaking the whole contraption, they were off. Dora had packed them some sandwiches, they had a couple of tin cups for water and the whole day in front of them. And Fenn was determined to extract payment from Sybs for her share in this extraordinary vehicle. When they found a place to picnic he would just insist that she try her legs instead of listening to her saying she could not possibly walk.

'C'mon, honey . . . just one more try!'

They had found a clearing beside a stream, eaten their sandwiches, drunk clear, cold stream water, rested, talked. Fenn had tried to find out a bit more about this guy Ralph, but apart from reiterating that he was Chris's brother and an old friend, Sybil did not seem inclined to discuss him. Fenn had such an itch of curiosity over Ralph . . . but he would have to wait until the next time Ralph came calling, which might, according to Sybil, be any day now.

'Of course, once I can walk things will be different,' she said lazily. 'I'll get a job and . . . well, things will be different.'

She was lying on her back looking up at the blue sky through a canopy of green leaves. Fenn, lying on his stomach but reared up on his elbows, picked a long stem of grass and leaned over her, tickling her nose.

'How different? Getting married, d'you mean?'

Sybil sneezed and grabbed the grass, turning it on Fenn, making it travel across his cheek, over his nose and up into his hairline.

'How mundane you are! Marriage – you'd think there was nothing else! I'm never going to get married.'

'Oh, yeah? Told Ralph yet?'

'Nope. Why should I? I'm going to have a career, aren't I? I'll get to be a head teacher if I stay single; if I marry all I'll get will be a husband.'

'What's wrong with that? I thought all you girls wanted to get married. I thought . . .'

'Well think again,' Sybil said crisply. 'I don't want to get married, I want to be someone. And now let's change the subject; is there any food left?'

'No, you gannet, there is not! And you'd best give me your hands, because I want you on your feet.'

'Oh. Are we moving on, then?' Sybil sat up and rubbed her eyes, then smiled at Fenn. 'I'm sorry if I sounded cross, but it's such a lovely day and I don't feel much like talking about the future. Everything's so – so uncertain.'

'Sure,' Fenn said peaceably. 'Now on your feet, hon.' He heaved on her hands and she came forward, protesting that it would do neither of them any good if he pulled her arms out by the roots. He knew full well, she said, that she could not get up from a sitting to a standing position without a good deal of assistance and he was just tugging at her hands.

'True; mustn't expect too much at this stage,' he said, releasing her when she was sitting upright. 'Now come on.'

He hooked his hands under her armpits and brought her to her feet. She swayed against him and he could smell the soft flowery scent of the soap she used and her fresh young skin. He put an arm round her, feeling once more the rush of protectiveness which touching her gave him. She was so heartrendingly dependent, so determined not to be!

'There. Now you lean against this tree whilst I get in front of you, because you, young lady, are going to walk back to the bike.'

'Walk? Me? All that way?'

He nodded, then took her forearms in a firm grip.

'Yup, you. Shuffle, honey!'

She protested that she could not, that she would fall, but even so she took two shuffling half-steps forward before pulling back against his grip.

'I'll fall on you and we'll both go down. Oh, Fenn, I am trying, but no more, not now. I can't, really I can't!'

She looked so frightened and big-eyed that he was tempted to whisk her up in his arms and carry her back to the bicycle and forget the walking lesson, but then he hardened his heart. Suppose he went off on his next mission and never returned? Who would teach her to walk then? Dora loved her very much but she was too afraid of doing damage, and not strong enough anyway to manhandle Sybs, light as she was. And look at the kid, she was pleased as punch over two miserable little shuffles . . . before this afternoon was out he wanted her to walk, really walk!

In the soft June afternoon they toiled on. Sybil managed a proper step, though she would keep bending forward from the waist, which meant that a step was difficult and of course she looked absurd, which made Fenn laugh and he did not want to laugh, he wanted to make her mobile.

'Stand up *straight*, honey,' he counselled her. 'You're getting your centre of balance all wrong like that, you really will land on your nose if you don't straighten up.'

'Then let's stop,' Sybil panted. 'I've done ever so well . . . please let's stop now, Fenn.'

'No, I've had a better idea. I'll get behind you, hold you from the back, then you won't be able to bend forward. See? Let's give it a go, Sybs.'

He manhandled her into the new position, then held her firmly by the elbows, his body acting as a sort of moving cradle, and it worked, she walked forward, wobbly but upright. She squeaked and said: 'I'm doing it! I really am walking!' and then, almost back at the bicycle, she over-reached herself, her knee failed to lock on the movement and she went down and Fenn, perforce, went too. They lay on the ground giggling like two maniacs whilst Fenn tried to ask her if she was all right and Sybil tried to tell him that if she wasn't she would know who to blame. And then he pulled her into his arms and kissed her.

It was not a brotherly kiss nor a cousinly kiss nor, even, a good-friendly kiss. It was an extremely passionate kiss and it involved a good deal of mumbling and squeezing and a lot of other things which Sybil really scarcely understood but found she enjoyed. What was more, Fenn, who had always been gentle with her, was suddenly rough – very rough. He crushed her against him and his mouth ignored her mouth's surprise at his sudden and violent behaviour and took hers in a manner which she found almost shocking. He had no right . . . it was her very private mouth he was plundering . . . oh Fenn, oh Fenn, oh Fenn!

The embrace seemed to last for ever and yet be over between one breath and the next. She lay against him, hearing the pounding of his heart and of her own. She was breathless, astonished, hungry, satisfied . . . she did not know what she was, save that she was not the same Sybil Cream who had ridden into the clearing an hour earlier.

'Oh, Sybs . . . oh, Sybs, are you all right? I'm sorry, I guess. Did I scare you? Did you like it?'

'You – surprised me,' Sybil said honestly. 'But I liked it . . . I think I liked it.'

Fenn laughed softly.

'Guess I was celebratin' all that good walking. You ready to ride home, now?'

She was not ready! She wanted more than anything to stay here on the ground in this wood whilst Fenn kissed her some more. And cuddled her some more. And squeezed her in some of the places he had started to squeeze before he had suddenly stopped. But she did not think a girl could say such things to a young man, especially such a young man as Fenn, who was probably just sorry for her.

'Right. Help me up, then.'

They rode home rather silently, both busy with their thoughts.

What's the matter with me, Fenn asked himself, pushing hard on the pedals and trying to think about the tea Dora would be preparing for them. What was I doing, making love to the kid . . . and her a cripple. Besides, she had Ralph. She was no good to him, he wanted a rich wife, a successful woman who could help him, not hold him back. Besides, the war was by no means over, he might never live to see his rich wife and it wouldn't do the kid much good if she were fool enough to fall in love with a guy who might die tomorrow.

Except that they were all in the same boat. That buzz bomb could have landed on the Creams' cottage and killed them all, himself included. So why not make love to her, let her live a little? She had an innocence which he found both touching and attractive, she liked him, had enjoyed what he had done to her, could be persuaded and kissed and cuddled into compliance.

But he couldn't do it. She might repulse him and then things could never be the same between them again and he found he valued her friendship far more than he would have valued a fleeting affair. Besides, she was a loyal kid – she might let him kiss her but there it would end because of that Brylcreem boy as she called him, that Ralph.

And you don't want her, not really, he reminded himself as they came out from the shelter of the woods into farmland once more. You don't want to be tied down. Even if she were free you wouldn't want her; even if she could walk she's no use to you. Little Sybil Cream, doomed to limp through life, always the bridesmaid, never the bride.

The thought pulled him up short. What on earth had made him think such a thing? She would marry if she wanted to do so, she was beautiful, intelligent, everything the average man wanted in a woman. She would be walking soon, he had felt the resolve in her.

They reached the cottage. She smiled secretly at him as he lifted her off the bicycle and carried her into the kitchen. He did not smile back. He dared not. She was nothing to him – nothing!

The weeks went by, with Fenn spending all his spare time at the cottage on Beach Road. He and Sybil used the tandem every day when he had leave and the weather was right and gradually Sybil's sense of balance improved and she began, tentatively at first and then with more strength, to apply pressure to the pedals as they rode along.

Together, now, they examined the wild flowers in wood and meadow and marsh. Fenn taught Sybil to walk when he wasn't teaching her to cycle and she taught him about the English countryside. He was a keen student too, though he often made her laugh with his absurd suggestions.

'If wild roses are called dog roses, and wild violets dog violets, what are these called?' Fenn said one day, twirling a stem of the dark pink wild flower which he had just picked on the cliff above the sea.

'That's a wild pea; I did tell you,' Sybil said. 'See, it's much showier than the vetches and vetchlings, but they're all the same family. And it's like the dog rose, it has no scent, though the cultivated ones, sweet peas, smell lovely.'

'Then if cultivated roses and violets and peas smell nice, the ones that don't should all be called "dog",' Fenn said in tones of such sweet reason that Sybil looked at him suspiciously. 'Why aren't these . . .' he twiddled the pink flower under Sybil's nose '. . . why aren't these called dog peas?'

'I don't really know,' Sybil confessed. 'I suppose . . .'

'Because if they were, I could tell Dora that you had been telling me about the dog pea on the cliffs, and encouraging me to collect some.'

'Oh, Fenn, you really are awful! Oh, and I never even saw it coming. I might have known you were only interested in the name of the flower so you could be rude!'

'Rude? Me, rude? Really, ma'am, that's a trifle harsh . . . ouch . . . ouch! Sybil, remember you're a lady . . . *ouch!*'

They had been sitting side by side on the sweet turf; all of a sudden Fenn was underneath with Sybil's elbows in his stomach and a handful of mixed wild flowers being remorselessly rubbed into his mouth.

'You're a devil, Fenn; say you're sorry!'

'Sorry? Who is it shoving flowers up my nose, whose elbow is that in my gut? This is no way to treat the guy whose cycled miles to give you pleasure!'

'Oh, no? Now what is this pink flower called?'

'It's a dawg-pea . . . no, no, I'm mistaken . . . it's a wild pea, of course!'

Later, when he had left Sybil at her home and was cycling back to the base, Fenn reflected on how good it was to see Sybil with colour in her cheeks and sparkling eyes, wrathfully jabbing him, being the normal girl he knew her to be instead of the quiet, repressed creature who thought she would never walk again. She was welcome to dig holes in his stomach with her elbows and half-choke him with flowers, if only she would continue to grow in confidence. She was improving with every day that passed.

Summer came. Sybil and Fenn continued to work hard, and gradually Sybil's confidence returned until she was able to walk a few steps by herself. Fumblingly at first, and awkwardly, but nevertheless she was mobile. She would not walk much in the street in case she fell but she walked about the house, in the yard, around the classroom. The kids were all impressed, she told Fenn wryly, they thought she was next door to a miracle; which was more or less how she felt herself.

In August Paris was liberated and the bomber crews noticed they met with less resistance when they overflew Germany, though there was still flak and a few fighters coming up to try to hassle them. Leave was easier to obtain and Fenn got time off when he could and came over to Pakeby to bully Sybil, make her practise. She was beginning to show confidence in her walking, she would turn her head in a natural fashion when you spoke, whilst continuing her onward progress. She would always drag one leg a little, Fenn thought, but what was that compared with the way she had been, tied to the wheelchair, dependent on the good offices of friends and family, never getting out into the countryside she loved? He told himself she would scarcely need him in a couple of months, and wondered at the cold and hollow ache which the thought brought in its train.

September came and Fenn went home to Manchester. What was more, he told people where he was going.

'To see relatives,' he said. 'To talk about staying in England after the war.'

Everyone talked about after the war now; there was not the almost superstitious feeling that if you said the words fate would pay you out by making it last twice as long. Fenn discussed what he should do in peacetime with Rachael and with Amos, and found them understanding and involved with his decision, not standing back, but letting him choose for himself.

'I know they say the States is the land of opportunity,' Rachael said timidly. 'But there's opportunities here, Fenn. You could work with Amos, learn the business – or do you want to go on flying? Amos says they'll need civil airline pilots after the war – bound to. There'll be a lot of flying, Amos says.'

'Dunno what I'll do, yet,' Fenn said honestly. 'Might go back for a bit, but I reckon I'll come home again. I was a mechanic working on automobiles pre-war; guess I could go back to that.'

In the evenings, when baby Mark was in bed, he and Rachael talked of all sorts of things. He told Rachael about the Creams, but explained that they were simply good friends whom he would probably never see again once the war finished. He talked about the sort of woman he wanted for his wife and explained that because he had had very little formal education he felt bound to search for a woman who was successful in her own sphere, whatever that might be. He told his mother that if he decided to stay in England it would mean fighting his way up before he could consider a family and suchlike responsibilities.

And then later in the evening he went off to the pub with Amos and they talked man to man and Fenn aired his new knowledge of the flora and fauna surrounding Pakeby and they discussed the war in all its aspects and how wonderful the peace would be, when it came.

And at the end of his leave Fenn returned to Flacton, warmly certain that Rachael and Amos understood that he intended to be someone and do something when the peace came, that they applauded his sensible approach to life, and his reasons for trying to meet the right woman instead of falling in love with just any girl who caught his eye.

*   *   *

The night he left Amos and Rachael cuddled in bed and talked, as they always did.

'He's a good lad, isn't he, Amos?' Rachael said presently, reaching out to switch off her small bedside light. 'A son to be proud of – and what about that girl of his, eh? Ah, she'll make him a grand little wife, grand.'

'His girl? Who might that be, sweetheart? He kept telling me he wanted to meet a woman who could contribute something to his life, who wouldn't just be a burden to him . . . I think he meant a rich woman!'

Rachael chuckled indulgently.

'Oh, that! He's met the girl for him even if he can't acknowledge it yet. Why do you think he talked so much about her? A fellow doesn't spend all his time with a girl unless there's more in it than friendship, dearest.'

'Well, who? The one called Chris? Not that Lizzie!'

'No, you great *schlemiel*! Sybil, of course!'

'But she's a cripple! Oh I know she's walking now, but she's still not right, and he was saying she'll not be right for a while yet.'

Rachael reached out a warm, lazy hand and curled it round her husband's neck.

'Amos, Amos, it's clear you've never raised a son! You don't listen to the *words* when you want the truth from a son, you listen to the way he says the words! It'll be Sybil, you'll see.'

Whilst Fenn was in Manchester – wouldn't you know it? – Ralph came home and spent a couple of hours with Sybil. Missed him again, Fenn thought to himself, but in his heart he was glad. It would have hurt and annoyed him in some peculiar way to see Sybs with another guy – not that he wanted her himself. I take no passengers, carry no supercargo, he reminded himself. I'll need all the help I can get to set myself up with some sort of business here in England – if that's what I decide to do.

'You saw Ralph, didn't you? What's he like?' Fenn asked Paul privately as he and the other young man walked back to the hospital one evening.

Paul had been saying goodbye to the Creams. He was going to a big training centre for the blind just outside London and wanted to remind them to write because someone would read him the letters, and he could type his own replies once he'd mastered the typewriters at the centre, he said.

'Don't know; never seen him,' Paul said. 'Never seen you, for that matter.'

'Oh, very funny,' Fenn said crossly. 'I don't know any other guy who can size people up quicker'n you, Paul, with or without sight. So what's he like?'

Paul considered. Fenn appreciated that commenting on Chris's brother might be difficult for Paul since it was common knowledge that Paul and Chris were going to get married when he was in a position to support her. He had bought her a tiny sapphire ring which she wore on the third finger of her left hand – and stared at so constantly that Fenn told her its image would be engraved on her brain patterns long before they got married.

'We-ell, he's Chris's brother, so I couldn't dislike him. He's not very like her though, not really. He's like all of us who've been through the war, pretty tired, damn weary of the whole business. But he laughed and kidded Sybil and considering what he probably thinks, he was nice to me. Polite, you know. Welcomed me to the family and sounded as if he meant it. He and Sybil went off a couple of times, but . . . I dunno, I didn't get the impression that he was all that keen.'

'Not keen? Not keen on *Sybil*? The guy must be every sort of fool,' Fenn growled. 'She's one of the best, is Sybs. Don't you agree?'

'She's nice. Tell me, what does she look like? I don't like to keep asking Chris all the time.'

'Well, she's tall and quite thin, really. Only a couple of inches shorter than me. Hmm . . . she's got streaky hair, brown and goldy and fair, all together. And good skin, very pale and clear. Her eyes are a very light brown – amber or the colour of clear honey, I suppose you could say. They're very wide open eyes, kinda round, with lashes only a bit darker than her hair. She's got a nice mouth, it's a good sort of shape and the lips are a nice clear pink, except when she wears lipstick, of course. Her teeth are small and even and always very clean. Umm . . . her figure's all right an' all.'

'Is that it?'

Paul seemed to be biting back laughter, Fenn could not imagine why.

'Yeah, I guess. Why? Have I left something out?'

'No, nothing. It's the most detailed description you've ever given me, Fenn. Ever stopped to ask yourself –' He stopped short.

'Ever stopped to ask myself what?'

'Oh, nothing. It doesn't matter. One of these days you must describe Lizzie to me. I think you're better at it than most.'

'Lizzie? Blonde, blue-eyed, pouting, pretty. Small, bosoms bounce when she walks, waggles her hips . . . what in hell are you laughing at?'

'Nothing,' Paul said. 'Except it's easy to see you don't really admire Lizzie, pretty though she may be.' They had been standing at the hospital gate but now Paul turned in, raising a hand. 'Goodnight, old chap. Thanks for your company.'

'It's all over bar the shouting,' Fenn said contentedly.

VE day had come and gone and the month of May was half over. Paul had returned from his course as a trained speed writer and typist and he could now read Braille. He was lodging with a Mrs Patterson on Florence Road and went by bus daily into the port to work there. There was talk of bringing the troops back from abroad; some soldiers and sailors were already beginning to appear in the streets, bronzed and jumpy, quick to throw themselves behind the nearest object if someone dropped a saucepan or shrieked to a friend. Gradually, the American air crews were being disbanded and men were going home. Henry was back, rolling in, hugging Dora, hugging Sybil, even hugging Fenn, though Fenn was sure that the older man was as surprised as everyone else to find himself with a GI not only in his house but in his arms.

It was a marvellous, disturbing, exciting time. More freedom was allowed to everyone, school children planned parties with their parents, street parties, village parties, even town parties. Sybil had got her first full-time job in teaching since her illness and was discussing the possibility of learning to ride a bicycle all over again. She was well aware, she said, that riding a tandem with Fenn doing most of the work was a good deal easier than a solo ride, but though she might limp a little on her own two feet she would scarcely limp on a bicycle, and it would make the journey easier and cheaper, for the school was five miles inland.

And inevitably, Ralph announced that he was coming to spend a day's leave in Pakeby and whilst there would make a momentous announcement. Lizzie would come over for the day too, and Paul would be there. Henry was still on disembarkation leave though he intended to sign on aboard a trawler when he did start work again. It would be a real family party.

'I'd better leave you alone that day, I guess,' Fenn said, but Sybil was immediately so distressed that he supposed, grimly, he would have to go through with it. See her engaged to this guy who, after all, was Chris's brother and had stood by Sybs all through her illness and her subsequent incarceration in the wheel-chair.

For if one thing was certain, it was what Ralph's momentous announcement would be. What else could he be announcing but his engagement? On reflection Fenn supposed it might be a hundred things, but he was still sure that Ralph intended to make it official between Sybil and himself. Damn it all, what else was there of sufficient significance to gather the whole family together?

The day arrived. Fenn wore his pinks and felt uncomfortably smart. He arrived at half-past three and there was great excitement in the Creams' cottage because the Wintertons, who had not been over to Pakeby except for fleeting visits during the war, were going to have tea with the Creams and then go on to Malverns to see what needed doing to the house before they could open it up again.

'Ralph's driving them over,' Chris announced, pink-cheeked. 'Do you realize they've only met Paul briefly – Paul, you'll love Mummy, and Daddy's most awfully kind. You'll like him as well.'

Judging from Paul's strained expression delighted anticipation of the treat was not his chief emotion, but he nodded dutifully and sat down in the chair which Henry drew up for him.

Lizzie arrived next. She was looking very smart in a cream linen suit and, Fenn saw at once, was also very nervous. But despite being rather pale she looked very beautiful – and to Fenn, not a patch on Sybil, who wore a blue gingham dress which was too small for her and old school sandals. But Lizzie had been earning good money during the war and was earning good money now, working in Tuttles gown department and enjoying every minute of it. Lizzie's boyfriend had been invited and might pop along, so Lizzie said, glancing a little self-consciously round the room.

'Ralph's bringing my parents over for tea, and then they're going to open up Malverns, or at least see what needs doing to it,' Chris told Lizzie excitedly. And who was to live in Malverns? Why, herself and Paul – she was sure that her parents were going to suggest it.

Fenn sat beside Sybil on the sofa and waited patiently. Henry's mother arrived next, with her son helping her along. Granny Cream had lost a good deal of her sharpness over the years – she was proud to tell people she was eighty-six – and she came in regally on Henry's arm and immediately took the best chair by the stove. Henry had wanted the family party in the front room but Dora was firm. Sybil still slept in there because she found the stairs very difficult and Dora did not want her disturbed. So everyone must make the best of the kitchen, she said decidedly.

Last of all, they heard the car draw up outside. There was scuffling and laughter and Chris flew across the room to let her parents in. Mr Winterton had lost most of his hair but grown a fine, dark moustache. He looked a decent sort of guy, Fenn decided. And Mrs Winterton was pretty and plump and had just a touch of that headgirl look which made all the other landgirls anxious to do as Chris advised.

Ralph came in. Tall, fair-haired, with the easy grin and the underlying seriousness which, Fenn thought, would be worn for some time to come by his and Ralph's generation. They had seen too much, lost too many friends, to be lighthearted in a wholehearted way ever again.

Ralph walked across the room. Fenn frowned. He had seen the guy before; now where would that have been? Lizzie stood up and smiled as Ralph came towards the sofa . . . and light exploded in Fenn's brain.

He jumped to his feet, swung his fist, and hit Ralph right on the point of the jaw. He knocked him off his feet and halfway across the kitchen and would have followed it up, would have killed him but for Lizzie, who flew at him, fastening herself on his wrist, her grip maniacally strong.

'You bastard, you bastard!' she shrieked. 'If you've hurt him . . . !'

Sybil was staring at him, a tiny frown etched between her soft, winged brows. Paul was saying in a low voice to Chris, who was on her feet, a hand flying to her mouth, 'What happened? Who hit who?'

Mr Winterton was saying, 'Now now, old chap . . . is it a touch of shell-shock, perhaps?'

Mrs Winterton was kneeling beside Ralph, trying to hoist his head on to her knee.

Dora and Henry just stared.

Fenn, hampered by Lizzie, was actually growling, his rage against this smoothly smiling Brylcreem boy so intense that he could only think how, as soon as Ralph got up, he would enjoy knocking him down again.

He had recognized him as soon as he saw Lizzie smiling up at him with that expression in her eyes. That two-timing little bitch – he flung her off on the thought and stood, fists clenched, staring down at Ralph – the two-timing little bitch had been cheating on her sister for years, and Ralph, damn his eyes, had been shagging Lizzie whilst pretending to court Sybil – *his* Sybil, Fenn's little love!

He had met them in the refreshment room on Thorpe station, when he had been on his way to Manchester for the first time. Lizzie, making love to Sybil's boyfriend! It had been going on for years, with poor little Sybs fondly believing that Ralph was true to her . . . he ground his teeth as Ralph began to blink and stir.

'Fenn?' That was Sybil, taking his hand, her small fingers cool and composed in his. 'Fenn? Shall we go outside?'

'He's – he's – Sybil, that guy . . .'

'Yes, all right. You come outside with me, now. We'll let someone else do the explaining in here, I think. Lizzie, come out in a minute, will you? I'd like to know just why you flew to Ralph's defence so lustily just now.'

Lizzie had satisfied herself that Ralph was not dead. She turned to her sister, ruefully smiling.

'Sorry, Sybs. No one wanted to hurt anyone else, that was the trouble, so we all got rather deeply enmeshed in unnecessary lies. Ralph and I have been engaged for a while; we're going to get married quite soon now. Ralph said you knew it was over between you, but . . .'

'What's it all about? Ralph's marrying *Lizzie?* Ralph, dearest, what is going on?' Mrs Winterton's confusion was mirrored in most of the faces in the room. She looked up at Fenn, no longer angrily but appealingly. 'Young man, why . . .'

Sybil shook her head. She put her arm round Fenn's waist and urged him towards the door.

'We've got something important to discuss,' she called over her shoulder. 'Ask Lizzie; I think she understands even more than I do!'

The door shut behind them.

In the room they had left, Ralph was sitting up, ruefully stroking his chin, staring up at Lizzie and smiling faintly.

'I probably deserved that – but why? I don't think I've ever seen the chap in my life before – has he gone off his rocker?'

'No, I don't think so,' Lizzie said coolly. 'He recognized you, Ralph. You won't remember, I doubt if you even saw him, but he tried to pick me up on Thorpe station when I was waiting for you to come home on leave once.'

'Ah!' Paul gave a satisfied sigh. 'He was defending Sybil, then. He thought Ralph had been cheating on her.'

'He was right,' Ralph muttered, scrambling to his feet. 'But last year I came over and saw Sybs and told her I'd met someone else. Only Lizzie didn't want Sybs to know it was her, and Sybs didn't want anyone to know that she and I had agreed to split up . . . so we all kept our mouths shut. But the war's over, I'm coming out of the RAF, and Lizzie and I want to make it official – get married and all that stuff. So we discussed it and decided to come clean at the family get-together.'

'I see,' Mrs Winterton murmured doubtfully. Dora saw that the Wintertons were by no means enchanted to discover that their blue-eyed boy was going to marry Lizzie Cream . . . then realized, in a sudden leap of understanding, that it was not disapproval of Lizzie but simply total bewilderment which beset them. They could not have been any too pleased when Ralph had seemed anxious to marry Sybil, but at least Sybil had spent time with the Wintertons, was Chris's best friend and a teacher, like their daughter. Lizzie worked in a shop and in any case had always held herself aloof from the Winterton clan, so that the family hardly knew her. But wouldn't Lizzie make a lovely bride? And she'd make Ralph a marvellous wife, she'd be so good at all the things solicitors' wives needed to do, she'd dress well, entertain, impress his clients . . . Dora could see that the Wintertons would come round in the end. And Sybs wanted to teach, she kept saying she had no desire to marry . . . things would work out for the best eventually.

'So we're to be sisters-in-law,' kind Chris was saying to Lizzie, giving her a kiss and a bit of a hug. 'I'm very glad, Lizzie, and very happy for Ralph. You aren't worried about Sybil, are you?'

'Yes, I'm very worried; but I'm so selfish that I can't let that keep me away from Ralph,' Lizzie admitted. 'Oh, Chris, what'll happen to Sybs?'

Chris chuckled and took Paul's hand.

'Oh, Sybs will surprise us all,' she said airily. 'Sybs will be all right, you'll see.'

Sybil and Fenn had walked away from the cottage, round the corner and out on to Beach Road. From there it was only a matter of twenty yards or so to the shore. Without a word they crossed the sand and settled themselves with their backs against the nearest beatster hut. Fenn was racking his brains for an explanation which would not involve telling Sybil that Ralph had been unfaithful to her for years when Sybil spoke.

'Why did you hit him?'

Immediately, all thoughts of being a real gentleman fled. Fenn glared; he could feel his brows getting closer together, positively beetling in fact, and knew his mouth was closing into a tight, furious line. With an effort he forced himself to relax.

'I saw them, see? Kissing. Only then I didn't know he was Ralph Winterton, your guy, I just thought he was another of Lizzie's fellers.'

'So you hit him. Why, Fenn?'

'Why? Because he'd done you wrong, Sybs. Because he was going to hurt you.'

'But that's no reason for you to hit him,' Sybil said softly. 'You could say it was none of your business if Ralph had two-timed me. You haven't really answered my question, Fenn. Why did *you* hit him?'

'Well, I guess I feel kinda responsible for you. Say, honey, do you realize that you walked across that kitchen and down to the shore here and you walked straight and tall, as though you'd never had nothin' wrong with your legs?'

'Did I? That's good,' Sybil said, but absently, as though it didn't matter very much. 'Do you know what, Fenn? I think you love me.'

There was a short silence whilst Fenn struggled to assimilate this totally new idea. Then he put his arm round her.

'I guess you're right,' he said. 'Guess I've loved you from the first moment I saw you that day on the beach, walkin' so straight and proud, with that heavy basket of fish on your arm and your little bare feet padding over the sand.'

'Good. Because I fell in love with you that day and I've just loved you more and more ever since,' Sybil said earnestly. 'So you really bopped Ralph one on the chin because you love me . . . is that right?'

'Yeah, I guess so,' Fenn said wonderingly. 'D'you know what, Sybs? You're the only person I want to be with, all the time. Sometimes I've wondered what in hell I'll do without you.'

'Why wonder? Why not just stay with me?' Sybil murmured. 'Fennimore Kitzmann, will you marry me?'

He began to laugh, then she saw that there were tears in his eyes. And then he stood up and seized her in his arms, turning her towards the sea.

'Oh, God, I love you, Sybs! I didn't want to, I didn't know it, and now we've got it back to front – it's the guy who proposes in my book. So will you marry me, honey? I've never felt this way about anyone before, I swear it!'

'Of course I'll marry you. I'm just glad you hit Ralph, if that was the only way to make you see we were right for each other. So you swear you've never loved anyone like you love me – what'll you swear it on? On Granny Pi-anny's best white wig? Her Sunday-go-Meeting wig?'

'You little devil! Don't you dare insult Granny Pi-anny because it's her that brought us together. Do you realize I ain't never told you a lie – not *as* a lie, anyway. We'll go home to Cheetham Hill just as soon as we can . . . my mom will be so surprised. You'll love Rachael, and my stepfather, my little brother . . . oh, God, Sybs, I want you!'

He took her in his arms, kissed her hungrily and then he put his arm round her shoulders and led her into the beatster hut. There, on a nest of old, soft nets, he began to tell her how special she was, how she was his first love and his last love, how stupid and blind he had been not to see what was right in front of his nose.

'I've heard it said that fellows don't respect girls who give in to them,' Sybil said presently, and Fenn assured her that with him respect and love would go hand in hand – and would she like to stop talking for two minutes, because he had a deep and terrible urge to kiss her?

'All right, I won't say a word,' Sybil said. 'Oh, Fenn, I do love you so very much!'

Up at the cottage, tea was laid and ready, the kettle hopping on the hob. Lizzie and Ralph had been congratulated, Chris and Paul had been offered the use of Malverns as soon as it could be made ready for occupancy, Henry's hopes of a berth on a trawler had been discussed. Presently Dora looked out of the kitchen window and then called her husband over.

'Henry, there's no sign of Sybs and Fenn – do you think you could go and give them a call? Tell them tea's ready. And tell Fenn we all understand and even Ralph's forgiven him – eh, Ralph?'

'Look, I'll go,' Ralph said quickly. 'Don't you worry, Mr Cream, they're probably down on the beach, talking things over. I'll just run down and fetch them up.'

But this Henry would by no means allow.

'I'll go myself, hev a word with the boy,' he said genially. 'I in't met many of these GI Joes, be nice to hev a word.'

He left the house and walked down Beach Road, seeing the ruined church as though for the first time, resolving to go over there tomorrow and just tidy up the grass a trifle. After all, the church was just about all the Creams could see through their front windows; might as well be neighbourly and keep the grass cut decent.

He could see that Sybs and that young Yank weren't in the church, nor on the cliff-path, and presently he could see that they weren't on the beach, either. But they could easily be behind the beatster huts, sheltering from the wind, having a good old chin-wag.

Henry went down on to the beach, crunched over the big round pebbles, over the shingle, and began to walk across the soft and yielding sand. He reached the first beatster hut, stopped short, stood for a moment and then hastily retraced his steps. Well, history repeats itself, he thought with a chuckle; who'd have thought it of Sybs, such a quiet, good little thing! And Dora swore that though she was fond of Fenn, couldn't be fonder, Fenn had absolutely no interest in her girl.

This time there'll be no interfering, Henry told himself as he regained the small cliff and began to walk up Beach Road towards his home. This time the choice will be theirs and theirs alone – but isn't it funny how things do go full circle? First, me and my Dora, last, Sybil and her Fenn (outlandish name!). Still, what did it matter? It's love that matters when all's said and done. First love, last love, what makes the difference so long as it's true love?

'They're busy,' he said briefly to Dora when he got back indoors. He gave her hand a bit of a squeeze. 'They're rare fond of each other if you ask me, though Sybil's still got that limp, poor kid. She drags one leg, kind of.'

'She always will. But Fenn won't either notice or care, you mark my words.'

And Dora gave a little smile and a sigh and squeezed his hand back to show she understood. Then she began to pour the tea.